THE SCARAB
MISSION

BAEN BOOKS by JAMES L. CAMBIAS

The Godel Operation
The Scarab Mission

Arkad's World

The Initiate

THE SCARAB MISSION

JAMES L. CAMBIAS

THE SCARAB MISSION

This is a work of fiction. All the characters and events portrayed in this book are fictional, and any resemblance to real people or incidents is purely coincidental.

A Baen Books Original

Baen Publishing Enterprises
P.O. Box 1403
Riverdale, NY 10471
www.baen.com

ISBN: 978-1-9821-9239-6

Cover art by Dominic Harman

First printing, January 2023

Distributed by Simon & Schuster
1230 Avenue of the Americas
New York, NY 10020

Library of Congress Cataloging-in-Publication Data

Names: Cambias, James L, author.
Title: The scarab mission / James L Cambias.
Identifiers: LCCN 2022046616 (print) | LCCN 2022046617 (ebook) | ISBN 9781982192396 (hardcover) | ISBN 9781625798978 (ebook)
Subjects: LCGFT: Novels.
Classification: LCC PS3603.A4467 S29 2023 (print) | LCC PS3603.A4467 (ebook) | DDC 813/.6—dc23/eng/20220928
LC record available at https://lccn.loc.gov/2022046616
LC ebook record available at https://lccn.loc.gov/2022046617

Printed in the United States of America

10 9 8 7 6 5 4 3 2 1

To my sister Maggie,
for letting me steal her books.

"And thorns shall come up in her palaces,
nettles and brambles in the fortresses thereof:
and it shall be an habitation of dragons,
and a court for owls."

—Isaiah 34:13

PART I

Scarabs

CHAPTER ONE

Yanai looked at Safdaghar and didn't like what she saw, not one bit of the image.

Yanai was fifty-five million kilometers from Jupiter—just behind and Sunward of its orbital empire, gaining fast. But she wasn't thinking about Jupiter. Her mind and her sensors were focused on a big wobbling wheel twenty kilometers behind her. That was Safdaghar, a space habitat, and Yanai was the first spacecraft in sixteen standard years to try docking with it.

Safdaghar was moving a little faster in its orbit than Yanai was, so the two were converging at about ten kilometers per hour. She could feel the occasional ping of debris on her hull, from the sparse cloud of bits and pieces surrounding Safdaghar. No danger at these velocities, but still annoying.

The danger was Safdaghar itself. Like most of the billion habs orbiting the Sun in the Tenth Millennium, Safdaghar spun on its axis to create the illusion of gravity for its occupants. But maintaining a stable spin requires constant management. After sixteen years of neglect—not to mention considerable damage—Safdaghar was completely out of control. Its axis was precessing like crazy, just like a spinning top about to fall over. And Yanai could see chaotic motions as well, likely the result of irregular mass distributions inside the structure.

Her task was to dock with this tumbling wreck, stabilize it, and then shove the whole thing into a new orbit which would take it closer to Jupiter. The king of the sky would then flick Safdaghar out into the darkness of the outer system, where in a few decades Yanai's clients would catch the wreck and take it apart. This was a once-in-a-millennium window, and even as the low bidder on the job Yanai expected to make a once-in-a-millennium profit.

If she could clamp on safely, and *if* she could get the tumbling ruin stabilized in time for a high-power burn. The problem was that Yanai was a big girl herself—three hundred meters long; five hundred tons of fuel, radiators, and fusion engines, with a little life-support system strapped on for her four biological crew. She had the power to move a city, but wasn't what anyone would call maneuverable.

So she took it slow, approaching Safdaghar very cautiously, analyzing its motion to pick the perfect time and place to grab hold. Until she was safely clamped on, Yanai had no spare capacity to keep an eye on her crew. They were on their own.

"Can I have a word with you?" Solana asked Atmin. The corvid was in the ship's galley, holding onto the back of a seat with one foot and daintily eating a layered meat-pop. He bit off part of the outer layer with his sharp beak and swallowed it whole before answering.

"You may have one word or many, though I think you will not have them long, but rather toss them out at me. My own mouth I shall fill with honest meat," said Atmin to the human woman.

"Who are those two?" Solana grabbed the back of the seat across from Atmin and with her free hand gestured toward the passage leading forward. In the observation bubble at the end of the passage, a raptor dino dressed in black stood next to a man-shaped mass of mismatched machine parts, watching the wrecked hab approaching.

"The dino's name is Pera and I guess from how she speaks her home is somewhere in the many Venus rings. She fights in others' wars for pay—or so she says. The borg is called Utsuro, and with that you know as much as I." He tore off another strip of meat.

"Why are they here at all? What's going on? Yanai won't talk to me."

"Yanai has more important work: not crashing into things. Those other two came on the ship when you already were in hibernating sleep. I know that Pera joined our crew to reach the Jovian moons. She works for passage, not for gain. I did not get the chance to ask Utsuro—he revived himself without my aid."

The maneuver alert tone sounded and the lights momentarily flickered orange. Solana swung herself into the seat and it grabbed her securely. "We don't need any help," she said.

For a moment the deck of the galley became the ceiling as Yanai fired her braking thrusters. Atmin ignored the fact that he was hanging rather than perching, and concentrated on digging out the soft liver core of his meat-pop before answering. "In truth I think we do. This job may want a broader set of skills than we possess. I judge the price of things we find, and you are good with tools, but neither would be any use to shift a heavy load. If nothing else, both Pera and Utsuro look quite strong."

"We can print up a bot if we need muscle. Are they getting shares?"

"A partial deal. As usual we two get five percent of gross, whereas they both will split that share of what remains when all the costs are paid. Yanai assures me that this will be fair to all."

"I don't care if it's fair. I just don't want to lose any gigajoules because Yanai decided to pick up a couple of strays."

"Yet here they are, and neither you nor I can change that fact. Why don't you go and say hello, and let me eat my food? It's been two years since last I had a meal."

Solana looked forward again, then spoke aloud, looking at the ceiling the way humans did when speaking to homes or vehicles. "Yanai? Safe to move about?"

"Next burn in forty seconds."

Solana pushed out of her seat and floated to the passage. Yanai's life-support pod was definitely a low-end model—instead of reconfigurable smart matter, the interior was partitioned with panels of plain graphene. But some long-departed crew member had attacked the walls of the passage with a paint pen and a surprising aesthetic sense. At the galley end of the two-meter passage an incredibly complex, detailed pattern of curving strokes in dark green covered the walls, almost hiding the hot magenta background. As Solana moved down the passage the pattern simplified and lightened, while the background got softer and paler, so that she emerged from a light mauve end lightly scored with spring green.

"Good morning," she said aloud.

The two in the observation bubble turned to greet her. Pera swung her seat around, while Utsuro merely rotated his head a hundred and eighty degrees. The cyborg's face, such as it was, featured an assortment of sensors on the left side, and an old-fashioned visual display panel on the right. At the moment it showed a single question symbol.

"Time for breakfast?" said Pera, showing a wide row of curved meat-tearing teeth.

Solana had never met a dino in person before. Pera was big—probably two hundred kilos—but she looked lean and swift rather than bulky. The word *predatory* came to mind. Her long tail coiled securely around the post of the seat she was sitting on, with her massive legs tucked in on either side. She wore a simple dark skinsuit with lots of pockets, and had gloves on her feet with openings for her huge hooked claws—which were coated in blue enamel. Her skin was dark gold and the crest of feathers on her head was brilliant blue, matching her eyes. More blue feathers ran along the outer edge of each bare forearm.

"You'll have to get it yourself," said Solana. "I'm Solana Sina, one of Yanai's *senior* crew. Tell me about yourselves. What are you good for?"

"I can tear apart any mammal who pisses me off," said Pera. "That good enough?"

They were interrupted by the maneuver alert. Solana launched herself at the third of the four seats in front of the diamond window and it secured her with a second to spare before Yanai thrusted to the left and then down.

"We don't need a ratcatcher," said Solana drily as soon as the lights went back to normal. "What technical skills do you have?"

"Combat engineer," said Pera, suddenly sounding a lot more professional. "Explosive ordnance disposal, hull and barrier breaching, general demolition. I've worked in freefall, surface, and tunnel environments. Served in two wars and three counterinsurgency operations—first in Kreyda hab militia, then as a volunteer in the Radunitsa Freedom Army, and after that as a contractor for Screaming Death Security Consulting." She tapped her wristband and a text box appeared in the corner of Solana's vision.

"All right, good," said Solana as she scrolled through the list of jobs, commendations, and impenetrable acronyms. Presumably Yanai had verified all of this during the voyage out from Vesta. "What about you?" she asked Utsuro.

"I'm afraid I have nothing to boast about," said the cyborg. He had a nice voice, probably some long-dead actor's. The display half of his face went from showing one question mark to a whole pattern of them. "My history only goes back nine years. I crewed on a sweeper ship, did some odd jobs in an industrial hab, and for the past four years I've been in the Ceres Rescue Service."

"Nine years? You mean nine Martian?"

"No, nine standard. That's all I can remember. The sweeper Marokintana Maru found me in space. I was wearing a fancy suit that had me in medical stasis, but I'd obviously been out way too long. Lots of radiation damage—and some major injuries, too. Marokintana Maru's crew were all mechs, with no bioprinter aboard. Their only medical gear was a little crash kit that nobody had opened since the ship was built. They couldn't heal me, so . . ." The cyborg raised one metal hand and flexed the three stubby fingers. "They fixed me instead. A remarkable job, given that they just had scraps and free printables to work with."

"You don't remember anything before that?" asked Solana, trying not to sound skeptical.

"Bits and pieces, but nothing useful. I seem to know a lot of languages, I recognize most music from Mars and Deimos over the past few centuries, and I have very good manners."

"Well, who were you before? What about your genome?"

"That's another mystery. I've sent out dozens of messages to search all over the system, but none of them found any match for my DNA. I looked about like this."

"No, don't—" began Solana, but before she could finish the display on Utsuro's face showed a very ordinary-looking man with black hair, light brown skin, and dark eyes.

"Do you recognize me?" the image on the cyborg's face asked.

"No! Turn it off!" she shouted, and shielded her eyes. Then Solana launched herself hard at the passage, bounced off the painted panels, and fell through the galley toward the crew quarters. She got into her own little cabin and slid the door shut, then floated in the center of the room, curled into a ball.

After a minute she heard Atmin's beak tapping on the door.

"Go away."

"Your introductions did not go as well as one might hope. If either of our new-waked crew did wrong, just speak and I shall deal with them in manner stern."

The image of a two-kilogram bird giving a stern lecture to a cyborg and a dinosaur a hundred times his mass almost made Solana smile. She swallowed and spoke a little hoarsely. "He didn't know. The cyborg. He displayed a face and I panicked. It's not his fault."

Atmin was silent for a moment. "The fault is ultimately mine. I failed to ask what visage he might show, nor did I warn of danger if he did."

"It's okay." She sniffled and wiped tears with her sleeve.

"I shall explain to Utsuro that he must needs hide his human face. Fear not: I will not tell him why. I go."

Solana heard the flutter of wings in the passage. She rotated two or three times more, uncurled herself and pushed against the ceiling, then grabbed the edge of her bed and reached underneath it to open the storage bin.

In an age of smart matter and printers, only the rich and the mad kept hoards of things. All of Solana's material goods fit into a single bag: a few unique items with sentimental value, or things she might need in a hurry without waiting for printer time. The goggles were both a tool of her trade and a comfort for her fears.

She slipped them on and her perceptions expanded. Now she could see everything, in wavelengths from nanometer soft X-rays all the way to centimeter microwaves. She could see polarization, phase and Doppler shift, and magnify a thousand times. They showed her electric and magnetic fields, and told her the composition of every surface. It was like having the senses of a mech, or even a ship.

But Solana needed her goggles for a different purpose. They could also filter what she saw. A simple software hack replaced every human face with a featureless oval. Whenever she went among humans—or even primates and human-shaped mechs—she kept her goggles on, stuck to her skin at maximum adhesion, with the face filter active.

A world of faceless people meant freedom.

Solana took a deep breath and opened the door. The others were all still up in the observation bubble. Solana headed that way, moving slowly, forcing herself to go on. She paused in the galley to get something to eat, and while her cheese dumplings printed she listened to Atmin's harsh voice from the other end of the passage.

"...and if I did I still would guard her privacy. So I will tell you only this: Solana must not see a human face. It causes harm to her, and injury to any one is deadly to us all."

"Please tell her I am terribly sorry," said Utsuro. "I promise it won't happen again."

"I just want to know what other little mines are hidden in her head," said Pera. "Salvage work is dangerous enough without worrying about whether one of your crew is going to decohere because of something she sees."

"Solana will not fail us on the job. Of that I am most sure," said Atmin. "She—"

"Came back to apologize," said Solana, drifting into the observation bubble. "What happened before was my fault. I was careless and didn't wear my protective gear." She tapped the goggles. "I'm safe now."

The lights went orange again, and Yanai's voice sounded through the crew pod. "Prepare for spin. Portside will be down."

Atmin and Solana got themselves secured as Yanai jolted from side to side, running her thrusters at maximum. The spinning ruin before them seemed to slow as the ship matched its once-per-minute rotation. But the second-order precession remained as the axis of the station swung around every five minutes.

"Contact in two minutes. Suits on and secure yourselves," said Yanai, and the lights went red.

Solana's loose coverall suddenly became skintight, protecting her against depressurization by sheer mechanical force. The cowl that she wore over her hair slid down to cover her face and went transparent, and the little air bladders on her shoulders inflated. A readout in her vision said she had four hours of oxygen, currently on standby since the crew pod was still pressurized.

Pera's suit did much the same. Atmin's suit came flying into the observation bubble from his cabin and snapped him up. Unlike the others, it wasn't skintight. The bird sat inside a diamond bubble with four limbs that could be either hands or feet, and thrusters to move about in microgravity. Utsuro merely turned off his convective cooling fans and extended a filmy radiator fin along the center of his back.

The ship wasn't aiming exactly at Safdaghar's axis. She was

off-center by sixty meters—deliberately, since she'd need some leverage to stabilize the hab. Even spinning in sync meant there would be relative motion when they touched.

Yanai extended her six arms. They were massive and strong, each twenty meters long and three meters wide where they joined Yanai's main truss. Like the rest of the ship's skeleton the arms were tensegrity structures of diamond fiber and graphene rods—and like the rest of her skeleton they were tremendously overdesigned. Each was tipped with a door-sized adhesion pad for a good grip. Cables ran from the back of each pad to Yanai's center of mass, so that once she clamped on there would be no flexing, no shear stress on her nose.

"Twenty meters," said the ship. "Nineteen, eighteen, seventeen." A meter-wide chunk of debris thunked against the observation bubble and went tumbling off into deep space, making everyone start in surprise. "Fourteen, thirteen."

"If any claims to feel no fear, I call that one a liar," said Atmin. "Six times have I aboard Yanai made lock-on with a tumbling wreck, and six times have I wished to be in some safe world instead."

"Three, two, one, *contact!*" said the ship. The final word was drowned out by the audible crunch of the arms slamming into the spinning hull, the creak and twang of Yanai's structure adjusting to sudden loads in new directions, and the clatter of some loose objects back in the crew quarters.

Everyone was silent for a second, looking about and listening. Then Solana and Pera said "Pressure check" aloud in unison. Solana almost chuckled.

"Crew pod pressure is steady," said Yanai, and the lights turned back to orange.

"I'm here," said Utsuro, and his voice sounded full of wonder and delight.

The next five days were uncomfortable and annoying. Yanai had to stabilize Safdaghar's wobbling axis before she could shift the hab's orbit. Steady thrust would make the precession worse. Instead, the ship had to give the habitat a precise shove once every revolution, over and over and over again. This meant a five-second burn at full power every sixty-four seconds, for more than a hundred hours. The inconvenience of living in fifty-nine-second intervals between rocket bursts meant all four of Yanai's crew spent most of that time in bed doing entertainments or chatting.

On the third day Solana lay flat in bed, linked up with Atmin and Pera via her implant. She had mounted her bed in the corner where the outer wall met the aft floor. Most of the time she felt a ghostly pull down, caused by the spin of Yanai and the habitat to which she was docked. But once a minute she found herself lying on her side for five seconds as the down vector swung around to the aft floor. The sheet held her in place so she didn't roll involuntarily. It wasn't ideal, but it would have to do. Images of Atmin and Pera floated in front of her.

"Okay," said Pera. "I've looked at the old design schematics, I've read the histories—so now give me the *real* story. What happened to Safdaghar?"

"We do not know much more than this," said Atmin. "It was a small and simple hab, with twenty thousand baseline folk aboard. What little wealth they had was made from art. The humans crafted things by hand, then sold the scans across the billion worlds. From time to time they even sent out pods which held unique original creations for the rich of Juren and of Mars."

"And then boom," said Pera.

"And then some fate—we know not what—wrecked Safdaghar and took the lives of all within. A single rescue mission came to search for any who survived, and found here no one but the dead. For sixteen standard years the lifeless hab has spun untouched."

"That's what I don't get," said Pera. "Why leave it? We're just beyond the Old Belt, a prime orbit. Plenty of habs within easy reach of this place in energy and time. You'd think it would've been repaired and resettled, or already taken apart. There has to be a reason."

"The rights to Safdaghar were caught in legal webs, and stuck there while the spider courts of Deimos, Ceres, Mars, and even Juren all drew strands about its corpse. No salvager could sell the scrap, no bank would lend to pay for restoration of the hab, no colonist could come with title clear to any place within. Add to that the tumbling of the wreck, the halo of debris, the unknown hazards still inside, and one can hardly wonder Safdaghar has had no visitors but dust."

"Then why are we here?" asked Pera.

"A Deimos group at long last won the fight to claim the wreck of Safdaghar, and paid off all the rest. With title clear they sold the mass to patient folk amid the outer ice. Yanai in turn put in the lowest bid to do the job of boosting Safdaghar to dance with Jupiter and send it flying out to Kuiper space."

"You didn't answer my question. Why are *we* here?"

"We four scarabs come in search of loot," said Atmin. "This hab, though small and poor and badly hurt, still holds the goods of all who once did call it home. Some few of them had modest wealth or came of ancient lines with heirlooms fine and rare. No inventory could be made before disaster struck, so who in Kuiper space, when finally the wreck arrives in forty years, can tell if anything is gone? Then, too, the main export of Safdaghar was creativity—what work of agile minds may still be here unseen?"

"You do your looting and nobody minds because the buyers out in the Kuiper Belt just want the metals. Okay. Still seems like a lot of work just to sell somebody's knickknacks and unpublished doodles."

"And yet there is a chance—not certain, but the odds are good—that what we four may find within may be worth more than Safdaghar itself."

"Somebody sell you a map to buried treasure?"

"The treasure hid in Safdaghar was not a hoard of thorium, nor some great Inner Ring device like magic to a baseline mind. It was, in fact, a man."

"Hardly a treasure," said Pera. "There's half a quadrillion men in the solar system. That drives the price down."

Solana spoke up for the first time. "The going rate for specialized slaves is ten million right now. There's nine thousand habs where it's legal to own someone, and forty thousand where it's illegal but nobody cares."

"And there's millions of habs where everyone's a slave because they have no rights," said Pera.

"I fear we stray from civil speech—" Atmin began.

"That makes it okay?" Solana demanded. "Doesn't it *bother* you that there are places where owning a human as a plaything is just fine with everyone?"

Pera's voice became a predator's growl. "It bothers me to see some scarab getting all righteously ionized about a few million crazy pervert mammals when there are trillions being oppressed and tortured and murdered by crooks and fanatics."

Solana was about to reply when Utsuro's image appeared alongside the others. "Please forgive my lateness," he said. "I was speaking to Yanai about a private matter."

"You did not miss the most important bits," said Atmin. "For as I was about to say, the wreck of Safdaghar may hold a treasure of great worth. There was a Martian poet known as Pasquin Tiu. Have any of you heard his work? His verse was famed on Mars and far beyond. In both Old Belt and Jovian space his words were loved—except in Deimos, where bold Pasquin gave offense. For those with wealth unmatched and sovereign might do tremble at a jest, and cannot stand to hear a laugh directed at themselves."

"I just looked him up," said Pera. "He disappeared twenty standard years ago."

"He dared to give offense and Deimos took it without grace. He took another name, another face, and took to hiding what he wrote. Thus hidden and suppressed his fame grew exponentially. The Martians found his verse on walls or read it printed out by hand in ink on cellulose. They whispered poems mouth to ear, and sang them set to famous tunes, so that the music soon become a kind of secret hymn.

"Assassins sought him out and nearly got him twice. His worried friends arranged for Pasquin to leave Mars to save his life. He wrote a final book of verse with brush on silk two decades past, and nothing since. But I have sought him out, and done research on twenty worlds, and put together clues that others may have missed, and so at last I tracked him down. I think that Pasquin Tiu was here at Safdaghar when sad disaster struck. If any works of his remain intact within this wreck, their worth would be immense—as much as all the mass of Safdaghar itself."

"But can we find them? It's a small hab, only two klicks across and half a klick thick," said Pera. "That's still a lot of volume. The plans show a lot of levels—the open landscape ring plus a whole bunch of farm and industrial space, not to mention transport, services..."

"Approximately ten square kilometers of floor space," said Solana. "Looks like most of the population were in the ring at the rim. If he really was hiding that would be the place to go."

"That's still, what, three or four square klicks—not including all the buildings," said Pera. "Most of them are two or three stories, and the plans show a couple of ten-story towers. That may not sound big by megastructure standards, but it's a lot of rooms to check."

"I'm sure there will be plenty of time to search," said Utsuro. "After Yanai finishes her burn we have forty days before we have to undock for aerobraking at Jupiter. There are four of us, plus however many bots we can print up. If we plan carefully we can search the whole hab with time to spare."

"Lost works by some dead poet are great if we find them, but I'd rather focus on real stuff we can carry," said Solana.

"Fear not. I have a list," said Atmin. "A list of names of those in Safdaghar with treasures we can seek. I even have addresses for a few. Whatever Pasquin Tiu's fate, we will not leave with empty claws."

"Tell me what to do and I'll get it done," said Pera. "I'm just here for the ride."

Solana looked at the three images in her vision. She knew what Atmin wanted. Pera's goal seemed straightforward enough. But what did Utsuro want in Safdaghar?

After eight thousand nudges from Yanai, the hab once again spun on a stable axis. The tug gave her biological crew a few hours of freedom to move about, then warned them back to their cabins. "I have to reposition myself to the hab's axis for the orbit-change burn. Once I'm settled in place you can do what you like, but it's safer if you stay put while I maneuver."

From Solana's perspective, that meant another hour of random jolts and bumps as Yanai disengaged from her off-center position and moved to the entrance of Safdaghar's docking bay. The bay itself was just a big open cylinder at the axis of the spinning hab, a hundred meters across and two hundred meters deep. A launch tube ran down one side, so that the hab could send out small payloads without wasting propellant.

Yanai's arms weren't long enough to span that space, so she nosed cautiously into the bay, matching Safdaghar's spin, until her arms touched the rear wall. Her rear third stuck out of the entrance, which gave her room to extend her radiator fins.

Thus anchored, Yanai could finally bring her engine up to full power. A plume of pale violet plasma shot from the lattice-work funnel of Yanai's magnetic engine bell. Solana, in her bed in the crew pod, felt a faint vibration carried through the ship's skeleton, but no sense of acceleration. The glow from Yanai's radiators lit up everything outside, as if Safdaghar had acquired its own little orange sun.

Yanai's powerful engine pushing Safdaghar's immense mass required twenty hours of constant burning to affect the hab's orbit. She was pushing the hab away from the Sun, changing its orbit from a near-perfect circle to an ellipse which would take Safdaghar close to Jupiter. Jupiter would give the hab an even bigger boost, flinging it out on a forty-year journey to the Kuiper Belt.

That was why the crew had a time limit. Changing Safdaghar's orbit would use up nearly all of Yanai's propellant. Only by aerobraking in Jupiter's atmosphere could she avoid accompanying the hab to the outer darkness. The scarabs would leave in forty days or never.

The acceleration felt so weak that Pera asked why they couldn't start salvage operations while Yanai was still doing her burn.

"I don't think that would be healthy," said Yanai. "The hab's docking tubes are all retracted so you will have to go out in suits to reach an airlock. With my drive running the radiation levels outside would cook you. Just wait a few more hours."

The four of them could and did move around the crew pod during the burn. Atmin and Pera were both glad of the chance to get some exercise. The corvid flew back and forth a hundred times along the length of the pod's main passage, not stopping until he had flown four kilometers.

Pera took over the observation bubble at the forward end for an hour of *longwu* practice against a projected image of another neoraptor. She dodged kicks and tail-blows, slashed at the air with her own wicked toe-claws, and kept at it until she was panting. As she fought, she sang—a mix of ancient military songs and some haunting wordless dino keening.

Utsuro didn't need exercise, of course. Solana did, and went through the regimen she had been taught as a child—but only in her own cabin with the door locked. It was even slightly embarrassing to her that Yanai might see.

All of them wanted to get inside Safdaghar as soon as possible, and so the whole crew gathered in the observation bubble, all ready to go, when there was still an hour left on Yanai's burn clock.

"I recommend double suits for Solana and Pera," said the ship. "As I pushed I could feel mass shifting inside the hab. There might be loose junk, shards of diamond, or reactive chemicals."

"My gear can stop hypersonic darts and most hostile nano-bots," said Pera, banging one gloved fist against the side of her battle armor. She had a large powerpack on her back above her hips, and a combat engineer's laser slung below her torso.

"This isn't a boarding action," said Solana. "If we see hazards we avoid them or contain them."

"I volunteer to go in first," said Utsuro.

"Your eagerness, while laudable, is puzzling to me," said Atmin. "What draws you to Safdaghar? What do you seek within this lonely wreck?"

"Myself," said Utsuro. "The mechs who found me tracked my vector. It originated at this hab. My guess is that I lived here once, and got out during the disaster. I've got a scanner keyed to my genome. If I can find traces of my DNA on board I might be able to learn who I was."

"You might not like what you find," said Solana.

"Anything is better than ignorance," Utsuro replied.

CHAPTER TWO

In Safdaghar's prime, the main entrances had been five diamond-roofed passages extending the length of the docking bay, with extensible passage tubes every few meters. They were spaced at the points of a hexagon, with the sixth point occupied by Safdaghar's magnetic launcher. All the docking tubes were safely retracted, and the pressure membranes had been sealed off by solid doors when disaster struck. So when Solana, Atmin, Utsuro, and Pera passed through Yanai's membrane, they dropped down to the deck of the docking bay and had to walk to an emergency airlock outlined in glowing green on the rear wall of the bay.

Solana made her shoes sticky, as the spin gravity was just a twentieth of a gee. Utsuro did the same, and Atmin maneuvered his diamond ball with little thruster jets. Pera showed off her combat boarding expertise by jumping to the wall beside the airlock directly from Yanai's hatch.

The bay was completely empty, without even the normal clutter of an active facility. No work pods, no cargo movers, no tool kits stuck to the floor, no coils of cable or hose. The sole rescue expedition, shortly after the disaster, had confirmed that no spacecraft were docked at Safdaghar. Over the years the

increasing wobble of the hab's axis had thrown anything left in
the bay out into space.

"*I volunteered to go first,*" Utsuro reminded the others via radio
link, and opened the airlock. It was a big one, a cube three meters
on a side, with doors that could accommodate a cargo container
or a small vehicle. The cyborg went in alone and cycled through.

"*No air inside, at least not up here,*" he told them when he
opened the inner door. "*Everything is dark. No power, either.*"

The other three squeezed into the lock together. Solana set
her goggles to light amplification and infrared. Pera turned on
her helmet lamps and Atmin turned on the spotlights at the
front of his spacesuit ball.

The inner door opened, revealing a short passage leading
straight ahead. It was decorated in the bland cheeriness of transport terminals everywhere. The walls were etched with images of
Safdaghar's habitat ring and events from its history. A small heap
of broken furniture and smashed planters had piled up around
the airlock door.

Utsuro was already at the far end, beckoning impatiently.
They followed the passage into an open concourse some ten
meters wide, open above so that one could see the floor curve
around overhead.

The only light came from windows looking out into the docking bay, and Yanai's bulk blocked most of it. The rest was dim
shapes and deep shadows. On infrared it was only marginally
better. "*It's all cold,*" Solana announced. "*Everything's a uniform
one hundred sixty kelvins. I don't see any active power.*"

The rear wall of the concourse had broad passages lined with
what had once been shops and offices. Above them was a huge
shattered window looking into what looked like a zero-gravity
sports and performance arena at the axis of the hab. Even with
her feet made sticky, Solana had to move with great caution. The
floor was littered with debris, including sharp diamond bits from
the shattered window.

Safdaghar wasn't like any of Solana's other salvage jobs. The
other habs had all been deliberately abandoned. The inhabitants
had taken everything they wanted, and what was left had been
sad and empty but not frightening. This hab was a snapshot of
destruction.

She could see big uba vines growing on the walls, dead and

desiccated from years in vacuum. A snack vendor's cart stood anchored near the exit from one of the docking access passages, and under its transparent dome Solana could see a heap of dehydrated dumplings in all colors. Above it a fabric sculpture made to float on air currents hung limp and still.

The launch tube facility was fifty meters to spinward, a big open space with cargo elevators in the floor and airlocks to the docking bay. The launcher itself was a diamond tube as wide as Solana's outstretched arms, girdled with magnetic accelerator rings. A row of superconducting energy storage banks flanked the tube where it passed through the hab's hull.

Solana could see that one of the magnetic power-storage loops was leaking a little heat. When she adjusted her goggles to show magnetic fields she was startled to see that it was still charged. About half the energy in it had dissipated over the course of sixteen years, but it still had about five gigajoules available. It was an inconvenient amount—enough to make it dangerous to try to take the thing apart, but not enough energy to be worth keeping.

"Shall I drain it?" she asked Atmin.

"No need to take that risk right now. Yanai can send a bot while we descend in search of beauty lost."

"Short it!" Pera suggested. "That's always fun to see."

"I don't think vaporizing wire is a safe pastime," said Utsuro.

Atmin's sphere maneuvered over to the launcher's loading door, a four-meter section of the tube's top half raised on telescoping pistons. "I see a payload set to launch. Solana, come and help me see what lies within," he called.

She could see a centimeter gap at the edge of the cargo pod's hatch. "This has been opened," she said.

"Careful!" Pera called. "Don't use your hands. Someone might have left a surprise behind."

"Allow me, then," said Atmin, extending one of his travel sphere's spindly mechanical arms. "I fear good Pera fears too much."

He flipped the hatch open and the two of them just stared for a moment.

Within the cargo pod were half a dozen suited humans, with an emergency life-support pack linked to their helmets by taped-together hoses. All of them were long dead and vacuum-mummified, with neat holes in their skulls.

"Why discard the dead?" Atmin wondered aloud. "I do not

think that Safdaghar was big or rich enough to waste the mass
of corpses."

"Biohazard, maybe?" asked Pera. "Maybe they had some bug
too dangerous to keep aboard."

"I do not see the need to furnish oxygen to those who do not
breathe," said Atmin.

Solana looked at the bodies. Their suits were brightly colored,
and a couple had patterns of kittens or chicks. They were all
smaller than she was. "These are children," she said.

"How awful," said Utsuro. "Who would do such a thing?"

"Such things are not unknown," said Atmin. "In habs where
food or air runs short. Or civil strife unleashing deadly hate."

"Leave them," said Yanai. "According to the plans, power control
and the backup generators are all three levels down. Main processors and data storage is one level below that."

"Stairs over here," said Pera, using her laser to light up an
inconspicuous doorway between two elevators.

The stairway was small, just a little local access route between
the levels of the hub—not the main spokes connecting to the
habitat rim. The emergency doors had slid shut at each level, so
there was just a flight of steps down ten meters and then a floor
sealing off the next flight. In the feeble spin gravity near the hub
none of them bothered actually climbing down the steps when
it was easier to jump down.

The door on the first level was not sealed shut, but bulged
out. "That's bad," said Pera. "It should open inward."

Utsuro got one hand into a gap between the door and the
frame, braced himself against the wall, and wrenched it open.
He looked inside. "Oh, dear," he said.

"What does that mean?" asked Pera.

"I see a great deal of damage on this level. I think something
must have exploded. Perhaps a capacitor failed, or a flywheel."

Solana followed Pera through the door while Atmin brought
up the rear. According to the plans this level had no windows,
so it should have been utterly dark. But she could see perfectly
well by daylight coming in through holes in the outer hull. Many,
many holes—ranging from millimeters to meters across. The spin
of the hab meant that the beams of light streaming in through
the holes constantly moved, creating endless shifting shadows.

"Move carefully. There is debris," said Utsuro.

Solana was glad of the carbon-fiber coverall she was wearing over her suit, because there was indeed debris. Debris everywhere. Graphene wall panels shattered into paper-thin daggers, sheets of aluminum wrapped around structural beams like flags in a strong wind, hanks of optical fiber and structural cable tangled around broken metal struts, and a layer of gritty shards and gravel on the floor.

Pera looked very tense and alert, and held her engineer's laser ready and powered up. She kept still, and watched the moving shadows.

Solana switched her goggles to spectrographic vision and looked at the patches lit by the moving beams of light as they swept around. "There's a thin layer of metal on all the exposed surfaces," she said. "Looks like a mix of silicon, copper, and tungsten."

"Antimatter containment," said Pera. "Something failed and the cells turned to plasma. Chain reaction. Must have been a couple of micrograms. Probably an emergency power supply. The decks held but all the interior walls blew out."

"That raises in my mind a question which I put to those of you with knowledge of such things," said Atmin. "Did this explosion cause the wreck of Safdaghar, or did it happen after?"

"I think it was after," said Solana.

"Why?" asked Utsuro.

She tried to keep her voice professional and clinical. "No bodies. Not even traces of hemoglobin. I don't know how many people worked in this part of the hab, but I don't think anybody died here."

"No broken mech parts, either," said Utsuro.

"I've seen habs survive much worse damage than this," Pera added. The dino's stance relaxed a tiny bit, though she still watched the moving shadows.

"Try to make contact with the main mind, or find a backup device," said Yanai over the link. "It would know what happened."

"And if we save a mind of level three from Safdaghar that means a rescue bounty for us all," said Atmin.

"It would be the right thing to do in any case," said Utsuro.

"The main processor assembly should be two levels down and about ninety degrees to spinward of your current location," said Yanai.

The four of them returned to the stairs and Solana got out her tool kit. The emergency doors were level with the deck, covering

the stairs down and the open shaft in the center. A two-meter
square over the stairs down glowed faintly green, indicating an
access hatch.

Solana's tool kit was her most expensive possession. The
tough smart-matter bag held an omnitool, a laser, a bonder, a
small printer, and a sensor. The bag itself doubled as an energy
supply, and could live on sunlight, burn chemical fuel, suck up
local power by induction, or actually plug into the local grid.

She chose the sensor and set it on the access hatch to see
what was on the other side. The device linked to her goggles.

"*No air,*" she announced. "*Temperature looks the same, too.*"

"*Want me to just cut it open?*" asked Pera.

"*I can get it,*" Solana replied. She used the sensor to find the
latches on the hatch, and cut each one out with the tool set to
molecule thickness.

The level below had a ten-meter ceiling, and appeared mostly
undamaged. Solana got the emergency doors open so they could
peek inside at a seemingly endless maze of pipes and reactors
for microgravity industry.

Atmin was pleased to see the machinery undamaged. "*A trove
of costly gear for us, convenient to the docking bay for hauling
out! Solana, we must come back here when rescue work is done,
so you can assay metal and determine what to take and what to
leave for Kuiper scarabs decades hence.*"

They cut their way down another level, to where Yanai said
the main processor was—or at least where it had been when the
plans were last updated. Getting to the right compartment wasn't
easy. From the stairway they followed an axial passage to one of
the main circumferential streets running all the way around the
level. At every major intersection the emergency doors were shut.
Once Solana figured out where the latches were on the first one,
they could open the others with a few shots from Pera's laser.

The passages on this level were littered with debris, but it
wasn't the complete devastation of the blast damage upstairs. It
was simply that anything which hadn't been stuck to the floor
had battered itself to bits against the walls during sixteen years
of Safdaghar wobbling on its axis. At first the force must have
been slight, but by the time Yanai stabilized the hab's spin the
passage had been lurching from side to side once a minute.

The result was that the lower meter of the walls on either side of the circumferential passage was completely stripped of paint. Where those walls met the floor a layer of fragments and debris had accumulated—fragments of plastic and graphene, shattered glass and diamond shards, and drifts of dust. Larger pieces were buried in the mess, but nothing looked worth stopping to pick up.

Safdaghar's main processor sat in a heavily shielded section, protected by massive doors of five-centimeter titanium with an outer layer of heat-absorbing carbon. The scarab crew could clearly see the cross-section of the door because someone had blasted a meter-wide hole in the center of it.

"Shaped charge," said Pera.

"I see a lot of nitrogen compounds on the walls," said Solana. "Nitrogen polymer, maybe?"

"It pleases me to see you two are working closely as a team," said Atmin. "Good Pera, have you thought at all of taking up a scarab's life?"

"Not for me. I can earn gigajoules by sitting in a nice safe hab. If I'm going to take risks it has to be for something important."

"If gigs aren't important can I have your share?" asked Solana.

"Not as long as I'm breathing," said Pera.

"You should not say such things," said Atmin. "Press on and let us learn the fate of that great mind which once ran Safdaghar."

Solana looked through the breach in the door. Beyond it she could see a sphere about fifteen centimeters across, suspended in the center of the protecting armored room. Coolant lines and power conduits connected it to the floor and ceiling, and a web of data lines ran from the sphere's equator to the walls of the room.

It was all quite cold. She didn't need to see the severed power and coolant feeds to tell that the main processor was dead.

But the dead brain wasn't alone in the vault. The floor was covered by a half-meter layer of jellied blue coolant compound. Two yellow-suited human figures were embedded in the gel, surrounded by a stain of rusty purple. One lay facedown, with an engineering laser like Pera's in one hand, but the other was looking up. Solana's filter hid the mummified face, but she could clearly see the deep slash across its front, from collarbone to hip, almost deep enough to cut the body in half. She had seen dead people before, but this was still shocking.

Pera peered over Solana's shoulder. "Looks like they blasted in here and then killed the brain. Who are they?"

"*Their suits say Safdaghar Emergency Response,*" said Solana.

"*That raises in my mind a worrisome idea,*" said Atmin. "*Could Safdaghar have died of civil war? Some strife between the ruling mind and all the lesser folk?*"

For a moment nobody said anything.

"*It happens,*" said Yanai over the comm link. "*Though more often to ships than habs.*"

"*I hope we do not give you cause for murderous intent,*" said Atmin.

"*Not yet,*" said Yanai.

"*We ought to see if there is a backup device,*" said Utsuro.

Solana moved cautiously through the hole in the door, being careful not to tear her suit. She looked down at the jellied coolant and then prodded it with one foot. It was soft, but not squishy. Very gingerly she put her weight on it. In one-tenth gee her forty-five kilograms weren't quite heavy enough to break the rubbery surface layer.

Avoiding the corpses, she made her way to the central sphere. The outer surface was warped and cracked from overheating. Some of the data lines had melted and snapped.

"*According to the design specs Safdaghar had a Juren Processor Designs type SCELSJ variant 66 main processor, rated at an intellect level of 3.2,*" said Yanai. "*The backup storage device should be at the bottom of the protective casing.*"

Just below the sphere, where the severed coolant line hung empty, Solana saw a boxy fixture still faintly glowing green. The slot within was empty. "*Someone took it,*" she called out.

"*One of those two, maybe?*" asked Pera, shining her helmet lamp down on the corpses.

"*I don't see anything.*" Solana scanned the entire floor once again, hoping to find it embedded in the blue jelly.

Atmin used the four arms attached to his life-support ball to crawl into the processor room. "*Though well I know the thought is vile, we nonetheless must search the dead. This nasty work may save a mind far greater than our own.*"

Solana suppressed a shudder and stepped across the jelly to join Atmin.

"*We'll just stay out here, then,*" said Pera.

The hands on Atmin's suit arms were smart matter, so the bird made two of them into cutting blades and deftly sliced away the jellied coolant covering the faceup corpse. He then proceeded to methodically search all the pockets and pouches on the outer coverall. As it was a rescue-service suit, there were a lot of them.

"*The man who wore this suit went well-equipped to death,*" said Atmin. "*Each pocket holds exactly what its label says, and nothing more. I find no backup unit here.*"

Solana grimaced and forced her hands into the goop, working them under the second body. She kept her back straight and lifted with her legs. At first nothing seemed to be happening, then all at once the jelly parted from the floor and the body flipped over. Solana lost her grip and shot upward, snapping hundreds of data channels as she bounced off the ceiling and fell back again.

She landed a couple of meters away and winced as she caught sight of the body, now faceup after sixteen years. This one had been protected by the coolant jelly—which meant that the corpse had rotted until it froze. The inside of the suit was a chunk of ice, colored a horrible swirl of red, yellow, and black. Two eyes, embedded in the ice, looked out at nothing.

Solana's visual filter saw nothing it recognized as a face, so she got an unimpeded view. She had to turn her back on it for a minute, fighting nausea and fear. Nobody—not even Pera—said anything. Finally she turned around and knelt again next to the corpse. She forced herself to keep it technical. Focus on the job. Ignore the eyes.

Like the other body, this one had a single, brutal slash across the front of its chest, cutting right through the rib cage almost to the spine, passing directly through the heart. The right forearm was also severed, dangling by a few threads of the coverall. The enhanced senses in her goggles meant Solana didn't need to open any of the dead woman's pockets. She could look through the tough silicon-fiber cloth, and saw no data device at all.

"*Excuse me,*" said Utsuro. "*But something just occurred to me. If these two individuals really did kill the main processor—who killed them?*"

"*Loyalists, maybe,*" said Pera. "*Couldn't stop them in time but wanted revenge? They might have taken the backup.*"

"*But where did they go? There are no other processors aboard Safdaghar capable of running a Level 3.2 mind,*" said Yanai.

"*Evacuated?*" asked Pera. "*Took the backup and got to a shuttle in time?*"

"*I'm afraid that doesn't make sense either,*" said Utsuro. "*We would not be here if the main mind had survived, as it would own the wreck.*"

"*Unless it had some reason to hide? Maybe Safdaghar screwed up, killed everyone, and then didn't want anyone off-hab to know. A high-level bot could have gotten the backup out,*" said Pera.

"*Even a near-baseline bot couldn't remain hidden once it reached some other hab or world,*" said Utsuro.

"*This chattering is wearisome,*" said Atmin. "*We do not even know what questions we should ask.*"

"*I know one,*" said Solana. "*What next?*"

The four of them returned to Yanai. Along the way they picked up a few kilograms of metal in order to print out some simple bots to make a survey of the hab's decks. Yanai had a standard hull-repair bot design on file, and she and Solana worked out some modifications before running off half a dozen.

Each bot resembled a horseshoe crab, with a domed outer shell of polymer and six legs with sticky feet on the underside. The edge of the shell could deform to make a seal with the hull surface, so that the bots could repair punctures without interference from rushing cabin air. The redesign replaced the repair tools with a simple drill, an atmosphere tester, and a probe with a low-light eye.

They sent the bots down the elevator shafts with instructions to stop at each level, drill a hole, check atmosphere and conditions on the level, then seal the hole and move on.

While the bots crept down toward the rim of the hab, the crew assembled in the observation bubble to make plans.

"I must confess I had not thought that years of Safdaghar's precession would have shaken up the contents of the hab as much as we have seen. If even near the hub it was so bad, out near the rim I fear that all will be reduced to dust," said Atmin.

"If anybody had a valuable collection of antique glassware we can scratch that off the list," said Pera. "We should just focus on heavy elements. What's our mass limit?"

"Ten percent of my full mass is a safe load for aerobraking," said Yanai. "Call it forty tons. I've got two thousand cubic meters of empty tankage to stow cargo in, so that's not a problem."

"I would like to check the rim section, if it's not too much trouble," said Utsuro. "Just to see what's down there."

"I too believe that though it may be shaken up, we yet should spend our time in that part of the hab," said Atmin. "The goods of all the citizens of Safdaghar must hold some value still."

"Simplest and safest just to clear out the decks near the hub," said Pera.

"I always like to maximize efficiency in time and energy," said Yanai. "Solana, you have not said anything."

She hadn't spoken up because she didn't know what she wanted to do. Yanai was probably right: maximize profit, minimize effort. They could stuff Yanai's empty tanks with all the heavy elements and intact machinery they could find, and get out with time to spare. That was the logical course of action.

The problem was Atmin. She liked the bird, and she knew how much time and effort he had put into tracking down his dead Martian poet. He would be disappointed, especially if she went against him. And Solana didn't want to risk losing his friendship. With other humans—and even some mechs—Solana always had the nagging suspicion that her conditioning affected how she felt about them. But a corvid? No doubt there. If she liked Atmin it was her own genuine emotion, and that was something to treasure.

"I guess it would be worth taking a look at the rim section, just to see what's there. If it's all too messed up we can pull back to the hub and concentrate on salvaging metals."

Utsuro's display screen showed a smiling icon, and Atmin fluttered his wings with delight. "Our councils then are at an end. We shall commence our salvage work by dropping to the farthest rim, then coming up one level at a time, until by systematic work the hab is stripped of all that we can take."

"Still seems like extra work to me," said Pera.

"Normally I would agree," said Yanai. "I tend to think of everything in terms of mass and vectors. But a kilo of hydrogen and a kilo of phosphorus aren't equal in value, even if they take the same amount of energy to accelerate. And a kilo of raw organics isn't worth the same as a kilo of DNA samples from a high-end designer. I'm not qualified to judge what is and what isn't likely to have value. I can appreciate an elegant maneuver, but I can't judge between two crude attempts at rendering an image by hand, using pigments on cloth or paper. Just a moment—" Yanai's voice didn't change but everyone could tell something was wrong.

"Bot three just failed. It was descending the elevator shaft to the service level above the habitat ring. I have video."

The image was a bot's-eye view as the little machine crept down the side of the elevator shaft. At that level the local gravity was nearly a full gee, so it kept at least three of its feet touching the wall at all times. The low-light camera showed nothing but a long dark tube, curving away with distance. The bot stopped at the elevator doors and settled its carapace down against the surface before drilling. The final image was motion-blurred, then nothing.

"The poor thing," said Utsuro. "I wonder what happened?"

"Something hit it," said Pera.

"Perhaps a piece of debris fell down the shaft," said Utsuro.

"An object of twenty kilograms or more dropping from the hub would have enough energy to damage the bot," said Yanai.

"So would a bullet," said Pera.

"Who would shoot a harmless bot?" asked Atmin.

"Something with a gun."

"The choice between a random bit of junk dislodged by Yanai's mighty push, or lurking snipers hiding out for sixteen years seems clear enough to me," said Atmin.

"I think we're all getting too excited about a printed bot failing," said Solana. "It's a big hab with plenty of loose junk in it. That's why we sent bots instead of Pera."

"Thanks, I think."

"The rest of the bots should finish their initial survey in approximately ninety minutes," said Yanai. "So far they have detected atmosphere on two of the seven levels of the hub section, three of the six spokes, and the entire rim habitat area. The air mix is breathable, but the bots have detected both chemical and biological contaminants: carbon and silicon dust, a variety of bacteria and fungal spores, complex hydrocarbons, ammonia, and some sulfur compounds. I recommend life-support gear even in areas with atmosphere."

"A curse upon all foul reeks and filthy dust," said Atmin. "Must I work inside a ball and never stretch my wings?"

"Indeed you must, unless you wish to sleep inside an isolation bubble in the hold," said Yanai. "For I will not have pristine decks and walls begrimed with living filth."

Ten minutes later bot number five failed. It had stopped at the main hab ring and drilled a hole for its probe. It sampled the air, then extended its eye. The screen showed a high-ceilinged area full of buildings, then suddenly the video cut off. A second later the bot itself, on the other side of the elevator door, went dark.

Solana sat in the observation bubble while she and Yanai went through the bot's final instants millisecond by millisecond.

"The camera failed first. The bot showed no input on the video channel," said Yanai.

"That sounds like something happened to the camera when it poked through the door," said Solana. "Do the elevators on that level have some kind of outer emergency door? Maybe cutting the probe hole tripped a detector."

"The plans don't show anything like that. Point nine seconds after the probe retracted, the bot sensed a whole cascade of failures in very rapid succession before data transmission stopped—probably indicating main processor failure. The signal continued for another one point two seconds before cutting off."

"Maybe something corrosive in the air?" Solana suggested.

"The atmosphere test revealed nothing dangerous," said Yanai. "I think we need an expert." Two seconds later Pera's image popped up in Solana's vision. "During the search for the main processor, Atmin raised the possibility of a conflict within Safdaghar. Could the damage to this bot be the result of some sort of trap?"

"Pretty simple and low-tech—exactly what you'd expect if two factions are fighting with just what's available. Yes."

"What other kinds of trap should we be watching out for?"

The dino bared all her big sharp teeth in a grin. "All of them. In a civil war nobody stockpiles standard weapons. They throw together whatever they can. Printing up crap from some template they found, and half the time it's utter noise. Building things by hand. Primary risk is things like tripwires, spring-loaded stabby things, monofilament, maybe sabotage to stairs and walkways. Lasers, of course. We should all wear goggles, not just Solana. Won't be a lot of explosives—no handy rock for mining here, so they wouldn't keep it around, and it's very energy-intensive to make. Guns? You could print up a mag rifle, or even build one. Maybe cobble together some kind of weapon using compressed gas in a tube."

"I confess I don't understand what there would be to fight over," said Yanai.

"Maybe one group was doing something bad, and the other group wanted to stop them," said Solana.

"Any reason will do," said Pera.

Yanai called the other four bots back from the rim. Three made it home. Bot six failed in the spoke just two levels below the hub. This time there was no data to analyze at all. One millisecond it was crawling steadily up the wall of the shaft, the next millisecond all signal stopped. Pera and Utsuro went inside Safdaghar to the hub section again and opened up the shaft, but found nothing.

"Before we conjure phantom foes, or deadly relics of a war between the realms of might and could, we must remember clearly that these bots were printed out of powdered junk, from templates Yanai got for free, and therefore worth their price," said Atmin when Pera and Utsuro reported in.

"I'll go down," said Utsuro before anybody had a chance to argue. *"I'm tough and strong. Tougher than those bots, certainly. And if something down there is dangerous enough to destroy me, then the rest of you really should just leave."*

"Wait a second," said Pera. *"Yanai, do you have any cable? A kilometer or so?"*

"I always carry ten kilometers of hundred-kilonewton braided carbon fiber, ready for use, and I can print out more given time."

"One klick will do. I just want to be able to pull Utsuro out of trouble."

Solana got three emergency pressure membranes out of Yanai's ready-supply cabinet, then suited up and took the end of the cable from Yanai's cargo bay. She pulled it to the emergency airlock, then paused to disable the automatic link on the airlock so that both doors could remain open. Then she sealed one pressure membrane over the inner door frame before pushing through it, pulling the cable after her. The membrane parted around solid objects but kept gases in.

She pulled the cable down the passage to where Pera and Utsuro waited. Pera bonded the cable to Utsuro's back, just below the neck joint. *"There. Now if something happens we can still sell your body for scrap."*

"As it happens, the mechs who built this body gave me a complete assessment of its value, so that I could pay it off by working for them. Excluding the cost of their labor, and shipping, my body is worth sixty thousand gigajoule equivalent credits. Yanai, how much would Pera's elements fetch on the open market?"

"Her water and carbon are almost worthless. Two kilos of phosphorus is worth about a hundred gigajoule equivalent credits, and three kilos of calcium would fetch twenty. Call it a hundred and fifty to cover any price fluctuations. As salvage you are four hundred times more valuable than Pera."

"Thank you. Here I go."

Solana sealed the second pressure membrane over the elevator doors and gave the third to Utsuro. Then she stood next to Pera in the empty concourse as Utsuro descended.

Utsuro pivoted his arms and legs back so that he could walk on the side of the shaft with sticky feet. He trotted briskly down, about the same speed as the little bots. Since he didn't have to stop for samples, it took Utsuro only twenty minutes to get from the hub down to the habitat ring.

He narrated over the link as he pried open the elevator doors, releasing a strong dusty wind. Utsuro pulled himself through the door and anchored his feet to the floor, then unrolled the spare pressure membrane to cover the doors.

"Well, I'm here," he transmitted back to the hub. "I'm disconnecting the tether."

"What do you see?" asked Solana.

"A mess. The structures all seem to be intact, but there must have been a lot of loose debris flying around. This elevator is in the middle of a plaza, and the pavement is covered by almost a centimeter of fragments. And—oh, dear. I see some bones. Humans. At least two dead people. No, there's a couple more over there in suits."

"What killed them?" asked Pera.

"Let me look." After a pause Utsuro transmitted, "I can't tell how the unsuited ones died, but both of the suited bodies were killed by hypervelocity needles to the head."

"How do you know that?" asked Solana.

Utsuro didn't answer for a couple of seconds. "I just recognize it somehow. Maybe I was a medic once." Another pause. "I'm afraid I'm going to need a lot of decontamination before Yanai will let me back on board. There's a lot of organic material here. Some kind of low-temperature mold growing on everything. We should probably get samples—it could be a new strain. That would be worth something."

Atmin's voice came over the link from inside the ship. "The

plan of Safdaghar that good Yanai displays for me suggests you stand amid a place of shops and restaurants where once the people showed their wares and met to socialize. Look south and tell me what you see. Is there a shop that sold the work of cunning hands and clever minds?"

"The sign says Figments Design."

"It was a group of artisans whose fame reached far beyond this little hab. Does anything remain intact within? A gleam of wealth amid the grim remains?"

"I think so, yes. There's broken glass and pottery all over the floor, but the display cases must have sticky shelves. I can see things inside them that look just fine. Vases, bowls, some kind of sculptures. They are very pretty."

"Rejoice!" said Atmin. "That means whatever doom befell unlucky Safdaghar did not destroy the things its people left behind. No pirates came to slay and loot, nor vandals in some civil strife did smash and burn in wanton rage. Those works of hand have value more than equal mass of iodine or platinum."

Utsuro moved out from the plaza in a rough spiral, zigzagging among the triangular blocks of the shopping district. "The buildings are in good shape. A few have smashed windows. Everything inside looks all shaken around. I see some more bodies, half a dozen of them, all inside some kind of café. They aren't too badly tossed around. All of them have needle wounds, and—oh! It looks as if some of the bodies were disturbed by scavengers."

"Carrion birds?" asked Pera.

"Or stupid reptiles feeding on the helpless dead?" Atmin added over the link.

"I hope it was just animals," said Solana. "What if there are survivors stuck in here?" She had a sudden mental image of bony, hungry humans crawling around in the cold and dark, and looked around the hub concourse carefully, trying not to shudder.

"We have not seen a single trace of anything alive," said Atmin.

"I will turn on my spotlights and call out," said Utsuro. Over the link they could hear him shout, muffled by the noise compensation. "Hello! We are here to help! We can give you food, medical aid, and protection! Come to the elevator plaza!"

Solana felt tears in her eyes behind the goggles. The skin pads efficiently wicked away all moisture. She remembered the Salibi soldiers blasting into Kumu hab all those years ago, the crimson *shi* signs glowing on their armor. They had said the same—that they came to help—but of course young Solana and her siblings had not believed them. Genetic and psychological conditioning made sure of that.

No time to dwell on that now. She concentrated on the feed from the rim. Utsuro completed a full circuit around the elevator plaza. *"I don't hear any answer to my calls,"* he said. *"It's all very cold and still down here."*

"Now let us follow good Utsuro's lead and travel down the elevator shaft. Our camp will be down at the rim, where we can search and gather loot efficiently—no time lost going up and down, no need to decontaminate our skin each day. Just one trip down, a few days' search, then bring our finds back to Yanai," said Atmin.

"That's a clever idea," said Utsuro via the link. *"I think we should."*

Solana looked at Pera in the hub concourse. *"Is it safe?"* She was still thinking of pale cannibals hiding in the ruins.

Pera lashed her tail. *"No, it's not. I say clear out the hub levels and call it done."*

"Yanai, a squad of simple bots could cut and carry scrap to fill your empty tanks," said Atmin. *"You hired me to choose what art aboard this hab has value greater than its elemental mass. All that is at the rim. If fear will keep us at the hub then let me hibernate again and wake me when the job is done."*

"We still don't even know what really happened here," Utsuro added.

"I see your point, Atmin," said Yanai. *"I do want to maximize profit from this job, and creative works are worth more gigajoules per kilogram than scrap metal. We've got thirty days before it's time to undock. You four can spend a week checking the town ring, but if you don't find anything I'll expect double shifts on scrap collection after that. Utsuro, find a place to camp—look for a structure with emergency power, if you can find one. I'll print out some equipment and rations for the other three, and they can carry it down with them."*

Yanai's four printers ran continuously for the next three hours, making the cabin air hot and dusty despite all the seals and cooling. The two in the galley created ten days' worth of compact high-energy food for the three who needed to eat. For Pera, Yanai made slabs of liver pâté, sausages blending meat from a dozen species, and wagyu carpaccio. Atmin got hominy polenta, armadillo jerky, and some realistic-looking whole skin-less rabbits. For Solana the ship made festively colored surimi, spicy peanut-butter dumplings, and peppers stuffed with a paste of olives and pistachios.

The materials printer made transport bags, sleep-sacks, more pressure membranes, extra coveralls, a hundred meters of cable, and two spare suit liners each for Pera and Solana. That machine finished first, but then Pera asked the ship for some extra items. "I need about a hundred square meters of isotropic cloth," she said.

"What for?" asked Yanai.

"Snipers. I don't want to wake up with a hole through my head."

"What do you expect to be targeting you in a dead hab?"

"I don't know, and that's why I want to take precautions. You asked for my expertise? Here's some expertise: hang isocloth around the camp. It won't cloak us, but it does turn individual IR signatures into a big featureless rectangle. Also messes with lasers."

The two equipment printers in Yanai's repair bay made lights, heaters, cutting tools, pulleys, a jack, prybars, two little flying bots, and a fuel cell for power. "I'll fill a tank of methane for the cell, and you can feed it feces and organic waste," the ship told Solana.

Solana took a nap until the printers finished working, then she and Pera hauled all the gear into Safdaghar. They piled everything into the two largest transport bags, and then used the long cable to lower each one down the elevator shaft to Utsuro waiting at the bottom.

"*I'll go next. You two follow together,*" said Pera. She held the cable with her gloved hands and feet, and let herself slide down. Solana watched as the lights from Pera's helmet disappeared down the shaft.

She was still watching when Atmin's travel sphere nudged her. "*Enough delay. We should descend.*"

Solana didn't have much experience with rappelling, so she used her multipurpose tool to grip the cable and then had Yanai lower her down at a safe speed. Atmin's travel sphere simply floated down next to her, and the two of them passed the fifteen-minute ride by speaking on a private channel.

"Do you think Pera's right? Could something still be alive in here?" Solana asked the bird.

"Right now in Safdaghar the temperature is just above a hundred sixty kelvins, deadly cold to anything alive. The wobble of precession which our good Yanai did work so hard to fix would toss a hapless person here from side to side with bruising force. Could anyone, however tough or mad, survive for sixteen standard years of cold and dark and constant shaking back and forth? I scorn the thought."

"A mech could do it."

"But even mechs must have a source of power to survive. This hab has none. And if some unit with a long-term power source could stay within the wreck, the question one must ask is why? When rescue came, long years ago, why not then heed the call and leave the spinning tomb? Or in the cold years since that time, why fail to send a cry for help?"

"Pera's worried, and that makes me worry, too."

"Our fearsome raptor is not part of Yanai's faithful team. She is not one of us and so she compensates by putting on a warlike mask. Like some old soldier on campaign, regaling new recruits with gory tales, she does it to impress us, and thereby conceal that she is ill at ease."

"You sound very sure."

"My ancestors, and yours, survived in social groups, so understanding other minds is built into our genes."

"I think dino brains are based on corvid architecture—and some human, too."

"No doubt. But none of you are quite as good as I. So have no fear, Solana. All the dangers in this hab are those of any wreck. Do not let foolish dread of phantoms cause distraction, as that is the greatest risk of all."

Solana looked down the shaft, mostly so that Atmin couldn't see her smile inside her helmet. "I'll be careful."

CHAPTER THREE

Solana's first impression of the habitat ring was grim. Every surface was covered with dust, frost, and black mold. Everywhere she looked, she could spot human bones or mummified bodies.

And yet, even without her enhanced vision Solana could see that under the dried black blotches and the gray shroud, the town had once been quite pretty. Most of the houses were low, with lots of windows and sliding wall panels opening onto wide galleries. Away from the commercial district the buildings were grouped in little hutongs around what had once been elaborate gardens. Years of uncontrolled tumbling had tossed the elegant ponds and streams into a layer of shattered dirty ice covering multicolored tile pavement and dead plants, but one could still see the decorative bridges and little pavilions standing empty.

"I found a perfect place for us to camp," said Utsuro, lifting one of the big supply bags. "There's a medical clinic a few hundred meters to spinward. It has its own emergency power, and I think we can start up air and water recycling so that you three can be more comfortable."

"Are there more bodies there?" asked Solana.

"Not many. I left them in place for the moment."

The four of them walked silently for a few seconds. Atmin's travel sphere took to the air using its lift fans. The three on foot went slowly to avoid stepping on bones.

Finally Pera spoke up. "Nobody else is saying it, so I will: this hab wasn't destroyed by accident. Somebody *murdered* Safdaghar. Killed all the inhabitants, messed up the main mind."

"And?" said Solana.

"What do you mean?"

"I agree with you. Somebody attacked Safdaghar and killed everyone inside. Sixteen standard years ago. What are we supposed to do about it now?"

"We can at least record the scenes of bloodshed and decay," said Atmin. "Bear witness to the crime done here, and document as best we can. Perhaps we may inspire some with power to pursue whoever bears the stain, that justice—though delayed—may yet be done."

"We won't get paid for that," she said.

"More to life than gigajoules," said Pera.

"I'm saving up to get my brain redone," said Solana. "That's not cheap. It takes a high-level mind and a whole bunch of nanoscale surgery. Do you know how much four hour's work by a Level Three intelligence costs? How much is justice going to make us?"

"There's no reason for us to quarrel," said Utsuro. "Looking for valuable salvage will require a lot of searching—and so will looking for clues to what happened here. We can do both at the same time. Here's the clinic."

The medical clinic was a sturdy-looking two-story cylinder, colored bright safety green. Unlike the rest of Safdaghar's structures the clinic had a sealed shell like a spaceship hull, with transparent window bands and pressure membranes at the entrance. At some point the membranes had failed and emergency doors closed, so that the crew had to use an old-fashioned manual backup airlock next to the main entrance.

When the inner door opened Solana almost gasped with astonishment. The clinic's interior was all self-cleaning matter, so even now where the light from Pera's and Atmin's lamps fell they illuminated pure white surfaces, free of dust or mold. The furniture was blocks of smart matter in various sizes, ready to take on any shape desired.

The only light inside the clinic came from glowing lines

where walls met ceilings and floors, outlining the entire interior like a diagram. Doors had outlines in different colors: green for rooms open to all, yellow and orange for partly restricted, red for hazards.

The center of the building was a two-story atrium which also served as a waiting area. A dead flowering vine still clung to a trellis shaped like a double helix which reached all the way to the ceiling. Utsuro climbed the spiral stairs to the second floor while Atmin poked into the rooms around the atrium.

"I don't get it," said Solana. "There's no damage. The furniture isn't even out of place."

"Spacecraft standards," said Pera. "Everything's got grip surfaces. The chairs won't move unless you tell them to let go. I bet those offices have some shattered bric-a-brac—no human's ever been able to resist putting decorative junk in a workspace."

"The printers are intact!" Atmin called out. "A bounty for us all. One for tissues, one for tools, and one that builds up molecules. Each costs a million gigajoules when new. Yanai may wish to keep one for herself."

"The air seems safe," said Solana, looking at her tester. "Open up?"

"Beware the chill," said Atmin. "This air can freeze the moisture on your eyes."

"I'm hot enough. Verify first," said Pera, and looked at her tester. "Mine says okay. Looks like a consensus." She pulled back her hood and inhaled. "Yow. That *is* cold. Smells nasty. Something went bad in here a long time ago." She sealed up again and climbed up the spiral stairs to the second story.

Utsuro was already at the top. "There are six fatalities. All up here."

Solana hesitated, then walked upstairs slowly, making herself take each step despite a strong urge to go somewhere else and let the others deal with corpses.

Upstairs the gallery around the atrium opened into twelve little rooms. Utsuro and Pera stood outside the treatment chambers, as if nerving themselves to go in. Solana looked past Utsuro's metal body and saw why.

The treatment tanks were occupied. Patients had been put in them for stabilizing. Dozens of slender branching limbs entered each body, immobilizing the patients, providing support, injecting drugs and nano, seeking out foreign objects, and knitting together torn tissue. Power, control, and matter came through conduits from the wall.

Except that someone or something had ripped the conduits apart. The power and data links hung useless, and ancient stains showed where matter-enriched liquid had sprayed. The patients had lain trapped, restrained, and impaled until they died, then rotted into soup before freezing. One had tried to get loose, even managing to get the lid open so that he had mummified instead of rotting. The dried flesh was shredded where he had pulled the treatment limbs out of himself before dying.

Atmin's travel sphere hovered over Solana. "I think that these machines should best be left alone. Their value to us scavengers is not the equal of the price the patients paid."

Utsuro picked up the dangling end of the armored conduit. "Who did this?"

"Somebody strong," said Pera. "A mech. A borg. Maybe a bio in a power suit. Not an accident, that's for sure. You said there were more?"

"In the surgeries," said Utsuro.

Those two rooms were worse. One held two bodies, the other three, all mummified by time and cold. The years of rough precession had left all the equipment neatly stuck in place, but the bodies had been tumbled back and forth until each was just a shapeless bag of leathery skin.

"Stabbed, I think," said Utsuro. "At least, the injuries don't look like those of the dead people outside."

"Patient on the table, medics working. One hole each. Whoever did this knew exactly how to kill someone and wasn't wasting time," said Pera.

"Where's the power supply?" asked Solana. "I'll see if I can get us more than emergency minimum."

"Downstairs, I think," said Utsuro. "What shall we do with these bodies?"

"Long dead, they cannot do us harm—yet I confess I would enjoy my sleep far more without so many corpses in the house. Can you two move them out? I saw a garden in the back, a fitting place for them to rest," said Atmin.

"You get the tanks, I'll get these," said Pera, sticking her laser to one of her massive thighs. She knelt and picked up one mummy. "Not heavy."

"I do not envy your lighter work," said Utsuro.

Solana found the service room at the back of the clinic downstairs, right by the door to the garden. As she worked she heard the tramp of Utsuro and Pera going back and forth, taking out the dead.

The emergency power unit was a standard radiothermal unit, as ancient and reliable as an iron axe. No moving parts at all. It was good for another half century of steady output. But the power-switching system wasn't working. Not hard to see why: the unit had been ripped away. Solana got out her tool kit and dismantled the room's manual light control, scavenging the important bits to cobble together a switch for the emergency power.

Utsuro had just deposited the second treatment tank and its horrifying occupant in the garden when Solana connected her improvised switch to the building power and turned it on. Lights came on, fans began to hum, and a dozen pieces of equipment began sounding emergency alerts.

Solana closed up the utility room and went through the building shutting down or resetting everything making noise.

"A lovely piece of work, Solana dear," said Atmin. "With light and heat this place looks good as new. We only need select a place to camp."

"Upstairs is safer," said Pera.

Solana thought about the bodies now lying in the garden. Which would be worse? Trying to sleep a couple of doors away from where they had died, or downstairs—with the awful choice of facing the door to outside or turning her back to it?

"We can use the isolation and recovery rooms upstairs," she said. "Nobody died there."

"I don't need a bed," said Utsuro. "I can sit out in the gallery on guard while you three sleep."

"You don't sleep?" asked Pera.

"I do, but with this body I don't need quiet or a comfortable place to lie down. I just mute my senses. The body wakes me if it detects anything."

"Atmin and I can share a room to give you more space," said Solana to Pera.

"I'll be fine. I once spent a ninety-day transit from Venus to the Main Swarm sharing a room that size with three other dinos and all our combat gear."

"I hope this talk of sleep does not imply that any wish to go to bed," said Atmin. "The wealth of Safdaghar awaits!"

"Split up," said Pera. "Two go out on patrol, two set up camp. Atmin, you and me." She trotted toward the airlock. Atmin clucked and got back into his travel sphere before following.

While they were gone Solana checked over the life-support system and tried opening her suit hood. The air was cold enough to stiffen the hairs in her nose when she inhaled. The old filters were doing their best but the odor of rotting flesh was still very strong. She decided that she could get used to the smell more easily than she could spend a week in a full suit.

Utsuro moved methodically about the medical center, as if inspecting it. He had extended some kind of sensor from his left arm, and was passing it over various surfaces—walls, seats, handrails, and doors.

"Find anything?"

"Not much. They must have been good doctors. Everything is very clean."

Solana didn't say anything for a moment. "It's a big hab. Molecules are small."

"Ah, but we biologicals are constantly shedding. If I was ever here, there's a trail of my DNA everyplace I went."

"And if you don't find anything?"

Utsuro scanned a chair with excessive thoroughness before answering. "Physics doesn't lie. I was here. Whatever happened here happened to me, too. Finding the truth is worth more to me than loot."

"It's not worth more to me," she said, not realizing how angry she was until she heard her own voice. "What I want is to see other humans face-to-face, instead of just a bunch of colored circles. My share of this mission will be enough to get my brain fixed—but not if you're just going to waste your time on some little side project."

"If my work is unsatisfactory, you are welcome to tell Yanai. She is the one who hired me."

Neither of them said anything else until Atmin and Pera returned half an hour later.

"Our time is short, the hab is large. Efficiency must be our guiding star," said Atmin. "Despite what Pera says I think we must split up. Divide the hab and each one search alone. My plan is this: Solana takes the side north of the central road, proceeding east, or spinward if you like. Utsuro goes the same way but will search the south. To westward Pera goes, and I. She takes the northern half and I shall cover what remains. Though separate in space we stay in touch by comms, so none of us is far from help."

"I still don't like it," said Pera. "In war or salvage or anything else, you work in pairs."

"We simply do not have the time. This hab contains ten thousand homes, plus shops and space for work. Yanai gave us a week to search—that means we each must check four hundred spots each day. A mighty task, but one we barely can achieve if all of us use all our wits. To go in pairs would leave the search half done."

"Better safe than greedy."

"That's very easy for you to say," said Utsuro. "You signed on to get passage to the Jovian system, and that is already accomplished. You have the luxury of time. We do not."

"Don't worry. I'll do the job. And if anybody gets hurt because we're taking risks, you'll have to listen to me say I told you so."

Yanai's voice spoke from their comms. *"Enough bickering. Eat some food, get some rest, and start up again in four hours."*

Solana woke promptly at zero hundred and ran through her exercises. She had not been in anything more than microgravity since boarding Yanai, and the muscles in her calves and back were not happy to be back in full gee.

She always exercised in private. The regimen of stretches, light aerobics, and isometrics she had been taught as a child was familiar and felt good, but like every other remnant of her early life in Kumu hab it was a bit overtly sensual to watch. Even a bird or a dino would notice.

After her half-hour workout she used cleaning goo and had a couple of peanut dumplings, then dressed in her suit and coveralls for the day's work.

The others were all ready by one. Pera wore her armored suit and combat engineer's laser. Atmin very reluctantly squeezed back into his travel sphere. Utsuro printed a flimsy set of coveralls to keep dust and mold from getting into his joints.

Yanai had printed up a couple of simple hauler bots—a flat

bed a meter square, a single arm, and four rugged wheels. They
waited patiently outside while Atmin explained the search plan.
"We each must check a rectangle, five hundred meters long and
half as wide, one corner here. What pattern used is up to you.
Just look for things, and flag the spots where those of value
rest. These two stout bots will take away the loot. Twelve hours
of work, rest as you must. When that is done we eat and sleep,
and do it all again."

The section assigned to Solana that first morning was laid out
in a grid, eight blocks by four. The streets were lined with trees,
though a decade of precession wobbling had shaken away all the
leaves and smaller branches. Aside from that the streets were
dull and utilitarian, faced by unadorned walls, often windowless.
The blocks faced in from the street, with houses and some small
businesses grouped around courtyards laid out as gardens linked
by footpaths at the corners.

It was only after about fifteen minutes of exploring that
Solana finally figured it out: the neighborhood was two grids,
superimposed on each other. The road grid, oriented parallel to
the hab axis and the circumference of the spin section, was for
bots—transport, maintenance and repair units, and emergency
response. The footpath network, skewed forty-five degrees from the
roads, was for people, and passed through the heart of every block.

She walked around the first court, trying to judge which
houses were worth entering. Most of the buildings were in good
shape. The vast majority of Safdaghar's structures were made of
simple, almost indestructible materials like graphene, diamond,
and aerogel. Those had survived years of slow, relentless shaking
with little damage. A few had lost doors or sliding shutters, and
the wide gallery on one house had come unfastened from the
building and slid into the frozen ruin of the garden.

No time to waste, she reminded herself, and directed her
steps to the nearest door. It was locked, but there was a single
half-centimeter hole disrupting the smooth red lacquer just at
Solana's eye level. She took out her tool kit and got the lock open
in less than a minute, then slid the door open.

A woman had been leaning against the door with her back
to it, and something had shot her in the head, right through the
sturdy silicon-carbon panel. Her body, now just bones and freeze-
dried skin, tumbled out at Solana's feet. There was no face for

Solana's goggles to filter out, just some bone and teeth sticking out of a mass of black mold.

Solana jumped back, heart pounding. After a minute of controlled breathing she scanned the interior. A table and a wooden chest had slid around the room battering themselves to bits, but there were built-in storage cabinets along the walls packed with cloth. Whoever had lived here apparently made clothing by hand, favoring light fabrics in bright colors.

Valuable? Solana found some finished pieces on the floor and shook the wood chips out. Nice-looking, probably comfortable... but nothing particularly unique. She stepped over the body and went to the next house.

Atmin checked in with her after an hour. *"What progress have you made in seeking costly things to take?"*

"Not much," she admitted. *"I'm only on my third court."*

"You cannot enter every house. I do not even try. Seek those which once were home to humans skilled in craft, or who accumulated rare things from afar."

"It's hard to tell that from outside. And I don't like seeing the people. I tagged one place—they had some seashells. Real ones, I think. Any sign of your poet yet?"

"The houses here hold neither brush nor ink."

After that she tried to be more efficient. She ignored the bodies, tried not to think of who these people had been and what their lives had been like. Just force open a door or find a transparent window, give the interior a quick scan, and move on.

She passed through one court which was much more badly damaged than the others. The houses had been built of real wood, which the years had reduced to piles of expensive splinters. As she passed into the next court she glanced down the service roadway and saw something written on a wall.

The surprising thing was that it was obviously painted by hand. In an age of self-cleaning surfaces and eyes everywhere, graffiti was almost a lost art. A few habs permitted or even encouraged it, but in most of the Billion Worlds a slogan scrawled on a wall wouldn't last more than an hour.

Solana approached it, making her suit lamps brighter and cranking up the magnification of her goggles. Despite years of cold, damp, and the ever-present black mold, the strokes of crimson paint looked perfect.

no hate as red and hot as love
hungry cubs born in blood

She stared for a moment, then shook her head hard. No time
for memories now. Time to work. The routine soothed her, and she
didn't even mind the bodies so much. Look, scan, tag, walk, look...

When Atmin checked in again she could report six more courts
checked. *"Twenty-one to go."*

*"Eight hours remain for checking them, so do not slow your pace.
What new loot have you found?"*

*"One house had a set of platinum coins from the Lunar Repub-
lic. Seventh Millennium; I couldn't tell if they were real or printed.
Also one place had some really nice paintings so I tagged them, too.
I don't know if they're worth anything."*

*"My greatest hope, and greatest fear, is that we find the work of
some great talent yet unknown."*

"Why fear?"

*"To know a genius died shot down in some old senseless strife,
with many works unborn within her head, should sadden anyone
that beauty loves."*

At ten o'clock Solana limped back to the clinic. She was tired,
thirsty, hungry, and her feet were swollen and bruised. She was
thoroughly sick of seeing abandoned houses and freeze-dried
bodies.

The others didn't look any better. Utsuro said nothing at all.
Atmin announced he was taking a nap for the next hour and
urged everyone to do the same.

Only Pera seemed unfazed by her day poking through the
remains of Safdaghar. "Any pets in your sector?"

"I saw a bird in one house, on the floor. I'm pretty sure it
was sub-baseline," said Solana. "I think it died of thirst."

"Found some feral cats in my area. They'd been chewing on
the dead humans. Froze to death, finally. All five of them were
curled up together."

"Did you see any sign of Atmin's poet?"

"Nothing handwritten. If he actually was here, my guess is
that he stored all his text in the hab's memory, like normal people
do. Which means it's all long gone. We should be up near the
hub moving machinery."

"Don't worry. There will be plenty of that before we leave."

"Utsuro?" Pera called over to the cyborg, who was sitting on the floor near the entrance. "Find your DNA?"

When Utsuro didn't answer Pera glanced at Solana and lashed her tail. "Guess not."

"I found a...a baby," said Utsuro, very quietly. "A human baby. I couldn't see any sign of injury. It was next to a woman, shot through the spine. I think it died of hunger."

Pera broke the silence a minute later. "We could move back up to the hub..."

"No," said Utsuro more firmly. "I want to find out what happened. If I am the only survivor I owe it to the others."

When Atmin woke, the three full biologicals had dinner, and then began the task of evaluating the day's finds. This meant Atmin surveyed the pile of loot the bots had put in the little vehicle parking area next to the clinic. At the bird's direction the others separated the items into things worth keeping and those which weren't worth the effort of hauling back to the hub.

Solana's suit did its best for her feet, injecting painkillers and anti-inflammatories, and making the inside of her boots as soft and snug as possible. But she still winced with each step. Pera didn't admit any discomfort, but Solana could see that she sat down as often as possible, and walked with her jaw clenched. Utsuro was as silent and tireless as a bot, picking up the heaviest loads without effort or complaint.

By the time they finished for the day Solana was dead on her feet. If she didn't concentrate on staying awake she found herself drifting into dreams as she walked. Even Atmin sounded tired when they returned to the clinic.

"How much is all this worth?" Pera asked, gesturing at the little pile outside.

"My guess is sixty thousand gigajoules, or maybe more," said Atmin. "Which makes your wage a thousand gigs an hour. Does that satisfy?"

"Sixty thousand?" Pera still sounded skeptical.

"That picture is an ancient print—an image made by metal pressing ink against a virgin sheet of paper made of cellulose from plants. From Earth; the date is Sixth Millennium, and I think that is real. Ten thousand gigs, if so. That set of bowls are modern work, but shaped by hand of Martian clay and fired. The set of six should fetch at least six thousand gigs. The table is of wood, a kind I have not seen before, with rainbow pigments in the grain. The table's worth may be ten thousand gigs, its genome half again that sum. Must I go on? I know my trade."

"No, I believe you. Never realized people would pay so much for stuff just because it's old or hard to get."

"Our errant children of the Inner Ring may be content to know that matter can be rearranged at will, and higher-level minds say that a copy printed up today is just as real as its original, five thousand years ago or more. But living things like you and I all wish for continuity, and love to hold the things which others held in vanished times. The wish for authenticity may be irrational, but that irrationality can make us rich. So do not sneer."

"If everybody was rational, soldiers would be out of work, too. I'm not complaining."

"Then let us do as soldiers should, and take our rest when now we can."

In the perpetual darkness inside Safdaghar, morning looked like every other time. Solana woke when Yanai called the team. *"It's zero hundred again. Time to get up and get to work. We have twenty-six days before undocking."*

Pera and Solana both groaned aloud as they got up, feeling every sore joint and muscle. Atmin had the opposite problem: he spent the days inside his travel sphere and got very cramped and fidgety. Utsuro, of course, woke instantly and got smoothly to his feet with no sign of fatigue.

They ate with good appetite. "We may need to get Yanai to send down more food in a few days," said Solana around a mouthful of surimi.

"We're definitely burning more fuel than expected," Pera agreed. "How about you, Utsuro? Need any groceries?"

"As long as I have energy I can recycle my nutrients. My power supply will last another standard year at normal output."

"I've thought about getting machined up," said Pera. "A lot of mercs go full borg, but that's dangerous."

"Why is it dangerous to have a more durable body?" asked Utsuro.

"You're strong and tough, but you'll never be as fast as a mech. Electrons move a million times faster than nerve impulses. I've seen too many idiots forget that."

"I shall try to keep it in mind," said Utsuro.

The four of them split up at the door. "Another day, another set of blocks," said Atmin. "As time goes on the distance we must walk will grow, so we must learn to do our work with greater speed."

Solana and Utsuro walked together along the main avenue which ran down the center of the town level. The center of the avenue was a strip of grass and shrubs, with a double set of tram tracks. All the plants were frozen and black with mold. They passed a tram car. The hab's years of wobbling had rocked it off the track and slid the car on its side into a bodypainting salon.

"There's nobody in it," said Solana as they passed the wreck. "I checked."

"I scanned it yesterday, too," said Utsuro. "I thought a public conveyance might be a good place to find DNA traces."

"Any luck?"

"No."

Half a kilometer down the avenue they parted company and began searching. This section had more of a mix of uses: about a quarter of the buildings had workshops or kitchens on the ground floor and living quarters upstairs. The workshops were fascinating, and Solana wound up tagging things in more than half of them.

For most of recorded history machines made things better than biologicals could. A bot's movements were more precise, they could withstand any conditions, and could labor without ceasing. Printers and utility fog just made that work more effortless.

But humans, most biologicals, and even a surprising number of mechs liked to own things made by another baseline being. Part of it was status display, of course: anyone could print something out for little more than the cost of materials, but owning an original handmade item showed both wealth and taste.

There was also the irrational but very strong desire for authenticity. A printed copy of a Washikyosho bracelet was identical to the original down to the atomic level—but buyers bid billions of gigajoule credits for the ones made by a young prodigy goldsmith living inside Luna, who drank vodka as he worked and spent months adjusting the alloy mix for each piece. The copies were just worth their matter plus a license fee.

All this meant that a hab like Safdaghar, with no matter or

energy to export, could earn precious foreign exchange wealth by selling goods made by human hands, either the originals or scans for printing. The result was the seeming paradox of finding potter's wheels and handlooms in a hab with matter printers.

Solana had been working her way back and forth across her search area when the alert tone screeched in her ears. *"Halt-halt-halt!"* said Atmin, in a ragged croak unlike his usual voice.

Two seconds later he spoke again, sounding a bit more normal—but obviously still rattled. *"Something struck my travel sphere a mighty blow. It knocked me half a block away. A trap or foe, I cannot say. All hold while I investigate."*

"Location?" demanded Pera.

"It struck me where the streets which bear the labels 12 and L upon our reference map do cross. But please do not approach me yet, until I find out what it was."

Solana looked around her nervously, wishing for a weapon even if she didn't know how to use one. Ignoring Atmin's command to hold in place, she retreated into the workshop she had just left, and took shelter behind a sturdy kiln made of silicon blocks. If there was some enemy lurking about she didn't want to be immobile out in the open.

About a minute later Atmin spoke again, sounding much calmer. *"A trap, it was: a wire strung across the road did trip a blade on springy mount which struck my sphere a glancing blow. A crude affair, it did no harm to me. I hope the three of you were not alarmed."*

"Improvised?" asked Pera.

"I judge it so. The bladed head appears to be a cerametal cooking knife. The springy arm which stored the striking force is simple carbon fiber rod. I think that even I could build this thing."

"Get back from it and wait for me."

"There is no need for you to come. My sphere can rise above this trap. Why it was set and why this place, I cannot say. Utsuro and Solana, have you seen the like in those parts you do search?"

"I have seen nothing," said Utsuro.

"No traps, at least," said Solana.

"Then we must not allow this harmless trap to frighten us. Proceed."

Solana looked around the pottery workshop and found a suitable tool—a two-meter metal pole covered in heat-resistant carbon, with one flat end like a spatula. The craftsman whose mummy lay in the corner of the room amid a jumble of broken porcelain had used it to move things around inside the kiln.

She left the shop carrying the pole in front of her angled forward and up, to snag any tripwires. Of the four of them she was the most vulnerable. Utsuro's chassis was metal and graphene, Atmin's travel sphere was diamond composite, and Pera had combat armor that could stop bullets up to four kilojoules. Solana's suit could handle less than a tenth as much energy—the kind of jolts and bumps produced by humans moving mass around or swinging tools. It might protect her from whatever had hit Atmin, or it might not. She preferred not to find out.

Carrying the pole slowed her down, and Solana was exhausted by the time they finished the day's search. The others must have been going more cautiously as well, as it took them all an extra hour to return to the medical center.

Atmin was already there when Solana and Utsuro arrived. The bird was out of his travel sphere and was putting a hull patch on it with help from one of the bots.

"I thought you said the trap didn't damage your sphere," said Solana.

"I did, and it did not, but still I think it wise to place a patch upon the impact spot in case of microscopic cracks invisible to me."

"Let me check." She peered closely at the diamond bubble with her goggles at high magnification, rotating the polarization to check for stress. Through the patch she could see a jagged scratch five centimeters long where ultra-hard cerametal had chipped at the diamond even as its cutting edge had shattered. The damage didn't penetrate all the way through the three-millimeter shell, but it had definitely made a gouge.

"Are you all right?" she asked Atmin. "That must have hit pretty hard."

"My sphere has safety webs which held me in a soft but firm embrace. I have no broken bone or bruise. Fear not."

Pera showed up last. "I checked your trap," she said. "Improvised, but pretty nasty. If you'd been walking or riding a vehicle, instead of flying around, it could have cracked your sphere open. Maybe your head, too."

"Then fortunate it was that I was not. The subject is unpleasant, let us speak of something else. What treasures have we found today?"

Their haul was pretty good—some original ceramics and textiles, a thousand-year-old formal vest from the Trojan Empire cluster with hand-embroidered designs in gold thread, a pair of ruby earrings that projected holographic images when the light caught them at the right angle, and a data stick holding ready-to-print scans of a hundred superb original meals.

"If we can't sell that one, I'd like to keep it," said Solana about the data stick.

"Getting a taste for the high life?" asked Pera.

"I plan to."

Pera turned to Utsuro. "Find anything today?"

"I'm not quite sure. There was one partial match, very degraded and noisy, but better than random chance. I found it on the central avenue, by that fountain shaped like a wing."

"Have you..." Solana began. Her throat was suddenly dry. "Have you checked the bodies?"

"I scan each one. If I could find a relative or a clone it would be wonderful," said Utsuro. After a moment he added, "I close their eyes, too. It seems appropriate."

"Everyone gets broken down for elements in the end," said Pera. "Eyes open or closed, it won't matter."

CHAPTER FOUR

Three days later Solana and Utsuro set off down the central avenue for their assigned search territories. The backaches from walking in gravity had faded and she had toughened her feet with generous slatherings of liquid skin. With Utsuro leading the way they could walk briskly without fear of setting off a trap.

"I find myself wondering what the people in the Kuiper Belt will make of this, when it finally arrives," said Utsuro. His face screen displayed a triangle colored soothing safety green.

"You mean all the bodies?" As she spoke they passed a pair of leathery corpses lodged against the front of a soil-building shop. Utsuro had already examined both of them so neither he nor Solana paid them much mind.

"Will they be horrified? Or just shrug it off as Pera and Atmin do, and feed them all into the disassemblers?"

"I met someone from the Oort once. There was a Salibi priest in Jiaohui when I lived there," said Solana. "Father Mijel. He came from an Oort hab called Eindbaken, about five hundred AU out. It took him fifty years in hibernation to get from there to the Main Swarm."

They walked in silence for a few steps before Solana continued.

"He never talked much about his home, but I know that he and all the other Salibi had to leave. He was a full-borg like you, but his body was more like a cephalopod—a ball for his brain and life support, and a bunch of tentacles. That's why they had him at Jiaohui, to work with us rescuees with slave programming. No face. He said the Salibi had to leave Eindbaken because some of the younger ones didn't want to get borged up and the hab community said their bodies were using too much life support."

"They sound like very unsentimental people—except your priest and his friends, of course."

"I think so. It could be just that one hab." She looked ahead at the transverse road which marked the end of yesterday's search. "Time to get to work. I've got the stadium today." They could both see it ahead on the left, a melancholy-looking oval of huge dead trees surrounded by what had once been gardens.

"A low-effort day for you," said Utsuro. "I doubt you will find much of interest in there. When you're done, go back to camp and take a long nap."

Safdaghar's full-gravity stadium stood in the center of a large park, with pavilions and playing fields among ponds and gardens. The ponds were frozen mud now, and the gardens were black and desiccated. Cafés and tavernas with outdoor seating lined the edge of the park. Solana checked the nearest ones.

Mercifully, those buildings were mostly empty of bodies—and of anything worth tagging. One had a display of team bodysuits for some local zukyu clubs, but those clubs and all their fans were mold-encrusted corpses now. Another had a diamond case holding a perfectly intact trophy made of gold and platinum. The base was inscribed "Safdaghar Fangshuo Champions" with the names of teams and dates below.

The trophy wasn't beautiful, and certainly nobody alive would care about the victories of local Fangshuo teams. On the other hand it was literally worth its weight in metal. She tagged it for the bots.

Over at the edge of the habitat ring she found one café by itself among some houses. This place had no sports memorabilia at all, and the tabletops were all covered with layers and layers of graffiti. One table, occupying a place of honor in the front center of the outdoor seating area where passersby could see it, had a diamond protective sheet over the graffiti-covered surface. Under the sheet she saw crimson characters, still faintly luminous.

pride's eye inflamed by truthful dust
hunts what it fears to see

Solana could certainly understand fearing to see something
and still hunting for it. When she saw a face, especially a living
human's face, the urge to submit was seductively strong. Qarinas
like her weren't just programmed to obey—they were programmed
to *want* to obey. All self-doubt, all guilt, all uncertainty just faded
away. In total obedience she could feel like a master herself.

The Salibi couldn't break that programming, not without alter-
ing her brain, and their weird superstitions didn't allow that. To
their credit, they hadn't tried to use her conditioning to convince
her of anything. It would have been ridiculously simple: if just
one of the human Salibi had spoken to her unmasked, she might
be among them still. They had never done that.

The cafés were a waste of time, she decided. Time to check
out the park and the stadium.

The gardens didn't have any obvious spots where tripwires
might be strung. Solana kept the potter's tool extended in front
of her anyway as she followed the path to the stadium. The path
was paved with an elaborate mosaic, but Solana couldn't really
keep her attention on the design. There were too many bodies.

She counted ten dead people along the path, and then stopped
counting. The dried mummies were covered in the black mold,
and each one lay in the center of a mold patch which Solana realized had once been a pool of blood. She picked her way around
spots and rivulets of black mold until the mosaic path merged
into the broad pavement around the outside of the stadium itself.

The stadium was an impressive piece of bioengineering. The
outer wall was an oval of huge acacia trees, surrounding an area
a quarter-kilometer long and a hundred and fifty meters wide.
The trees were quite tall, nearly sixty meters. At the top their
branches merged to form a leafy canopy covering the whole
stadium and the surrounding pavement.

Solana could see entrances in the three-meter spaces between
trees. Some led to the field, some to stairs up into the stands, and
some opened into spaces under the seats which had once been food
stalls or storage areas. It looked as if all of the entrances into the interior of the stadium were blocked by piles of boards and metal panels.

She spotted one entrance which was open. The occupants had

evidently broken down the barricades from inside, and surged down the stairs, dying as they went. The stairway was covered in black mold and skeletons. Solana knelt to get a better look at them. All had severe injuries. Not neat little bullet holes, but massive gashes where something had sliced through clothing, skin, and bone in a single stroke.

"Uh, Utsuro? Can you come to where I am? I need your help," she said over the comm.

"I will be there as quickly as I can," said Utsuro.

Atmin made a disapproving noise but said nothing.

Solana waited outside the stadium, fighting the urge to run away. The darkness and cold now seemed almost malevolent. When Utsuro's lights came into view across the central avenue Solana almost cried with relief.

He sprinted over with mechanical smoothness. "What have you—oh," he said as he saw the bodies piled in the stairway. "Oh, dear. I suppose we ought to look inside. Please allow me to go first in case there are traps."

Solana handed him the rod, and Utsuro held it vertically in front of him as they picked their way up the stairs. It proved impossible to avoid stepping on bodies, as they were stacked three deep in some places.

They emerged at the top of the stairs, halfway up the sloped tiers of seats which grew from carefully trained branches of the acacia trees. Solana surveyed the entire stadium with her goggles at high magnification.

"Most of the exits are blocked from the inside, and there's a lot of stuff piled up down on the field. Looks like food printers and a stack of blankets."

"Perhaps they were planning to be here for several days," said Utsuro.

She could see weapons, too: spears made of graphene rods, a few laser cutters like Pera's, some printed mag pistols and air guns, and even a couple of combustion-powered shotguns.

"So ... they fortified themselves in here, with supplies and weapons. But then something happened. All of them tried to get out at once."

"There are about twenty armed men down on the field. Did they attack the place? Are they what everyone was running from?" asked Utsuro.

"I'm not sure." Solana zoomed in her vision on the hundreds of bodies scattered around the interior, especially the ones with weapons, trying to see any way to differentiate among them. Was it a rebellion? A faction war? A coup? Were the ones with weapons the murderers?

"Okay," she said. "Most of the bodies are pointing *that* way, antispinward, lying facedown. I think they were trying to get out, and got cut down. But the bodies with weapons are *behind* them, back on the field, and it looks like most of them were facing the other way when they died."

"Those were the last defenders," said Utsuro. "They stood down there with their handmade spears and scavenged guns, facing an enemy coming from spinward, trying to buy time for the rest to escape."

"And all of them died," said Solana.

Solana had seen a real battle in her childhood, when the Salibi raiders came to Kumu. The Salibi soldiers and mechs were not amateurs. The biologicals wore power armor with smart surfaces, surrounded by a cloud of nanobot interceptors. The mechs were just as well protected, and moved with blinding speed. They targeted Kumu's security bots and slave trainers with hypervelocity needles and self-targeting minimissiles.

Against power like that, Safdaghar's scratch militia would have been helpless. It wouldn't even take a full squad to massacre them all.

"But why?" she asked aloud. "Safdaghar wasn't at war. Nobody looted the place. None of this makes any sense!"

"Once I traced my orbit back to here I did a lot of research," said Utsuro. "I checked archives in every hab I visited, and sent out some autonomous queries to search all the major worlds. Not many people noticed when Safdaghar went dark, but there were some rumors that it was an attack by Deimos."

"It still doesn't make sense. Even if they had a reason, why would Deimos send troops to hack apart the people of Safdaghar one by one? They've got petawatt lasers and relativistic mag launchers—they could vaporize this hab from half a billion klicks away."

"Most wars don't make sense when they're over."

"There's nothing here for us. I'm not going to search the bodies for loot. Let's get out of here."

"I want to scan them. You go on and I will catch up. Be careful."

Solana left the stadium, wincing as the brittle freeze-dried bodies on the stairs crunched under her feet. There was nothing here she wanted to take. She walked around the outside and stood on the far side, looking across some practice fields at the remaining structures in her section for the day.

A flicker of movement caught her attention, and she zoomed in. The building was a shop selling frozen desserts. The front door swung lazily, as if someone had just gone through.

But...Utsuro was in the stadium. Pera and Atmin were a couple of kilometers away to antispinward. Yanai had stabilized Safdaghar's spin. There was no wind. What could leave a door swinging? Her old fears of pale blind hungry survivors lurking in the dark returned, and she clutched the rod tightly.

Utsuro emerged ten minutes later. If he noticed her standing there fighting panic he didn't mention it. "No traces at all. None of those people shares much of my genome."

"Let's get back to camp," said Solana.

"I still have my section to search."

"Can you maybe walk me back? I'm kind of scared. Please?"

"All right," said Utsuro. "I will accompany you. Now that you mention it, I feel a bit creepy myself."

On the walk back to camp Solana couldn't keep her head from swiveling. The goggles did have one flaw: they limited her peripheral vision. Normally in the dark of the abandoned hab that wasn't a problem, but now she couldn't avoid the feeling that there might be something lurking just beyond the edge of her field of view. If Utsuro noticed her swiveling her head about, he didn't mention it.

Getting into the well-lit medical center was a huge relief to Solana. She could actually feel her shoulders relax as they cycled through the airlock. After just a couple of nights it was home—or at least as much home as anyplace else Solana had ever known since leaving Kumu.

"Are you all right now?" asked Utsuro. "I need to get back to search my section." He waited long enough for her to nod, then hurried off. She saw him through one of the diamond-pane windows, sprinting tirelessly away up the central avenue.

With nobody about, Solana peeled off her suit and wiped

her skin down. She decided then and there that as soon as she reached some hab with gravity and clean water, she would indulge in a long hot soak. She put on a clean suit liner and then made some adjustments to her multitool.

Multitools were another long-established technology: a rod of smart matter with a handle, programmed with hundreds of different configurations. It could become a cutter, a gripper, a drill, a clamp, a wrench, a hammer, a punch, a puller, and so on through the whole menu. Solana's was a serious technician's model, and included a whole range of settings for work down at the submicron scale.

The default setting was a featureless rod. Most users had a short list of favorites which could be called up by turning a control ring on the handle, without going through the whole rigamarole of selecting from a menu. Solana edited her preferences now, choosing a new favorite tool setting and picking the "grip selection" option.

From now on, when Solana held the handle of her multitool in her fist, it would automatically shift into a twenty-centimeter chef's knife with a sharp point and a molecule-thin slicing edge. It might be utterly useless against a mech or a borg, but just having it made Solana feel a little safer.

Two days later, Solana was searching a large, rambling house which had unwalled rooms opening into gardens, almost like a series of pavilions except that people had obviously lived there full time. She found a couple of bodies, and the possessions of a good many adults and children, but whether they were separate families sharing the space, or a single group marriage she could not tell.

Utsuro commed her as she was looking through a collection of seeds, evidently handpicked and carefully sorted. *"Solana? I think I need your help this time."*

"Me?" It was hard for Solana to imagine anything Utsuro would need her help with.

"Yes. I will explain when you get here. I am spinward of you, at the lake."

Safdaghar's interior had two lakes—more like ponds, really, but the construction plans called them lakes, so the Scarab crew did, as well. They were placed opposite each other on the rim, and functioned as part of the water-recovery network and the hab's internal ballast system. By pumping water among various reservoirs around the rim and the hub, Safdaghar's controlling mind could regulate spin, damp out wobbles before they got serious, and even shift the hab's orientation to keep facing the Sun.

Pera had scouted out the lake on the opposite side of the rim; that one was part of a wilderness area, set amid a tangle of old trees and understory plants which had been allowed to grow mostly unmanaged. The one on this side was more obviously artificial, part of a formal-style park, and included a large swimming pool.

She spotted Utsuro's glowing face on the far side of the frozen lake. The ice was all shattered and smashed, then frost-welded into a rough and treacherous-looking surface. Solana elected to go around. The park was dotted with dead trees, and the ground was almost covered by leaves and twigs.

Utsuro stood in the center of a group of bodies. Like all the others, they were blacked by mold and mummified by cold and dryness.

"What do you need me for?" she asked when she was close enough to speak aloud.

"I found it. Here—a clear signal. My DNA. It's unmistakable."

"Congratulations, I guess," she said. "Do you remember being here? Is anything coming back?"

He stood, an immobile machine, for several seconds. "Nothing. None of this looks familiar."

She looked at the bodies. Her goggles didn't even need to filter out their faces; few were even recognizable. "What do you think happened?"

"I can't tell," he said. "I was hoping you might be able to help."

"It's a mess," said Solana. She cycled through the entire spectrum her goggles could image. Unlike all the other bodies she had seen, these were much more badly hacked about. The other dead of Safdaghar had been killed with quick precision—a single shot, a single slash. These bodies covered with dry leaves by the frozen lake were nearly dismembered. "There are weapons—the same kind of improvised stuff we saw at the stadium. No way to tell which side was which, or who won. I guess this was another last stand. Looks like the fighting was pretty brutal."

"I noticed that, too. But why here? The stadium at least made sense as a refuge. This place is wide open. What were they defending?"

"I'm no soldier. Maybe Pera could tell you. So where did you find your own DNA?" she asked.

"It's all around here," he said. "Highest concentration is here." He pointed to a spot in the middle of the mass of bodies. "There's a lot of it. I think I must have been injured."

"You think this is where it happened? Whatever nearly killed you?"

His face screen displayed a stick figure shrugging. "Hard to say. From what the mechs told me about my injuries I would expect to find some actual body parts, but none of these are mine."

"Oh! Can you find a trail? Scan around the site, see if you can track yourself."

Utsuro paced a wide circle around all the bodies and patches of mold, scanning the ground. Then he took a few steps outward and did it again, and then a third time.

While he searched, Solana zoomed in on the ground, looking past the mold and dead leaves. "There's some kind of fiber here," she called out.

"A tripwire?"

"I don't think so. It's not under tension."

"Is it attached to anything?"

She took hold of the three-millimeter strand of braided carbon which threaded its way under the leaves and bodies. After a moment's hesitation, Solana held her breath and pulled.

For a horrifying instant she thought she had fallen into a supernatural entertainment. All around her the leaves and bodies began to move. Then she realized it was just the long cable she was reeling in, stuck to bodies by ice and dried blood.

It went taut in one direction, and Solana saw that it led to a colder spot amid the dead leaves, about five meters away. "There's an access hatch here."

"Wait until I finish. It might be dangerous. Be careful you don't fall in."

He seemed to take forever to make his final circuit of the site, now at a distance of about a hundred meters. When he finally finished and walked toward Solana, his screen showed the standard cargo container icon for "empty."

"I couldn't find anything," he said. "Plenty of DNA here, none in the surrounding area."

"Maybe you left this way," she said, pointing to the hatch.

"Maybe."

They picked their way through the scattered corpses to the hatch. It was a square, a meter across, set among the fused regolith pavers of the walkway. The metal-and-carbon hinged lid lay flat open. One end of the cable was tied to the top rung of a ladder which led down into darkness.

"According to the plans, the next level down is all infrastructure—transport, data and power, raw materials storage and conveyors," said Solana.

"That would be a good way to sneak around," said Utsuro. "Perhaps my comrades and I tried an ambush here, striking at the foe from below when they did not expect it." He scanned the ladder and the sides of the shaft, then did it again. "Nothing. Let's have a look at this cable." He gripped it and began to pull.

"Any idea what it was for?"

"A cable can be many things. You can pull with it, use it as a guideline, tie something down . . ."

"A snare? Some kind of trap?"

"There are many possibilities," said Utsuro. "This is quite strong. I'm not sure I could snap it."

He reeled in the other end of the cable. It was attached to a blackened hollow tube with a barbed tip. "A rocket?" he wondered aloud. "Ah! Now I see. Yes, it was an ambush, and was part of a trap. The enemy passed through this park, the defenders launched this from hiding and then attacked. And . . . it seems we failed. Many were cut down, perhaps most. I was wounded but somehow escaped."

He was silent for a long time.

"I'm sure you did your best," said Solana.

His head swiveled to show her his screen displaying a quizzical green cat face, not human enough to activate the filters in her goggles. "I am not afraid to learn I ran away," he said. "Obviously we were outmatched. There is no shame in fleeing a foe you cannot fight. I only hope we managed to hurt them, even just a little. That would satisfy me."

Solana looked around at the dead park. "So what now?"

"Now that I've found one place I was, I need to find others. Create a heat map. The place where my DNA is most common is where I lived. Perhaps I can find my home and my name."

"Well, how about searching my section? You can scan for DNA and help me make up for lost time."

"That sounds fine," said Utsuro.

They walked through the park, heading back toward the residential area she had been searching. At the edge of the park Solana observed, "We still don't know why they started killing each other."

"I no longer believe that is what happened."

"What do you mean?"

"If this was an internal conflict, why were there no survivors? I simply can't believe the two sides were so evenly matched that they fought to mutual extinction."

"Weirder things have happened. Let's try this place," said Solana, leading the way into a house built over a series of frozen fishponds, her potter's tool held out in case of traps. "What's your explanation, then?"

"I think it was an invasion. Some outside force did this."

"We didn't see any hull breaches, except that place where the energy storage blew up."

"I asked Pera about hab assaults yesterday," said Utsuro. "While you were doing whatever it is you do with the door closed."

"Exercising. The way I do it bothers some people."

"I see. I meant no offense. As I was saying, Pera claims that more than half the time the invaders use normal docking facilities, with infiltrators opening the hatches for them. That could have happened here." Utsuro picked up a bronze statuette from the mass of broken furniture and smashed crockery on the floor. "How about this?"

"I don't know. Tag it. We'll see what the bird thinks."

Utsuro did so. In Solana's field of view a virtual text box appeared, in an attention-grabbing yellow-green shade.

After a moment's silent searching, Solana said, "But there's still the problem of survivors. If someone invaded the hab and killed everyone, where are they? Why didn't they take the place over? Or sell it?"

"Perhaps it was pirates, or predatory salvagers. The mechs who rescued me told me there are outlaw scarabs who prey on small, poor habs like this one, especially in the outer system. Slag the main mind, declare the biologicals to be sub-baseline, and scrap the whole hab. Nobody cares about a few hundred people among a billion worlds."

Solana found a carved wooden chest about half a meter long,

wedged into a corner. It looked intact, and was very pretty. She pulled it into the middle of the floor and tagged it. "Yanai said the same thing. But...if it was pirates or salvagers, why didn't they scrap Safdaghar, then? Or at least take stuff? Even if they couldn't recognize artworks the way Atmin can, they'd grab the metals and expensive printers. We haven't noticed anything missing."

"That box looks nice. Is there anything in it?"

"Oh, right." The box was locked, with a hand-forged iron mechanism which couldn't resist Solana's shape-changing multitool for more than ten seconds. Inside was a dress which made her gasp as she held it up. It was silk and lace, all obviously hand-made and very old. Under magnification the threads even looked biological rather than printed. A mindless bot or a printer could make it in a couple of minutes, but some human centuries ago had spent weeks at the job.

"Wonderful," said Utsuro, as Solana folded the dress carefully and put it back in the box. "Another possibility occurs to me. Slavers."

"Why kill everybody if you want slaves?"

"Other than that one infant, and the children in the launch capsule, I have only seen dead adults."

Solana frowned behind her goggles, trying to remember if she had seen any children. There certainly had been children in the hab—she'd found toys, playgrounds, and child-sized clothing. But Utsuro was right: no bodies.

Even without the gene mods and prenatal tinkering which had made Solana a perfect slave, there were older, cruder methods to enforce obedience. The masters at Kumu had used them, too. Solana knew that for some customers, the process of destroying a victim's will to resist held more appeal than the actual result.

"Wait," she said. "That would take a ship—a pretty big one, too, even if they put all the captives in stasis. Yanai said there weren't any ships tracked leaving Safdaghar when the disaster happened. And you can't hide a spaceship."

They crossed the icy garden toward the house next door. Utsuro pushed through the brittle hedge dividing the lots, snapping branches and leaving a gap Solana slipped through easily. "Actually, you can hide a ship," he said. "If you know exactly where the observer is located. Put up a completely nonreflective refrigerated shield and keep your ship entirely inside the sensor shadow. If you don't occult anything, the observer won't see you. The technique is seldom used, if only because most sensors are networked. I don't know how many eyes were watching Safdaghar when it happened."

"Where did you hear that?"

"I just know it. I don't remember how."

The next house was built in and around a twenty-meter banyan tree with dozens of subsidiary trunks. The nine rooms of the house were linked by bridges and ladders, and the walls were little more than cloth screens. Three of the rooms had torn loose from their attachments during the years of constant wobbling, littering the ground with bits of wreckage and sad little bundles of moldy fabric.

"Hold me up and I'll look inside," Solana instructed. Utsuro raised her up on one hand and moved carefully around the banyan while Solana balanced herself and looked into the treehouse rooms. In addition to making her obedient, the gene designers had given Solana perfect balance. She could stand on Utsuro's upraised palm as he walked around as easily as she could stand on a floor.

"Nothing in this one," she said after poking her head through a rip in the cloth wall of one room.

Just then the cyborg froze. *"Please keep silent,"* he said directly into Solana's head via the comm. He lowered her to the ground slightly slower than dropping her. Solana looked around but could see nothing beyond the ruined garden and the broken hedge.

After twenty seconds Utsuro spoke over the comm again. *"I thought I heard something creak in that first house we searched. Wait here."* He stepped to the hedge, moving swiftly but placing his feet precisely on spots where the ground was clear of anything that might make noise. As he reached the opening in the hedge he dropped to all fours with his arms and legs bent like a spider's, his body just clearing the ground. Then he looked through, making a quick scan before pulling back. *"I don't see anything,"* he said through the comm.

Solana stayed in one place but turned slowly around, scanning on visual and infrared with no lights. Anything that could move would give off heat, and against the uniform chill of Safdaghar's interior that should show up like a beacon. All she could see was blackness, and a few spots on the ground where Utsuro's footprints were cooling back down to equilibrium.

Still in four-legged mode Utsuro crept through the hedge and across the garden of the house next door, then raised his head to look through a window. He stood for a long time, absolutely still. Solana watched him and his surroundings.

After a minute of watching and listening the cyborg looked around once more and then walked back without trying to be silent. "Nothing," he said aloud. "Perhaps we moved something and it fell over."

Solana looked around once more, then up before answering. "I thought I saw something the other day. Near the stadium."

"This place is making us jumpy," he said.

"I can't imagine why," Solana answered with a laugh that was more nervous than amused. "Still, I think maybe from now on we should work together, no matter what Atmin says about efficiency."

"It will slow us down. I want to scan as much of the hab as possible."

"Could we at least be closer together? Maybe alternate blocks or something?" Solana tried not to sound as if she was pleading.

"I suppose that would work," said Utsuro. "If it will make you feel less nervous, we can do it that way."

"Don't you get nervous?"

"Not in the same way you do. No adrenaline, no fight-or-flight, no panic. I don't even have some of those glands anymore. But I can still feel a sort of existential horror about what happened here. It isn't the fear of something sneaking up on me in the dark, so much as the knowledge that someone was capable of doing this."

"People are capable of all kinds of awful things. All bios. Mechs, too. Basically everybody. How can you even be surprised?"

"I suppose I am an idealist at heart."

For another two hours they searched Solana's section, staying within a hundred meters of each other. Their methods were very different. Utsuro was methodical, doing a DNA scan of each house and checking all the rooms systematically. He could do that while moving with mechanical speed, never needing a rest.

Solana had to rely more on judgment and context clues to pick out houses and workshops which looked like good targets.

Sometimes she skipped whole blocks if they didn't look interesting. The result was that she leapfrogged ahead of Utsuro, even a couple of blocks at a time, but he inevitably caught up and passed her.

When the four of them gathered back at the medical center to eat and rest, Pera began the meal with an announcement. "Atmin and I have been talking about the way we're searching, and we've decided to work as a team, even if it's not as efficient."

Solana fought to keep a straight face, but of course Utsuro could manage a perfect deadpan, his screen showing only a question icon in blue. "What is the reason for this change?" he asked.

"Both I and Pera are afraid," said Atmin. "She worries that more traps are hid in houses, streets, or passageways. My fear is likely just a morbid fancy yet I must assert I think that something is at large within this hab."

"At large?" asked Utsuro. Solana suddenly didn't feel like giggling at all.

"He thinks he saw something," said Pera. "I'm not sure."

"I did, too," said Solana. "And Utsuro heard some noises."

"Though nothing certain," said Utsuro quickly.

"This means our search will take more time," said Atmin. "With double shifts it can be done—a sprint of work to search the rim, and then withdraw to Yanai and the hub for simpler toil."

"Double shifts?" asked Pera.

"Eight hours of search, a rest, and then eight hours again before the daily meal and sleep. The pace is hard but surely you have served in worse conditions while at war?"

"I just signed up to get a ride." The dino lashed her tail. "None of this makes sense. It can't be a bio, not after so long. A mech? Why not show itself and get a ticket off this wreck?"

"I was discussing what happened here with Solana," said Utsuro. "I wonder if we've made a mistake in assuming all this destruction was created by some sort of internal conflict. Maybe Safdaghar was attacked. A mech or high-level bot could remember that and assume we are the same sort."

"What sort?" asked Pera.

"Pirates or slavers," said Utsuro.

"We noticed that there aren't a lot of kids among the dead," said Solana. "Maybe somebody took them. Like those kids in the launch tube."

Pera cocked her head and looked thoughtful.

Then Atmin spoke, slowly and sounding very tired. "I sadly must report that you are wrong. Two days ago I found a theater, which desperate folk of Safdaghar had fortified. A score of guards with scavenged arms lay dead outside. Within, still sitting in their seats, were near two hundred children, shot. I do not think that anyone of any age survived what happened here."

"Why didn't you mention that before?" asked Utsuro after a moment.

"I did not wish to cause you fear, or rage, or sorrow for the dead. I thought this was a tragic tale, of factions in a hab gone mad with hate. But if the folk of Safdaghar were victims of attack, that changes all. We should record their fate, and after leaving tell the worlds what happened here."

"And our mysterious lurker?" asked Pera.

"If it exists at all—and still we do not know—we should extend the hand of mercy if we can. From now on if you think you see or hear some hidden watcher, call to it and offer help."

"We should have done that anyway," said Utsuro.

The array of tagged items outside the clinic covered the dead lawn and spilled into the street beyond. When she and Utsuro headed out after waking, Solana walked past paintings and ink drawings, sculptures, antique furniture, handmade ceramics and glassware, metalwork, even an ancient spacesuit.

The morning walk was long—by now the four of them had searched almost half the hab, and had to travel more than a kilometer to the part of the hab ring yet to be gone over. But for the darkness and the mold-covered mummies, it might have been a pleasant stroll. As it was, Solana and Utsuro tried to distract themselves by talking about their future plans.

"If I may ask, what do you intend after your brain modification? Will you continue working for Yanai as a scarab?"

"One or two more voyages, to build up some savings. But after that I want to go to one of the big habs, or a planet. Juren, maybe, or even Earth. Someplace with a whole lot of people, where I can fall in love and have messy breakups and it'll all be what I choose, not some compulsion in my neurons."

"Isn't love just another kind of compulsion?"

"I don't know," said Solana. "I've never been in love. How about you?"

"I can't remember. I suspect I have been—the word is attached to a very strong feeling. But I don't remember who or when."

"Do you think it was one of them?" Solana gestured at the darkness and death around them.

"I'm afraid so. Otherwise... why wasn't anyone searching for me?"

"Maybe they think you're dead."

"I hope I wouldn't give up so easily."

Just then Solana caught a flicker of motion off to her left, from a house she had checked days before. Something had ducked out of sight from a window, she was certain. She clutched Utsuro's arm and said *"Something's there—left!"* on the comm. They both froze.

"Hello?" Utsuro called aloud. "Whoever you are, we mean no harm. We can help you!"

Of course there was no response.

"I'm going to see what's over there." Utsuro moved slowly, arms outstretched to either side, hands open. He repeated his announcement aloud as he approached the house, and waited nearly a minute before sliding the door open.

Solana remembered that house: small, cramped and cluttered inside, evidently inhabited by bad housekeepers before the disaster. The floor was a churned mess of broken furniture and dishes, with mold thick on every surface. She had given it a quick scan and moved on.

Now Utsuro stepped inside, cautiously placing each foot, making sure the surface was stable before putting his weight on it. He went in, poked his head into the two adjacent rooms, and pulled himself up to the sleeping space upstairs.

"I don't see anyone here at the moment," he said. *"How certain are you?"*

"Mostly," she replied. *"I wasn't recording, so I can't review the image."*

"I'll take your word. Anything which could move around in this mess would have to be very light or very agile. A bot?"

"Plausible."

"Wait a moment. I don't think I—" His comm went silent.

"Utsuro?!" Solana felt momentary panic.

"I'm all right. Don't worry. I just did a quick DNA scan, and I got a match here."

"Your genome?"

"Strong match, good signal. I was here!"

She hurried over to the house, circling through the barren garden to the rear, where the house faced a shared courtyard with seven other houses. A fountain now sheathed in ice stood in the center, and much of the ground was icy from a long-ago broken pipe.

The other houses facing the courtyard had broad porches and upstairs galleries, with sliding doors open to the inside. Judging from the furniture scattered about, the people had spent a lot of time sitting on their porches. It must have been a jolly little place, she thought. But all those open doors and alleyways meant a couple of dozen ways for someone to flee.

She looked at the ground, seeking any heat traces, but found nothing.

Utsuro came out of the untidy little house and scanned the porch facing the courtyard. "Nothing here," he said aloud. "I only got a signal in one room."

"Not your house, then. That's good. Whoever lived here was a slob."

"I thought the same." He made a circuit of the courtyard but shook his head when he returned to Solana. "I could have sworn I scanned this place already."

"Maybe you skipped that room. I wonder why you were here, back then."

"I think the resident was a singer. One room is soundproofed but there are no instruments."

"Can you sing?"

Utsuro thought for a long time before answering. "I suppose it's possible. I certainly remember a lot of music, and the mechs said I had some smart-matter hardware in my larynx. A variable voice."

"Maybe the two of you were rivals. You and whoever lived here."

"Or collaborators. Preparing a duet."

"See? We're figuring out all kinds of stuff about you."

"All speculation. With a variable voice I might just as well have been an actor or a comedian."

"You don't seem like the comic type. You're too dignified."

They returned to the main avenue and pushed on toward the next search area. The route took them past the stadium and the park. Despite the fact that she had passed that way several times already, the two massacre sites still made Solana nervous. She let Utsuro lead the way, and kept looking to the sides and behind them.

Just past the park, the avenue passed by a shop which had once sold frozen desserts. The pavement blocks in front of the dessert place were painted to form a gigantic mosaic image of a bowl of frozen custard. Utsuro stepped onto one bright yellow stone and both of them heard a loud click. The cyborg froze. "Get away!" he said.

Solana didn't argue. She sprinted ten meters to where a solid-looking planter made of glass blocks and filled with dirt offered protection.

"What happened?" she said over the comm.

"I don't know. I stepped on a paving block and it shifted a tiny bit under my weight. You heard the click? I'm afraid it might be a trap. Like the one Atmin found."

Solana raised her head over the edge of the planter and scanned the whole area around Utsuro at high magnification. "I don't see any spring-loaded blades or anything like that."

"I am more worried about an explosive. A mine."

Solana switched to the general channel. "Pera! Utsuro stepped on some kind of trigger mechanism. He's afraid it's a mine. What do we do?"

"Did it explode?"

"No."

"Then don't do anything. Stay put. I'll be there as quick as I can."

Solana provided Pera with their location, then got up and walked back to where Utsuro stood, his right foot on the booby-trapped paving stone, his left just raised behind him.

"Are you okay?" she said aloud.

"You shouldn't be here. There might be other traps."

"Well, I'm here now. Are you okay?"

"I am slightly off-balance. If you could please provide me with something I can use to stabilize myself I would be very grateful."

She handed him the long-handled pottery tool, which he gripped in one hand. With the end of it on the ground he was a tripod, much more steady.

"Thank you. Now you really should get to a safer spot."

"How do we know what spots are safe? I thought this road was safe—we both passed this way yesterday."

"Evidently neither of us stepped on the right block."

She knelt behind him and peered at his right foot and the yellow block underneath it. It had definitely sunk, a good half-centimeter.

"So how do these things work?"

"Typically there's a trigger—like a pressure pad or a proximity sensor—and an explosive charge. The bomb is often surrounded by shrapnel. Other versions place the explosive elsewhere, such as in front, firing at the entire area. There are also incendiaries, nanoburn sprays, goo bombs, and so forth."

"You seem to know a lot about them."

"Perhaps. I may have learned it here. This might be my own handiwork. I do know one thing about mines, though: putting your face right next to one is a very bad idea."

"Pera won't be here for twenty minutes. Do you really want to stand here that long?"

"Now that I can balance, it is no hardship."

Solana drew her multipurpose tool. Following her new presets, it immediately turned into a big sharp knife. She called up the control interface in her goggles and made the tool into a long thin probe with an eye and a light at the tip. Then she worked it into the crack between the block under Utsuro's foot and the one to the right of it.

Her goggles displayed the view from the probe. She seemed to be soaring through a very deep and narrow canyon. On either side, the walls were glossy and rippled like calm water. Here and there groups of straight parallel gouges marred the smooth surface.

Looking down she could see that the smooth wall of the glass paver ended at a layer of adhesive, bonding the block to a shock-absorbing layer. Below that was the graphene sheet of the habitat deck.

But beyond the intersection at the edge of the block, she could see something weird. The underlayers were roughly cut away, and below was an empty space. According to the hab plans, that was just available volume for piping and wiring.

The probe showed that the depressed block was mounted on a simple metal rod, which in turn connected to a very primitive-looking spring-loaded pressure switch. Solana couldn't see any explosives, but wires connected to the switch ran off in six directions under the floor.

She described what she saw to Utsuro. "I'm just amazed none of this got set off during all that time the hab was wobbling back and forth."

"One can hardly call it a fortunate chance."

Solana tried to trace one of the wires under the floor. Her probe was only a meter long, and even at maximum extension with the light cranked up as bright as it could go, the wire just led off into darkness.

"This is quite a trap. It looks like it sets off half a dozen bombs."

"Some might be fakes. Decoys to delay and distract the person attempting to clear the mine. Solana, *please* wait for Pera to get here. She is a trained combat engineer."

"She can place mines and breaching charges, and maybe clear them by setting them off, but I've got the microtools and vision. Even if she was here I'd still be the one doing the work."

"That's true, but you could have waited," said Pera's voice, making Solana jump. She switched out of probe view mode and looked over her shoulder. The dino was there, breathing rapidly.

"How'd you get here?"

"I ran. You said it was important, so I ran. I can run a kilometer in ninety seconds."

"Oh." Solana considered Pera's long legs, her horizontal body and massive rib cage, all obviously built for speed, and blushed. "Well, now that you're here, how do I disable this thing?"

"Take a look at the pressure switch and describe it."

Solana examined the switch unit again. It was bulky and crude, as if it had been made by hand, without even a printer. "There's a rod glued to the bottom of the paver, and a steel spring which is compressed right now. I can see an electrical contact at the bottom."

"Classic design. Very low-tech. Of course, if it was advanced you'd both be slush by now. The spring's to keep it from going off if anything too small walks on the trigger. As long as you keep weight on it, the contact is closed. That sends an arming signal to the charges. When you release the contact, boom. Or whoosh, or ft-ft-ft, or whatever the weapon systems do. If we're very lucky, the power supply is long dead and no signal got sent, but I don't think we want to test that right now."

"So all I need to do is make sure that contact stays established even if Utsuro lifts his foot?"

"Right. Bridge the gap between the contacts, or extract the spring. Both, ideally. What you *don't* want to do is sever any of the leads to the weapons."

"Got it."

Solana rummaged in her kit and found a spool of micron-thick wire. She fed it into the handle of her tool and set it to spin ten centimeters of wire out at the tip, just between the tiny eye and the tiny light. Once the wire was in place she adjusted the tool again to make a little gripper, which she used to set the wire in place, one end on each metal contact. Another adjustment and the tip of the probe glowed white-hot as she spot-welded the tiny wire to the contacts. Then, just for safety, she did it all over again on the opposite side.

Pera stood nearby, singing softly to herself. When Solana was done she sent an image to the display inside Pera's helmet. The dino nodded, and then both of them retreated back behind the heavy planting box ten meters away.

"Okay!" Pera called to Utsuro. "Your best bet is probably a vertical jump. Go!"

Utsuro crouched and let go of the pottery tool, then leaped a good two meters straight up. He came down a meter or so past the trigger stone.

Solana realized she was holding her breath. After a moment she looked at Pera, who had taken a small mirror on a telescoping handle out of one of the many pockets on her armored suit, and was surveying the site while keeping her head below the edge of the planter.

"Utsuro, are you all right?" Solana called out.

"I appear to be."

She risked a look and saw him walking calmly toward them. Solana and Pera managed to get to their feet before Utsuro reached the planter.

"Now what?" asked Utsuro.

"Now you two stay right here. I'm going to clear the site."

Pera cautiously approached the yellow paving block, studied it for a moment, then took a small disk out of another pocket and placed it delicately atop the block. She returned the way she had come, and then gestured for everyone to shelter behind the planter again. Only when they were all down did she transmit a short code.

The disk suddenly turned into two jets of blue-white plasma, one pointing up, the other down. The upward jet looked like a glowing sword three meters high before dissipating into vapor, and the downward one shattered and melted the paving block and the switch underneath it.

Three near-simultaneous bangs followed immediately, and then a rattle echoed around them as hundreds of tiny needles buried themselves in every surface facing the mine.

Pera gestured palm-down and the three of them waited a full minute before she gave thumbs-up and they could stand.

"Thank you, to both of you," said Utsuro. "It was terribly careless of me to step on that thing."

Pera lashed her tail irritably before speaking. "This changes everything. There could be others, maybe more dangerous ones. We should pull out now."

"No, please! Not now. I've been finding traces of my DNA. I just need a little more time."

"This is crazy. You're crazy. All of you are crazy. We're pulling out. Come on." She switched to comm. *"Atmin, get back to the camp. Fly as high as you can and do not set down anywhere."*

She set out at a cautious pace back to camp, looking intently at the ground before her. After a moment, Solana followed, trying to step where Pera had walked.

Utsuro stood still for several minutes, then walked straight down the center of the main road, heading for the camp.

CHAPTER FIVE

Sixteen years earlier...

She was gently kissing the back of a Master's knees when the harsh buzz of the alarm sounded. Solana looked up at the Master's face and saw him looking back, just as confused as she was. A voice over the comm network replaced the buzzer.

"Danger! Hab under attack. Not a drill. Get to emergency shelters immediately. Danger!"

"I guess we'd better. Where's the nearest shelter?" asked the Master. He was a visitor to Kumu habitat, one of hundreds who spent years in hibernation to make the trip for a few weeks of unbridled excess before going back into the freezer for the journey home—possibly with a Qarina in the next berth.

"In the hall," said Solana, and launched herself at the door. In Kumu's microgravity environment she could move with ease, but her Master was clumsier. She led him out of the play suite into the corridor. All along it frightened Qarinas and Masters of all sexes emerged from doorways, mostly without clothes. Solana's own temporary Master suddenly looked self-conscious about being naked and sporting a huge erection. The drug cocktail he'd taken would make sure that wouldn't fade no matter what happened.

"Clear the way!" A squad of human and mech guards hurried down the hall from the direction of the nearest transport stop, bouncing off walls in their haste. They were accompanied by a swarm of weapon bots. The humans were in armor, currently colored high-vis orange, but the weapon drones were sinister tactical black.

The Qarinas, obedient to a fault, flattened themselves against the sides of the passage, but some of the Masters tried to accost the human troops with questions. The response was a shouted "Shelter! Now!" followed by an augmented-strength shove in the direction of the nearest glowing green door.

A sudden loud bang left Solana unable to hear anything but the ringing in her ears. Ahead she could see a new hole in the ceiling. Mechs and humans came swarming through, all in white marked with a red *shi* symbol.

The security troops stopped and hesitated for a split second, which was too long. The intruders sent a hail of smart darts and micromissiles down the passage, blasting mechs and bots to scrap and punching holes in the chests and heads of the humans.

They advanced down the hall, separating the panicked crowd as they went. Qarinas were gently but firmly passed back toward the hole in the ceiling. Masters and staff got a needle through the head.

Salibi. Solana had heard about them from one of the trainers. "They're dangerous fanatics who hate Qarinas like you. If they catch you they'll lock you away and never let you give pleasure again. But don't worry, little one. There's only a few billion of them and they're down in the Main Swarm. They can't get you here."

Solana dove into the nearest open doorway, another play suite set up for restraint. She swung herself around a big pillory in the center of the room and shot into the bathroom. She'd be safe there. The door could be pressure-sealed and she'd have water. Once the guards chased the bad guys away she could come out. She curled herself up into the cabinet under the sink and waited, barely daring to breathe.

She tried to use her comm implant but the Kumu network was dark. It occurred to Solana that the invaders might be able to detect her signal so she silenced it. She waited in the dark, utterly isolated, listening to the shrill noise of alarms, distant explosions, screams, and amplified voices giving orders too garbled to understand.

After a time the noises died away, and Solana began to wonder if it was safe to come out. With no Master, no trainers, nobody to tell her anything, Solana had a rare opportunity to think for herself.

Qarinas didn't get much education, but Solana was curious and had learned things in her few idle moments. She knew that Kumu was very far from the Main Swarm, far from anything, really. Even a fast sail took a standard year to get from Jupiter to Kumu. There wasn't really any way to sneak up on the hab undetected. The Salibi must have come in a disguised ship, masquerading as a regular dumb cargo payload.

She had seen a cargo pod being unloaded once. It was certainly big—a couple of thousand cubic meters—but Kumu itself was a kilometer across, thousands of times bigger. Could the Salibi really hope to keep control? Would they even want to?

But leaving an enemy hab left them open to retaliation, What if the trainers got Kumu's laser working before the Salibi were out of range?

Solana suddenly felt very alert and cold. The Salibi couldn't leave an intact hab behind, nor could they hold it. Which meant they would likely try to *destroy* Kumu when they left. Including any little stray Qarinas hiding in cabinets.

She checked the network, to see if there were any announcements. Still dark. After a couple more minutes she crawled out of the cabinet and groped her way to the door. It opened, which meant there was air outside. That was encouraging.

It slid open when she touched the control, and in the quiet it seemed incredibly noisy. The passage beyond was lit by red emergency lights, dazzling after the dark cupboard.

Where to go? The shelter door at the end of the corridor had a big black-edged hole cut in it. She could see bodies inside, spattered with blood. None of them moved.

What was the safest place in Kumu? Where could any survivors hold out? Well, the hab couldn't survive without power, so the fusion reactors were in the core of the structure, with literally all of Kumu as armor against damage. She went to the nearest vertical shaft and pushed herself down. She fell very slowly—Kumu's mass was just a million tons, so she weighed just a few millionths of a newton—and with each deck she dropped the force pulling her diminished.

The security bots had tried to hold this shaft. About a hundred meters down Solana came to a barricade. They'd closed a pressure hatch and then backed it up with layers of construction foam and graphene. But the attackers had cut through the wall into a laboratory, cut two decks down, and outflanked the defenders. Solana followed their trail and found the next section of the vertical shaft riddled with holes and scorch marks. A few shattered bots clung to the walls.

Down near the core she found another defense line, also breached. Blood-spattered corpses in armor outnumbered the broken bots. None of them were Salibi. Surely Kumu's defenders had managed to kill at least a few? Maybe the invaders had taken their dead. Solana remembered something else she'd heard from her trainer: the Salibi claimed that every dead person's mind was archived by an infinitely high-level intelligence existing outside of normal spacetime, and at some point in the future all the dead would be reactivated. That was why even human Salibi fought like disposable mechs.

The shaft ended at Deck 4. Below that was the armored sphere holding Kumu's power reactors and oxygen reserves. There was only one entrance, and she didn't know where it was. Qarinas weren't allowed down here, at least not normally. Solana found a door into a passage around the equator of the core. It looked like a control space. More signs of fighting.

A mech with an armored white hemisphere shell came scuttling around a big coolant pump and stopped. "May I help you, child? This area is not safe for biologicals. There are toxins and unexploded warheads."

She turned to run but the mech caught her with a burst of machine speed. Arms popped out of armored ports and grabbed her by ankle and elbow. Solana writhed and fought, flailing with her free limbs. The mech carried her back to the vertical shaft, and she saw a pair of white-armored humans descending to meet them.

"Found another," said the mech. "Poor thing was trying to join those despicable creatures inside the core."

"I don't despise them," said one of the humans. "They are cunning and strong, and glory in their sins. I *hate* them. May God forgive them because I certainly can't."

"Amen," said the mech. "Now take her to the staging area. I have to finish planting charges."

Solana hadn't tried to fight the mech, but humans were different. They could feel pain. As soon as the mech released its grip she aimed a kick at one human's abdomen. When the other one tried to grab her she bit and punched and wriggled. These two were not frontline troops. They were wearing protective suits, not heavy combat armor, so a foot in the groin from a girl in perfect physical condition could actually hurt.

For one glorious moment she struggled free and launched herself down the corridor. Then behind her she heard the muffled pop of a launch pistol, and a tranq round hit her bare back. It spread out and she felt a faint prickle. Then her muscles stopped obeying her, and all she could feel was an overwhelming desire for sleep. The very last thing she heard before sinking into darkness was the voice of one human. "Poor things. They'll fight to the death to stay slaves."

She woke once, briefly, in a converted storeroom where a couple of human medics were moving among dozens of unconscious Qarinas lying on stretchers. Solana tried to move, but there were medical sensors stuck to her skin in a dozen places, and the humans noticed at once. They had clear face masks on, to avoid spreading microorganisms, but as soon as they turned they made the masks opaque, a blank white field with a red *shi*.

"Don't worry, child," said one. Her voice was calming. "No harm will come to you. We're just prepping you all for hibernation. Soon we will all be out of this hellish place."

"No," she murmured and kept struggling to get up. Her muscles were weak and didn't do what she wanted.

"Nothing but death for you here," said the other. While he spoke the first one touched a patch to Solana's bare chest, and in just a couple of seconds everything faded away.

When she woke again she was about five kilos thinner, sitting in a chair with soft but unbreakable restraints keeping her in place. She felt the tug of Mars-level gravity, pressing her down into the seat. The room looked like a medical clinic, and a human wearing white coveralls and a face-concealing mirrored visor stood just out of arm's reach.

"Welcome to Jiaohui," the human said. Her voice was pleasant but wary. "If you're willing to behave yourself I'll release you."

"Let me go!"

The woman just waited.

"I won't try to fight," said Solana.

The woman's head nodded and a second later the restraints withdrew into the chair.

"You've been hibernating for two standard years, and right now you're in the Main Swarm. Do you know what that means?"

"A long way from Kumu. Near the Sun."

"Very good. I confess I've been shocked by how ignorant some of the other children we rescued are. Now, do you know why I'm wearing this?" The woman tapped her faceplate. "I could make it transparent. Show you my face and order you to behave. Why didn't I do that?"

Solana didn't know. None of this made sense. When trainers wanted obedience, they gave orders, and sometimes backed it up with punishment. These lunatics had taken her prisoner, hauled her across the solar system, and now were . . . *pleading* with her? It was insane. She shook her head mutely.

"Well, I'm sure you'll figure it out. In the meantime we're going to educate you. Teach you some basic knowledge about the world and how to live in it. Give you tools to help overcome your conditioning. Once that's done, you can decide what you want to do."

"I want to go home. I want to go back to Kumu."

"That's one thing I'm afraid you can't do. It's a dead hab now. We made sure of that. All the slavers are dead, the genomes destroyed. We did take off a lot of financial data, and some friendly high-level minds are trying to crack the encryption. Find out who their customers were, their suppliers, their backers. Find any other operations in the same filthy trade. But Kumu itself is nothing but cold scrap full of vacuum."

That hit Solana like a blow. She had never known any place but Kumu. The dormitories, the playrooms, the training center, the Masters' suites, and the cafeteria had been her entire universe. The scents, the images, the infinite variety of textures and sensations. Now? This silent white-painted place wasn't home. It would never be home.

The mirror-faced woman seemed to understand what she was thinking. "I'm sure you're sad right now. Leaving home is hard, no matter what kind of a place it is. But we've brought you out of that so you can have a better life. See more than the inside of a sex dungeon."

Solana's surge of anger surprised even herself. She leaped at the woman, teeth bared and fists clenched. If her coverall hadn't been tough carbon fiber Solana might have been able to do some damage. As it was she flailed and struggled and eventually the restraints reached out of the chair and hauled her back.

"Fighting will get you nothing," said the woman, shaking her head. "Harming yourself won't accomplish anything, either, so please don't try anything like that. If you really want to leave, cooperate. Learn. Show you can get by on your own and we'll let you go. I can see you're quite intelligent. This should be easy for you."

"What if I don't? What will you do?"

"We'll feed you and take care of you and keep you from harming yourself or others. And we'll wait."

Madness!

She decided to trick them. She'd pretend to go along with their crazy scheme. Do what they wanted her to do, learn the things they wanted to teach her, and fool them into letting her go. And then...then she would find a Master. Do what she was meant to do. Serve, and obey.

After a sleep and food—the food was surprisingly good, though the spices were different from what Solana was used to—she found herself facing the same masked woman again.

"What do you want me to do?" Solana asked.

"Well, today I thought we could start teaching you. You're literate, but I don't know what else you know. What shall we study—numbers, history, tech? Or something else?"

Solana was nearly paralyzed. How could she please this woman? She gave no orders, her face and body were hidden, and even her tone of voice was unnaturally even. For nearly a minute Solana simply stared at her.

Finally she just picked the first thing the woman had said. "Numbers."

"Of course. Let's begin with the basics and see how much you already know."

For the next couple of hours Solana explored a new world. She could count, and had a vague understanding of adding and taking away. The mirror-masked woman taught her about dividing numbers and multiplying them, and how they were really the same thing, just in reverse.

She actually felt a little disappointment when the masked woman sighed and stretched and said, "I'm sorry, Solana, I'm afraid we'll have to stop for now. My voice is giving out and I haven't had a drink since I woke up. Would you like to continue tomorrow?"

"Yes!" she said—and then remembered that this was all still part of her plan to trick them. "I mean, whatever you want."

"Perhaps we can try solving some basic problems tomorrow. In the meantime, I'm giving you access to the instruction we've been doing. You can play with it as much as you wish. Unlike me, it won't wear out."

She saw only masked Salibi for two weeks, until they were sure she wasn't dangerous. Then Solana was moved to a room with three other female Qarinas about her age: Alipina, Lele, and Laruan. All four were starved for skin contact and the conditioned reward of giving pleasure. The Salibi wisely left them alone until they were sated.

But Solana began to tire of their endless play after a couple of days, and when her next numbers lesson came up she went off enthusiastically to work with the masked woman.

From numbers they moved on to the workings of the physical world—the motions of planets and habs, the behavior of photons and electrons, energy in all its shifting forms, and the iron laws of conservation and entropy. Solana found she could lose herself in that magnificent complexity just as well as in the rules of numbers. The way that just a few simple principles could generate, well, everything in the Universe, was endlessly fascinating.

Of course, all of that was just a game she was playing. Everything she learned was a cover for her secret plan to escape. Her training back at Kumu was good preparation. Many times she had been ordered to do things she hated, and the trainers made sure to punish any signs of resentment or resistance. Solana had learned to find something, some tiny element she could put herself in, apart from the awfulness.

The same principle worked here: she found a refuge in the things the Salibi wanted her to learn. She taught herself to use numbers, to understand physics, and to manipulate tools at the nano scale. They thought she was expanding her horizons, becoming a new person, but she was fooling them. Hidden deep inside herself she held to her plan: get out of Jiaohui, find a Master, and never worry about anything again.

✧   ✧   ✧

She was studying one evening in her dormitory, exploring a virtual world of molecules and chemical bonds via her data implant, when she became aware of shouts and jolts happening in the physical world. Lele and Laruan were fighting and Alipina sat in the middle of the floor, crying loudly.

"All of you hold still and be silent!" Solana shouted. The other three obediently shut up. "Lele, tell me what happened."

"I just wanted to play with Alipina, but Laruan didn't want to share."

Solana could see Laruan looking furious and impatient. "All right, Lele, you keep still. Laruan, tell me what happened."

"She's lying! 'Pina was listening to music and dancing by herself, and Lele started bossing her around like a Master. I told her to stop, she told me to quit interfering, so I told her she couldn't touch Alipina. That's when she slapped me."

"All right, stop. Alipina, let's hear from you."

'Pina was the youngest of them, a very sweet girl who hated to see others disagree. She wiped her nose with the back of her hand. "I just wanted to dance. I wish Lele and Laruan wouldn't fight all the time. I'll play with Lele if she wants, I guess."

Solana tried to be patient. "None of you should be doing anything you don't like. 'Pina, you can dance all you want. Lele, you shouldn't have hit Laruan and you shouldn't use Alipina like a toy. And Laruan, even when you're right you sound incredibly annoying. Now, I would *appreciate it very much* if you three could try not to fight while I'm studying."

She dropped back into her virtual environment, but couldn't concentrate. The other three were being quiet, so what was the matter? With a physical sense of shock she realized that she had sounded just like the Salibi—insisting on free choice, telling the younger girls not to use each other for pleasure by command.

And she realized she wasn't just doing it to fool anyone. Somehow in the past few weeks she had started thinking like a Salibi, without realizing it.

So where was Solana? What did *she* really want?

Halfway through the next session her teacher paused the instruction and turned her mirror mask to Solana. "When you got here I asked you a question: Why don't I show you my face and give you orders? I could make you a believer in five minutes. Have you figured out why I haven't?"

"You believe we should make choices," said Solana.

"Exactly. Ordering you to believe won't save your soul. I'd be no better than those selfish bastards who created you."

Soul was a word the Salibi used a lot. It meant personality, and identity, and even the capacity for independent action. In their ideology it existed as a separate thing from the brain, even separate from a person's knowledge. The Salibi spent a lot of time worrying about their souls—far more than they bothered about their bodies. After Kumu, where bodies were everything, it was hard for Solana to understand.

"Is there any way for me to change my brain? Make it so I don't have to obey every human I see?"

"Oh, it's possible. Your brain is just matter, after all. What can be done can be undone. Now, we don't have access to the tools and knowledge to do it here in Jiaohui, but I'm sure you could find someone who does, in some other hab or world. We don't do that sort of thing. There are philosophical objections."

"Philosophical?"

"Your brain may have been built by a gang of sadistic perverts, but it's the one you've got. Our faith teaches that brain alteration of any kind is unnatural, and therefore contrary to God's will. Even to correct other tinkering like what was done to you. These are tests. Faith will help you endure it."

"But I don't want to endure it! I want it fixed!"

"It's your choice, and I certainly won't stop you. In fact I'll pray for you. What I won't do is help you edit your brain."

"What's your name?" Solana asked her.

The woman hesitated. "We're not supposed to form attachments. It's too much like what you were rescued from."

"Please? I want to know."

"I'm called Jian. But I am just your teacher and therapist. That is the full extent of our relationship. Am I clear?"

"Yes," said Solana.

Time passed. Solana moved to a little solo room where the others couldn't disturb her. She adjusted to wearing clothes all the time, although she still ditched them whenever she could. She learned. And six months after waking her up, Jian came to Solana as she finished a day absorbed in microcircuit repair.

"How are you progressing?"

"I finished the Level Ten instruction today!"

"That's enough to get certified as a tech in some habs. Wonderful!" Jian sat down next to Solana, maintaining a ten-centimeter separation as always. She held a box in her left hand. "I think you've learned about as much as we can teach you here. For better or worse, you're done."

Solana blinked. Done? "What happens now?"

"Now you've got a choice to make. You can join our order and stay here. Help us save others, and devote yourself to God." She looked at Solana and shook her head. "I think your answer to that is no. Correct?"

"I'm afraid so," said Solana. "You've been very kind, and I owe you everything. But I can't make myself believe the way you do."

"I hope that will change someday. You still have two other options. You've heard of Biara? It's a hab entirely populated by Qarinas. They obey nobody but each other. Up in the Neptune Trojans. I've heard it's a nice place. A completely altruistic society. You'd be safe there."

"No," Solana said with decision.

"May I ask why not? If you don't mind, that is."

"Will you keep this a secret?"

"Everything you've ever said to me is confidential."

"All right. It's just...I don't really *like* being around other Qarinas very much. They wear me out. They're too...too..."

"Needy?"

"Yes! I mean, they're always nice. But sometimes I just want them all to leave me alone. And then I feel terrible."

Jian's voice had a smile in it. "It's perfectly fine for you to feel that way. A lot of the legacy humans and cyborgs here have the same problem—and more than a few of your fellow Qarinas, too. That's one reason we rotate staff to other projects."

"If I don't want to stay here and I don't want to go to Biara, what does that leave?"

"Everything else. There's a billion worlds out there. Go out and find what God has prepared for you. You'll need visual filters to protect yourself—or spend all your time away from humans. It will be hard, and your freedom will be in danger all the time."

Solana was silent for a few seconds. "I think that's what I want."

"I expected that," said Jian. "From the first time we spoke

together. I'm so proud of you, Solana! I don't think anyone has managed the transition to full autonomy as quickly as you have."

Solana laughed aloud. "You know why? It was all a trick. Back when we started I decided I was going to fool you. Make you think I was making choices for myself, but really I was just doing it to get out of here, so I could find a Master and go back to being a proper Qarina."

Jian's masked head tilted. "And will you do that? At this point I don't think I can stop you."

This time Solana laughed aloud. "You were teaching me not to take orders, and I was secretly trying to disobey you! It's crazy!"

Jian laughed with her.

"Will you do one thing for me?" asked Solana.

"Anything."

"Show me your face. I just want to see what you look like."

Jian hesitated, then she pulled the mask off. Solana was surprised at how creased and loose the skin of her face was, how thin and gray her hair was.

"You're crying," said Solana. "I'm sorry. I didn't mean to make you sad."

"Not sad," said Jian. She kept wiping away tears but she was smiling. "I'm so proud of you, my dear." Very tentatively, she reached out and patted the back of Solana's hand, then pulled away as if she was afraid Solana's skin might burn her.

"This is yours now," she said, passing Solana the box. It opened at her touch, revealing a pair of multifunction goggles. "They've got image filters. Try—I mean, I think you'll be pleased when you try them on."

Solana touched them to her face and felt the edge mold itself to the skin around her eye sockets. Everything was a little bit brighter, a little sharper. She looked at Jian and was startled to see a skin-tone oval with two black dots for eyes in place of Jian's face.

"These will protect you," said Jian. "If you wear them whenever you're around humans, nobody can make you do anything against your will. Your choices will be your own. May God protect you."

CHAPTER SIX

"I understand your fears, and share them to a great extent myself," said Atmin. "Yet every salvage job includes a share of risk. If here that means we must beware of traps then so we shall—but after spending so much time in search we cannot simply stop."

"Sunk-cost fallacy," said Pera. "Bad logic and bad economics. We've got some good stuff and we're still alive. Haul it all back to the hub, fill Yanai's holds with metal, and leave. Profit is profit, even if you don't get as much as you wish for."

Solana had done the math. Her share wouldn't be enough for major brain modding. She would have to spend another year saving up, or more. Her goal always fluttered just beyond her fingertips.

"I'm willing to stay a little longer," she said. "We've avoided any harm so far."

"If you jump off an orbital tower you're perfectly fine until you hit the ground," said Pera.

"I am a good deal stronger and tougher than the rest of you," said Utsuro. "Why don't the three of you pull back to the hub and let me finish searching this section? Atmin can evaluate things I find remotely, and I can complete my DNA scans."

"I like it. What does our centro think? Yanai?" said Pera.

The ship spoke in their heads via comm. *"I can't judge. If Atmin's right, the artworks and antiques of the rim section are more valuable per kilo than the industrial salvage of the hub. Continuing the search is sound economics. As to safety, I can print some additional bots to accompany each of you."*

"You're all letting your greed override your common sense."

"I must dispute your words," said Atmin. "For now I think we have a second goal more worthy than the first. This wheel of death did not acquire its grisly load from internecine strife, we all agree. No civil war or faction fight could leave all dead, efficiently and swiftly slain with skill. We do not stand amid a suicide. Instead I state this is a murdered hab. We should record all that we see, and make it known in Juren and beyond. Let justice be our goal, and profit next."

Pera lashed her tail again. "Oh, you're good. That's fourth-level intellect stuff, right there. Justice for the dead—even as we rob their corpses!"

"The people here cared much for craft and art. The Kuiper folk would see all that they made as so much matter to reclaim. What you call robbing I prefer to think of as preserving what they did. It honors them."

"While we're at it, why not grind 'em up for phosphorus? It goes for thirty gigs a kilo and we can say we're honoring their memory by putting it back in circulation. I bet there's five or ten tons here, at least."

Atmin gave an angry croak. "I will not hear a mercenary thug condemn the way I get my meat. How many gigs per corpse do *you* get paid?"

Pera lunged forward and snapped her teeth but Atmin took to the air and circled out of reach above her.

"Please!" said Utsuro, trying to position his metal bulk between the two. "Let's not quarrel."

"Attention!" said Yanai. *"I am detecting another spacecraft attempting to rendezvous with this hab. It's a dumb shuttle out of Scapino habitat. Pilot isn't answering my calls."*

"Scapino?" said Utsuro. "That hab is full of criminals, isn't it?"

"I don't know about that," said Pera. "But I've heard of some pretty shady military contractors based there. Mercenary thugs, I guess you'd call them."

"I fear they may be coming here to loot the hab," said Atmin. "Scapino lies within the Jovian retro ring, and only from those backward-circling habs could looters match our course without expending energy too great to leave a profit from the trip."

"*I got a message back at last,*" said Yanai's voice inside their heads. "*They say they're freelance rescuers, looking for a survivor bounty. I told them everyone on board is dead but their centro insists on docking and taking a look.*"

"Rescuers?" said Pera. "That's a lot of hot dust. This hab's been dark for years. I'm with Atmin. They're coming here for loot."

"Just like us," said Utsuro. "Perhaps we can work out some kind of an arrangement. There's plenty for all."

"No. We should just take what we've got and leave right away," said Solana. She tried to keep her voice calm but her heart was pounding.

"*They are on final approach,*" said Yanai. "*I estimate no more than forty minutes before the shuttle enters the docking bay.*"

Forty minutes, Solana thought, trying to stay calm and rational. Could she get back to Yanai in that time? Sure, but there would be no way to move all their salvage before the newcomers arrived. Abandoning it all would mean more years to save up for her brain mods.

The newcomers might actually be freelancers looking for a rescue bounty as they claimed, or just some desperate scavengers who could be bought off. And if it came to trouble, between Yanai, Utsuro, and Pera there wasn't much this team couldn't handle.

But she couldn't quite shake a sense of things slipping out of control, of nagging worry, of lurking dread.

Solana took a deep breath. "I guess we have to let them come," she said. "Can you three handle meeting them? I want to stay out of sight."

"They might not be humans," said Utsuro.

"I thought your goggles filter out faces," said Pera. "That's what you said."

"Yes, but I can't keep them on all the time. Like I said, I'll just stay out of sight if they come down here."

Atmin gave a startled croak and jumped off the upstairs gallery where he had perched. As he soared down to his travel sphere he called out, "We must to work at once. The goods we tagged and stored outside might tempt a thievish hand. The shop next door has space upstairs: let's hide our loot at once!"

Pera groaned but got into her suit again, as did Solana. They went outside and the three biggest members of the team formed a relay, passing items into the shop and up the stairs while Atmin's flying sphere picked up small objects and carried them through an open window. Solana had the first stage, taking items from the garden to the street. Pera carried them next door and into the shop, and Utsuro hauled them upstairs.

As they worked Yanai sent bulletins on the approaching vessel. *"It looks like a small intra-Jovian shuttle. Lots of nonstandard modifications. No obvious weapon mounts or targeting sensors. If the crew are biologicals I doubt it can hold more than half a dozen of them. Mechs might double that. The centro's definitely a human."*

"Yanai? Just out of curiosity, when did the shuttle leave Scapino hab?" Solana asked as she picked up a framed painting, carried it out of the garden to the street, and handed it to Pera.

"Assuming no major vector changes in flight, it must have left Scapino just after I started the burn to put Safdaghar on a Jupiter intercept course."

"Isn't that kind of suspicious? How did they know?"

"The sale of Safdaghar's mass to a Kuiper syndicate was a matter of public record in Deimos, Juren, and elsewhere. Scapino hab was in a good position when I began my burn."

Solana selected a smoky glass statue of a winged woman from the pile and lifted it with a grunt. "It sounds like they were waiting for us."

"They may have been keeping an eye on Safdaghar, yes. It would not be hard for a baseline or higher mind to deduce the path I was putting the hab on. Simple physics, really."

She handed the statue very carefully to Pera. "I guess I was just being antsy."

"They have matched vectors and rotation with Safdaghar, and are approaching the docking area. Fifteen minutes."

"I think we'll need more time to get this stuff out of sight. Can you stall them at the hub a little while?"

"I will try."

Yanai sent a camera feed to the four of them, showing the intruder as it neared the hub. The shuttle looked tiny next to Yanai, which Solana found reassuring. Even if the people inside wanted to make trouble, the scarab team's mighty friend was right there, strong enough to move worlds.

The newcomer was obviously patched together from bits of

other spacecraft. The command module had the pointed nose and flattened bottom of a spaceplane, but behind that the fuel tank was a simple cylindrical can reinforced by struts. On either side were boxy cargo containers held on by more struts, and the dorsal side had a smaller cargo pod shaped like a flat hexagon. At the rear a pair of fusion motors doubled as power plants, with cooling provided by fan-shaped radiator panels that were just folding up against the sides of the shuttle as Yanai's eyes watched.

Whoever was piloting that shuttle was very good. It got lined up well aft of Yanai's giant engine, and then just drifted slowly down the length of the bigger ship and into the docking bay with just a couple of low-power thruster puffs to stay properly aligned.

As it crossed the threshold of the docking section the shuttle's nose thrusters slowed it to just a meter per second, and then a complete stop. One tiny puff from the dorsal side let it settle belly-down onto the floor of the docking bay, just behind Yanai's crew section and a short walk to the emergency airlock into Safdaghar.

Nothing happened for about ten minutes, which was enough time for the four at the rim of the hab to finish hiding their treasure. After that sprint of adrenaline-fueled work, all of them except Utsuro needed a rest. They sat in the medical center drinking flavored water and watched the camera feed Yanai sent down.

Then the shuttle's pointed aerodynamic nose opened up like a flower and a trio of suited figures pushed out through a pressure membrane. Two were humans, one a chimp. All wore different suits with no sign of a unit emblem or a six-armed blue starburst, or an octagon, or anything even hinting at rescue. The chimp went to check out the emergency airlock, but the two humans walked to a point just under Yanai's observation bubble. The shorter of the two moved with bouncy confidence, the other followed with demure short steps, hands clasped in front.

The shorter figure waved up at Yanai, and a second later a video feed cut in which Yanai relayed to the rim. It showed a cheerful female human face with iridescent purple skin and shiny gold eyes. She looked like she was ready to go to a party. *"Good morning!"* she said via comm. *"I'm Jaka. Anybody on board?"*

"My name is Yanai. Currently my crew are inside the hab."

"Pleased to meet you, Yanai." Jaka looked down Yanai's length with evident admiration. *"You're a big one, that's for sure. Moved this whole hab by yourself?"*

"*I did. My crew are just making a final inspection of the structure.*"

"*Good for them. We're going to be looking around as well. How many are there? Your crew, that is.*"

"*Enough to do their jobs,*" said Yanai. "*Nothing you need to worry about.*"

A kilometer away Solana let out the breath she had been holding as she listened.

"*Leaving anytime soon?*" asked Jaka, still cheerful.

"*I plan to undock a hundred hours before periapsis. What are your plans and purpose here?*"

"*Just looking around, like I said. I can't wait to meet your crew. Where are they in the hab?*"

"*Various locations. Sometimes it is difficult to track them all.*"

"*You're a tight-lipped one, aren't you? Why the secrecy?*"

"*The quality of the information you give me determines the quality of my responses.*"

Jaka laughed. "*Okay, then. My friends and I are here to see what we can steal. Honest enough for you?*"

"*Yes. Having adjusted the hab's orbit, that is our purpose as well. I wish to avoid conflict. There is enough material of value in Safdaghar for both groups.*"

"*Oh, of course, of course. No point in wasting time fighting when there's plenty of loot for everyone. Great to hear we're on the same vector. Simplifies everything. Now: what can you tell me about the hab? No point in duplicating all of your team's work, is there?*"

"*I am sending you an updated schematic of the habitat, with damaged and depressurized areas marked. None of the hab's main power and control systems are working. Just a few emergency devices.*"

"*Thank you. Very helpful. I think we're going to get along just fine.*"

Meanwhile, down at the rim of Safdaghar Pera added her own commentary. "I don't like this. Not at all. They knew we'd be here and they came anyway. The easiest way to get good loot is to let someone else do all the work of finding it and then take it from them."

"As Yanai said, there is plenty for all," said Utsuro. "Even a thief would not wish to fight if there is no need."

"Tell them we've searched this part already. Make them go somewhere else," said Solana.

"*I didn't want to tell them where you are,*" said Yanai. "*But if you think they will agree to divide up the interior I will suggest it.*"

"It sounds like the most reasonable course," said Utsuro.

"Pull back to the hub and let them spend their time dodging booby traps," said Pera.

"I feel no need for company beyond us gathered here. If these intruders are content to stay as far away from us as can be done, I will not make complaint. We all concur, let it be so," said Atmin.

The four of them peeled off their suits and ate dinner as they watched the feed from Yanai's eyes. For variety Solana tried one of Pera's multi-meat sausages and some of Atmin's hominy. She had to drown the sausage in hot sauce to cover up the faint putrescine flavor, but it made a welcome change from her regular fare.

Instead of everyone having a little inset window in their vision, or flipping back and forth between their own eyes and Yanai's, Atmin set his travel sphere to project an image of what was going on at the hub. That way they could eat and watch as the newcomers unloaded their gear from the shuttle and carried it into the hab.

There were six of them up at the hub: the stylish-looking woman who called herself Jaka, her companion who seemed to be another female human, the chimp, a large male human, an absolutely average-sized male human, and a little eight-legged mech.

It took two trips for the six of them to move all their gear through the emergency lock into Safdaghar. Their gear was an eclectic mix, just like the suits they wore.

"What's in those cases they're carrying?" asked Pera.

"Tools, I expect. We certainly brought some with us," said Utsuro.

"Might be tools. Might be weapons," said Pera.

"Yanai, I wish to know: can you detect the slightest hint of motion on their ship, now that the new arrivals have all passed into the hab?" asked Atmin.

After about a minute Yanai answered. "*Hull vibration shows only mechanical systems and thermal noise. There could be mechs or bots aboard in dormant mode, but definitely no bios.*"

"You see?" The bird perched on Pera's head. "They leave their shuttle with no guard, right next to mighty Yanai's hull. A twitch of gripping arm or cutting laser flash would wreck it, stranding them aboard dead Safdaghar. They dare not cause us harm."

The feeling of relief that came over Solana was physical, as if she had stepped into a sauna. She could feel muscles relax that she hadn't even realized were tense. Yes, they were safe. Everything was going to be okay. Yanai would see to that.

"It would be nice to invite them over for a visit," said Utsuro. "Perhaps offer to exchange some meal templates."

"I would prefer, I think, a neutral site. I do not wish to let them spy upon our lair and study it too well," said Atmin.

"How about the stadium?" said Pera. "That's a fun place."

Yanai had one bot inside the hub, positioned on a support cable with a good view of the whole interior. From its eyes the crew followed Jaka's team as they spread out through that part of the habitat. The newcomers almost duplicated their own movements from a week earlier. The four humans kept their feet stuck to the floor, and did a very efficient room-by-room search. The chimp and the little spider mech climbed around the innermost parts.

After about an hour the spider mech made its way to the cable where Yanai's bot was positioned, and climbed to a point just a meter away. The mech maneuvered its smooth safety-green back to face the bot's eye and displayed a text message. "I can tell this bot is active. Enjoying the show? Blink lamp if you're watching."

Evidently Yanai blinked the bot's lamp, because the mech displayed another message. "It's rude to spy on people," it said, followed by a paragraph of the filthiest insults Solana had ever seen. Then the feed from the bot cut out.

"*That mech appears to have disabled my bot,*" said Yanai.

"I think that was very rude," said Utsuro.

Solana retreated to her room and got herself ready for sleep. She rubbed herself all over with cleaning goo, then touched the little empty jar to her bare stomach and pressed the recall button. The goo flowed over her, avoiding surfaces like her eyes and lips which she had left uncoated, carrying along a gray sludge of oil, dead skin, dried sweat, and plain old dirt. Everything wound up back in the jar, where the cleaning goo began digesting the sludge for fuel. A tiny residue of molecules the goo couldn't use accumulated in a compartment at the bottom of the jar, but enough room remained for several days more before Solana would have to empty it.

She woke four hours later when Pera contacted everyone via comm. "*I see lights over by the elevator plaza. They've followed us down here. I say we go tell them to get the hell out.*"

Solana pulled on her suit in frantic haste. "*Yes! Make them go away. We were here first.*"

"*I think a polite reminder would be best,*" said Utsuro. "*There's no need to pick a fight.*"

Solana emerged into the central space of the medical center, where the other three were already gathered.

"They've already picked a fight by coming here," said Pera.

"I refuse to join any violence," said Utsuro. "Neither Atmin nor Solana have the strength or training to fight these new arrivals. You would face them alone."

"You mean that?" asked Pera. "Seriously?"

"If we are attacked I will do all I can to defend the three of you. But I will not make threats to someone who has done nothing to harm us."

"Yanai? You can wreck their shuttle. Tell them to clear out."

"*I don't want to make a threat I'm not willing to carry out. I don't want to strand anyone here, no matter how rude and pushy they may be. And I certainly don't want to take them on board myself. I'm sorry, Pera. I don't like it, but I'm afraid we can't stop them from going where they please.*"

"This is how you get things like the Kendraraj genocide. Nobody wants to be unpleasant."

"You go too far," said Atmin. "To link a crime like Kendraraj to this affair is ludicrous. Though pushy these new rivals show no sign of murderous intent."

"Yet."

"I'm leaving," said Solana.

"You can't go up the spoke these newcomers are using," said Utsuro. "And we don't know if the others are safe."

"Not back to Yanai. I just don't want to be around if strangers come. Too many faces."

"My dear Solana, have no fear. Your goggles do protect both eyes and mind. No need to flee."

"Just until they go away. It's safer. I can spend a few more hours in my suit."

She didn't wait to argue the point. If Pera could see the lights of the newcomers, then they had probably spotted the illuminated medical center. Solana went dark, making her suit zero-reflective, going without lights, relying entirely on passive light amplification and infrared for vision. In case she had to wait past mealtime she brought along some peanut dumplings. Her suit had a little pressure membrane over the mouth so she could pass food inside if necessary.

The buildings around the medical center were all mixed-use, with shops or services on the ground floors and living space upstairs. All had rooftop gardens.

Across the street and a little way to spinward was the tallest building in the neighborhood: four stories high, with a taverna on the ground floor, a dance studio on the second, and apartments above them. The fourth floor was smaller than the others, a whimsical domed penthouse surrounded by what had once been a lush garden of uba vines trailing down the sides of the building. It offered good concealment and a wide field of view.

Solana took up a position at the corner of the garden, hidden by vines, and watched down the street in the direction of the elevator plaza. After just a few minutes she saw movement. Four humans and a chimp were coming up the central avenue.

They moved oddly. First one human and the chimp dashed forward about forty meters, then stopped and crouched behind planters or in doorways. After a moment the other three sprinted past them, leapfrogging to positions about twenty meters in front of the first pair. And then the original two moved again, past the second group to a new spot twenty meters beyond them. The entire team advanced about sixty meters a minute that way.

Solana was no soldier, but she had seen people move that way before, when the Salibi invaded Kuma. These newcomers weren't puttering about like her group, snooping and searching. Nor were they just walking openly. They moved like attackers.

"Be ready for trouble," she said to the others via comm. *"They'll be here in two or three minutes, and they don't look friendly."*

For a moment she wished for a laser or a gun, but then dismissed the thought as silly. She wouldn't know what to do with one if she had it. An armed drone would be far more useful than she could ever be.

Still, she thought, this rooftop garden seemed like a perfect place to put a sniper or a scout. She could easily see those figures darting from hiding place to hiding place down below, and they hadn't noticed her at all. If she did know how to use a weapon they would be in tremendous danger. Why hadn't they thought of that?

"Please don't be an idiot," said a voice behind her. Solana whirled to see the little spider mech standing about two meters away. Its surface was zero-reflective black like her own suit, save for a glowing green icon of two eyes and a line below. "I don't see any weapons but you might have something sneaky like a crossbow or a spring gun, and that might put a hole in one of those squishy morons. Put your hands out to the sides and move away from where you're sitting."

Solana started to comply and then realized the mech wasn't holding a weapon, either. So she ran as hard as she could for the opposite edge of the roof and made her gloves and shoes sticky as she swung over the parapet. The climb down was ten meters and she jumped the last three. After that she ran, zigzagging through alleys and yards, trying to get as far away as possible. With her suit dark and her goggles to see without lights, she would be hard to spot in the dark emptiness.

She took refuge in what had been a bathhouse a block away, where people had once gathered to drink subfreezing infused alcohol and poach themselves in scented steam. The place had evidently been empty at the time of the attack, and self-cleaning surfaces kept the interior utterly immaculate as the hab died around it.

"Atmin? What's going on?"

His response was to send her the live feed from the eyes in his travel sphere. Atmin was inside the medical center, looking out and down from one of the front windows, where a clear space had been wiped in the beads of water frosting all of them on the inside. The four human intruders and the chimp stood in the little front garden, facing the airlock entrance, where Utsuro stood barring the way. Pera was nowhere in sight.

Jaka, the purple-skinned woman with golden eyes, stood slightly in front of the others, wearing a transparent bubble helmet and a clingy skinsuit like something one would wear to a party in vacuum, with a more utilitarian vest of many pockets over it. She had a pair of sleek minimissile pods stuck to her upper arms. Solana knew they could be loaded with harmless stun rounds, webs, strobes—or deadly explosives.

The others were also armed. The largest human wore a suit with armor-gel layers over vital spots and a face-obscuring helmet, and carried an unmistakable needle rifle. A smaller human in a crude-looking old-fashioned suit wore a backpack with a laser emitter sticking up over one shoulder. The chimp had minimissile pods on his forearms. The slender woman stood behind Jaka, in an identical party-time skinsuit and bubble helmet. She had a plasma breacher in her hands, but she carried it as if she had just found it on the ground and was looking for whomever it belonged to. All of them except the leader and the laser bearer had large backpacks on.

Solana could see that the humans were watching Utsuro, the chimp was glancing around to the sides as if worried about a trap, but the slender woman only watched Jaka.

"...And I'm sure we all want to start things off on the right foot," said Jaka as the image appeared in Solana's vision. "You know me already, I'm Jaka—Jaka Layala. And these are my people: Ulan, Anton, Adelmar, and Tanaca. Freelance rescue and salvage entrepreneurs. We're not just a crew, we're more like a family." She pointed at them as she spoke. Ulan was the big man in the armored suit. Anton was the smaller one in the old-fashioned outfit. Adelmar was the chimp, and Tanaca was the silent woman standing two paces behind Jaka.

"Ask her about the mech," Solana said to Atmin on comm.

After a moment's delay while Atmin forwarded the suggestion to Utsuro, the big cyborg spoke. "Isn't there another member of your crew? Yanai saw a mech while you were unloading your shuttle."

"Oh, that one. Yes, I'd forgotten all about it. The mech goes by Daslakh. New guy on the team. It's not very social. Never mind, what about your little group? Who are you?"

"My name is Utsuro. My companions are Pera and Atmin. Pera is the dino, Atmin is the bird. I believe you have already met Yanai at the hub."

Jaka smiled and waved a finger in mock admonishment. "Now *you're* the one being forgetful. Not a good way to win my trust. There's another person around here somewhere, hiding out in the dark. Who is it?"

"I neglected to mention another member of our crew, a human who does not wish to meet anyone. She suffers from a severe phobia."

"Phobia? You mean she's afraid to meet us? Some habs do that to criminals—make them scared of whatever they did wrong. Is your missing woman a dangerous person? Is she armed? I need to keep my people safe, you understand. Can't have some sociopathic murderer hiding out in the dark."

"You have nothing to fear," said Utsuro. "If your group needs a place to camp, I suggest—"

"Camp? You want us to sleep outside, in all the mold and dust, with dead people everywhere? While you're all warm and comfortable in there with lights and power? Maybe you can live out here but my people need to be able to take off their suits once in a while, maybe have a hot meal. We'd be very much obliged if you let us join you in this building."

"I'm sorry," said Utsuro, "that's out of the question. There simply isn't room."

Jaka spread her arms. "No room? This place is huge! You could fit dozens of people inside—unless you're hiding something."

"Remember you are here only because Yanai chose to allow your shuttle to dock. She can change her mind if you cause difficulties."

"Wait, wait, wait. We're down here right now. Our shuttle is up at the hub with your boss. She can't get at us. All she can do is mess with our shuttle. Without the shuttle we'll be stuck here, and eventually die. Are you telling me you're willing to *kill* us rather than let us camp in this building? Seriously? Is your ship listening?"

Utsuro stood motionless, his face display still showing a diagonal red bar. But on the comm channel he sounded very upset. "*What shall I say? She's right—Yanai can't destroy their shuttle and maroon them here. That would be murder.*"

"*Invert it,*" said Pera. "*Ask her if she's willing to risk that just to come inside.*"

"*Do we even have the right to keep them out?*" Utsuro continued. "*We don't own this hab any more than they do.*"

"*We were here first.*"

"*Solana, let us know what your opinion is,*" said Atmin. "*I know that Pera does incline to keep them out, but what of you? I think I know what you will say but I would hear it in your voice.*"

"*I don't want to keep my goggles on all the time. Ask them to leave.*"

"*I thought as much. My own thought is to let them in, and thereby let this Jaka see we have no treasure hoard. The work of searching here is hard, and all of us agree the scenery is grim. I say we let them come, for I expect they will not stay.*"

"*That's two and two,*" said Pera. "*Yanai, break the tie.*"

"*I must protect my crew—which means I think you have to let them in. I can wreck their shuttle, or knock it off into space. But then you're trapped in a hab with armed beings who have nothing to lose. And in a fight, there's no way to predict who might get hurt. Cooperate until you can get up to the hub.*"

"Very well," said Utsuro to Jaka. "Your people may come into the medical center. You may use the downstairs area. We will remain upstairs. Please use the decontamination wipes in the airlock." Via comm he added to the rest of the scarabs, "*If they try anything I will protect you.*"

"*I'll stay where I am,*" said Solana. The bathhouse was comfortable enough, there were no dead bodies, and she could live on peanut dumplings for a day or two.

"*Why so scared? You've got your goggles, right?*" asked Pera.

"The face filters mean I'm not compelled to obey anyone who looks human," she said. "But . . . there's always a faint urge. I was made to be a slave and the ones who made me did a very good job. I'll just stay away."

"*They won't stay long. I'll make sure of that.*"

PART II

Jackals

CHAPTER SEVEN

Jaka sent Ulan in first. His suit had the toughest armor, so it made sense. The poor fool actually sounded proud to be the stalking horse. "Affirmative, Captain!" he said and marched toward the airlock with his head high.

Anton knew better than to comment, but he did roll his eyes. Inside his reflective helmet visor, with no video link, he could at least do that without Jaka noticing. He glanced back and forth between the airlock and the big frosted window over the main entrance, where the dino and a bird in a travel sphere looked down at the four of them, their outlines indistinct behind a curtain of condensation.

If it came to trouble, his orders were clear: stand still and let the laser do its job. The targeting bot in his backpack was far below baseline, but it could identify and shoot the targets Jaka had preselected much faster than Anton's sluggish biological nervous system. And if that made him an obvious target to draw enemy attention while Jaka got away, well . . . from her viewpoint that wasn't a problem so much as an added benefit.

He looked up at the dino, who had a combat engineer's laser in her hands. Anton was well within range, and the dino could tune it so that the diamond window wouldn't absorb any of the energy at all. She'd probably aim at his chest. He would feel the stab of heat, and then the water in the skin and muscles of his chest would explode. If she had good aim, that might stop his heart right away, and this antique suit wouldn't be able to keep him alive.

Do it, he thought. I'm an obvious threat. You can see the laser emitter. Kill me now and save yourself. Save both of us.

But the damned dino disappeared from the window, repositioning inside to cover Ulan as he cycled through the airlock.

"Adelmar, you're next."

The chimp didn't bother to reply. He just ambled forward, no rush, no evasion, nor any show of enthusiasm. Anton smiled a little at Adelmar's utter lack of concern. The chimp knew Jaka was sending him into danger ahead of herself, but he didn't mind at all. He would do the same, so he didn't complain.

"You wait out here until we're inside," she told Anton. "Make sure nobody's sneaking around in the dark. The mech said they had a scout up on the roof across the street, and it doesn't know where she went."

"Yes," he replied.

"Yes what? Do you understand what I said?"

"Yes."

Jaka gave an annoyed sniff. Inside his helmet Anton couldn't keep from smirking. That tiny, passive defiance felt so good!

Jaka went to the airlock, Tanaca following a meter behind as always. She stood patiently outside while Jaka cycled through, and did not look around as she waited.

Movement caught the corner of his eye. He turned in time to see a black spider shape hurtling directly at his face. It struck him and clung to his visor. Anton gave a sigh of relief. The black underside of the spider mech displayed the word BOO! in bright red letters.

"You're lucky my laser didn't zot you," said Anton.

Daslakh displayed a smirking cartoon face. "That won't happen. During the ride down I had a long chat with the bot brain you're carrying on your back. Strictly private, digital only. Nothing you meat brains would understand. Anyway, I'm now on its permanent supersecret Do Not Target list. I worked out a similar understanding with the missile pods."

"Clever of you."

"I'm old and cunning. The smarter the weapon, the easier it is to hack. Ulan's needle rifle is too dumb for me to mess with. Appropriately."

"Aren't you afraid I'll tell Jaka?"

"You're not exactly chatty with her."

"She could order me to tell."

The image on the mech's underside turned into a stick figure making a shrugging gesture. "I don't mind if she's a little afraid of me. I didn't sign on for a long-term relationship. As soon as we dock someplace after this job, no matter where, I'm going to find a ship or a payload leaving the Jovian system and get as far away from Jaka as I can."

"Can you see if Tanaca's gone through yet? There's a chunk of debris blocking my visor."

"She's decontaminating. Not that it will help much. In a week there'll be as much mold inside that med center as there is out here. You sweaty chunks of meat give off too much delicious skin flakes and mucus. A banquet for microorganisms. Looks like she's done." Daslakh moved up to the top of Anton's helmet.

The rim of the airlock glowed green, indicating it was safe to use. Anton went in and used half a dozen wipes to clean off his suit, stuffing the used ones into the top of the dispenser to be broken down and reassembled with all the dirt and biologicals removed. Daslakh helped him get his back and the laser backpack.

"There! Perfectly clean, except for the millions of spores hiding out in crevices those wipes can't reach, ready to start feeding on you. This lock really needs a hard UV lamp, but I guess the builders never thought the hab could ever get so messed up."

Anton passed through the inner door into a short corridor where everyone else had dumped their suits and the backpacks full of supplies. Jaka and Tanaca still wore their skinsuits, minus the bubble helmets. The entire team stood facing off against the crew of the big tug in the central atrium of the medical center.

As he peeled off his own suit Anton had a look at the opposing side. The cyborg stood in the center, hands raised for quiet, his face screen displaying solid white. The dino stood next to the borg in full armor, holding an engineer's laser. Her helmet was opaque but her posture set off all kinds of atavistic alarms in Anton's hindbrain. *Predator! Danger!*

The bird hovered above in his travel sphere. Anton could see now that he was a corvid. The sphere didn't look armed, but that didn't mean much. No sign of the mysterious fourth person.

Daslakh slipped between Anton's feet, and changed color to match the floor. It scuttled silently to one side, lurking behind a planter holding the crumbled remains of a fern. Anton had no orders, so he just stood at the back of Jaka's group, next to Tanaca.

"I'm sure you've already grabbed the best stuff, and that's fine with me," said Jaka. "Plenty for everyone here. My team just need a place to rest where we can feel secure. All these weapons are making everyone too jumpy."

"I do agree no good is served by standing tense with weapons drawn," said the bird, who seemed to be the centro of the other crew. "As you outnumber us you can display good faith by being first to lay aside your arms."

"Okay!" said Jaka cheerfully. "Ulan, put up your rifle. Safe enough?" she asked the corvid.

"Missile pods," said the dino.

"Even if I take them off I'm still linked," said Jaka. "The same goes for Adelmar. You'll just have to trust us."

"Perhaps you could leave them outside," suggested the big cyborg.

"And let them get all dirty with mold and corpse dust? No, thank you." Jaka looked around the medical center. "By the main door—that looks like a closet. Why don't we stow the pods there? We'll want them when we go out, of course."

"And the laser backpack," added the dino.

"This whole conversation has taken a very hostile turn, and that makes me sad," said Jaka, though she still looked as cheerful as ever. "I detest violence, so I agree to your paranoid demands. Anton, take the pods and the backpack and put them in the closet."

He did as he was ordered. It was a little awkward to manage four missile pods and the laser backpack at once, but he got them into the closet without dropping anything.

"Your turn," said Jaka. "Stash that laser and whatever else you're carrying."

Pera slipped off the powerpack and set her engineer's laser down on the floor.

"We came aboard to search for certain things amid the wreck, and did not plan to fight. Aside from Pera's useful laser tool we have no arms to stash," said Atmin.

"No internals in the borg, or in your little sphere? None you'll admit to, I guess. That's fine. See how much I trust you? I won't even ask to scan anyone."

Jaka and the bird arranged a division: the earlier group would get the second floor, Jaka's crew the ground floor, and the teams would continue operating independently outside.

Once the others had retired upstairs, Jaka ordered her group to bed down right in the central atrium, where they could see and be seen. Over private comm she told them, *"I want these selfish fools to understand that I'm not afraid of them at all. All of you: act like this is our place and they're the guests, understand?"*

The little mech spoke up from under the chair Jaka had occupied, and it pleased Anton to see her startle just a little. "Why are we even here? They've already grabbed any artwork that survived. We should be up at the hub ripping out processors and power systems."

"My reasons are my reasons," said Jaka. "You'll see soon enough. Now: I want everybody rested up for tomorrow, so bed down right now. Use sleep inducers. In six hours we'll all be up and outside." Via comm she added, *"I want to find that extra person they keep forgetting to mention. These junk-pickers have some scheme running, and I want to know what it is. Daslakh: you keep watch tonight. If you see anyone outside, wake me at once. And if you hear them talking, record everything."*

"I hear and obey," said the mech aloud, and positioned itself by the main entrance with a good view through the diamond doors.

Anton found a clear spot of floor near Adelmar. The chimp was an old pro, and didn't need an inducer to sleep whenever the opportunity presented itself. Anton envied him that ability: even back in Fratecea habitat before being traded to Jaka he'd been terrible at falling asleep. He would lie in his narrow bunk, utterly exhausted, but his brain would race out of control.

No risk of that anymore. His brain was now *very thoroughly* controlled. The compliance implant included a sleep inducer, so that whoever held his codes could knock him out at will. He could access the inducer himself, and yet he hesitated. With Jaka and the others asleep, he had a rare moment of something he could pretend was freedom.

He wished for a way to warn the other crew. Jaka was planning to betray them. That was just a fact, like the law of gravity. He had seen it many times before. Once her crew had enough information, she'd kill or chase off the salvagers and take their stuff.

At least it would be quick. None of the tug's crew were humans, so they'd be eliminated with brisk efficiency. Not humans. Jaka had uses for them. Anton knew that better than anyone.

He didn't like the direction his thoughts were heading, so he sent the inducer code and was rewarded with swift oblivion.

Five hours and twenty minutes later Anton awoke. The view through the windows was unchanged, but Jaka's crew were busy getting into their protective suits. She retrieved the weapons and handed them out as the crew went out through the airlock.

Outside she gave them their orders. "I want to know where the other person is. Daslakh said it looked like a woman, some kind of human. Find her. Adelmar: you search spinward on the right-hand side of this big street. Anton: you take the left side. Ulan: you go antispinward on the right, Tanaca and I will take the other side. Daslakh: see if you can track her from where you spotted her in the first place."

The mech raised one limb, turning the smart-matter foot at the end into a miniature flesh-colored human hand. "Captain Jaka? What do we do if we find some loot in this hab we're supposed to be looting?"

"Leave it. We can come back later if it's worth taking. My guess is these other guys have tagged all the good stuff already— maybe even hidden it. That's not important right now. Just find the woman. Get moving."

Anton headed out, grateful for the opportunity to be alone and under nobody's direction but his own. He had his orders, of course, but how to carry them out was up to him. So his search was diligent but not especially brisk. He turned on the twin headlamps of his antique suit and poked into all the houses, trying to flush out the mystery woman.

The dead didn't bother him. They were old, dried out and covered with mold and carbon dioxide frost. They were anonymous. Just bodies. He didn't know any of them. He hadn't killed any of them himself.

Safdaghar hab must have been a nice place, once upon a time. Anton liked the little courtyards with their dead gardens, and the tree-lined streets. The people who designed and built the hab had tried to make it attractive and comfortable. Almost any random spot would be a good place to sit down and listen to music, or chat with a friend.

They had spoiled it, of course. People always did.

Anton entered a new courtyard and froze. He thought he heard movement in one of the houses. No way to tell which one. He went to the center of the courtyard, where lawn furniture and blueberry bushes lay tangled together in a heap. He moved as slowly and quietly as he could, listening intently.

In the center he stood and listened, slowly turning to shine his headlamps into each of the houses around the courtyard. He had completed about three-quarters of a rotation when he heard a stealthy sound behind him.

Anton whirled and saw movement: the curtain in one doorway was swaying as if someone had just passed through. He ran in pursuit, taking the two steps up to the broad porch in one bound, and bursting through the curtain into a large studio cluttered with overturned furniture and scattered tools. It was a woodworking shop, so in addition to workbenches and tool cases there were chairs, a decorative cabinet, and a suit rack made of wood and aluminum.

He stood in the doorway, listening. There were no other exits, save for windows above head height on the far side, and those were closed.

"I have a laser," he said aloud. "If you try to attack me it will fire. I know you're here, so come out." If his quarry had somehow gotten away, he hoped she couldn't hear what he was saying.

A figure crawled out from beneath a workbench. Anton was slightly amazed that anyone could fit in the space. She stood—a small, slender woman, obvious even under the coverall she wore over her skinsuit. Her helmet mask was opaque black.

"My name is Anton," he said. "I was sent to find you. We've worked out an arrangement with your crew so you can come back now."

"I don't want to," she said. Her voice was lovely. "It's not safe for me to be around other humans. Please don't make me go back."

"Do you have any weapons?"

"No," she said. "Just my tools. I'm a tech, not a soldier."

She moved like a dancer, he thought as she stepped out into a clear patch of floor so he could see her better.

He reviewed Jaka's orders. She had said she wanted to know where the woman was. She had told all of them to *find* her. Well, he'd done that, hadn't he? Jaka hadn't said anything about what to do next. Eventually he'd have to report, but he felt no urge to rush.

"My name is Anton," he said. "I'm part of Jaka's crew from Scapino hab. She got a tip from someone that this wreck was being moved, and figured there might be some good loot on board. What's your name?"

"Solana," she said. "I'm with Yanai, the tug. We're just taking off some artworks before it's time to aerobrake at Jupiter periapsis. There's plenty of stuff for everyone. You can go somewhere else in the hab."

"My centro and the bird worked out a deal. We're all staying in the med building."

"I can't go back there. I have to get to the spoke. Have you told anyone where I am?"

"No," he said. "Not yet. You can talk to me a while before you go. Please? Where are you from?"

"I live on Yanai. As I said, it's difficult for me to be around other humans. I mostly stay with the ship or nonhumans."

"I'm sorry if my presence is disturbing. Why can't you be around humans? Is it some kind of implant?"

"Something like that. It's hard to explain. You're not in any danger, or anything like that. It's me. That's why I need to get away." Her voice was fearful. It had been a long time since anyone had been afraid of Anton, but he remembered the sound.

"Look," he said. "My centro—Jaka—told me to find you. If I don't report in she'll get suspicious. I've got an implant of my own, and she can access my senses. So—" He stopped speaking.

"Too late," said Jaka over the private comm. *"You're a smart guy, Anton, so I like to check on you pretty often. More than you realize. Now, it sounds like you're trying to do something clever, and I can't allow that. Bring her back to the med center now. No delays."*

"—you..." he finished when the implant released control of his muscles. "I'm sorry. Jaka just told me to bring you in. She might make me use the laser if you don't come along."

"You don't have a choice," she said. "I understand. It's all right."

✧   ✧   ✧

Jaka and her satellite Tanaca were waiting inside the med center when Anton and Solana arrived.

"Here's the mysterious fourth person," she said as soon as Anton and Solana cycled inside. "We've been dying to meet you. Let's see who you are. Come on, dear, don't be shy. We're not about to bite you."

Solana hesitated, then retracted the cowl of her suit. Without the black faceplate, Anton could see a lovely human female face with flawless golden skin. Only the eyes were covered by a bulky pair of multifunction goggles.

"See?" said Jaka, "No need to go about all masked. You could even ditch those goggles so I can admire your eyes."

Solana took a step back and shook her head. "I can't. I need them all the time. It's a neurological problem."

Jaka scrutinized Solana's face in silence, then broke into a big happy grin. "I understand. Don't worry about a thing. We were just about to have some brunch. Want some? Anton, make some food."

In the kitchen he heated up a couple of ration packs that seemed vaguely breakfast-like—rice omelets and smoked fruit. When he brought them out, Jaka was sprawled on a couch in the atrium with Tanaca on one side of her and Solana perched nervously on the other.

"Here we are. He's so useful. So, which hab are you from, dear? Someplace in Jovian space?"

"I live aboard Yanai."

"I heard that when you told Anton. But surely you weren't born on Yanai. She doesn't have a shikyu, does she? Where did you grow up?"

Solana cleared her throat nervously. "I lived on Jiaohui for a while. That's in the Main Swarm, about point eight AU."

"Jiaohui . . . isn't that a Salibi hab? You're far too pretty to be one of them."

"I, um, they took me in when I was little. My home hab was destroyed."

"How terrible! When was that?"

"About fifteen or sixteen standard years ago. I don't like to talk about it."

"I don't blame you. Not one bit." Jaka took a big bite of smoked pear and smiled at Solana as she chewed. "Now, I'm very sorry to snoop, but I did happen to overhear you telling Anton you're planning to go back up to your ship. I'm very sad to hear that. I was hoping we could be friends. You, me, and Tanaca here. All friends together."

"It's my neuro problem. The same reason I need the goggles. I'll be safer on Yanai."

"Hard luck for your teammates, isn't it? They're left to do all the work while you sit up there at the hub doing entertainments and eating fresh-printed meals."

Solana didn't respond, but she shifted uncomfortably.

Jaka patted her knee. "It's all right. Medical necessity and all that. Have you thought about getting any treatment? A higher-order mind can do amazing things with neural pruning. Not cheap, though."

"Yes," said Solana. "I'm saving up."

"Good idea! You're certainly in the right place to find valuables just lying around for the taking. It seems silly to waste the opportunity just because of some irrational fears."

Anton stood in silence, watching Jaka with a mixture of admiration and horror. Her ability to use words to box people in was worthy of a higher-level mind.

She continued, "I like you, Solana. I'd like to help you. I presume you're getting a share of what your team recover in salvage? Because I'd hate to cut into that. You need it. You shouldn't have to postpone your medical procedure for lack of gigajoules. Let me help. Stay here and earn your share. I'll guarantee your safety. Watch your back. What do you say?"

Solana's perfect forehead was furrowed. "I guess..." she said.

"Wonderful! It'll be great. You'll see. Don't worry about a thing." Jaka finished her brunch and noisily sucked her fingertips clean. "Oh, by the way: I imagine you're a little concerned about me eavesdropping on Anton. Don't worry about that. It's a safety thing. I have to monitor him. You see, he's a convicted criminal. There's no telling what he could get up to if I don't keep him in line. You can't believe a word he says, either. Don't trust him. Only me. You can trust me with your life."

She looked over at Anton and feigned surprise. "Oh, you're still here! Go start searching for heavy elements. Potassium and up. Bring back whatever you find, and be sure to tell the others."

✧   ✧   ✧

Anton spent the next several hours in blissful solitude, going house to house in search of valuable matter. The devastation made him curious. What had happened to Safdaghar? The hab structure was intact, and it wouldn't be difficult to get power and data running again. Had some tyrannical movement taken power, then destroyed everything in a relentlessly tightening spiral of political purity? Likely, he thought. The scum always rose to the top.

He rigged up a little sledge out of a bed frame and some ropes from a swing, and dragged it behind him as he wandered semi-randomly among the empty buildings collecting junk. At one point his path took him between two houses, in a little alley with blank walls on either side. He saw that somebody had written on one of them in bright crimson paint, "snap blind with broken fangs tearing with no care or will."

A slogan? he wondered. Or maybe a quote from some protest song? He recalled the early years of the Movement in Fratecea, when he and other activists had done their own share of slogan-painting. Their graffiti had been more prosaic: "Down with the Board!" and "Transfigurance Now!" He liked this surreal scrawl better.

So...had whoever painted this been afraid of being killed for it? Or had they later turned killer, executing those who simply would not agree with whatever it meant? No way to find out. They all were equally dead.

He had been out for six hours when Jaka finally recalled him. *"Thought I'd forgotten you? No chance of that. Meet at the children's playground a hundred meters north of the med center. There's some stuff we have to discuss in private."*

Anton dragged his sledge back to the clinic building and left it in plain sight of the entrance, then made his way to the playground where Jaka and the others were gathered. It was a small park, no more than fifty meters on a side, all done in bright colors that showed through the black mold. The play surface was tough and spongy, dotted with things to climb, water sprays now embedded in ice, sandboxes, long-dead musical plants, and a cellulose spinner for making dress-up costumes.

Jaka beckoned them over to one of the parent benches along the edge of the playground. *"Private channel only, encrypted. Friends, we've found our treasure. Forget all this nonsense about art or valuable scrap. That woman's the real prize."*

"*Doesn't look that special to me,*" said Adelmar.

"*Oh, but she is. That face, that figure—that's a custom genome. Somebody paid for her to be perfect.*"

"*Hardly perfect.*" Adelmar tapped the side of his head.

"*Exactly. She isn't perfect. She's got some mysterious neuro issue. Has to wear goggles. The others said she's got a phobia about people. Odd, don't you think?*"

Anton spoke up. "*She might be a failed prototype. The neuro issues could be unexpected side effects.*"

Jaka looked at him in surprise. "*You can talk? I forgot. As to your idea, I won't say it's impossible, but that doesn't happen very often nowadays. A fourth-level mind can simulate the whole process of development from zygote to adult and spot any problems before anybody hooks up a single pair of nucleotides.*"

Adelmar made an impatient tell-me-more gesture. "*Okay, so what makes a girl with a bad brain worth a fortune?*"

Jaka smiled, enjoying his frustration. "*As I said, accidental brain flaws are vanishingly rare nowadays. Maybe they still get them in low-tech habs where they fertilize by fucking and women bear children like wild animals. But that girl's too perfect to come out of some sweaty vagina. She was designed, which means her brain was designed. That neuro 'flaw' is a deliberate feature.*"

"*Oh!*" Adelmar gave a soft hoot and drummed on the spongy ground with both palms. "*You think Kumu, maybe?*"

"*She's old enough. And that explains the goggles, and why she's flying with that crew. None of them look human.*"

"*So what?*" asked Daslakh. "*We're thieves and scavengers, not slavers.*"

"*I know some people,*" said Jaka. "*Back at Scapino. People who know people.*"

Anton had no idea what Jaka was talking about. He sent a query to the sub-baseline brain aboard the shuttle, asking for data on Kumu relevant to the past thirty years. The little internal library had fifty results—ships, companies, towns, some people with that name, a political movement which once ruled a trillion people. But the obvious answer was a hab.

Kumu was a criminal hab in the Kuiper Belt, about 43 AU out. For a century it was notorious for the creation of Qarinas, humans optimized as sexual playthings. Other worlds and empires had denounced the practice and Kuma's ruling junta, but did nothing to stop it. Finally in 9934 a shipload of Salibi fanatics had raided the place, taking off several hundred Qarinas, killing most of the hab's rulers, and wrecking all the molecular-scale printers and gene banks they could find.

Jaka might be right: the woman called Solana might well be one of those liberated Qarinas. The thought made Anton queasy. With Kumu out of business and other Qarina creators running dark for fear of Salibi attacks, the price for a human sexual slave was probably immense. And Jaka had contacts back at Scapino who could find people willing to pay that price.

His former comrades in Fratecea were missing a golden opportunity, Anton thought—but then he wondered if they *were* missing it. There had been a handful of politicas who'd been taken out of the dormitories and never seen again, all of them notably attractive. Anton had assumed they'd been taken by members of the inner Party, but suddenly he wasn't sure. Had they been exported in order to improve Fratecea's balance of payments?

"How to find out?" Adelmar asked Jaka.

"I just have to get her to take off those goggles she's so desper-ate to keep on."

"The dino won't like it."

"Don't worry. I'll arrange things so that she does it entirely of her own free will." When Anton happened to look at Jaka he saw her staring back at him with a big smile on her face.

They spent a couple of days working, making a big show of how serious they were about collecting scrap to remove. Twice a day they made a big pile of stuff in the street and then Daslakh would crawl over the pile identifying the composition of each item. It picked up a shiny chain necklace. "Looks like silver— nope, just platinum. Forget it," it said, and tossed it onto the junk heap. It selected a tool. "Now, this is the real stuff! Fifteen percent tungsten! Definitely a keeper!" The tool went into the much smaller pile of salvage to haul back to the hub.

They saved beryllium (what little they could find), tantalum, thallium, gold, silver, rare-earth elements, and mercury. More than once Daslakh reminded everyone, "You know, I bet most of the useful industrial elements are stored up at the hub. Scav-enging people's personal electronics and hand tools seems like a big waste of time."

To which Jaka replied, more than once, via the private channel, *"Be quiet and keep working. I want those idiots to think we're serious about salvaging metals."*

Since Anton couldn't know when Jaka might be looking through his eyes, or listening with his ears, he did his best to avoid the other team. In person he might be tempted to try warning them.

He wound up doing most of the scrap-picking himself. Tanaca kept close to Jaka, who recovered maybe half a dozen items per day. Adelmar was a little more diligent, at least when anyone could see him. He improvised a sack from some curtains and brought it back full of junk.

The bird had warned them about the possibility of booby traps. Jaka was skeptical, but agreed to keep her team close to the medical building, where the others had already searched pretty thoroughly. Privately she told her crew, *"I think they're just trying to scare us off."*

Ulan was the only one to risk going out into the unexplored sections. He was fascinated by Solana and kept trying to cross paths with her "accidentally" until Jaka finally gave him a direct order: "Stay away from her until I tell you otherwise. We don't want to spook them."

"I'm just…" he began, obviously with no idea what he was going to say next.

"I said stay away. I don't want you sneaking looks at her tonight, I don't want you trying to watch her cleaning up, and I don't want you following her tomorrow. *Avoid* her. Got it?"

"This is shit."

"Put up with it for a day. You're a big boy. You can do that."

Anton spent another relatively pleasant day looking for metals worth keeping. With Daslakh's tutelage he was getting better at spotting them. He did wish that the heavier elements could have a wider range of colors and properties. Too many were shiny gray and dense. Whoever had created this simulation had gotten lazy past mercury, concealing the issue by making most of the heavier elements short-lived so nobody would notice.

He paused for lunch at a stadium made of trees, crowded with dead people. Anton found an unbroken chair among the debris, and set it next to a mosaic-topped table bolted to the ground in the plaza outside the stadium. Nobody but corpses watched him eat. His primitive suit didn't have a membrane to push food through, so he had to make do with sipping fish broth through a straw.

Safdaghar was very quiet. Back in Fratecea there had always been the sound of vehicles, loudspeakers making announcements, people talking, animals, and machines. Scapino had been much the same—fewer animals, more loud music. The shuttle had been noisy with gurgling sanitary systems, buzzing life-support fans, buzzing cooling pumps, and the voices of Jaka and her crew. But inside Safdaghar there was nothing to make noise. No machines, nothing alive. Nothing but his own breathing and the hum of his air filter.

And something else. He kept himself still, resisting the urge to see what was making the sound. It was an irregular pattering, like hard-gloved fingertips tapping out some chaotic improvised music. The sound was moving, getting gradually louder and closer. Air currents blowing debris? Condensation dripping from the ceiling high above? Some thermal effect?

Finally Anton couldn't keep himself from turning around, shining the twin headlamps of his helmet around the plaza. The noise vanished as soon as he moved. He looked around, panning methodically across the whole area. Corpses, dead leaves, some unidentifiable mounds of debris, a few tables like his own standing undamaged and unused.

"Is anybody there?" he called aloud. "Anybody?"

"Yes," said Daslakh via comm. "I want to talk to you. Sit tight." A moment later Anton heard the little mech's feet clicking rhythmically on the pavement—very different from the irregular pattering he had heard before. Daslakh jumped onto the table, its shell glowing wine-red, with the silver Gemini design of Fratecea's emblem shining brightly on its back. "Greetings, Resident! Are you working hard for the greater good of the community?" it said aloud.

"What do you want?"

"I want to talk."

"I might not be the only one listening."

"Hey, Jaka! You're a filthy slaver and you cheat at tic-tac-toe. Wave Anton's hand if you can hear me."

"Just reminding you."

"I can hear your implant's broadcast frequencies. It's not talking to anybody right now so maybe we should quit wasting time. I'm kind of worried about her little scheme to sell the Qarina."

"Fighting exploitation is what got me here," said Anton. "But I didn't think you cared."

"Bios being awful to each other is a pretty constant feature of the solar system. But this particular awfulness is a bigger problem than most. First of all, we could all wind up on some bounty list if anyone finds out. I don't like drawing attention."

"You should have thought of that before you signed on with Jaka."

"Getting off Scapino was very important to me right then. I didn't have much choice. Anyway. The second problem is that Jaka also has to know that slave-dealing is a serious offense almost everywhere. We're witnesses. It's a lot easier to enjoy ill-gotten gains if nobody knows how you got them."

"If she wants me dead there's nothing I can do about it," said Anton. "She can kill me with a thought."

"And anyway, just because trillions of people are being awful every second doesn't mean we have to help."

"Are you being...*moral*?" asked Anton, only partly in sarcasm.

"Never mind. It's—" Daslakh's tone suddenly shifted. "But then I found out that the loan shark had hired the mercenaries to do debt collection, so that instead of protecting me, *they'd* be hunting me, too. Needless to say, I had to find a ship out of Scapino right away. Fortunately, our beloved leader Jaka happened to be looking for a technician, because apparently none of you sausage-fingered biologicals knows which end of a hammer to use for welding optical fibers. One short-term contract later I was on the shuttle with the rest of you getting myself out of there, body and mind."

"What?"

"Of course if I had known I would wind up inside a wrecked hab full of mold and emotional drama I might have taken my chances with the loan shark after all. Anyway, from here I figure I'll make my way outsystem. Maybe the Uranus Trojans. And... she's gone."

"Jaka was listening?"

"Couldn't you tell? Your implant's signal traffic went up by two orders of magnitude. Back to quiet mode now. Point is, the Qarina plan is dangerous. I'm going to try to convince Adelmar. He's a realist. Can you talk to Ulan?"

"Anyone can talk to him. He never listens."

"True—doubly so right now. It's shocking to see what happens to his blood flow when that Solana person is around. You're bad enough, but with him I'm kind of surprised there's enough oxygen reaching his brain to keep him conscious. I guess his brain doesn't really need that much to begin with."

Anton got up and panned his helmet lights around the plaza again. "Did you sense anything moving around here before you pinged me?"

"No. Can't say I was looking for anything, either. Why?"

"Never mind. I guess I'd better get back to work."

Just then he heard Jaka's voice inside his helmet, on the group channel. *"All of you, come back to the clinic. I've got an announcement to make and I want you all here."*

"What do you suppose that's all about?" asked Daslakh.

"I'm afraid to find out. Let's go."

When Anton and Daslakh got back to the medical building, everyone was gathered in the atrium—both Jaka's team and the group from the tug. Jaka gestured impatiently when Anton cycled in. "Get out of that suit and come here."

He shucked it off and skipped the wipe-down stage. She pointed to a spot on the floor right next to her, so he stood there.

"Sorry for the delay, but I couldn't start without Anton. He's the reason I called you all together." Jaka got up and began to circle him, gradually spiraling out beyond arm's reach.

"You see," she said, "Anton's supposed to do what I tell him. That's part of his criminal service mandate. But the other day I gave him an order and he tried to get clever and disobey me. It was a simple order: find your missing teammate. After all, a wrecked hab is no place for one person to be wandering alone, and I was worried about her. But silly, *silly* Anton thought he could play games with the exact wording of what I told him, even though he knew what I meant. He found her, but decided not to say anything. If I hadn't checked up on him, poor Solana might still be out there."

"I—" he began, and then his mouth and face froze.

"No, don't try to confuse everyone with your excuses." She turned to her audience. "He's very clever about that kind of thing. He used to make propaganda for a vicious dictatorship. Don't believe a word he says."

Jaka circled around behind Anton, so she could see everyone

at once. "So now he has to be punished. I want everyone to watch, so you can see that you're in no danger from this convicted political extremist. His compliance implant is under my control."

She turned to face Anton and sent the command code via comm. He felt the compliance implant activate, and suddenly Anton was just a spectator, unable to do anything but watch as his brain and body obeyed the implant instead of Anton.

He could see the others ranged about the room—Ulan watching the scene eagerly, Adelmar paying more attention to the spectators, Tanaca oblivious as always to everything except Jaka. Daslakh had disappeared. The members of the other crew watched over the edge of the upstairs gallery that ran around the atrium. The cyborg's face screen was blank, the dino cocked her head and lashed her tail in puzzlement, the bird was motionless and attentive, and Solana's mouth was open in horror.

"Anton, I want you to bite off the top joint of the little finger of your left hand," said Jaka. This was all for show. She could move his muscles at will.

"No!" Solana called out as Anton raised his hand to his mouth.

"Stop, Anton," said Jaka. She turned to look up at Solana. "You don't want me to punish him?"

"Please don't," said Solana. "He didn't do anything wrong. I asked him not to tell anyone, that's all."

"You're telling me you're the one to blame for his disobedience?"

"I guess so." Solana sounded a little puzzled.

Jaka paused for a second, as if coming to some important decision. "I'll tell you what: I won't punish Anton for disobeying me if you take off those goggles."

Atmin gave a loud caw of alarm. "Solana, do not let yourself forget what will befall if you should do as this intruder asks."

"Well?" asked Jaka. "I'm not going to wait. Take them off now."

"I need them," said Solana.

"Anton, do as I told you."

Anton's finger was between his teeth. He could feel his jaw muscles tense, and the pain from his joint, and the crunching sensation as teeth met cartilage.

"Stop!" Solana called, and pulled off the goggles. Underneath her eyes were closed.

"Anton, stop."

He stopped. He didn't taste any blood in his mouth, which

was good. His finger joint felt crushed. Anton wanted to wiggle it, to see how bad it was, but of course Jaka hadn't given control of his body back to him, so he couldn't.

When Jaka spoke again her voice was soft, almost affectionate. "You did a very brave thing, Solana. Look at me."

"I can't. Please."

Jaka's reply was a scream of pain, or at least what sounded like one. Solana's eyelids flickered open just for a moment, and Jaka repeated "Look at me!" There was no softness in her voice anymore. Solana's eyes met Jaka's and froze there. She had lovely eyes, Anton thought, huge and dark.

"Solana, put—" Atmin began, but Jaka cut him off.

"Give me the goggles. Understand? You don't need them. Isn't it much nicer without them?"

The cyborg's screen showed a man's face, but Jaka noticed it first. "Don't look at the cyborg. Ignore him. Only look at me. Toss those goggles over."

"No," said Pera. From one of the pockets of her suit she produced a pistol—a dino-scaled pistol with a muzzle as wide as Anton's thumb. "Stop it."

"She wants to do what I say. Don't you, dear?"

Solana nodded. Her face had relaxed, and was now almost masklike in serenity. She looked at the goggles in her hand, then at Jaka, and tossed them down.

"See? Entirely voluntary. Not like poor Anton at all. She *wants* to do what I ask."

"I said no." Pera pointed the pistol at Jaka. "Give them back."

"You shoot, you die," said Adelmar, and tapped one of the missile pods on his suit with a finger.

"*This is ridiculous,*" said Yanai over everybody's comm at once. "*You, Jaka, there will be no fighting. Do what Pera says. If you attempt any violence against my crew I will destroy your shuttle and maroon you here.*"

"*Look at my shuttle and tell me what you see,*" Jaka replied.

"*The external cargo—oh,*" said Yanai.

"Freelance rescue and salvage is a dangerous job," said Jaka aloud to the room. "You never know what kind of people you'll run into. My shuttle doesn't have any weapon mounts, but a few years ago I got hold of a surplus plasma lance warhead. That's mounted in the external cargo pod, and right now it's pointing at your ship. I've set a deadman switch so that if anything happens to me it will fire. I'd also recommend against trying to tamper with it."

"That's just random noise," said Pera. "I don't believe you."

"Test it, then. Fire that gun. You can probably kill me, then Adelmar will kill you, and your ship will be crippled. A Koenig Mark LXIX series 4 medium plasma lance warhead at point-blank range will cut your ship's spine in half even if it doesn't vaporize the main processor. I'm not sure what will happen after that. The shuttle might survive, and some of my team may get out alive, but your crew will spend half a century trapped in here on their way out to the Kuiper Belt. You'll probably starve before you go crazy."

"Yanai, we work for you. What orders do you give your crew?" asked Atmin.

"I've identified the device on the shuttle. She's telling the truth. Pera, no shooting. Not now, at least. The rest of you, no fighting. Jaka, my crew are free agents. They listen to me only because I'm paying them. There are limits to what they will tolerate. And I've got a backup stored at Osorizan hab. Kill me and I just lose a few years of memory. So there are limits to what I will tolerate, even with your weapon aimed at my hull."

"Naturally, naturally. Same for my people. We just want fairness."

"Be specific. What do you want?"

"We want a fifty-fifty split of everything both teams find. Including whatever goodies your crew have already stashed somewhere. If you think about it, you guys actually come out ahead, since there's six of us searching for stuff and only four of you. I think an even split is more than fair."

"What about Solana?" asked Pera.

"I want her as insurance. You and the cyborg might decide to try ambushing my people one by one. Without those goggles she's the only one of you I can really trust. I'll give them back when it's time for us to leave."

The bird, the cyborg, and the dino went silent—presumably conferring by secure comm. Anton could see that neither the bird nor the dino were happy. Pera lashed her tail and scratched the floor with the big sickle claws on her feet. The bird fluttered about restlessly. The cyborg stood absolutely motionless. After several minutes the bird perched on the gallery railing near the top of the stairs.

"Reluctantly we do agree. Each team shall have an equal share of all the items found aboard. Before we leave this hab you will return Solana's gear. Do you agree to all I say?"

"Sure! Like I said, all we want is a fair shake. This won't cost you anything. Now that we're all working together on the same team, I guess we shouldn't waste any time. Let's all get some rest so we can get started first thing in the morning!"

Anton's finger joint throbbed all night, but he ignored it. He had slept through worse pain back in Fratecea, after his arrest. Once he had complained to a guard about conditions in the political prisoner dormitory. Fratecea had printers—the regime could provide mattresses to sleep on and something better than printed ration sticks to eat. It was perfectly logical to treat them well. The guard had looked at Anton with an expression of weariness and disappointment, then wordlessly struck him across the face with his baton. The blow had knocked Anton down, dislodged his left upper canine tooth, and fractured his cheekbone. The bone took weeks to heal, and still ached at times. He did not complain again.

CHAPTER EIGHT

The teams divided up in the morning. Jaka and the bird conferred and assigned search territories. They also established a shared network so that the teams could see each other's virtual tags and stay in touch.

"My team has run into some booby traps about the hab," the bird said. "It would be safer if we work in pairs."

"Great idea!" said Jaka. "We can mix and match from both teams, get to know each other better. Build trust and teamwork."

Anton wound up paired with the bird, Atmin. On Jaka's instructions, he left the laser backpack behind that day. "If you get into trouble, see what the bird can do. And don't disappoint me again."

They suited up and left the medical center. The bird's travel sphere hovered about four meters up, behind Anton and to the right as they headed up the main street of the rim toward their search area.

"Do you know what happened here?" Anton asked, gesturing at a pair of blackened mummies.

"My friends and I have theorized that some vile group of evil folk did somehow manage to get into Safdaghar, and then they slew all here within. The reason for such butchery remains unknown."

"You mentioned traps."

"I did. On three occasions that I know some members of my team have triggered snares. One of them was crudely made, but only one. The other was a cunning mine which might have maimed or killed had not Solana used her tools and skill to disengage the trap. Be wary where you place your feet."

The two of them walked in silence for a hundred meters or so. Then Anton asked, "What kind of salvage are we looking for?"

"Old Safdaghar did not have vaults of heavy elements, nor cutting-edge technology. It was a simple hab, autonomous in energy and mass. Its people got their food as much from gardens as from print. What wealth they had was in their brains and hands—for Safdaghar exported art, and crafts, and perfect meals, and suchlike goods that other living things would buy. Of course, they mostly sold the printer scans of what they made, so on a given day across the Billion Worlds a million people dine on meals created here, or decorate a room with art from Safdaghar. A tiny group of mighty wealth might even own originals from here, identical in every way to prints, except in provenance and price."

"I know a fair bit about art," said Anton. "Main Swarm contemporary stuff, anyway."

"A mech or even bot could say the same. That does no good, for art that's known is art that someone owns. No, we are here to find the unknown gems—items never scanned which we can claim. Your knowledge is irrelevant, but have you taste?"

Before his fall from favor Anton had spent two standard years evaluating works in terms of how well they fit Fratecea's ruling ideology, not caring whether they were good. "I might have a remnant."

"Then let me be the brain, and you the hands. From all that I have seen of Jaka's crew, the role is one you can put on with ease."

They reached the day's search area, a lower-density sector. The blocks were larger, and each had just a single house surrounded by vegetable gardens and fishponds. The watering systems had kept working for a while after the temperature in the hab dropped below freezing, and all the plants were encased in glossy ice. Mold or pests had consumed most of them, but here and there a green sprig or even a whole fruit showed bright color.

The sector had few trees, so it was easy for both of them to notice one house which was very different from the others. The structure itself was unremarkable, a two-story building with the usual broad galleries and a flat roof. But the gardens around it had been hacked down and the house itself was heavily damaged. Windows were shattered, walls were pocked with bullet holes, and the roof had a crude parapet of bricks and sandbags around the edge.

"I think we should begin our search with that one," said Atmin, and his travel sphere buzzed over toward the damaged house.

Anton followed on foot. The gardens around it had been cut down deliberately, and in a great hurry, bushes and plants hacked off and left where they lay. The stakes supporting tomato and squash plants had been pulled up and tossed down. As near as Anton could tell, someone—several someones, most likely—had cut down everything standing more than about half a meter above the ground. It didn't fit anything Anton knew about growing vegetables.

Then he looked at the house and understood. They had cleared the ground to defend it. No enemy could use the gardens for concealment. Guards on the roof would have an unobstructed shot at anyone or anything approaching the house.

Not that it had helped. As he stepped up onto the wide porch surrounding the house he could see the bullet holes in the walls. Most were single shots, with a few perfect little equilateral triangles of holes.

Atmin entered through a shattered window. Anton slid the door open and went into the main room of the house. It extended all the way through, with smaller rooms opening onto it on the sides. He counted a dozen bodies in the room, all wearing combat suits marked with the sword-and-wheel emblem of Safdaghar's militia.

Most had been shot in the face, but he could see a few who had suffered limb injuries. Their suits' first-aid systems had inflated tourniquets to keep them from bleeding to death, and squirted medical foam all over the wounds. The injured men had kept fighting until hits to the head or heart had finished them.

The main room was empty of furniture. It had all been shoved into side rooms, blocking the windows. Most of it looked intact, except for one room where a barrage of hypervelocity needles had turned everything into a pile of fragments.

Atmin's travel sphere touched down in the center of the main room, where two uniformed corpses lay atop the body of a third. "Lend a hand to move the two atop this man," said Atmin.

Anton dragged the two militia soldiers away, revealing the dried mummy of a man in a Martian-style tunic and tights, lying on his back. He had a small hole in the left side of his head, and a much bigger hole on the right.

Atmin extended two flexible arms from his travel sphere and began searching the body.

"What are you looking for?" asked Anton.

"I search for sheets of paper bearing poems written down in strokes of ink." Atmin opened the tunic and rummaged in an inside pocket. He pulled a dried-out brush and a palette carved from Martian redwood. "No pages here."

"Who is he?" asked Anton.

"I think it is a man who used the name of Pasquin Tiu in life. A Martian known for loving Mars, and mocking Deimos to the point he had to flee to stay alive."

"Looks like he didn't flee far enough."

"Too true. Now help me search the house. Leave nothing unexamined in this place. A single scrap of writing may be worth—" The bird paused and cocked an eye at Anton. "I cannot tell its value 'til I see. To work!"

The two of them searched every room, opened every drawer and case, and even looked for loose panels in walls, ceilings, and floors where something might have been hidden. Anton found a ream of handmade rice paper, blank except for some spots of mildew. Atmin uncovered a steel box inlaid with thin slices of Martian basalt forming the arrowheaded phi sigil of Phobos—their lost moon was a hugely significant cultural icon for Martians. The box held a set of self-inking brushes ranging from micron-thin to one as wide as Anton's hand. But nowhere did they find so much as a lone character written down.

After three hours in the fortified house the bird gave up. "If Pasquin wrote a single verse in Safdaghar I do not see it here."

"Maybe he just wrote normal text, instead of fooling with paper and ink."

"He never did before—but then, on Mars he wrote in secret, pasting sheets to doors or putting paint on walls while cameras were blind. In Safdaghar he may have thought it safe to save his thoughts as insecure electrons in a net."

Anton sipped water from his helmet's funny-tasting reservoir. The dust they'd raised inside the house made his throat feel dry despite his suit.

"If I may ask, why are you here?" said Atmin. "You seem to

be an educated man, unlike the ruder members of your team. How did you come to work with them?"

"No choice," said Anton, tapping his faceplate over his forehead. "I've got a compliance implant. Jaka's got the codes. When it's active I'm a puppet."

"A dreadful situation, to be sure. Who put that implant in your head—and can it be removed?"

Anton straightened a little. "I'm a criminal. Guilty of memetic sabotage against Fratecea habitat."

"What sabotage did you perform?"

"I told a joke." He felt his face getting hot inside his helmet. "I got kicked out of the Party, lost my citizen rights, and wound up in the work dormitories with other enemies of the hab. Because I'm a *fool* I thought it was all just a mistake. If the Party leadership only understood what I was saying they'd realize that and let me out. So I didn't shut up. I filed protests, I complained to the guards, I smuggled out a description of what it was like in the dorms, and I tried to organize protests among the other politicas. I got beat up, I got stuck in solitary, I got screamed at and humiliated in reeducation sessions, but I was stubborn and didn't give up. I believed in the Transfigurance Movement and wanted to help. Finally I got results: they stuck an implant in my head and sold me out of the hab."

"This implant which enslaves you is a thing which someone might remove, unlike Solana's traitor brain. Cannot you take it from your head?"

"Pulling it out would turn my brain to slurry. I may do that someday, when I can't stand it any longer."

"Then I suggest you leave with us. Whatever signal Jaka sends cannot reach out across the gulf of space. As soon as you are out of range—"

"If I get too far from Jaka—and I don't know how far that is—the implant will stimulate my pain center until I die. That's also why I can't harm her."

"This implant—does it speak to her?"

"When she activates it she can see and hear with my eyes and ears. When it's off I don't think she can eavesdrop." Anton thought for a moment, wondering. At times Jaka did have an uncanny way of knowing things. Was she spying on him without his knowledge? Daslakh had mentioned something like that. Or was she just good at figuring people out? "I'm not sure," he added.

"I beg your pardon if the things I said may cause you future pain. I shall restrict my speech henceforth." The bird rotated his travel sphere once more, looking around the room. "I sought to find a treasure here, but that was not to be, it seems. My hope of finding Pasquin's verse to sell on Mars is lost. There still remains the loot of Safdaghar's dead crafters and the systems of the hab itself. Come on."

Atmin led the way out of the house with Anton following, and they crossed the killing zone around it, heading away from the main road.

Just then a commotion broke out on the comm system. *"I'm hit, I'm hit!"* cried Ulan.

"What's happening?" Jaka and Atmin demanded at the same instant.

"A spread of darts punched through his armor," said Pera, who had accompanied Ulan on that day's sweep. *"Torso. I'll get him back to camp."*

Without any discussion, Atmin and Anton abandoned the day's search and hurried back to the medical clinic. The low humming sound of the lift fans on the bird's travel sphere rose to a sustained soprano's high note as Atmin sped off. Anton had to jog behind in his clumsy antique suit, so that he was sweaty and winded when he finally got to the clinic.

He got there just as Pera helped Ulan into the emergency airlock. Anton could see a cluster of darts sticking out of Ulan's torso, and his own stomach tensed in sympathy.

When he got inside everyone was gathered in the downstairs atrium. Ulan lay on the floor in the center of the room, moaning and writhing. Solana and Daslakh were cutting off his armor while Pera slapped stabilizer drug patches on his neck. Jaka and Atmin watched tensely and Tanaca sat huddled against the wall. Only Adelmar and the cyborg Utsuro were missing.

Seven darts had pierced Ulan's armored suit, marking the corners and center of a perfect hexagon centered roughly on his breastbone. "I can feel them, I can feel them," said Ulan. "Aah! It hurts! I'm all torn up." His face was gray and slick with sweat, and he was breathing shallowly and very fast. Anton disliked Ulan, with good reason, but for a moment he felt a pang of pity to see the man so helpless and afraid.

Working as quickly as they dared, Daslakh and Solana cut a

circle out of the suit's armored breastplate around the darts. As soon as the cut was complete the woman lifted away the entire front of Ulan's suit, leaving the darts pinning a disk of layered armor and fabric to his body. His exposed skin looked grayish and he was sweating.

Daslakh slid a couple of its limbs between the surface of the disk and Ulan's skin to look around. "Not much bleeding," it said.

"Which one looks the worst?" asked Solana. "We should get that one first."

"I've got a better idea," said Daslakh. In a single swift motion it yanked the disk and all seven darts off of Ulan.

Ulan screamed. Everyone froze.

Then Pera very deliberately smacked the side of his head. "Shut up, you fool."

On Ulan's bare, damp torso Anton could make out seven small cuts, oozing a little blood. The deepest might have been half a centimeter. The tips of the darts barely protruded from the inside of the armor.

"Pera, do not hit the man but check his wounds for any trace of chemicals, or nanotech, or deadly bioforms," said Atmin.

"Scanner says he's clean. Nothing on the darts."

Ulan raised his head, trying to see over his own bulky chest without bending his body. "How bad is it? Am I gonna die?"

Jaka gave a bark of laughter. "You big baby. Hold still and let Solana fix you up."

"Don't worry," said Solana, and ran a wipe over the cuts before gluing them shut.

"Pera, please, inform us all of what befell poor Ulan and yourself. Leave nothing out, no matter if it seems too small to tell," said Atmin.

"You told us to search around the genetics lab, two klicks spinward. I already did a quick sweep of the lab, but I didn't get into any of the apartments or the test gardens. There's a circular plaza in front of the lab campus, with some three- and four-story buildings around it. Ulan and I checked those first. Not much—one apartment had an ornamental vine that isn't in Yanai's library, so I took samples." She dug in a pocket on her suit and held up some leaves that refracted the light from the ceiling in abstract patterns.

"Nice," said Jaka. "Be sure to put it with the rest of our stuff."

"Continue, if you please, and tell us where and how poor Ulan was struck down."

"After the apartments we crossed the plaza to the lab campus. Right at the entrance there's an arch, a double helix made of glass, about ten meters high. Ulan went ahead of me—"

"Why?" asked Jaka, sounding suspicious. "Did you send him in first?"

The dino lashed her tail, thumping against a couch. "No, the idiot went charging in even though I told him to be careful. As soon as he passed through the arch the dart launcher fired. After that I was too busy getting patches on him and lugging his worthless sweaty ass back here to look around much."

"Hang on," said Daslakh, the little spider mech, who moved to stand directly in front of Pera. Its outer shell was now high-visibility orange. "This trap was at the entrance to the lab campus, right?"

"Yes. I don't know if it was a tripwire or a switch under the pavement. I'll go back and check—you can help."

"I'll hang back and record everything when you get killed. But I thought you said you'd already visited the genetics lab. Did you go in the same way?"

Pera cocked her head to one side, for a moment looking oddly like Atmin. "Yes..." she said slowly. "Pretty sure I did."

"No darts in your face?"

"No. Probably not a tripwire, then."

"My question is, was it there before?"

"Are you attempting to accuse good Pera here of setting up a trap herself, in order to waylay Ulan? It makes no sense—she saved his life," said Atmin. "Or would have done, had he been truly hurt."

"No, no," said the mech. "That's ridiculous. I think I would have noticed a half-ton dino sneaking out while the rest of you were snoring. No, I'm wondering if there's something else in the hab."

"We thought of that when we arrived," Atmin replied. "But nothing biological could stand the cold and dark for sixteen years—and if a mech remained, why would it hide at all?"

"I can think of about half a million reasons, and that's without using my full processing power. Maybe it thinks we're all a gang of pirates, come to loot the place? I mean, we *are*, after all."

"Even if a mech believes that we are villains come to rob and kill, the hab is now on course for Jupiter to fling it out into the Kuiper dark. What mech would rather spend four decades here alone, when it might strike a deal with us to leave?"

"A mech with a functioning brain, who doesn't trust a bunch of greedy biologicals? Or maybe one who's loyal to this hab and doesn't like to see you looting it? Or—I don't know—maybe one who thinks it would be easier to just kill you and take your ship."

"That would be unwise," said Yanai, who had been listening over the comm net.

"Might not be able to hijack you, but a competent machine could steal our shuttle. Point is, you can't rule it out."

"If there is something else in the hab..." Jaka began, then switched to comm. *"Adelmar, check in. Where are you and the cyborg?"*

"Main avenue, half a klick west. North side, third floor. How's Ulan?"

"He's recovering from his ordeal. Situation?"

"He found some bio traces."

"The highest concentration of my DNA yet!" Utsuro cut in. *"A very good match, better than any other traces I have found."*

"I think the two of you should come with haste back here to camp. The DNA can wait another day," said Atmin.

They bandaged Ulan's chest—more to salve his feelings than for any medical reason. Once Adelmar and Utsuro arrived, Pera briefed the assembled company on how to look for booby traps, how to avoid them, and what to do if they discovered one.

"Simplest and best advice: get away," she concluded. "So far everything we've found has been short-range or contact. One explosive, the rest were mechanical. That dart launcher sounded like compressed gas. Distance is the best protection for all of those. Hard cover as soon as you can reach it—put a building or a wall between you and the device. Soon as you're safe call it in. I'll try to deactivate the device, or mark it. Yanai, a couple of extra bots would be a big help."

"I am already printing some. I'll send them down as soon as they're cool."

"A couple dozen paint grenades would be nice, too, if you can print them. I can make shields out of materials down here. We should all carry them."

"Maybe you big squishy people need them, but I'm not lugging a sheet of graphene around. It would only slow me down," said Daslakh.

"My travel sphere is tough as any shield might be," added Atmin, "and belike Utsuro's hide is tougher still. But, yes, I see the need."

"Excellent!" said Jaka. She smiled at Pera. "You get to work making them. Daslakh, you help her. Anton, get dinner ready for everyone. I'll assign teams for tomorrow."

Anton went to do his job. The two groups shared the little kitchenette on the ground floor, though their food supplies were rigorously separate. Certainly Anton had no desire to sample either the dinosaur's gory food or the corvid's carrion-scented rations.

As he was working Jaka stuck her head in. "Solana will be joining the rest of us for dinner. Make some extra for her."

He was improvising a soup from the ration packs Jaka had bought to fill the shuttle's supply bins, so it wasn't hard to stretch it. He used protein chips for soup stock, carb sticks to thicken the broth, and vegetable cubes for flavor. A little salt, one scrap of pork jerky finely minced, and a generous dash of fish sauce and you had a meal fit for . . . well, a gang of shady salvagers and occasional hijackers who were used to getting by on far worse. A little more salt and half a liter of water did the trick.

"Can you use some extra ingredients?" said Solana as she entered the kitchenette. She rummaged in her group's half of the refrigerator and took out a package of a dozen peanut dumplings. "Will these go with what you're making?"

"Yes," he said. "I'll put them in right at the end. Don't want them to get overdone."

She stood watching as he stirred the pot. "I've never seen anyone cook before. Don't you have a printer?"

"Jaka got the shuttle from a salvager who was getting ready to scrap it. No food printer, no oxygen recycler, and no power plant. She could only afford two of the three. So instead we have a hundred kilos of Trojan Empire emergency rations, only thirty years older than I am."

"Where did you learn to cook? Did you create templates?"

"No," he said. "Back in my home hab everyone learned how. We grew wine, too. And I used to cook for the other people in the dormitory."

He didn't explain that he'd learned in order to stretch the meager food provided. Pooling rations and making soups or stews let everyone feel as though they'd had a real meal. What he cooked back then had been even more watery and a lot more bland than what he was making now, of course. Printer templates were allocated on the basis of service to the Transfigurance Movement, and the politicas, by definition, were of no value at all.

Jaka bustled in again. "There you are! Solana, dear, I've got a question for you. Be honest: do you trust the dinosaur?"

"Pera? Yes, absolutely. She can be kind of gruff but she keeps her word."

"Mm. Because it occurs to me that Atmin and Yanai might be trying to scare my team away with these stories of traps and something lurking in the darkness. Tell me, do you know anything about that?"

"No. That's just not like either of them. Besides, Atmin and Utsuro both ran into traps before you even got here."

"Did you actually see them?"

"I was right there when Utsuro stepped on a mine! I kept it from going off so that he could get away. I was there!"

Jaka put up her hands, palms out, and laughed. "Now, now. Don't get excited. It's just so hard to trust anyone nowadays." She glanced over Solana's shoulder at Anton, saw that he was watching, and smiled. "See you at dinner."

The six of them—Jaka, Tanaca, Anton, Ulan, Adelmar, and Solana—squeezed into the little dining area to share the soup and dumplings. Ulan sat a little apart from the others and said nothing. After some prodding from Jaka, Adelmar described what the cyborg had discovered.

"Checking an apartment. Second floor, good view of the main road. No bodies, nothing worth taking. Utsuro scans the place, gets excited. Says it's full of his DNA. Checks bathroom and gets quiet. I ask, he says frozen shit in toilet full of his DNA. His shit, he says."

"That's bizarre," said Jaka. "Solana, tell me why is the cyborg doing these DNA scans at all?"

"He came from here," said Solana. "Utsuro was found in space by some mechs, who rebuilt him. He can't remember anything before that. His orbital path intersected this hab at the time of the disaster. That's why he joined Yanai's crew for this job, to see if he could learn who he really is."

"And now he's found proof. Interesting. Whose apartment was it?" asked Jaka. "Any way to find out?"

"We toss the place good," said Adelmar. "Looks like a herm couple live there. Pics, some clothes, personal stuff. Pics don't look like him, none of his DNA on the clothes. Not his place, he figures."

"Wait," said Daslakh, who had been sitting quietly on the ceiling with its shell matching the beige panels. "How could his feces last for sixteen years?"

"Frozen," said Adelmar. "Toilet full of ice and frozen shit on top."

"What color was it?"

"Do we have to talk about this while I'm trying to eat?" asked Jaka. "By the way, Anton, good job with the soup. And thank *you*, Solana, for the dumplings."

"Yes, as a matter of fact we do have to talk about it," snapped Daslakh. "Adelmar, was it brown?" Daslakh's shell turned a convincing shit color. "Or was it black with mold like every other gram of organic matter inside this hab?" As it spoke a web of black spots and lines covered it until only a few visible flecks of brown remained.

"Brown," said Adelmar.

"Fresh," said Daslakh, reverting to safety green.

Nobody said anything for a moment.

"Intriguing," said Jaka, looking gleeful. "Let's all keep this quiet, okay? If the others don't figure it out, this might be useful as a bargaining chip. Solana, that means you, too. Understand? Do not tell any of Yanai's crew about this."

Solana didn't look happy, but she nodded. She had no choice.

"One more thing, dear. I think it would help all of us be less suspicious if you would join us downstairs tonight. Separate quarters seems so standoffish, don't you think."

"I like my room upstairs."

Jaka looked directly into her eyes and spoke clearly and slowly. "Solana, from now on you will sleep downstairs with us. Understand?"

"I understand."

"Good! You can be over with me and Tanaca. Just us three girls." She caught Anton's eye as she said it, and gave an exaggerated wink.

✧   ✧   ✧

Ten years earlier...

Anton composed himself as the bots brought in the next prisoner. Just before dawn a raid on a subversive meeting had netted more than a dozen enemies of the community. As centro of Fratecea's Memetic Safety Committee, it fell to Anton to judge them.

His eyes met those of the prisoner and he barely kept himself from flinching. It was Dejan. Anton hadn't seen him in months, not since joining the Committee. Dejan's hair was still a mess, and his mouth still bore a trace of his mocking smile, but the eyes in between looked older and sadder.

Anton didn't waste time with formalities. An image appeared in the air between them, of Dejan sprawled on some cushions in a converted storage space. He held an unlabeled bottle of red wine in one hand and his other arm was draped around a shirtless young subversive named Jovan.

Jovan had not yet been sentenced.

In the image Dejan took a long pull from his bottle and then called out in his wonderfully penetrating baritone. "I heard a good one yesterday! The Transfigurance Movement had a party to celebrate four years of Fratecea's new society. Anton Verac gets up and proposes a toast. He says, 'The Movement isn't just about changing society, it's about changing all of us! Look at Dina—she used to be a basic biotech, looking for algae and fungus. Now she's an administrator, writing reports about contamination!' The whole room claps. Anton continues, 'Or Milan here—before the Movement he worked as a musician, playing at parties for the rich Board families. Now he is a Protector, ready to lay down his life to defend our hab!' More clapping, but Anton's not finished. 'Or Osiv Cismar! Once he was a drunk, a liar, a bully, and a thief, but look at him now: the leader of the Movement!'" The room erupted in laughter, and then Anton froze the image.

Dejan chuckled quietly.

"You can't say things like that," said Anton.

"I'm sorry I used your name," said Dejan.

"It's not that. You can't insult the leader of the Movement."

Dejan raised his chin a fraction of a centimeter. "It's all true. That's why it's so funny. How can the truth be an insult?"

"You know it can. Back when the Board families ran everything you used to joke about them."

"What's got twenty-one dicks but no balls? The Board of Directors," said Dejan. "You laughed at that one."

"And a year later the Board were out of power. Words can be weapons. Weapons must be regulated."

Dejan's eyes looked sadder. "What's it going to be? Chip in my head? Recycle my biomass?"

"We aren't monsters. You'll spend a year in the work dorm. Show that you can be a good citizen and you'll be released."

"Gosh, that sounds simple enough!" For a moment Dejan's face had its old impish look. "Thanks, Anton!"

He allowed the bots to lead him out, but just as he reached the door Dejan looked over his shoulder, still smiling. "See you soon!"

Anton walked home that afternoon. He still lived in his parents' house, but there had been some adjustments. His mother and father kept to their quarters on the second floor when they were home. Anton needed the entire first floor. The main room had become his office, and nowadays the front steps always had a dozen people waiting, hoping to speak with him.

He got past them by not stopping, not meeting any eyes, not responding to their pleas. They knew better than to touch him.

But inside he was confronted with a visitor. Sari, Dejan's mother. She sat at the dining table which he now used as a desk. His father sat beside her, holding her hand.

"Anton," said his father.

"No. He made a memetic attack on the Movement. I can't give him special treatment just because our families are friends."

"Must it be the dormitory? Can't he stay at home?" said Sari. She was crying.

"That's impossible. He's spreading harmful ideas. He has to be isolated. You wouldn't leave a vine covered in mold with the healthy ones, would you?"

"It was just a joke!" said Sari. "Can't he tell a joke?"

"He's a grown man. He knows what is and isn't appropriate. What's funny to some people is hurtful and dangerous to others."

"Maybe you could just give him a warning. He's smart, he'll keep quiet," said Anton's father.

"It's too late for that. I can't change my decision."

"This Movement is worse than the old Board!" said Sari. "They cheated the growers and hogged all the export credits, but they didn't have work dormitories or compliance implants. If they'd thrown you and Osiv and the rest of your Movement out the airlock we'd all be happier!"

"Sari, don't get excited," said Anton's father, with a panicked look at Anton. "She's just upset. She doesn't mean it."

"She should be more careful. Now I've got a lot to do before dinner. If you don't mind?" Anton gestured at the door.

"Come on. I'll take you home," said his father, and led the sobbing Sari out.

Anton was always an early riser. He liked to be the first one at work in the Safety Center. There wasn't really any reason for him to work in a room in the building, but being there meant everyone could see him. He could set an example for the others.

But this morning he wasn't the first in the building. Renzo stood by Anton's workspace, looking about. "Can we have privacy?" he asked before Anton could say anything.

"Do we need it?"

"Oh, yes. Both of us need it."

Anton used his implant to impose privacy on them. The hab's eyes and ears could still sense them, but only someone with higher-level clearance than Anton—*and* a need to know—could get access.

"All right. What's up?"

Renzo stared at the floor, working his lips silently for a moment, then took a deep breath and met Anton's eyes. "I know someone on the Justice and Redress Committee. Your mother helped develop the Ruby 22 strain."

"Yes. Everyone knows that. It's a popular variety. A big seller off-hab. The whole community benefits from her work."

"She gets a percentage."

"A quarter percent! Same as the rest of the team."

"Justice and Redress decided that all royalty holders are complicit in the crimes of the old Board. And their families."

Anton's throat was suddenly dry. "What's the redress?"

"It's being decided case by case."

Anton knew what that meant. The Justice and Redress Committee could use it as a weapon: settle old scores, blackmail rivals into cooperating, destroy enemies.

"Thank you," said Anton.

"Good luck," said Renzo, and then hurried away.

He needed to move fast, Anton realized. Get himself protected before J&R could move. And there was really only one person who could do that. He requested a meeting with Osiv Cismar. He spent ten minutes on the verge of panic before a reply came: in six hours he could have five minutes of the leader's time. He hoped it would be enough.

During one of his personal breaks that morning he did contact his mother, under a privacy seal which was almost certainly unethical. "You have to get rid of your royalties now."

"Which ones? I worked on dozens of strains."

"All of them. And any credits you got. Donate it all to the hab now."

"That's all our savings! What's going on?"

"Do it. Right now. Empty all your accounts. I'll explain later."

It might help or it might not. The credits would be forfeit sooner or later anyway.

The six hours felt like weeks passed before Anton hurried to see Osiv. He arrived fifteen minutes early for his five-minute appointment—and wound up cooling his heels for nearly an hour in an anteroom.

The leader of Fratecea's Transfigurance Movement was a short, bouncy man with a wide toothy smile. "Anton! Good to see you, brother! Work keeps us too busy—I haven't seen you in weeks!"

Anton's implant started a five-minute countdown as soon as he was called, so he didn't waste any time. "It's wonderful to see you again. Osiv, I heard some disturbing news this morning. Justice and Redress is moving against royalty holders. Is that true?"

"Yes, yes. Necessary. Board families used to hand out fractional shares to their clients and supporters. Buying their loyalty. Some stayed bought. We have to root them out."

"But many people earned their shares by service to the hab—developing strains or vintages which still bring in credits from off-hab."

"Your parents," said Osiv, looking Anton right in the eyes, no longer smiling. "They did well under the old system."

"Yes, among many others. I can assure you they're loyal. And consider: this new policy of J&R is a memetic hazard. Transfigurance is all about a new start, not holding on to old grudges.

When you abolished the Board you said, 'The past is gone. It has no power.' Punishing people for complicity gives the past power again—especially if the Committee has to judge what people did and why. It's an inconsistency. It makes the Movement look like hypocrites. We can't afford that."

Osiv studied Anton's face, as if looking at a sculpture. "I remember you hated that the Board made rules that didn't apply to themselves."

"It's inconsistent. Unjust. For them and for us."

Osiv looked off beyond Anton's shoulder for a couple of seconds, then met his eyes and smiled again. "You're right. I'll tell the Committee they have to adopt a single uniform policy on fractional shares and enforce it equally. That good for you?"

Anton hadn't realized how nervous he was until he felt himself relax. Osiv would fix this terrible mistake. All was well. He smiled, really smiled for the first time in—how long?—and gave Osiv an old-fashioned bow of respect. "Thank you, Osiv. I knew you'd understand."

"Goodbye, Anton," was all Osiv replied.

When Anton got back to the Safety Center half a dozen Protectors in full gear were standing idly by the entrance. He didn't give them much thought until one moved to block his path to the door. The others formed a ring around him.

"Anton Verac, you are charged with being complicit in the system of repression perpetrated by the former Board of Proprietors. Come with us." They had a privacy bubble around them; the hab wouldn't relay any signals from his implant. He knew better than to offer resistance.

They had a little van with windows set to opaque. Anton felt the gaze of passersby as the Protectors led him to the van. He found himself blushing with embarrassment. Arrest by Protectors was something that happened to enemies of the Movement, to the stupid and corrupt who refused to transform themselves. Not to him! It was almost a relief when they shoved him into the back seat and shut the door.

Justice and Redress met in what had once been the house of the Oseminte family, one of the richest of the Board. It was directly across the street from the medical center the Osemintes had endowed, now renamed simply Main Medical Center.

One tenet of the Transfigurance Movement was that formal laws and procedures were all expressions of oppression. Consequently the Justice and Redress Committee didn't bother with any nonsense about lawyers. Anton stood in a room, with a couple of others awaiting their hearings. The seven members of the Committee sat casually on couches and comfortable chairs, as if they had simply managed to get to the room first and grabbed all the seats. The bots hovering behind the prisoners made sure nobody approached closer than five meters to the Committee members.

He knew them all, and he knew that only two of them mattered: Adina Catran and Toma Penaj. The other five were ciphers, who seldom spoke and always voted along with Adina and Toma. Adina's parents had worked with his own in the viticulture labs, but they hadn't developed any lucrative strains. He and she had played together as children.

Toma was an older man, one of Osiv's cronies from before the Movement. Everyone assumed he was Osiv's mouthpiece on the Committee. When he began speaking, Anton's heart sank.

"Anton Verac. Your mother owned partial royalty rights to sixteen wine-grape strains controlled by the Tarm family, nine strains controlled by the Scutrosa family, and one controlled by the Zana family. She spent the revenues resulting from those royalty shares on goods and services for you and your father as well as herself. She directly transferred funds to you which were derived in part or entirely from those shares. Therefore your entire family was complicit in the system of exploitation and oppression perpetrated by the Board of Proprietors."

"Some of those strains brought wealth from other habs. The whole community—"

"In addition," said Toma, not stopping, "you have recently taken steps to conceal your family's participation in a repressive system, and abused your position as an official of the Movement to influence official policy in order to avoid the consequences."

Anton looked at them. Toma's expression was slightly contemptuous. Adina kept her eyes on something above and behind Anton the whole time, never meeting his eyes. The other five spent their time looking back and forth between Toma, Anton, and the floor.

Toma waited. Anton opened his mouth to begin a defense, a justification, and then stopped. It was useless. He knew it was useless, they certainly knew it was useless.

He swallowed, and then looked directly at Toma and made himself smile. "I heard a joke the other day. The Movement had a party to celebrate four years in power. Osiv Cismar stood to make a toast. He said, 'The Transfigurance Movement didn't just change society, it has changed all of us! Dina was once a simple biotech but now she's an administrator.' The whole room clapped. Osiv went on. 'Or Milan—before the Movement he was a musician, playing for the rich, but now he is a Protector, defending Fratecea!' They all clapped some more but Osiv went on. 'Or Toma Penaj! Before he joined the Movement he was a liar, a crook, and a chronic masturbator, but look at him now: he's on the Justice and Redress Committee!'"

Did Adina's mouth twitch just a little? Anton wasn't sure. He would have to work on his delivery of the joke. He was going to have plenty of time to practice.

Anton was not prudish. His time in the work dormitory had ground any modesty or squeamishness out of him. And he knew that Jaka had an exhibitionistic streak. Making people uncomfortable was a source of power, one she enjoyed using.

But her performance—and there was really no other word for it—after lights out was more blatant than anything he had seen since she had bought his control codes. Not only was she on display but she compelled Solana to do likewise. There was no attempt at quiet or concealment. Jaka wanted to make sure everyone knew what was going on, as if daring Yanai's crew to object.

Anton's spot that night was next to Ulan, and he had orders to keep the big guy from trying anything. He couldn't stop Ulan from peeking through the crude partition of chairs and planters separating them from the "girls," but he himself kept his back to it and watched Ulan.

"Daaamn," muttered Ulan. "That Solana's hot. Fusion hot. Makes Jaka look like a Europan or something."

Anton gave a disapproving sigh.

"Don't know why she's wasting her time with Jaka and a buncha toys when there's plenty of hot meat right here."

"Just ignore them," Anton murmured.

"Listen to 'em, man!" Ulan whispered, almost groaning. "That girl is off the tether." After a minute's silence broken only by the gasps and giggles from the other side of the partition, he asked, "So is it true? About her? She's a Qarina?"

"Evidently so."

"I did an entertainment once. Really hot. It was a hab fulla Qarinas. All of 'em hot and ready. Never thought I'd see one for real. You think it's true? They do whatever you tell 'em?"

"Best not to think about it. Get some sleep."

"I don't wanna get some sleep. I wanna get some of *that*."

"Please be quiet."

"I don't have to listen to you," muttered Ulan, but he did quiet down. Shortly after Jaka bought control of Anton, Ulan had tried to push him around. He was big, with lots of boosted muscle, but Ulan had never done hard time. He'd been a guest, briefly, at a detention facility in a hab where prisoners still had rights and the guards carried only tanglers or sonics. By contrast, Anton had been in work dorms where the deaths of political prisoners was considered a feature of the system, not a problem. The one time they had come to blows, Ulan had broken two of Anton's ribs and smashed his nose—but Anton had gotten one of Ulan's eyes out before Adelmar pulled them apart. After that Ulan left Anton alone.

Anton closed his eyes and did his best to ignore Jaka's noisy grunts from one side of him and the sound of Ulan stimulating himself from the other. The thought of finding a grip tool and ripping out his implant was very tempting, but sheer fatigue won and he dropped off to sleep.

He woke a few hours later. Everyone else was still asleep, except for Daslakh, who sat on Anton's chest, gently prodding the tip of his nose with one limb. "Get up and keep quiet. There's something I want to show you before these other idiots."

Anton got silently to his feet and followed the softly glowing mech to the front door of the clinic. He looked through the frost-webbed diamondoid doors but didn't see anything. "What's up?"

"The window, stupid."

He refocused on the pane a meter in front of his eyes and then he saw it: opaque lines on the clear material, spelling out words.

GET OUT NOW

CHAPTER NINE

As soon as Daslakh sounded the alarm Solana joined the others as they crowded around the front door. She managed to pull on her discarded suit liner, for modesty as well as warmth. The message on the front door of the medical center was a welcome distraction: she, and everyone else, could focus on the mystery and not think about the night before.

Pera suited up and went outside, checking the airlock and the surrounding area for any tracks or booby traps. After about half an hour she reported back.

"Nothing. No traps, which is good. No sign of entry attempts—but from now on we should lock the outer airlock door when everyone's inside. No footprints or thermal traces."

"How was the message even made?" asked Utsuro.

"Thermal spalling on the outside surface of the panes. I'd guess a laser tuned to hard UV."

"Can your laser do that?" Jaka asked. Unlike Solana, she hadn't bothered to dress beyond putting on her utility vest and gun belt.

"I can crank it down to a hundred nanometers, but it's hard on the power cell. Why?"

"Just wondering." She looked around. "Daslakh?"

"Right here," said the mech, standing on the ceiling above her.

"Did you happen to see when this happened?"

"No. I noticed it right before I called everyone. Before that I was in the room with the emergency generator, charging myself."

"Wouldn't have made much noise," said Pera. "And if they tuned the laser right, all you'd see is a little red patch tracing the lines."

"Can any say with certainty that it was not inscribed upon the panes before we ever came to Safdaghar? For all of us have used the airlock rather than this door to come and go. I know that I myself have only looked upon this pane with the briefest glance, and might have missed these words," said Atmin.

"I'm sure," said Pera. "When we moved in I checked for cracks. I would've seen any writing."

Solana saw Jaka and Adelmar staring at each other, and guessed they were using private comms. The chimp made a nodding motion with his right fist, and Jaka smiled at him.

"Never mind how it was made," said Daslakh. "Pay attention to the message. Someone wants us to leave, and I second the motion. We've got some good loot—maybe not as much as all of us would like, but better than nothing. I say we take the most valuable items we can carry, and get out of here."

"The mech's right. There's something weird here, and I don't like it," said Pera.

Jaka pushed through the crowd to Solana, and looked directly at her. She spoke by private comm. *"Tell me the truth: is this a ploy by the bird and the dino to scare us away?"*

Solana shook her head.

"Are you sure? Could they have cooked this up without telling you?"

"Atmin would never do that."

"If you say so. Still, go along with what I'm about to say." Jaka smiled again and turned away from Solana. "I think someone's trying to scare us," she said aloud.

"More accurate, I think, to say that someone has succeeded," said Atmin.

"But that's all they're doing. Look at everything that's happened: those ridiculously feeble traps, this warning. Some doubtful sightings."

"Don't forget the loss of a bot," Yanai put in.

"Exactly! A bot, not a person. I think someone's trying to scare us. Drive us away and get the good stuff."

"Excuse me, but I think it's important to remind you that I did step on a mine," said Utsuro.

"What would have happened if it went off?" asked Jaka.

"Fill him with darts," said Pera promptly.

"Would any of them even pierce his shell?" she asked triumphantly. "There's lots of very efficient ways to kill people, even mechs and borgs. Why not use them?"

"Can't use what you don't have," said Pera.

"Then we've nothing to fear. Let's put it to a vote. Who wants to run away?"

Pera raised one hand, and Atmin, after a moment's hesitation, spread his wings.

"Utsuro?" asked Pera.

"I'm not ready to leave yet. I still have questions. Maybe the rest of you could go back to Yanai until I'm finished."

"The only answer you will find in Safdaghar is just a blank," said Atmin.

"Looks like we've got a clear majority in favor of staying," said Jaka.

"Solana?" Pera looked at her, head cocked quizzically. "Are you okay?"

"I'm fine," she said.

"Really? You're still part of our crew. You don't have to do what she says."

Jaka kept silent and watched Solana with a faint smile.

"Don't worry about me," she said. As she spoke she realized she meant it. Ever since the Salibi soldiers had taken young Solana away from her masters, she had felt a constant nagging worry. Worry about what she should do. Worry about what other people would think. Worry about whether she could succeed at things. Worry about the future. Worry about past mistakes. It never ended. Apparently other people felt that way all the time.

But with her goggles off and Jaka's face before her, all those worries vanished. Solana had only one concern again: obedience. It made everything simple.

At some level, in the most analytical part of her mind, she knew that sense of serenity was the result of genetic engineering and prenatal brain modification—a hardwired reflex to make her a perfect slave. It didn't matter, though. The dopamine rush from obedience was very real, and drowned out those abstract concerns about free will.

"Let's pair up and get to work," said Jaka. "Anton, you accompany Utsuro this time. Adelmar, you go with Pera. Tanaca and I will tag along with Atmin. Ulan, you keep an eye on Solana."

Solana could see a look of disgust on Anton's face. Ulan wore a mix of amazement and glee.

They all suited up and left the medical center, splitting off in twos and threes as they headed for the shift's search areas. By the time Solana and Ulan had gone about half a kilometer down the main road to spinward, they were alone together.

He managed to restrain himself for another ten minutes, then said, "Hey, c'mere," and then half-dragged her into a house with walls made of woven living vines, now dry and brittle. "Get that suit open. Lemme see you."

The desire to please drowned out her sense of disgust. She obediently undid her suit, smiling at him in the way she had been taught.

"Oh, yeah. *Oh,* yeah." He put his big hands on her bare skin. "I bet you're gonna like me better than Jaka."

With her goggles off she liked everyone. She loved Jaka's masterful ways and diamond-hard will. At the moment she loved Ulan's brute power. Even his clumsy fumblings were erotic.

There was no call for any skill on her part. He was too desperate, almost comical in his haste.

"Here, get on top," he said. "How do you like that, huh? Bet you," he said, and then stopped. Ulan's eyes unfocused, then closed, and he flopped back onto the floor and began to snore.

Solana looked at him, puzzled, and then noticed the little orange dart sticking in the left side of his neck. She looked that way, toward the open doorway and the courtyard beyond. Without her goggles she could see only darkness—and maybe a quick movement of something blacker than the shadows outside.

She tried to wake Ulan but he was completely unconscious. With no way to please him she had to help him instead. He was too heavy for her to lift. What to do? She knew, intellectually, that she needed to do something, that there was danger, but her brain kept telling her to obey Ulan.

"Pera, are you there? I need help."

"Situation?"

"I'm in a house, about six hundred meters west of the clinic, north side of the avenue. Ulan just went unconscious. I think he's been shot. Some kind of dart. I can't tell if it's tranq or poison."

"He stable?"

"I think so. His suit's giving him something." She could see the fabric of Ulan's left sleeve flex and pulse as the suit's support system hit him with different drugs.

"Get out of the building, get some cover. I'll be there in two minutes."

She stood and sealed up her suit, glad to shut out the chilly air. She'd have to clean herself and decontaminate the suit, too. No telling what kind of spores she had on her now. After a moment's consideration she sealed up Ulan's suit, too.

His needle rifle was beside him, within easy reach. Even with Solana for his plaything Ulan didn't want to be unarmed. Solana considered the weapon. Should she leave it? Ulan would want it when he woke...

...But for now he wasn't awake, and he hadn't given her any orders about it. What would be the most helpful thing for her to do? Take it. Protect him. And protect herself from whatever was lurking in the shadows. She grabbed the needle rifle and slung it over her shoulder.

Outside the house, alone in the dark with nothing but an oval of light from her helmet lamp, she felt a shudder of revulsion. The urge to please faded with no humans in sight. It was still there—she even felt a pang of loneliness because there was nobody around to command her—but at the moment Solana could obey her own will instead of someone else's.

After a moment an unstoppable wave of anger overwhelmed her sense of disgust. Solana wanted to get a heavy chair and bash Ulan's face in. Jaka's, too. Maybe even Tanaca, for her eternal acquiescence. Why hadn't anybody *done* anything?

This wasn't the first time she'd felt this way. At Jiaohui there had been a moment when Solana had looked back on her previous life and finally understood what had been done to her—done before she was even born, slavery literally built into her genome. She had spent weeks filled with rage, seething when she was alone and exploding when others were around.

Could she hide? Stay away from the others until they got

tired and went away? Pera and Atmin could bring her food. She wished she had her goggles. Then she could sneak around in the darkness of the hab without shining a light and giving away her location. Go back to seeing human faces as blank ovals.

A noise made her start, and she spun to see Pera approaching, moving with obvious caution but covering the distance efficiently.

"Why aren't you in cover? Whatever got Ulan could pick you off out here."

"It could have shot me at the same time as him. He's in there." Nevertheless she crossed the street and crouched behind a sturdy-looking bench.

Pera went into the house, only to come bounding out again a second later. She reached Solana's side in four strides, and touched one hand to her helmet to create a secure link.

"You really did a job on him. I don't know how we're going to hide that."

"What?"

"Ulan. How'd you cut him up like that?"

"I didn't do anything. He was unconscious when I left him, but he was alive. Good vitals."

"Well, right now he's in about eight or nine chunks. Blood all over the place."

"Are you joking? He was fine just a couple of minutes ago. How could—" Solana felt a stab of panic. The two of them were very exposed out in the street. The darkness beyond her helmet lamp seemed infinite, full of dangers. She crouched, pulling Pera down beside her.

"Did he try anything?" asked Pera.

"I couldn't say no."

"How'd you break the conditioning?"

"I didn't. I told you—he had his helmet off and his suit open. Some kind of dart hit him and he passed out. That's when I called you."

Pera finally understood her. The dino's pose changed. She had been crouching next to Solana, offering comfort. Now she shifted into a combat-ready posture, scanning the area for danger. She drew her engineer's laser in one swift motion. "Turn off your lamp." She switched to public comm. *"Ulan's dead. At least one confirmed hostile in the hab. Location unknown. Get to safety. Use caution."*

Pera went back to her direct link with Solana. "Okay, safest course is to move fast, frequent changes of direction. We'll move spinward to the next cross street, then cut south and double back along the next parallel road. Then—"

"I can't go back. Not without my goggles."

Pera lashed her tail. "You can't stay out here! We'll figure something out at the med center. Maybe a blindfold. Or maybe I'll just tell Jaka that I'll fry *her* unless she gives them back. Now come on."

Solana followed Pera, running as fast as she could, aware that the dino was holding back in order to let her keep up. They followed a very roundabout course, crossing the main road twice and actually going beyond the medical center before doubling back.

A block away they paused at the corner of a building, all lights off, keeping still and silent. Pera watched for more than five minutes. "Final sprint. I'll run ahead, then cover you. Ready? Move!"

The dino took off at maximum speed, covering more than two meters with each step. She reached the door of the medical center and turned, laser at the ready, scanning the rooftops...

Solana wasn't there. As soon as Pera sprinted off across the street she ran as hard as she could in the other direction.

"*Is your brain misfiring? Get back here!*" said Pera over the private link.

"*No. Even if I wear a blindfold she'll figure out a way to make me see her.*"

"*Not going to happen. I'll make sure of it. Jaka's lost one of her goon squad; the male human and the chimp don't look like they want to die for her. But you have to come inside. We don't know what's out there.*"

Solana cut all her comm links and turned off her lamps. For a minute she stood in utter darkness and silence. As her eyes adjusted, she began to make out the faint glow of the medical center's lights reflecting off the ceiling of the hab ring, a hundred meters above her. It wasn't quite enough to see, but it did give the world a little definition: she stood in a black canyon under a barely perceptible sky.

During her years in Jiaohui, Solana had learned to orient herself in a rotating hab with a couple of head nods. Spinward was to her left, which meant she was facing south. The med center was behind her.

The buildings in this section were one- and two-story affairs built right up to the broad sidewalk, and were joined together or separated by narrow alleys. By trailing her hand along the wall she could follow the block. At the corner she stepped cautiously into the street, sliding her feet along the ground to avoid tripping over anything, and feeling ahead with outstretched hands.

With almost nothing to see her hearing felt hypersensitive. She could hear her feet sliding through the dust, and her own breathing, and the faint hiss of her helmet filters. With each step her water reservoir sloshed a little. She strained to hear anything beyond her own body.

She went another block south, then turned antispinward. She stopped and crouched down, listening for any sound of pursuit. Pera had excellent night vision, and might be out there without a light. But after several minutes Solana satisfied herself that nobody was nearby.

She activated the direct comm link to Yanai. *"I need to get out of here,"* she said. *"I can't go back without my goggles."*

"Of course," said the ship. *"Get back to me and I'll print you a new pair. We'll figure out a way to do the blocking software. You can stay on board as long as you need to. Nobody will argue about shares. I'll see to that. Can you make it on your own?"*

"I have to," said Solana.

"Good. I've got a question for you: do you think Jaka's crew would interfere if I tell Utsuro and Pera to start moving the salvage out of there?"

"Jaka wants her cut. She'll do anything to get it."

"We will have to find out what her price is. For now, you get to the elevator."

Now that she had a goal and a plan, Solana wasn't as fearful. She walked in the direction of the elevator to the hub. If she could make it to the shaft, she'd be safe. Just a one-kilometer vertical climb. She could do that. Her suit gloves and shoes could become sticky as needed, so there'd be no danger of falling. She was in good condition. She could do this. She had to.

When she had put a few more blocks between herself and the med center, she asked Yanai to send Pera a message and key to set up a new secure comm channel.

"Where are you?" the dino asked after a couple of seconds.

"I'm safe. That's all I'm going to say. What's going on?"

"Jaka tried to convince everyone that you and I murdered Ulan. Nobody believes it, but you can't argue with her. Atmin finally admitted it was possible and Jaka started acting like we'd both been tried and convicted. She and the chimp went out—she said they're going to bring back Ulan, but I think they're looking for you. You sure you're safe?"

"I'm well away from the clinic and I'm staying dark."

"We still don't know what's going on. There's something out there," said Pera.

"I'll be careful."

"Do you have a weapon?"

Solana started to say no, but then realized that the weight banging against her side was a needle rifle. "Of course. You be careful, too."

She shut down all her comms again. If she was going dark, no point in carrying around a big bright wireless beacon. The only part of the spectrum she couldn't make entirely dark was infrared. Her body couldn't stop generating heat.

Navigating entirely by touch and bearing, Solana crept down the side street. A few times her sliding feet bumped against dry corpses in the roadway. The second one had actually shifted a little when her foot bumped it. That inspired the horrible idea that some lurking killer might deliberately impersonate a dead body. Maybe more than one. She'd heard about military nanobots which could turn a corpse into a puppet, living off fat and dead tissue. Casualties turned into enemy combatants. They might be *all around her in the dark.*

She crouched and unslung the needle rifle, then activated her implant and tried to talk to it. If Ulan had been careful, the gun was security-linked to him and him alone.

He hadn't, and it wasn't. The gun powered up and informed Solana how many needles were in the magazine, how much juice was in the power cell, how many days it was overdue for maintenance, time-to-failure estimates, and all its mechanical twinges and gripes. It handed targeting information to her implant, which put up a little crosshair in her vision to show what the gun was pointing at. Unfortunately, the gun had no vision system of its own, so the icon just floated against a dark background.

Solana clutched the rifle and listened for a long time, forcing herself to breathe slowly until the feeling of panic subsided. Then she got to her feet and resumed shuffling toward the elevator plaza, holding the rifle at the ready, with her finger on the trigger.

Time check: her implant said it was less than three hours since she had left the med center with Ulan to begin the work shift. It felt like three days.

Groping in the dark made for slow progress, especially when she kept pausing, freezing in mid-stride trying to hear...something. Something maddeningly just out of hearing. It might be Jaka and Adelmar, it might be the mystery killer, it might be debris shifting, it might be all in her head.

After another hour of cautious progress she stood at the edge of the elevator plaza. The light from the medical center was barely visible here. The curve of the hab meant she could see it directly, a very faint cluster of lit windows far off above the nearer buildings. The elevator was a black shadow in the center of the dark plaza.

She waited, huddled against the corner of a building, watching and listening. Jaka had her goggles, and might be wearing them, but she didn't know if the chimp had any kind of night-vision gear. If they were searching they'd have to be moving around. Surely she'd be able to hear them? She hoped so.

Five minutes passed and she saw no lights, heard no movement or speech. Time to move. She shuffled forward across the plaza, sliding her feet through the gritty dust and debris on the pavement, going as fast as she dared.

Her outstretched left hand touched the wall of the elevator shaft. She felt her way along it until she came to the little vestibule with benches for passengers to wait for the next car to the hub.

A light flashed on, nearly blinding her. Her finger tightened on the trigger of the gun and let loose a stream of needles into the wall of the elevator shaft. Jaka stood before her in the vestibule with a lamp aimed at her own face. She grinned. "Boo!" she said. "Don't close your eyes."

As she looked at Jaka's face, Solana felt her anger and shame and worry diminish—as if those parts of her were locked in a tiny cell, screaming and banging on the walls, but they were so thick she could barely hear anything. None of that mattered, anyway. The only thing Solana could care about was the human in front of her, and how to please her.

"All better now?" asked Jaka.

"Yes," said Solana, bowing her head.

"You know, you're a much nicer person without those goggles," said Jaka. "You're not selfish or greedy or angry. I like you much better this way."

The praise gave Solana a rush of happiness. The tiny screaming part of her mind couldn't stop it. She smiled, and felt herself blush.

"Come along home," said Jaka, and set out along the street toward the med center again. She kept her lamp on so they could walk normally. "It wasn't hard to figure out where you'd be going, not really. Your ship was surprisingly quiet on the open channel. Now, a few days ago she was willing to let herself get blown up if anything bad were to happen to you, so obviously she cares about your welfare. Not like *some* digital minds I could name. I guessed the two of you were speaking privately, and that told me where you were going. Wasn't I clever? Tell me how clever I was."

"You were very clever to guess I was going back to Yanai," said Solana. Jaka was always so smart, so wise. Her attention made Solana feel happy.

"Oh, by the way—*did* you kill Ulan?"

"No," said Solana. "I was serving him when something knocked him out, and then I called Pera for help and when she got there she said he was all cut up."

"Ah. Who might have done that, do you suppose? Maybe a large reptile with sharp claws? You, I can trust. She could be lying. Listen to me: when we get back to the med center I'm going to propose some changes in how we run things. I want you to support me. Never mind what Yanai says, or Atmin, or Pera. They didn't go out in the dark to find you. I did. I'm the one you should trust. Keep me in sight at all times."

They walked some more and then Jaka spoke again. Silence seemed to irritate her. "I've heard about Kumu hab and the Qarinas," she said. "I can't imagine some of the horrible things you must have gone through."

"I don't want to talk about it."

"I understand," said Jaka. She stopped and put her arms around Solana. "People can be awful. I've been through some tough times myself. The others don't know, but my early years were as bad as yours. Maybe worse. The hab I grew up in was falling apart, almost like this place. Whole sections were uninhabitable. The place was controlled by gangs. They fought each other and preyed on everyone else. My parents died when I was little. Murdered. I can't"—she choked back a sob—"I can't remember their faces."

Solana never had parents, but it sounded as though Jaka thought they were important, so she patted the other woman's shoulder sympathetically.

Jaka rested her head on Solana's shoulder, and her voice dropped to a whisper. "I had to sell myself to survive. Not like a Qarina. No super-rich owner keeping me as a pet. Just one dirty, brutal thug after another, using me and tossing me aside. I learned to steal, fight... even kill. Did you ever have to do that?"

"No. Not for real, anyway."

"It does something to you, in your mind. I know that I look selfish to other people, or callous. Maybe even cruel. But I've been worse, and I don't want to be that way. Do you understand?"

"I think so," said Solana, and patted Jaka's shoulder again.

"I just want my fair share," said Jaka. "Just enough to live quietly. Someplace safe. That's all." She raised her head and looked into Solana's eyes. "That's why I need you. To help me forget."

They remained that way for half a dozen heartbeats, and then Jaka turned at the sound of Adelmar's approach.

"Ulan's in a bag," he said, and looked at Solana. "She do it?"

"She says she didn't. Do you think the dino could have done it?"

The chimp shrugged, palms up. "Clean cuts. A blade, not a claw. Strong, too. Right through bone."

"The dino and the cyborg are the strongest ones here. Nothing to prevent Pera from using a knife, especially if she didn't want blood on her feet. She seems like a tidy kind of person."

Solana couldn't tell if Jaka actually believed what she was saying, or was merely trying to find a convincing argument. Her absolute confidence made it hard to oppose her. Solana found herself accepting Jaka's reality even when she knew it was false.

The three of them reached the medical center and cycled in. Jaka went first. "Good news, everybody!" she called out as soon as she was inside. "I've got Solana back, and she's all right. Whatever murdered Ulan left her untouched."

Solana came in at the end of this, and stripped off her suit. She could see little black flecks on her suit liner and skin, and immediately got her cleaning goop to stop the mold before it could spread inside the building.

"With Ulan's unfortunate death we need to make some plans," said Jaka.

"I'm sure we all agree in light of that macabre event," said Atmin. "The time has come for us to leave this hab of death."

"You think so?" said Jaka. "I'm more interested in finding out who killed him."

"Something's in the hab," said Pera.

"There are a lot of things in the hab, including us. I'm very sorry to have to point this out, but it's very likely that Ulan's killer is here in this room right now. Adelmar, you saw what happened to Ulan. He was killed by powerful strokes with a sharp blade, correct?"

"Right through bone," the chimp repeated.

"I can't do that. Neither can Solana. Nor Anton or Tanaca. Adelmar, you were with Pera when Solana called for help. I hope nobody thinks you can run faster than a dino, so you can't have reached the scene before Pera. Utsuro was with Anton the whole time. The only person strong enough to kill Ulan, who also had the opportunity, is...you, Pera."

"You're crazy," said Pera, slamming her tail down on a chair hard enough to shock the smart matter, so that it reverted to a simple cube. "Solana said he got hit by a tranq dart—*while he was trying to rape her.* Who shot him?"

Jaka looked wide-eyed and innocent. "That's a good question. Maybe it was one of the booby traps infesting this place. As you say, he was quite irresponsible and may have overlooked a tripwire in his haste."

"Doesn't make sense. Why zero a trap on some random patch of floor?"

"It's equally unlikely that your hypothetical lurking killer went to the trouble to tranq him, only to slice him apart a few minutes later. But someone *outraged* by his deplorable behavior might do it upon finding him helpless." Jaka looked rather pointedly at the cube that had been a chair.

Solana watched the others. Utsuro's face screen showed a question glyph. Atmin's head was cocked to one side. Tanaca stood silently at Jaka's side. The little mech Daslakh was stuck to the side of a planter, colored rescue orange. Adelmar had edged forward to have a clear line of sight on Pera. Anton stood off to one side, staring at the floor with a pained expression. Did they believe Jaka? Should she believe her?

"Not going to put up with this," said Pera. "Where's your proof? Scan me for blood, show me a blade big enough to cut through a man. Find the trap that shot him."

"Daslakh, check her."

"I live to serve," said the mech, and scuttled over to Pera. It crawled over her, looking closely at the exterior of her suit and poking into pockets and pouches. "A little hemoglobin on the soles of her feet. Nothing on the claws. Tool kit has a five-centimeter multitool. You could certainly turn that into a blade, but there's no way to cut a human in half with it. Laser hasn't been used since its last recharge, and even a biological could see the difference between a laser burn and a blade cut."

"These houses have cooking tools. There are plenty of knives about. Here's a suggestion," said Jaka. "Pera, prove me wrong. You and Daslakh go examine the crime scene and see if there's a weapon. Look for something which might have launched the dart. Give us some facts to work with."

The mech took up a position on Pera's back, just behind her head, where she couldn't reach. It changed color to resemble Pera's black combat suit, then played a trumpet fanfare. "First Irregular Safdaghar Cavalry Regiment, advance!"

As soon as Pera and Daslakh cycled through the airlock, Jaka turned to face the rest of the company, smiling as always. "I think we all should cut our comms so we can speak *privately*. There are important things to discuss."

"I cannot think of anything that we must speak about which can't be heard by Pera or Yanai. What secret plot do you wish to concoct?" asked Atmin.

"Oh, it's nothing like that. Put your mind at rest. I just want to talk about how we're going to manage Pera when she comes back here with no evidence of any monsters hiding in the shadows."

Solana watched her but followed orders and said nothing. It was really impressive to watch Jaka work the group.

"What do you mean by 'manage'?" asked Utsuro. "I'm afraid I don't understand."

"Well, she's gone off to look for proof that she didn't kill Ulan. I don't think she's going to find any, because, well, I think she *did* kill him. Not that he didn't deserve it, of course. But still—is anyone really *comfortable* with a heavily armed murderer among us?"

Atmin fluttered down to land on the back of the broken chair. "If Pera slew vile Ulan as he rested after rape I do not call that murder but think it justice done."

"I'm certainly not going to defend his conduct, but even if Pera did believe she was dealing out some rough justice that doesn't really make the rest of us any safer, does it? I mean, what if she decides someone else has violated her private moral code?"

"I see your point—and know an easy way to cure your fears. You and yours can simply leave. Take half of all we've found and then embark. Once in your shuttle and away from Safdaghar, you will be safe from any sense of right and wrong," said Atmin.

Jaka never got to reply because just then everyone jumped at the sound of someone pounding on the diamondoid front doors of the clinic. They all looked, and all froze in amazement.

A man in a white environment suit stood at the door, banging with one fist. Daslakh stuck to the next pane over, displaying the words Open Up Idiots on its lower carapace. Pera leaned on the man for support, standing on her left leg. Her right leg was missing.

CHAPTER TEN

"Lost a lot of blood," said Adelmar, reading Pera's vital signs from her suit. With Utsuro's help they had gotten her onto an examination bed, lying on her left side with the stump of her severed leg easily accessible. The end of her right leg was covered by a white sheet of smart bandage, which also displayed her vitals and listed what treatments it was administering.

"She left about five liters on the ground," said Daslakh. "I don't know why she's still conscious."

"That bandage is giving her stims and painkillers. It should keep her stable. She needs a lot of fluids right away," said the stranger. His suit had changed shape and color inside the medical center, so that he now looked like a boulevardier from one of Juren's million cities, in a stylish maroon velvet tunic over midnight-blue trousers and a high-collared canary-yellow shirt. The cowl of his suit had turned transparent, revealing a pleasant but absolutely ordinary face and a head covered with black stubble.

"Who are you?" asked Jaka.

"Okada. Sabbath Okada. And you are Jaka Balavan, lately of Scapino habitat. You have at least three other names, but never mind about them," he said. Then he turned in place, jabbing a finger at each person in turn as spoke. "No need for introductions. We have here: Tanaca Mamua, Atmin of lineage 8504-RC, Anton Identity Cancelled, Utsuro, Solana Sina, and Adelmar de Malapert. Our patient is Pera Stodesyat. The only one I can't identify is you," he said to Daslakh.

"Good," it replied. "Now tell us how you got here and why."

"I'm here to save your lives. There's a combat mech in this hab. It's damaged and quite likely insane, but it's still very dangerous. You need to leave at once."

"Do tell us first how Pera's leg was severed from her hip, and how you came to bring her here," said Atmin.

"A booby trap at the house where Ulan died," said Daslakh. "A loop of monofilament stuck vertically to the walls, floor, and ceiling. When she passed through it, the loop pulled tight. Don't know what the trigger was. Pera ducked aside so it didn't cut her completely in half, but it got her leg. Mr. Fancy Suit came in a second later and got that smart bandage on her before she could bleed out."

"And since Daslakh is too small to support Pera's weight, I had to use my fancy suit to help her get back here," said the stranger.

"Very convenient, you being close by when the trap went off. Especially since it wasn't there earlier," said Jaka. As she spoke she moved to her left. Adelmar went the other way and flopped into a chair behind Sabbath.

"Did I mention the combat mech? I thought I heard myself say those words. It set those traps. At first they were crude, because when you got here the mech was barely functional, maybe even sub-baseline. But while you've been poking around looking for junk to sell, it's been repairing itself, getting stronger, smarter—more deadly."

Anton felt a little spark of hope. This Sabbath Okada—or whatever his name was—didn't seem afraid of Jaka, or confused by her. He looked *free*. Anton hadn't seen that in a while. Even the crooks and pirates in Scapino had been bound in webs of fear and desperation.

Jaka didn't show it, but Anton knew she was feeling a touch of new fear herself: the fear of losing control. She might have a remote-control for Anton's brain, and have Solana enslaved by her genome, but Adelmar and Daslakh and the others could turn against her in an instant. Only fear and distrust kept them in line, and Jaka had to work constantly to maintain those feelings.

She raised one golden-haired eyebrow. "It's a plausible story, but I can think of one just as good: *you*, Mister Sabbath Okada, are the one who's been skulking in the dark, laying traps and trying to scare us off. You want all the loot of this station for yourself. Maybe you didn't intend to hurt anyone, but now Pera's lost a leg and you had to reveal yourself. So you come up with a bogeyman story. I'm not going to buy it without proof."

"How can I persuade you I'm telling the truth? Time is short."

"Daslakh? What can you tell me? Is he lying?"

"I don't know. He's got absolutely perfect autonomic control. Pulse and respiration are rock-steady, pupils haven't changed size at all since he came inside, and his suit is regulating his temperature."

"I had a rather repressive upbringing, I'm afraid," said Sabbath. "I blame society."

"So you're stuck with using your own intelligence and judgment," said Daslakh to Jaka. "Sorry."

"Well," said Jaka, "I'd be more inclined to trust you if you weren't standing there in a suit of smart-matter combat armor."

Sabbath looked more amused than anything else, and Anton could tell that was getting on Jaka's nerves. "All right," he said. "If that's what it takes to convince you."

He stood a little straighter and held his arms out from his sides. The suit flowed off of him, forming itself into a little bundle between his feet. It left him nude, but he didn't seem to mind. His physique was flawless, unlike anything Anton had ever seen. The guards back at Fratecea and some of the pirates at Scapino had been bulky with muscle, but none of them had Sabbath's effortless grace. The only person who compared to him physically, Anton realized, was Solana.

"Satisfied? Or were you just hoping for the chance to ogle?"

Jaka and Adelmar moved simultaneously. The chimp propelled himself out of the chair with one shove of his powerful arms, and grabbed Sabbath from behind. Jaka dove at his feet, grabbing the suit and rolling into his legs. Sabbath tumbled forward and landed with Adelmar on top of him, pinning his arms in a full-nelson grip.

Jaka tossed the suit bundle to Tanaca. "Put this in the freezer and lock it. Anton: get the restraints out of my bag and stick them to the wall in that exam room. We'll secure him there." She stood up, looking pleased with herself, and pointed at the minimissile pods on her arms. "Try anything and I'll blow you to bits."

"You are making a tremendous mistake," said Sabbath, not resisting as Adelmar half-carried him to the exam room. "I am not your enemy. You're all in terrible danger!"

Anton grabbed Jaka's bag and found the restraints: simple strips of flexible smart metal. He followed Adelmar into the exam room. The chimp slammed Sabbath against the wall and held his left arm out. Anton sighed and pressed a restraint strip against Sabbath's wrist. The smart metal stuck to the wall and contracted to hold the man's hand securely.

"This isn't going to help. Don't do this!" said Sabbath.

"Sorry," Anton muttered as he got a strip onto his ankle, then a second onto the other leg.

With a final restraint on Sabbath's right arm Adelmar could let go. Their prisoner stood against the wall, wrists and ankles pinned. Despite being naked and bound, he looked more annoyed and impatient than afraid. "Why do you even listen to her? What is imprisoning me going to accomplish?"

"No more traps," said Adelmar. "No more ambushes."

"That's all wrong. The mech is still out there. You're all in danger and you need me."

The chimp pressed one forefinger to Sabbath's lips and then took a step back. Then he slammed one massive fist into the prisoner's belly. Sabbath jerked forward, gasping, then hung from his restraints.

"For Ulan. A shit, but you shouldn't have cut him. Keep quiet or get hit again."

Anton made sure Sabbath was breathing, then followed Adelmar into the atrium. The chimp gave Jaka a thumbs-up.

"Great! Now that our mystery stalker is locked up there's no more danger. We can decide what to do with him later. Yanai! Do you recognize his name?"

"*It's not in my personal memory. I can send out an autonomous message to search for it.*"

"Good idea. We can check his genome, too. That name sounds fake to me."

"You should know," Daslakh muttered.

"What was that? I didn't quite hear you."

"I said that even if this guy did kill Ulan, we aren't totally safe. No telling how many traps are out there."

"Very good point," said Jaka. "He's still dangerous even if he's restrained. See if you can get anything from his suit."

"I know some tricks." The little mech scuttled off to the kitchen and inserted one limb into the freezer. But just a couple of seconds later it snatched its limb out and turned bright hazard red. "That thing is just crawling with defenses," it said. "Soon as I tried to link up it started sending nasty little attack programs my way. Very advanced stuff. If I wasn't so old and cunning I'd be overwritten by now. All of you: don't make any contact with it if you don't want your implant hardware going dark or trying to kill you. Probably should avoid linking with him, as well."

"And now it's time for everyone who doubted me to apologize," said Jaka. She really did love to twist the knife, Anton thought.

After a moment of silence Atmin spoke up. "Your tricking him was neatly done. If truly he is false then we are in your debt. But if his words were true—"

"They're not. It all fits. That suit's as strong as Utsuro, and could easily make a blade. You saw how it frightened Daslakh. This Sabbath person is obviously the one who killed Ulan, and probably set the traps as well. Some of them, anyway."

"How did he get here, and why?" asked Utsuro.

"How? Good question. Some kind of little stealthy boat launched on an intercept from Jupiter's main ring. Low emissions, cold thrust. That's how I'd do it," said Jaka. "And why? I still think he was trying to scare us away to get the best loot for himself. But it's equally possible he's some kind of psycho murderer. Did you say something?"

"Not me," said Daslakh. "I'm too scared, remember?"

"What are we to do with the poor fellow?" said Utsuro. "Even if he is as you say, it would be inhumane to abandon him when we leave."

"You want him, take him," said Adelmar. "Plenty room on Yanai."

"*I will gladly take him to the synchronous ring,*" said the ship. "*Utsuro, can you get me a gene scan? It might tell us more about who he is.*"

"Anton, help him," said Jaka, with a surprisingly serious look. He wasn't sure how he could help the cyborg use a built-in scanner, but he followed Utsuro into the exam room.

Within, Sabbath stood upright again, looking relaxed and

mildly curious despite the enormous bruise already forming on his abdomen. "I've decided to confess," he said. "I'm actually an interplanetary assassin with the death sentence on me in a dozen different jurisdictions. I've got a special offer for you: give me back my suit and I'll take out that woman for free."

Utsuro ran his gene scanner over the man, and then after a moment did it again. "Who are you, really?" he asked. "I would very much like to know."

"I told you. Sabbath Okada. Can I rely on your discretion?"

"Yes," said Utsuro.

"No," said Anton. "Jaka controls my implant. I'll tell her anything she asks. That's why I'm here."

"I begin to see," said Sabbath. "You, and a Qarina who'll obey anyone—what about the other woman and the chimp? What's she got on them?"

"Tanaca...I can't tell if she's terrified of Jaka or if she's in love with her. Maybe both at the same time. Adelmar's just in it for the money."

"She certainly has no hold on me, nor on Atmin or Pera," said Utsuro. "But these results are—"

"Yes, they are," said Sabbath. "If you let me go perhaps I can explain in more detail. Privately."

The cyborg took a step back. "I'm not sure if I trust you."

"Link up, then? My comms are secure."

"No," said Utsuro. "Not at present. According to the mech your suit has very aggressive countermeasures. You might have something similar in your head. I cannot afford having my own systems corrupted."

"Is there any way I can get you to trust me?"

"Perhaps if you reveal your true identity."

"I did that already, twice. I'm Sabbath Okada, professional killer. Really."

"I'm afraid that doesn't help."

"Well, if you want to chat stop in any time. I'll be here." He still looked amused as Anton followed Utsuro out of the room.

Jaka set up a roster of guards to watch the prisoner. "Two people here, the other six gathering goodies outside. We'll keep working in pairs in case there are more traps. I'll take the first shift, with Adelmar. The rest of you, get back out there and find something worth our time."

Anton was paired with the corvid Atmin, Solana with Daslakh, and Tanaca accompanied Utsuro. It did not escape Anton's notice that the two best-armed members of the group were safe inside the medical center. Despite Jaka's boasts, he suspected she was still afraid of something in the dark.

He followed the bird along the main avenue. For safety Atmin trailed a line below his flying travel sphere. Anton watched the hanging thread, fluorescent blue in the light from his helmet lamps, alert for any sign of a snare or tripwire. After a few blocks Atmin spoke. "Good Anton, tell me what you think of our new guest. Do you believe he slew Ulan? I am not sure."

"That's what Jaka thinks."

"And are you but a puppet on her hand? I want your thoughts, not hers."

"I don't think we know everything. Why would he kill Ulan but save Pera? It doesn't make sense. He's keeping something secret, though," said Anton.

"A single man who came by stealth could not remove much loot. He either came in search of some specific thing...or is not here for that at all."

"But why would he come here, then?" Anton protested. "And why now? The hab's been derelict for years. Plenty of time to get something, if he knew what he was after."

"Why now is obvious: Yanai has stabilized the spin of Safdaghar. Without her work it would be near impossible to dock or move around within the tumbling wreck. But what he seeks is not as clear. It seems to me the only things within doomed Safdaghar to draw attention now would be ourselves."

"He's going to be disappointed, then. None of us are worth much. Except maybe Solana."

The bird didn't appear to catch his hint. "That is not the thing I mean. I do not think this Sabbath wants us, not at all. Instead it strikes me that he may be here to stop us doing something that he does not wish to see occur."

"That sounds a lot like Jaka's idea, that he's trying to scare us off."

"A mystery, I do admit. I cannot work it out."

Their abbreviated search shift turned up some nice items: an actual bound printed paper book, which had escaped the all-pervasive mold by virtue of being sealed in film; a set of gold medallions from Psyche; and a set of little porcelain bots which performed erotic dances when Atmin opened their box.

All that was about as much as Anton could comfortably carry, so the two of them turned back toward the clinic, with Atmin leading the way once again. To get back to the main road the bird chose a diagonal route via courtyards and alleys, through a section already searched.

As they went through one courtyard where an elaborate water garden had been churned into muddy ice fragments, Atmin switched his travel sphere to hover mode and paused. "I thought I heard a noise. Did you?"

Anton stopped and listened. Yes, there it was, a faint staccato tapping sound coming from his left. "Over there." He turned and let his helmet lights shine on the house making up that side of the courtyard. It was two stories, and the walls on this side were made up of sliding panels, mostly open. The light shining into the rooms made odd shadows behind the jumbled broken furniture.

"Look there!" said Atmin, and aimed his own spotlight at a room on the second floor. At first Anton could see nothing—but then what looked like a shadow suddenly moved. It reached the edge of the balcony in an eyeblink, its many limbs drumming arrhythmically on the floor as it moved.

In the glare of two sets of lights the thing was still pure black. Anton's eyes couldn't make sense of it: he saw limbs, lenses, wires, assorted boxes and spheres of various sizes, all jumbled together with no symmetry or plan.

Curiosity gave way to panic. Here was Sabbath's killer mech, a dark nightmare come alive. Anton dropped the stack he was holding and ran for the alley. Atmin made a heroic dive at the thing to distract it, swooping his travel sphere within a couple of meters of it before veering off after Anton.

The mechanical shadow remained immobile for an instant, then leaped down from the balcony and pattered after Anton. Its sharp feet made chips of ice fly as it crossed the frozen pond.

Inside his head Anton could hear Atmin putting out a general alarm on comms. *"Alert! A black machine with bladed limbs is chasing us and looks to be a foe. We are six hundred meters from the camp, to south and spinward, running fast. Please help! We are unarmed."*

Anton ran harder than he had ever run before. His antique

suit felt like a sheath of lead. The air in his helmet felt hot and damp as his breathing overwhelmed the filter system. When the visor started to fog he fumbled at the latch and got it open, sucking lungfuls of cold musty air, ignoring the bitter gritty dust.

Behind him the rapid arrhythmic tapping of the machine's feet got steadily louder.

Atmin dragged a decorative rug off a rooftop terrace, so that it fell onto the machine. For a moment it flailed about while Anton ran even harder and got around a corner, out of sight. He heard cloth rip and then the irregular footsteps again.

Now he was on a lateral street, heading for the main avenue that circled the habitat ring. Over the comm channel he could hear half a dozen voices asking questions and giving orders, but Anton couldn't spare the attention—or the breath—to speak at all.

He looked over his shoulder but couldn't see it. Atmin's travel sphere floated above him. "Wh—where?" he gasped out.

"I do not see the shadowed foe. It may have run away."

Anton skidded around the corner onto the avenue, fell, rolled, and scrambled to his feet again. He could see the lights of the clinic ahead, just a couple of hundred meters. Almost there...

And then the black machine emerged from a building to his left, just a few meters away, too close to escape. It sliced the air with a couple of bladed limbs. He swerved aside, hoping to get around it, but the machine got directly in front of him. Anton tried a sudden change of direction but his heavy suit tripped him up and he stumbled.

"*Down! Down!*" came over the comm. He couldn't tell who was speaking but he dove for the ground, rolling sideways as a blade raked the pavement, sending up a shower of chips. He saw an upraised blade silhouetted against the lit face of a building, ready to impale him.

Then the shadow machine twitched and jerked as a stream of needles struck it. Its black surface bloomed with lines of tiny orange specks marking each hit. Then four minimissiles hit home at once and exploded, blasting the thing apart in a shower of parts.

Anton sat on the pavement, gently probing his face for cuts. His ears felt as if they were full of water, so that he couldn't make out what Atmin was saying to him until the bird switched back to the comm channel.

"*Did any harm befall you? Can you walk?*"

"I think so." He got cautiously to his feet. After that run his muscles were already feeling sore, and his knees gave off sharp pains when he put his weight on them. He coughed and got a mouthful of dusty phlegm, and spat on the ground.

The others began to gather around. Daslakh crawled about the wreck of the black machine, poking and probing with its limbs. Solana came over to Anton and helped him up.

"Hold still," she said, and reached for his face. She pulled a splinter of graphene out of his cheek, just a centimeter below his left eye. He hadn't noticed.

Jaka, of course, was practically incandescent. "Killer mech status: fragged! Whatever comes along, we can deal with it." She bent over the wreckage and picked up what looked like a sensor cluster. Three of its five lenses were cracked. "Not so tough now, are you?" she asked it.

The biologicals headed back to the clinic building, although Daslakh stayed behind with the ruined machine.

When Anton cycled through the emergency airlock the rest were already crowding into the exam room where their prisoner was shackled to the wall. Jaka stood before him, brandishing the smashed sensor cluster. "We got your killer mech. Adelmar hosed it with needles and I gave it a full barrage of missiles. Boom! No more mech! What do you think about that, Mr. Sabbath Okada? Still afraid of the big bad machine?"

The man pinned to the wall wasn't looking at Jaka. Instead his eyes were on the broken sensor cluster, and his face wore an expression of extreme puzzlement. When she finished gloating he finally looked up. "Very well done, but there's one little problem: you've killed the wrong mech."

For a moment nobody said anything. Even Jaka was silent.

"Have any of you actually seen a modern, high-end combat mech?" Sabbath continued. "Not security mechs or mercenaries from some matter-harvesting hab—I'm talking about the kind of weapon system you'd see Juren or Luna deploy."

"Saw one once," said Adelmar. "In the test area at Poincare. Me and a friend snuck in looking for weapons or scrap. Hid behind a boulder, absolutely ambient cold. The rock turned into a giant, looked just like my friend's uncle. Didn't say anything, just pointed at the rim. We ran."

"A top-quality combat mech is just a big blob of smart matter," said Sabbath. "It can take any shape it needs to." He jerked his chin at the broken piece in Jaka's hand. "Certainly not a collection of spare parts like that."

Daslakh strolled into the room on the ceiling. "I'm afraid he's right," it said. "That thing you shot up was just a bot, barely autonomous. Its main processor was from a cleaner. Calling it a mech is an insult to digital intelligences everywhere and I demand compensation."

Jaka tossed away the sensor cluster. "Okay, if it's just a bot with a salvaged brain—who made it? Who told it to attack Anton?"

"I told you," said Sabbath. "The real combat mech that's still out there somewhere. It put that thing together out of scrap."

"Ha! If this mech is so advanced, why would it want to build a clumsy scrap bot? Tell me that!"

"Maybe as a probe," said Sabbath. "To get a sense of what weapons we have at our disposal."

"I can think of another reason," said Daslakh. "Adelmar, how much is left in that needle rifle?"

"Magazine's at ten percent," said the chimp.

"And Jaka used up four explosive minimissiles. How many do you have left?"

"Enough to mess up anyone who tries anything," she said.

"Your mech's got a point," said Sabbath.

"I'm not *her* mech, I'm *my* mech," said Daslakh.

"I humbly beg your pardon."

By that point Anton's appetite for bickering was more than satisfied. He hurt all over and wanted above all things not to hear Jaka's voice. When all eyes were on Sabbath he slipped out of the exam room and over to the office, hoping for some quiet.

But when he opened the door he found Solana already there. She couldn't quite hide the look of despair when she saw him, although her expression quickly changed to cheerful attention. It didn't look creepy at all.

"Turn around," he told her. She spun slowly, raising her arms and stretching to display herself. "No, no," he said quickly. "I mean face away from me. Does that help?"

"Yes," she said after a pause. "What do you want from me?"

He glanced over his shoulder, but all the others were still arguing loudly in the exam room. "We have the same problem. Why don't we help each other?"

"No one can help me." Her voice was flat, stating a fact.

Anton took the little doodle sheet and stylus out of his pocket. Keeping his eyes aimed at the ceiling he scrawled, IMPLANT SEES AND HEARS WHAT I DO, ALSO COMMS. CAN YOU DISABLE? He hoped his blind writing was legible.

"I like to do microtech work," she said after reading it. "I'm pretty good at it, too. Especially when I've got my goggles on. I really wish I still had them—I'm looking forward to doing more tech work in the future." A little of the deadness in her voice went away.

"I'm sure you'll get them back," he said, and wrote: WHERE ARE THEY?

"They have an image filter," she said. "Faces look like blank ovals. Now that Jaka's got the goggles safe in her hip pouch, I can see faces again."

"Did you ever miss seeing them?"

"Well, it meant I couldn't do any cybernetics work. Can't work on a human if all you see is a big blue triangle or something. I've never worked on mechanical limbs, or implants, or anything like that. Just machines."

"Do you think you could do that if you tried?"

"I've never worked on a living person before. I'd be terrified of doing something wrong. What if they start bleeding? What do I do?"

"I'm sure you can think of something," he said, and wrote: FILL HOLE WITH MED FOAM AND TAPE OVER. WILL RISK IT.

"You know," she said, sounding very dismal, "when I look at someone, like you or Jaka or even Ulan, that person is the most important thing in the world at that moment. I'll do anything to please them. No one else matters."

"I've never understood why anyone would want a Qarina," he said. "If you want a partner who can't say no, why not get a sekkurobo and have done with it?"

"We don't just obey our masters. We *love* them. We want to please, and we can do that on multiple levels. When I see Jaka again I'll want to make her happy, whatever that takes."

In other words, she might reveal the plan. "You must be very good at that." He scribbled: KEEP HER TOO BUSY TO ASK. "How do you spend your time when she's not around?"

"When I'm out working, I'm working. Usually I'm paired with

one of her crew. She keeps me close when we're in the building, especially when it's sleep shift. I'm sure you've noticed." Both of them were all too familiar with Jaka's tendency to wake up at least once per shift and demand "stress relief" to help her get back to sleep. "Sometimes I just want to go back to being a Qarina all the time. Let other people make all the decisions."

"I know what you mean. I'm fighting a losing battle against this implant. Every day it gets easier to just go along and do as I'm told. I'm starting to *want* to obey her."

"Just like a Qarina. Tell me, Anton: why don't you simply order me to do what you want?" She turned around and looked into his eyes. "Come on, you know I'll obey you." As she spoke her voice and her expression softened. She no longer sounded bitter and sardonic, but sincere. "I want to serve you any way I can," she said, and he could tell that she meant it—for the moment, anyway.

Anton became aware of a sound outside. One of the others? It wouldn't do to be found conspiring with Solana. He shifted his hand to the back of her neck as he lightly touched his closed lips to hers. His other hand went around her waist, barely touching. He felt her lips trying to kiss him back, and her body pressed against his. It felt perfectly natural, perfectly real. It would be so easy...but he rejected the thought.

"Hey," said Daslakh. "If I can interrupt your dubiously consensual sex activity for a minute, the other biologicals want you to get to work in the kitchen."

When Anton turned to follow the mech he didn't have to pretend to be embarrassed and flustered. In the instant before he looked away from her he saw Solana smiling at him, but he couldn't tell if it was real or not.

CHAPTER ELEVEN

Sabbath Okada was a model prisoner. Shackled to the wall of the exam room by Jaka's smart-metal strips, he didn't scream or curse or make demands. He was always willing to make polite conversation, and occasionally expressed regret about the urine and feces streaking his legs and the wall.

Jaka had them watch him in pairs, and it was no coincidence that each pair contained someone allied with her or under her control in some way. The following day Solana wound up partnered with Utsuro. For safety she hung back, keeping her eyes on the floor or the walls, anywhere but Sabbath's face.

Utsuro cleaned him up and then gave him some soup through a straw. "Thanks," said Sabbath when he was finished.

"I would release you if I could," said Utsuro. "This is inhumane."

"You could rip these restraints off the wall with one hand," said Sabbath. "I promise I won't stop you."

Utsuro didn't answer for a moment. "Not now. I still don't trust you enough. Besides, it would tear the skin off of your arms."

"You've wiped my ass for me, why can't you believe what I say?" asked Sabbath.

Another pause, and then Utsuro said, "Your genes and mine are identical. Why?"

Sabbath glanced from Utsuro to Solana, then shrugged. "Made in the same lab. We came out of adjacent shikyus within hours of each other. We played and trained together for twenty standard years. We had the same job and the same boss."

"*Who am I?*"

"Are you sure you want to know?" asked Sabbath, and he didn't sound as if he was joking.

"Yes. Please tell me, I beg you."

Sabbath took a deep breath and expelled it. "All right. Your name is Basan Okada."

Utsuro was silent for several seconds. "Say it again."

"Basan. Your name is *Basan*. Remember when we snuck down to Pavonis?"

"We rode on the outside of the elevator capsule, and glided down from ten kilometers up. Three of us. You, me, and...Ikkita."

"Anything else coming back?"

"I went to Titan. Ikkita was there, too, I think. She and I—"

"You were lovers, and both of you thought you were keeping it discreet. We all thought it was hilarious."

"After the mechs fixed me I tried to remember my life, and there were other bits but none of them fit together. I remember being a man, a neuter, a woman, and a herm. Was I a dragon, once?"

"That's all you. We were both dragons—working undercover in the Magonia cycler."

"Undercover? You make us sound like detectives, or spies."

"Operatives. Do you remember who we worked for?"

"Major Gaulteria," said Utsuro promptly, and then hesitated. "But who was she? I don't remember."

"It's complicated, and I'll explain everything once we get away from this bunch of idiots."

"Just tell me why I was here in Safdaghar—was it a mission?"

"Yes. A little covert op. You were part of a team. It all went wrong."

"What happened?"

"I don't know all the details. You and a mech were infiltrated into Safdaghar, inside a cargo pod with sensor masking. Your job was to bag a subversive hiding here. Shortly after the mission was to commence, Safdaghar went dark. Our bosses aborted the retrieval. That's all I know."

"Please don't lie to me. If any of what you say is true then obviously you must know far more than that. Who was the target? Who was the mech? What was the plan?"

"I wasn't part of the mission so I don't know the plan, and all of this got wiped after... whatever happened here. You were teamed with a mech named Kamaitachi. I never met it, but Kamaitachi had an excellent combat record. You two worked together before. This should have been a piece of cake."

"The target? Was I sent to kill someone?"

"You weren't the one to pull the trigger. That was Kamaitachi's mission. Your job was to identify and locate the guy. He was a Martian dissident. All we knew was his pen name: Pasquin Tiu."

For a moment Utsuro said nothing, his face displaying a question mark. "I think I understand why you asked if I wanted to know. From what you've said, it sounds as if I was some kind of professional killer. I wish it wasn't true, but it matches what I remember."

"We did all kinds of ops. You were one of the best." Sabbath hesitated just a second. "Okay, look, I've been spying on all of you for a while now. I watched and I listened. And I recognized you. Right away, I could tell. Inside that cyborg shell, with no memories of who you are, you're my brother Basan. But it's as if you've been reset, or something. You're more like what I remember from when we were kids. Kind. Helpful. Always looking for the best in people. All the cynical callous professional agent stuff is gone, and I can see the real you again."

Just then Utsuro stopped and turned his head to face the door. A second later Solana heard footsteps and saw Jaka and Adelmar approaching. Utsuro stepped out into the atrium to meet them.

Jaka had been talking about something but she went silent as she saw the cyborg standing in the doorway. His face screen showed a red hazard symbol.

"I insist that you release this man Sabbath at once," said Utsuro, with his speaker volume cranked up so that everyone in the building could hear what was happening. "He is not trying to rob us and he was not responsible for Ulan's death, or anything else that has happened. Your treatment of him and all of us has been cruel and inhumane."

Jaka regarded Utsuro for a moment, still with a faint smile on her face. "Hormone dispenser giving you extra testosterone today? Or did our guest sell you some sob story?"

"Release him now. Your thumbprint will deactivate the restraints."

"No. Are you going to pull it off?" She held up one fist, thumb upraised, and wiggled it. "I think you've spent enough time with that guy. He's messing with your brain. Go look for something valuable."

After a moment Utsuro replied, "I will not give up. You will release him."

"Maybe so, but not today."

Utsuro went outside, leaving Jaka in possession of the field. She smiled and looked into the examination room. "Solana, take a break. We'll let Okada think up some new improbable story. Maybe he's secretly Adelmar's father. I'm looking forward to hearing it."

Everybody in the building heard the confrontation between Utsuro and Jaka, and everybody outside got the news in seconds. The tension between Yanai's team of scarabs and Jaka's crew had been building for days, and now they all were waiting for the storm to break.

Solana was doing some much-needed maintenance on Anton's laser backpack when Atmin fluttered down to perch on her shoulder. "I think it would be helpful if you do not get this done before Utsuro comes again. The fewer weapons Jaka and her group can wield, the better it will be for us."

"She told me to cycle the batteries and lubricate the tracking servos."

The bird's claws tightened on her. "You cannot see her face right now. Why do you still obey? I beg you, leave the work undone."

Solana felt herself blush. Why hadn't she thought of that herself? She was reverting to her childhood self, eager to serve and obey. "I'll finish with the servos, but I'll leave the batteries dry."

"That leaves all the armaments on Jaka's arms and Adelmar's. We need to separate the two and leave her with no backup in a fight."

"It won't be easy."

"I do not wish to see a fight break out. If violence can be minimized, will you at least stand with our team?"

"I don't know. Without my goggles—"

"Have you no free will at all? I beg you to resist the urge to give her your obedience."

"It's really hard. I'll try to keep my eyes closed."

"Do what you must. Stay out of sight of her if that will help. When you are done with this, join me upstairs at Pera's bed of pain. Whatever Jaka says, the time has come to send our injured friend back to Yanai."

She hurried through the work, then cautiously looked out. Jaka wasn't directly in sight, so she sprinted to the stairs and got up to Pera's room without interference.

The dino lay on her left side, with the bed supporting her torso, a chair piled with pillows holding up her head, and her tail stretched across the floor. She still wore the top half of her armored suit, but the rest was heaped in the corner of the room. The stump of her missing leg was at eye level for a standing human, and Solana couldn't help staring at the smart-matter bandage.

It had sealed itself over the exposed stump of Pera's leg, and Solana could make out where it had formed tubes to link itself into Pera's circulatory system, pulsing with her heartbeat.

"Damned thing's made for humans," Pera grunted. "Can't make enough painkillers. Hurts more now than when that snare got me."

"I tell you now that pain relief awaits you at the hub. Yanai can care for you but we must lift you to her care."

Pera raised her head to look at Atmin. "You going to hold me in your beak? Or use both feet?"

"All we need to do is get your bulk downstairs. The bots can bear your weight from there, at least to take you to the spoke, where with a sturdy cable good Yanai can draw you up a kilometer to the hub. In micrograv, with other bots to help, you can proceed to Yanai's care."

Pera nodded. "Sounds good—but what about you? And her?"

"I hope to send Solana up with you, to help you make the lengthy climb. Once there she can remain as safe as you." Atmin cocked his head at Solana. "I trust you will approve that plan."

She nodded, but inside felt a mixture of emotions: fear that

Jaka would find out and stop her, fear of *disappointing* Jaka by leaving, and down below all that a spark of hope.

"Utsuro," said the dino. "I heard him laying down the law to Jaka. He won't go."

"I understand his righteous rage at how our prisoner is kept. But frankly I admit I cannot find that man Okada worth the life of any one of us. I do not like to leave him here, but if we must, we shall."

"He says he's Utsuro's brother," said Solana.

Bird and dino exchanged looks. "Is he?" asked Pera.

"He knows things about Utsuro. Helped him remember. If they aren't brothers, they were close somehow. And he looks like that reconstructed image of his face Utsuro showed us."

"It matters not to me," said Atmin. "We still must get poor Pera to Yanai. Utsuro must decide what he will do."

"Pretty cold," said Pera.

"Would you wait for his return? I fear some conflict will result, and how then will we get you out of here?"

"Okay. Get my suit on me and find my laser," said Pera. "Whatever happens, I'm going to need them both."

Getting a two-hundred-kilo dinosaur into her armored suit took a lot of time and effort. Even with the suit's quick-seal systems and self-adjusting material, Pera had trouble getting it on. Solana had to help roll her from side to side, and more than once wished Utsuro was on hand to lend his strength.

Atmin went in search of the laser, and came back using his sphere's limbs to crawl awkwardly along, dragging the powerpack on the floor with the actual laser weapon trailing at the end of its power cable.

With Pera fully dressed, Solana improvised a pressure seal on the missing leg of her suit so she could manage in the airless hub.

"I wish we'd kept the leg," said Pera.

"An extra fifty kilograms of meat and bone would be a lot to move," said Atmin. "By now black mold and other filth has spread upon that limb, and cells within are dead. Simpler far to grow one fresh for you. Now we should not delay. Solana: find the bots and ready them to move our Pera to the spoke. All other preparation I can do."

Solana hurried downstairs and found her own suit, but just

as she prepared to seal the hood over her head she felt a tap on her shoulder.

It was Jaka. "What's up?" she asked cheerfully.

"I need to check the bots."

"What for?"

"Maintenance."

Jaka stepped in front of her and looked directly into Solana's face. "It makes me sad when you try to lie to me," she said. "What's going on?"

"Atmin wants to use the bots to help Pera get to the spoke, so Yanai can pull her up to the hub."

Jaka's eyes narrowed, but then she smiled again. "What a great idea! That bird's a clever one. I'll see if Adelmar can help. If we all pitch in we can get your dino friend moved safe and sound up to Yanai. Go on, get to work. Sorry to interrupt."

Solana sealed up and went through the airlock. Outside the silence seemed even more oppressive. The bots were nowhere in sight. She sent out a ping on their channel. No reply. She tried again, then linked up to Yanai.

"*Where are the bots?*" she asked. "*I need them. Atmin wants to move Pera to the spoke.*"

"*They aren't responding,*" said Yanai. "*The last status check was four hours ago—they were responding to a tag on the opposite side of the ring.*"

"*We haven't checked that part yet,*" said Solana.

"*Can you move Pera without them? It will take time to print a new one and send it down.*"

"*She's heavy. We'll need someone strong. Maybe Utsuro can do it.*"

"*He is approaching your position now, but has shut off comms.*"

Solana spun around and saw the big cyborg marching stiffly up the center of the street. His face screen still showed the hazard glyph, and the bright red in the darkness looked very sinister.

She waved to catch his attention. "Are you all right?"

"I am well," he said. "I have been thinking. I didn't want to act on impulse, or do anything unwise. But I have made up my mind: Jaka must be stopped. Her treatment of Sabbath Okada is cruel and unjust, and I fear she is putting all of us in danger by ignoring his warnings."

"Atmin wants to move Pera first."

"That is a good idea, but I think we should take Mr. Okada with us. I will not leave him behind."

"Be careful, Utsuro."

"I will be fine. Letting us all leave is the most logical thing for Jaka to do. She will have the entire wealth of Safdaghar for herself. There may be some posturing to satisfy her ego, but I'm sure she will agree."

He cycled through the airlock. Solana followed, still fearful.

Jaka, Adelmar, and Tanaca were in the atrium, sitting on couches facing the entrance. Solana couldn't see Anton. But she could see that both Jaka and Adelmar were armed. They had their missile pods on, and Ulan's needle rifle was on the floor within reach of Adelmar's right hand.

"Get out here. Utsuro's back," she sent to Atmin.

The cyborg walked into the atrium and stopped about five meters from the couch. "Jaka, I must insist you release Mr. Okada. We will take him back to Yanai now and depart Safdaghar."

Her golden lips were smiling but she shook her head. "Sorry. He's too dangerous. If I let him out of those restraints he could kill us all. How about this: why don't you and Adelmar help the dino get to your ship? Much more sensible. Then we can talk about it all together. Maybe take a vote."

"I will not listen to your words. You twist the truth and distract everyone from what is important. If you will not release Okada I will do it myself."

He turned toward the exam room where Sabbath was shackled, but Jaka leaped up from her seat on the couch and hurried to block his way. "No, no, no, you don't! This affects all of us. You can't just decide on your own. We should reach a consensus."

"Get out of my way."

"No. You're being unreasonable. We should talk it over."

Utsuro took a step forward. "I'm afraid I won't take no for an answer any longer. You will do as I ask."

"Or what?"

Utsuro took another step toward her. "You cannot stop me."

"Don't touch me!" shouted Jaka. "He's threatening me with harm!"

"I am not threatening you. Get out of my way."

Solana saw Adelmar behind Utsuro, reaching for the rifle. She wanted to scream, to jump down to the atrium floor, do something—but all she could manage was to clutch the top railing of the gallery and watch in horror.

Utsuro and Jaka spoke at the same time. "Don't come—"

"Please let—" He reached for her.

"Help!" Jaka screamed, and Solana screamed with her, involuntarily. Four minimissiles shot from the pods on Jaka's upper arms.

One struck Utsuro's face, shattering the screen and his sensor cluster. The second curved around to strike the back of his abdomen, where the power unit was. The other two shot straight forward at the armored sphere in his chest holding his brain.

All four of the little shaped-charge nitrogen-polymer warheads went off simultaneously. Utsuro's head blew apart into glitter, his power unit sparked and began to emit black smoke, while clear support fluid gushed from the ragged holes in his chest.

Still upright, Utsuro clamped one metal hand onto Jaka's wrist, and Solana heard a staticky comm signal. *"Please . . . Don't . . ."* The comm shut off and Utsuro fell heavily to his knees, still holding Jaka's arm.

"Shoot it!" said Jaka, tugging desperately at her trapped arm. Adelmar obediently emptied the needle rifle into the kneeling cyborg. White-hot pinpoints blossomed all over Utsuro's back, and dark red streaks appeared in the leaking fluid.

"Help him!" cried Atmin, swooping past Solana to dive at Adelmar's face with claws extended. The chimp stumbled back, flailing with his free hand, but the bird swept past untouched and circled back to land on the bleeding cyborg.

Solana took the stairs in three jumps and grabbed the emergency kit from the pile of gear just inside the entrance.

Jaka finally managed to pry Utsuro's fingers open and stepped away from the body, breathing heavily, her eyes fixed on the motionless shell. "He was going to hurt me! You all saw! I had no choice!"

Solana struggled to even find how to apply the treatment patches to Utsuro's metal body. She tried wrapping one around a broken tube but it didn't seal on.

"I've got no vitals from Utsuro," said Yanai inside her head.

Solana used her all-purpose tool to get the blackened metal of Utsuro's chest open. The brain tank inside was cracked, and she could see burned wires and severed tubes everywhere.

"Jaka, I need my goggles," she said.

It took Jaka a second to shift her attention from Utsuro to Solana. Then she shook her head and backed up a few steps. "No. Not on your life. Not now."

"He's going to die!"

"Dead already," said Adelmar quietly. He pointed with the barrel of the rifle at four needle holes in the back of the brain case.

"You planned this in advance. You murdered him—and who will now be next?" Atmin croaked.

The accusation snapped Jaka out of her panic. In the face of physical danger she showed real fear, but in the realm of words she was once again supremely confident. "I was in danger. You all are witnesses. He grabbed me. I'm just a legacy human, much weaker than a big machine like him. He could have killed me. I think he might have broken my arm." She rubbed it, a bit unconvincingly.

"Utsuro never would do harm to any living thing. The only danger was that he defied your power here and threatened to deprive you of a victim for your spite."

"You're crazy. Everyone saw it. Adelmar and Tanaca can back me up. It was self-defense. He shouldn't have attacked me."

"I will not hear your lies," said Atmin. "Begone and take your pirate thug band with you. This we should have done before you set a single foot upon the decks of Safdaghar. Begone, I say."

"Who's going to make me leave?" said Jaka, calmly and quietly. "None of you are armed. I guess that puts me in charge, not you. It's for my own safety. From now on everybody does what I say or else."

"Or else what?" said Pera. Solana looked up to see the dino supporting herself on the parapet around the upstairs gallery. She had her laser in one hand, pointed at Jaka.

Solana stood frozen, helpless. She wanted to please Jaka, but watching Utsuro die was more than she could bear. Out of the corner of her eye she noticed Daslakh crawl under a chair. Anton stood in the kitchen, his posture oddly stiff—as if Jaka had told his implant not to let him do anything.

"Well, hi there," Jaka called up to Pera. "I didn't expect to see you up and about. How's the leg?"

"Take off your missile pods. Tell the chimp to do the same."

"Of course, of course. If that's what will make you happy." Jaka pulled the pods off her upper arms and set them down on the floor in front of her, then nodded to Adelmar. The chimp tossed down the needle rifle and then took off his own pods, but kept them in his hands. "See?" said Jaka. "Safely disarmed. Now you put away that laser."

"No. Leave. All of you. Now."

"If you really want us to, fine. I wish I could stay, though—it'll be pretty entertaining to watch you get all the way back to the hub with nobody to help you but the bird."

"Solana and I can manage."

"Solana's coming with me—aren't you, dear?"

She didn't want to. She wanted to help Pera. Somewhere deep inside her she wanted to smash Jaka's grinning face. But what she said was, "Yes, if you wish."

"See? We've bonded."

"Give her the goggles and then let her choose."

"I don't have them on me. I've got a better idea." Jaka looked directly into Solana's face as she spoke. "Solana, please take Pera's laser away from her. It will make me very happy if you do that."

Solana didn't hesitate. All the horrible conflict went away once she had a task to perform, and someone to please. She trotted briskly up the stairs.

"No, Solana. Stop this," said Pera, still watching Jaka. "Listen to me, I'm trying to protect you."

"Give me the laser." She held out her hands.

"No. Go away. You don't have to do what she says."

"Please?" When Pera didn't respond, Solana took a deep breath and then grabbed at the laser in the dino's arms.

Needless to say, it was no contest. Pera's arms looked small and weak compared to her massive legs and torso, but they were still bigger and stronger than any un-augmented human's. Solana might as well have tried to arm-wrestle a construction mech.

But her futile tugging did get Pera to glance at her, and that was all the distraction Jaka needed. She snatched up her missile pods and rolled behind a couch for cover. An instant later four micromissiles arced up from her hiding place and curved toward Pera. At the same moment Pera pulsed her laser at the couch hiding Jaka, setting it on fire.

Then the beam went wild, scrawling a black line all over the atrium as everyone downstairs scrambled for cover. The missiles struck Pera's arms but did not explode. Solana heard the hiss as they injected something through the armor.

"Stim. Hip pouch. Hurry..." said Pera, and then fell over like a tree toppling.

Jaka watched for a second to see if she moved, then called up, "Solana, would you get that laser pack off her? I think we can all agree it's safer that way. Anton, Adelmar, get that stupid lizard back into the treatment room and see if there's any way to restrain her or lock the door from the outside."

"And what of me, for only I remain now free of your control?" asked Atmin. "Shall I return to Yanai and depart, my work all forfeit to your greed? Or will you murder me in turn?"

"Nobody murdered anybody. Your cyborg pal was threatening me. I have a right to protect myself. The same with Pera. You'll notice I even used tranq rounds on her. That shows restraint. She'll recover in a few hours, good as new. Except for the leg, of course."

"Or did you scorn to use a lethal round to strike at Pera as she stood in pain because you had none ready then to fire? Yanai, I think it time for us to leave. My plans have failed, and nothing now remains to keep us here."

"Have fun moving your one-legged dinosaur," said Jaka.

Yanai spoke via comm, limited now to just Solana and Atmin. *"You have to get Solana out as well."*

"What reason do I have for doing that? She has betrayed us all."

"Not voluntarily."

"That matters not a bit. If she can make a choice, then treason has she picked. If she cannot, then neither you nor I can change her mind. No matter if she merits pity or deserves to suffer blame, the end result is still the same. I say, away, and leave her here."

"No," said Solana. *"I want to go with you. Please?"*

"If Jaka bid you stay with her, what would your answer be?" asked Atmin.

She couldn't respond.

"Atmin," said Yanai, *"do you believe this Sabbath person? You are better at reading humans than I am."*

"Of him I cannot say if he speaks truth—or simply has great skill at telling lies. The former is my guess, for I do not believe in Jaka's claim that he has come to scare us off and so reserve the choicest loot. This hab is big. Far simpler would it be for him to

hide from us, and gather goods from places we have yet to check, then leave with us no wiser than before. I do not think that he would injure Pera then reveal himself to save her life."

"That means there really is some threat still hiding in the hab. The bots are gone. You need the help of the others to get Pera out. The chimp, at least. You have to win his loyalty away from Jaka."

"And how shall I accomplish that? I have no bribe to offer him, for anything of value he can simply take from me. I am no threat. And I would be a fool to even try appealing to his sense of right and wrong."

"As I said, you're better at interactions with biologicals. Figure something out. Change the conditions."

PART III

Dragon

CHAPTER TWELVE

With no one left to challenge her authority, Jaka moved fast. After dinner she decided it was time to interrogate Sabbath. She took Solana into the exam room with her and set her to work preparing the tools. "I'll need some heavy-gauge metal wire, and a heat source. Also a couple of scalpels and a strong piece of carbon rod, about a meter long."

Once everything was assembled, Jaka took a seat facing Sabbath, with a cold drink handy. She motioned for Solana to stand next to her.

The prisoner, as always, stood calmly against the wall in his restraints. He'd been like that for days, yet Solana had never seen him even relax. He hadn't slept at all. The only sign that he was actually a biological rather than a mech was the urine on his legs and the floor.

"All right, dear, is the wire hot?"

Solana took it off the resistance heater, using her own tool set to maximum insulation. The ten-centimeter length of wire glowed yellow, and sagged a bit under its own weight.

"Hold it up to his face. Feel that? Feel how hot it is? Do you want to feel it on your tongue, or in your eye? I'm prepared to be reasonable, here. Just tell me what I want to know. What did you come here to get?"

Sabbath shook his head sadly. "I've told you the truth. I came here because there's a killer mech on the station. You're all in danger. I don't want any of the stuff here."

"Solana, touch it to his lip. Now."

Solana winced almost as if it was her own, but obeyed Jaka's instruction. The glowing hot metal touched Sabbath's lower lip and a wisp of white smoke came from the point of contact. It stuck to him and she had to yank it free. The smell of burning flesh was awful.

He didn't scream. Jaka seemed disappointed. "You've got more skin than that, some of it more sensitive. No point in grandstanding."

"I'm a professional. This isn't going to work." His speech was a little distorted by the burn on his lip, but Sabbath showed no sign of noticing.

"Well, eventually you'll just die. Keep that in mind, because if you don't tell me anything useful I've got no reason to keep you alive."

"There is a combat mech in this hab, and it's going to kill you. That's a very useful thing to know."

"Liars get punished. Solana, write your initials on his chest."

She felt tears in her eyes. "Please, don't make me do that."

"I'm helping all of us. Besides, you heard the man: he's a professional. He won't mind. Indulge me, Solana. Write your initials on him."

"I'm sorry," she whispered, then scrawled a quick SS just over his clavicle. He looked more annoyed than in pain.

"Let's try this from the other end," said Jaka. "Who do you work for?"

"Major Gaulteria. She's based on Juren. I do covert ops for her."

"Never heard of her."

"Of course you haven't. I said covert ops—naturally she keeps a low profile. This is pointless."

"Not if I find out what she sent you here to get. Why else would you come? Solana, heat up the wire some more, it's getting cool." The metal was still visibly red, but Solana obediently put it on the resistance heater again.

"I'm telling you the truth. I'm not here for salvage. I came here to warn you. Hurt me more and I'll just start making up lies to please you."

Jaka smiled. "That might be fun."

"He's right. You're wasting time," said Daslakh from behind her. It was clinging to the wall behind them, just below the ceiling, and had been wearing the same greenish-beige color as the wall panel. No telling how long it had been there. Now it turned deep blue—attention-getting but not aggressive. "He's obviously had training, and probably some nerve work as well. You can make him into yakitori and he won't talk if he doesn't feel like it."

Jaka glared over her shoulder at the mech. "He'll never tell us anything if he hears you talking that way."

"It's called realism. You're showing more physical response than he is. Get your jollies when the mission's over."

"You weren't so bossy when you begged me to get you off Scapino."

"Then, I had a bunch of debt collectors tracking me. Now I'm more worried about this combat mech."

"Assuming it even exists!" Jaka turned back around and looked at Sabbath with a sulky expression. Then she got up and very deliberately kicked him in the testicles. "Maybe you can ignore the pain, but I can still damage you. Next time it won't be a hot wire, it'll be a cutting blade. Understand? Come on, Solana. I'm tense."

When Solana finally managed to get away, all the biologicals were asleep and Daslakh had vanished into some private universe, like a cat or an odd sock.

She contacted Yanai. *"I think I know how to get Pera out of here,"* she said.

"The bots haven't checked in. I'm printing up another one but it will take time. I had to send out one of my maintenance units for some scrap."

"All we really need is some kind of wheeled cart. I'm sure I can put one together pretty quickly. The others are all asleep."

"Can you make it with materials from inside the building? Wandering alone outside is too dangerous."

"Working inside would make too much noise. I'll stay close by." She got into her suit slowly and quietly, and remembered to mute the airlock chime when she cycled out.

Without her goggles she had to use a hand lamp to see, and the beam was maddeningly narrow and faint. Being able to see just one cone of light in the darkness of the hab made her very aware of what might be hiding in the places she couldn't see.

She remembered finding a food vendor's movable cart with wheels, lying wrecked against a building in the next block. She tried to walk silently—not because she had any illusions about being undetected by a machine which could certainly see her shining in infrared, but so that her own straining ears might hear it approach.

It took her forever to walk half a block, and the lights of the med center looked infinitely far away. Her nervousness kept threatening to bubble over into outright panic. The cart was where she had seen it, and she knelt to take a look. All four wheels were intact, which was a relief. They had actual bearings and were big enough to get over the debris in the street. The frame was made of sturdy carbon rods, but some of the joints had cracked. It was no longer a structure but a mechanism. Putting Pera's mass on it would flatten the whole thing out.

The first step was to cut away the upper section, the aluminum and ceramic cooking surfaces, the broken fuel tank, and the insulated drawers which had once held farm-grown prawns and peppers but were now lined with mats of mold.

She stopped, suddenly terrified. She could hear a humming mechanical sound steadily approaching. She switched her tool to knife mode and stood up, ready to fight or flee. The humming grew louder, and then she almost giggled as she realized it was above her. Atmin's travel sphere.

"To be out here alone is madness, courting death or harm. What purpose brought you here when all do sleep?"

"I can make a cart for Pera. You two can get to the spoke."

"And what of you? I dread whatever Jaka may intend."

"At least I can help you two. Maybe once you're away you can do something. See if any of the big habs around Jupiter might intervene. A little obscure group like the Salibi managed to bust up the Kuma operation all the way out in the Kuiper. Surely a giant hab like Juren or Chac could do as much right in their backyard."

"The life of one mere human, even of a hab like Safdaghar, is not of value to the great. But be assured that I, along with Pera and Yanai, will work unceasingly to find and rescue you."

Solana felt tears start in her eyes, but just then Anton's voice came over the common channel. *"Atmin, Solana, please check in. Are you all right?"*

"We two are well and still in sight of home. You need not fear."

"Jaka woke up and saw you two were gone. She wants you back here right away."

Over their private link Atmin said, *"This all was my idea. Remember that, and let me deal with Jaka."*

Solana was dreading what would happen when they got back so much that she forgot to be fearful walking in the dark. Atmin was less sanguine, constantly flicking his spotlight around.

Jaka met them in front of the medical building. She had Pera's engineering laser in her hand with the power pack slung over one shoulder. "Have a nice stroll?" she asked.

"We sought a cart to move poor Pera's bulk," said Atmin. "Your summons made us stop that vital work."

"Mm-hm. I'm getting very tired of everybody trying to lie to me. I start talking about what hidden treasures might be here, and you two sneak away in the middle of the night without telling anyone. It doesn't take a fourth-level intellect to figure out what's going on. So: what is it, and where did you hide it?"

"It is a cart for serving food to passersby or spectators at festivals and sporting meets. It lies upon its side, not eighty meters hence, just over there. Its value is too low to count in gigs—or infinite to us, for getting Pera safely out."

"Then why were you sneaking around? I think getting that dino bitch out of here is a fine idea. You both know that." Her eyes narrowed inside her bubble helmet. "You're trying to fool me, but you won't. I'm smarter than any of you. Solana!" She looked directly at her as she spoke. "You help Tanaca: start lining up the loot right here. And get me a chair. We're going to find out what the bird is hiding."

She sprawled in the chair and refused to let Atmin go inside while Solana and Tanaca worked. After about twenty minutes two dozen items stood facing the clinic, spaced a meter apart down the middle of the street.

"That looks good. Now, Mr. Atmin, this is your last chance to stop lying to me."

"I have not lied to you, nor did I violate the terms agreed. Unlike some people I do not go back upon my word."

"I wish I could believe that, but I don't. I've looked at all this loot and none of it is worth the trouble of coming down to the rim and searching houses full of mold and corpses. You could make just as good a haul up at the hub."

"Perhaps we could. My own opinion is that handmade goods hold value greater than mere mass."

"Oh, I'm sure you can find some idiot with more gigajoule-equivalents than brain cells at Juren or someplace who's willing to buy these things just because they're unique. But let me propose an alternative hypothesis, one that fits the facts just as well if not better. I think you know about something, some particular thing here in Safdaghar that's worth more than a cargo hold full of heavy elements. And, being a clever bird, you didn't bother to mention it to me because you're afraid I'll grab it."

"I swear to you there is no thing that you could take which I would lie to keep."

"Yeah, but that's just what you'd say if you were lying, isn't it? So instead I'm going to do something called an experiment, to test my model against observed phenomena. It's a unique opportunity and I'm not going to pass it up. See that statue? The blue glass one?" She took aim with the laser and lit up the statue with a sustained pulse of orange light until it shattered.

"I do not understand what purpose you pursue by vandalism of this kind," said Atmin.

"How about that ink painting?" Jaka adjusted the laser tuning and then set the paper on fire. They watched it burn for a moment. "See, most of this crap is useless to me. You claim you can find buyers at Juren or wherever, and maybe you can. I'm pretty sure the goons and grifters at Scapino won't give a pinch of dust for any of it, so even if I get half it's half of nothing. What's that thing?" She put a red targeting spot on a rectangular object covered in cloth.

"A book, of paper sheets, with words inscribed by hand and illustrations likewise done. It tells a story, like an entertainment but in text, of conflict in an ocean under ice."

"Any hot guys in it?"

"There may be one or two."

"Can you have them fuck?"

"The story has no way to choose. The author did not write it so."

"Too bad, then." She played the beam over the book until it blazed merrily. "If an entertainment has hot guys and no fucking, what good is it?"

"I beg you, do not waste these things we have put so much work into retrieving. Although you think they have no worth, I say that you are wrong."

"I'll make you a deal: you tell me what you're really after, and I'll put away the laser."

Atmin hesitated, then flapped his wings inside his sphere. "Then hear the truth. I did not tell you this before, but now I will because I cannot stand to see you wantonly destroy these things of beauty wrought by human hands. We came down to the rim to seek a treasure of great price, as you indeed have guessed. A poem, by a Martian bard, unknown to any data net, the last work of a man who died with Safdaghar. His name was Pasquin Tiu—at least, that was the name he signed to what he wrote. The value of a poem from his mind, all new to those who read, might be in petajoules or more. Enough to make it worth our while to search."

In answer Jaka aimed the laser at a rolled-up handwoven carpet and ignited it. The odor of burning wool penetrated everyone's filters. "That's ridiculous. How can anyone tell if it's real? You could just make up some handful of dust and claim this Pasquin guy wrote it."

"A baseline mind can analyze the text and style, and greater minds exist which can do more."

"I bet forgers can, too," she said. "Nice try, bird, but I'm not buying it—any more than anyone's buying some poem by a dead guy. Whatever you're looking for, it's not that." She methodically melted the face off of a metal statue. "So where is this poem?"

"My search has failed. If Pasquin left behind a final work, he did not write the words on paper with a brush, as usual for him. I fear it was inside his head, unfinished, on the day when death arrived to silence him for good. Which means each work you burn is one we cannot sell."

Jaka tuned the laser to infrared, then used it to score the surface of a mirror-finished egg until bits fell off. "You know, this laser's got preset frequencies that go right through diamond. Minimal energy loss. I could set your feathers on fire and boil your little brain."

"Remember that Yanai can still avenge her crew. I tell you just the truth. As Sabbath did. Why can you not believe what you are told?"

"Why should I? If I trust him—or you—I come out of here with some craft projects which may or may not be valuable. But if I believe there's a treasure, something small and priceless, then I'll keep questioning you and searching. Maybe I'll find it. You see?"

"This is a waste. A waste of time, of energy, and worst of all a waste of precious things. I will not watch you do this anymore." With as much dignity as a bird inside a clear hovering bubble could muster, Atmin flew away.

This has to end, Solana thought. I have to stop this. We have to get out of here. But what can I do? I can't disobey Jaka. I can't fight her and Adelmar. I can't do any of those things.

What can I do? she asked herself again.

She followed Jaka inside the medical complex and got out of her suit, even the liner. "Jaka, I had an idea about Sabbath. What if I question him?"

"You?"

Solana stretched in a way that had always affected visitors to Kumu like a dose of current to the brain stem. "What if I can make him want to cooperate?"

Jaka smiled, almost a leer. "Probably won't work but it'll be fun to watch anyway. Okay, give it a shot." She planted her chair just outside the exam room door and flopped down in it. "Hey, Sabbath—take a look at this."

Solana walked into the room and struck another pose, inviting and seductive.

"See? She's a Qarina. Ever heard of them? Bred to be the ultimate sex partner. Even better than a virtual experience. She can be yours if you give me what I want."

His burns were already blistering, he was tired and filthy, and Solana could tell Sabbath didn't believe a word of Jaka's promises. It didn't matter. Jaka was enjoying herself.

"Clean him up and put some foam on those burns. Show him how nice you can be."

Solana began by smearing him with cleaning goop, then calling it back to the tube. He didn't react to the touch of her hands, but he did give a little sigh when she rubbed the medical cream onto his burns. ("Work it in all over!" Jaka called out.)

Then, since his own arms were still pinned to the wall, she used a squirt bottle to pour broth into his mouth.

"Thank you," he said after his first long drink. "At the moment that's the finest meal I've ever had. Hunger is the best spice." He looked into her face. "Are you really a Qarina?"

"That's right," she said. "What are your wishes?" She looked him straight in the eye, her expression serious rather than seductive. "What do you want me to do?"

"It has been a bit cold and lonely in here," he said. "I'd love to feel your skin pressed against mine."

Solana didn't hesitate. She flattened herself against him, avoiding the burned places. Behind her Jaka gave a cackle of delight. "See? She'll do whatever you want. Ready to tell me why you're here?"

Sabbath nuzzled her ear. As he did, he whispered, "Tell your friend on the wall behind you to open the freezer where my suit is."

Using the pretext of baring her throat to his lips, she risked a glance over her shoulder and saw Daslakh standing on the opposite wall of the exam room, out of view of the doorway. The little mech's skin turned safety green, then reverted to a beige exactly matching the wall.

"Please tell the mech to open the freezer. That's all I need."

Solana gazed into Sabbath's face. "Why not me?" she murmured, trying to make it sound like something seductive.

"I don't want you to be punished if anything goes wrong. That mech seems old and cunning. I figure it'll be fine."

She opened a link to Daslakh and passed the message.

"Perceptive little monkey," said Daslakh.

"Don't be shy!" Jaka called from where she sat watching the show. "Show him what you can do!"

"Dance," suggested Sabbath.

Solana took a step back and began one of the routines she had learned during her childhood in Kumu: an utterly sensual display guaranteed to capture the attention of every human in visual range. As she turned and writhed she could see Jaka, completely fascinated. Anton stepped into view behind her, also unable to look away. Even Tanaca showed more interest in Solana than in anything since her arrival at Safdaghar.

The attention was intoxicating. Solana knew it was mostly conditioning and genes making her feel that way, but she enjoyed it anyway. As long as she danced, *she* was the master. All eyes

were on her, and every human watching desired her. Her movements commanded their minds and bodies, and she knew it,
and she loved it.

With all of them watching her, nobody had the attention to
spare for a little beige mech quietly crawling along the ceiling
and out the door.

She took Sabbath's air of detached amusement as a challenge.
She went all-out, bringing her bare body close to his but never
quite touching, displaying herself and then turning away, and
pantomiming desire and submission. When she saw him reacting,
she felt a glow of triumph. She was irresistible, even to a man
who could control his own heartbeat.

"*Okay,*" said Daslakh over their private link. "*It's open.*"

She spun closer to Sabbath again, brushing her lips against
his and whispering "Open" before pulling back.

"Long sobs of autumn violins," said Sabbath loudly, in archaic
Altok. An instant later Solana heard a loud crash from the kitchen.
She didn't stop dancing.

But whatever was going on had stolen her audience's attention. Jaka looked alarmed and dove for cover behind a planter,
dragging Tanaca with her.

Adelmar hadn't been watching her performance, having little
interest in displays of human flesh. He'd been dozing on a couch
but the noise from the kitchen brought him awake at once. He
gave a loud snarl and hurled himself at something outside Solana's
field of view. She heard a meaty *smack* and the chimp went flying
across the room and struck the opposite wall with a loud grunt.
He slid to the floor, looking groggy.

"You might want to get out of the way," said Sabbath. Solana
flattened herself against the wall as what looked like a two-meter,
starfish-colored rescue orange cartwheeled into the room. It leaped
at Sabbath, wrapping itself around his body and limbs, forming
itself into a suit. The smart matter severed the restraints from the
wall and Sabbath stepped forward. The suit completely encased
him, and then its surface shifted and changed color. The head
and hand coverings turned transparent, while the suit coating
his body became a very flattering black formal outfit with gold
embroidery at the collar and cuffs.

He looked down at himself and gave a little smile of satisfac-
tion. "Much better. The whole time I was shackled to the wall

I was keenly aware of how shabby I must have looked. It was a very painful experience."

Jaka stood up from behind the planter. "If you try anything I'll destroy you," she said.

"No, I don't think you will. Though I wish it were otherwise, I am not your biggest problem at the moment. We all need to get out of here right away."

She gave a snort. "What pile of dust are you going to unload now? Why do we have to leave?"

"Sixteen years ago, before his body was destroyed and he had to be borged up, Utsuro came here as part of a team on a mission. He was named Basan back then. The mission failed and he was nearly killed. The other half of the team was a combat mech named Kamaitachi. Not their first pairing; the two of them worked well together. In revenge for Basan being injured, Kamaitachi killed the entire population of Safdaghar. Shot them until it ran out of needles, then sliced them apart or smashed their skulls. You *killed* him. What do you think it's going to do?"

"I don't believe any of this," she said.

"I don't care what you believe." He raised his voice. "We are evacuating now. Suit up and gather enough supplies for a climb to the hub. Call the bird back here. Arm yourselves. I'll help Pera. No time for delay."

Solana pulled her suit liner back on and then hurried upstairs for her gear. Jaka didn't stop her.

Twenty-five years earlier...

It was the party of the year. The Jovian year, to be precise. Every 11.86 standard years, Voskemat Urvakan hosted an elaborate ball at his palace in the giant habitat Juren, which occupied the L1 point between Jupiter and the Sun. Over the course of four centuries Voskemat's party had become one of the most important social events for the richest and most famous biologicals in the solar system.

Voskemat declared that his thirty-fourth Jovian Year Ball would be an "intimate affair for my most fascinating friends" with a guest list limited to just 1,156 people. This created a social shock wave that destroyed friendships and marriages and sparked one actual shooting war between habs in Jupiter's Outer Ring. To maintain the "intimate" tone, the host prepared two hundred extremely realistic duplicates of his most attractive body, each fitted with full-sensory telemetry back to the tank where Voskemat's brain floated in bodiless tranquility. A near-baseline autonomous mind inside each skull could fill in when his attention was elsewhere.

The palace itself was an endless maze of pavilions and arcades sprawling through a square kilometer of gardens stocked with custom-designed plants. The whole thing stood atop a three-story disk holding all the mundane systems and services necessary to keep the place running, which in turn was supported on pylons half a kilometer above the waters of a lake surrounded by other fancy private estates, as if held up for less exquisite beings to admire. During the week before the party the entire structure was surrounded by a privacy shield, a great mirrored bubble to keep snoopers with bots or powerful telescopes from peeking at the guests. Other security measures, less visible but considerably more potent, ensured the safety of the partygoers. The triumvirate of superhuman minds that ruled Juren had a strong and direct interest in maintaining security and took no chances.

As the ball got underway, nobody noticed that there were three extra copies of Voskemat in the palace. Who expects the host to crash his own party? Even Juren's powerful intelligences couldn't match Deimos's ancient agencies for subtlety.

Sabbath Okada took a roasted candyfruit off a hovering tray and smiled at the half-dressed girl reaching for one at the same moment. His implant informed him that she was Arrat Heshtot, currently the acknowledged Ascended Master of the Ninety-Fifth Level of Initiation in the Mysteries of the Hidden Emperor. She had conducted a ten-week sexual affair with Voskemat eighty standard years ago, was three hundred forty years his senior, and was seven hundred million gigajoule-equivalents in debt to the Quantum Bank of Callisto.

He flagged her as potentially useful, gave her a wink, and turned away. That brought the target for the evening into view: Pavo Neskuita, a nice young man who was the avatar of Titan Psychoactives, an autonomous corporation taking human form in order to conduct a dynastic merger with the ruling family of the comet Oterma.

Sabbath, Basan, and Ikkita were at the party to counter a plot centered on young Pavo. Someone among the thousand other guests was secretly an operative of the Trojan Empire, with orders to sabotage the upcoming marriage by engineering a humiliating faux pas for the young man.

Unfortunately, weeks of investigation hadn't revealed who that Trojan operative was, which meant that Sabbath and the others couldn't simply arrange for an inconvenient accident or unexpected delay to keep whoever it was away from the party. And for Deimos to reveal an interest in the dynastic affairs of Oterma and Titan Psychoactives would wreck other long-term projects. So the three agents had to accomplish their mission on the scene, in complete secrecy.

Besides, it was more fun that way, Sabbath thought.

At the moment, Pavo was talking biochemistry—and showing genuine understanding and insight—with an elephant-headed man. Sabbath's implant identified the gentleman with the trunk as Xiu Li, a drug artist from Luna. His origin alone made him worth keeping an eye on. The rivalry between Deimos and Luna was an immutable law of nature. Sabbath pantomimed spotting someone beyond the pair and walked in that direction, pausing as he passed them.

"Enjoying yourselves, gentlemen?" he said, and patted Xiu's bare shoulder. Voskemat was notorious for making skin contact, which meant it was easy for the sensor web in Sabbath's hand to check Xiu for anything unusual.

They smiled and nodded and said inconsequential things, he smiled and nodded and said inconsequential things back to them, then edged past Pavo and waved at nobody in particular. Meanwhile Sabbath's implant processed the molecules on Xiu's skin. Water, sebum, salts, urea; a whole suite of tailored organisms; a lot of aldehydes—he must be on his second bottle of spiced brandy already; a mild euphoric produced by one of his symbiotic bacteria strains; and the chemical background noise of the room and other guests.

Still, it might be worth intervening. See if Xiu displayed any reluctance to be separated from Pavo. Sabbath didn't rush, but circled the pavilion on a seemingly random course over the next ten minutes. He bit into a pickled prawn and followed it with a shot of subzero vodka. Nice fringe benefit of this job—actual once-living food and top-quality liquor. Sabbath appreciated the finer things.

By the time he drifted back to Pavo, Xiu had gone off to have a dip in the cold pool, so Sabbath just hung back and watched the young man. Pavo was tall and good-looking. His corporate parent had wisely avoided any of the fashionable faces, instead picking a set of features that made Pavo not just handsome but *interesting*. People would remember him.

His clothing, of course, was flawless: a classic Titan-style loose tunic with a high collar and turnback cuffs, worn over hose that showed off well-shaped calves. Sabbath could see that the outfit was made by human hands, from cloth combining smart matter and real animal-hair fibers. Exactly right for a young man with enough wealth and status to ignore mere fashion, yet conveying respect for tradition and confidence in his position.

Behind that interesting face was a brain which would be genuinely fascinating to any neuroengineer. Translating an autonomous corporation—which existed chiefly as a set of policies and heuristics—into neurons and glial cells had required building the boy's brain on a nanoscale scaffolding, training dendrites like the branches of the topiary figures in Voskemat's garden. Combining that with high intelligence, psychological stability, and the right blend of flawless social skill and controlled aggression had cost Titan Psychoactives about a billion gigajoules. Licensing some of the new techniques had offset that expense, but the royal marriage to Oterma was a prize well worth the effort.

A young woman dressed as a pre-spaceflight Earthwoman with a tricorn and a gold mask stumbled and bumped into Pavo. With hardwired good manners, the young man took her hand to steady her. Their eyes met and both smiled.

Sabbath instantly went on high alert—leavened only by sheer incredulity at how amateurish it was. Would the Trojans actually try something that obvious? He pinged Basan and Ikkita, and hurried forward, as if to help.

"Is this brute manhandling you, darling?" he said, in a flawless imitation of Voskemat's meta-ironic manner of speaking. "As soon as you give him a good thrashing, I'll have him thrown out." He patted her shoulder to see what she might be dosed with. Would it be aphrodisiacs? Hallucinogens? Perhaps a subtle enzyme to interfere with alcohol processing?

"I'm all right. Just learning the gravity here," she said. Curiously, she gave Sabbath a cheerful wink before turning her attention back to Pavo.

Ikkita checked in. *"She's a fake. Name's Enkoyito Tifi, but that identity's only twenty hours old. Can you genotype her?"*

His implant was on it. *"No matches in Juren."* An anonymous genome was a sure sign of a covert operative. The sensor web on his palm had turned up some interesting results. The young woman's skin was well-garrisoned with defensive nanobots and tailored organisms, but he couldn't find a trace of any offensive chemicals. No sign of any intoxicants, either. Elevated estrogen, but within natural parameters for her apparent age and condition.

"How did she get in if she's got a brand-new identity?" asked Basan. *"Maybe we should just tip off Voskemat's security."*

"We *got* in," said Ikkita.

"Yes, but we're the best," said Sabbath.

Separating the two young humans required all three of them.

Basan homed in on Pavo, feigning brisk concern. "Master Neskuita, a word with you, if I may. There is an autonomous message from Titan asking to be allowed into my house network. It insists it is for you and has an authentication code. Do you know anything about this?"

"Probably junk," said Pavo. "I'm not expecting any messages. Please ask it to redirect itself to my suite, and I'll deal with it when the party is over."

"Normally I would not have troubled you," said Basan. "People who get messages at parties are generally too dreary to bother inviting. But there was a combination of urgency and mystery about this one that intrigued me. Are you enjoying yourself?"

"Yes, thank you," said Pavo. His body was already half turned away, but Basan in his Voskemat disguise wasn't ready to let him go.

"Have you visited the game room yet? There is a marathon session of Tiedao in progress. You might enjoy playing a few rounds."

"I'm afraid I don't gamble," said Pavo, now looking around in bewilderment. "Do you know where Miss Tifi has gone? I was just talking to her."

In point of fact, Sabbath and Ikkita had moved to bracket her as soon as Pavo was distracted.

"Come with us. No time to explain," said Ikkita. They led her to one of the balconies off the salon and set the privacy filter on the window so that it only showed silhouettes. Ikkita guarded the door while Sabbath gently guided the young woman to a chair and stood over her.

"All right, honeytrap. Who are you, really?" he demanded.

She looked puzzled. "It's me, Uncle Vosko," she said, and took off the mask. "What's wrong?"

Sabbath had no idea who she was—but evidently she expected Voskemat to recognize her. Time to be cagey. "I know who you look like, but that could be fake. State your name so my devices can see if you're lying."

She drew herself up proudly, sitting straight-backed as if the chair was a throne. "My name is Ausarta Calent, Princess of the House of Buntala, Baroness Entawru, and Heir-Apparent to the ownership and sovereignty of Oterma. *Now* will you tell me what's going on?"

Oh, hot dust, Sabbath said to himself. He had forgotten that there was another class of people whose genomes were kept secret, besides spies and operatives: extremely rich and powerful people who had to worry about impostors or personalized viruses.

"Just a passing whim. I am ruled by impulse," he said in Voskemat's voice.

"*But what's she doing here?*" asked Basan. He and Ikkita were on an open loop, seeing and hearing everything along with Sabbath.

"*Yes, what possible reason could she have for coming here and checking out the kid created specifically to marry her?*" said Ikkita. "*Almost as if she's hoping their relationship won't be a loveless legal fiction. How crazy is that?*"

"*Voskemat must be in on it,*" said Sabbath over the private loop. "*He's known her father since they were in school together, before Ezten married Queen Sabela.*" To Princess Ausarta he smiled, and said aloud, "Forgive me, my dear. I didn't recognize you in that outfit at first, and my suspicions got the better of me. I feared you might be some impostor attempting to prey on young Pavo."

"*We've been played,*" said Ikkita. "*Whoever planted that story about the Trojans trying to interfere must have known she was coming and set us up to interfere.*"

"*Well, no problem, then,*" said Sabbath privately, and then, "I hope this brief interruption doesn't spoil your rapport with the lucky fellow. By all means, go back to what you were doing, and good hunting!"

"*Guys? Problem,*" said Basan, and let Sabbath and Ikkita see what he was seeing.

Another woman had taken advantage of Ausarta's absence

to claim Pavo's attention, and she was doing a superb job of it. Her outfit was a swarm of glowing microbots whose movements and color changes were carefully crafted to tantalize, revealing glimpses of a flawless body without being blatant. All coupled with a cloud of pheromone perfume and disinhibitors to prepare the sexual battlespace.

But her real weapon was how she could play to her target. Every movement, every gesture just oozed sexuality. She was mirroring his movements, continually reducing the distance between them, and she kept her eyes locked on his with pupils dilated to display utter fascination. Even if Pavo recognized he was being manipulated, it would still be flattering to see that such an attractive person found him worth manipulating. And the centuries-old Autonomous Corporation mind was incarnate in a human boy in his teens. Not exactly a hardened target.

"Meili Tewu," said Ikkita. "Ident is ninety-five percent certain."

"Looks like the Trojan agent story is true after all. Hey, Sabbath, remember that time she poisoned you?"

"Vividly."

Meili Tewu was a freelancer, an operative clever enough to do the deniable jobs that great powers preferred to use outside talent for—and cunning enough to survive the inevitable tidying-up afterward. They had crossed paths three or four times, including one attempt to tidy her out of existence after a bit of false-flag wetwork.

"How do we get her away from him?"

Sabbath considered his inventory of weapons and other covert devices. He had monofilament concealed in his hair, diamond-edged fingernails, and binary poison glands in his thumbs. One tooth contained a tiny pellet of nitrogen polymer which could blast a hole in armor plate. He knew a dozen ways to kill a human with just his bare hands. "Um . . ." he said.

Basan took a bowl of ras malai from one of the circulating serving bots, cleared his throat, and announced, "And now I think it is time for an intimate little FOOD FIGHT!" He hurled the bowl with perfect accuracy, hitting Meili right in the face with a mass of sweet spiced cheese in cream.

Evidently Basan had sensed some unspoken zeitgeist in the room, for the other guests joined in with gleeful abandon. Ascended Master Heshtot pelted a chimp in a fabulous lace gown with a berry tart. The angel nuledor Sierra Hal ducked a thrown bombe and swung her shrimp brochette in a wide arc, sending a volley of curried crustaceans into the crowd. A cyborg entertainment-writer, who didn't even eat, dumped a plate of avocado croquettes inside the trousers of a famous mercenary captain—who responded by smearing a handful of durian marmalade over the diamond sphere holding the borg's brain.

Sabbath blinked in astonishment as the room devolved into a culinary version of the Sixth Martian Uprising, and then urged Princess Ausarta forward. "Now's your chance!"

She grinned and charged at Pavo with a plate of jellied escargot. Sabbath went to "assist" Meili, dabbing at her eyes with the corner of his silk toga. "Now, now, my dear. It will be all right," he said in a loud voice. More softly he added, "Come along or I'll have to kill you."

Meili looked at him, then both of them glanced at Pavo and Ausarta, who were trading shots of unagi mousse. When Pavo paused to lick some of it off Ausarta's collarbone, Sabbath smiled.

"Drat," said Meili.

"Looks like you've failed your mission," said Sabbath. "I've heard the Trojans can be pretty harsh about that. Have you considered changing employers?"

"Not until this minute, but yes."

"Let's discuss it while we exfiltrate."

"Certainly," she said. "But first—" She snatched a plate of vindaloo from a passing bot and dumped it over his head, blinding him with bubbling-hot sauce and intense spices. By the time he could see again she was gone.

Just then smart-matter hands gripped him very firmly in six places, as a pair of servitor bots lifted him off the floor and carried him over the heads of the crowd. He didn't break character as Voskemat, waving cheerily at the other guests as several took potshots at him with falafel balls and giant carp eggs.

"*Time to fade now,*" he told the others, but even as he said it he saw a second Voskemat in the grip of three bots on a converging course.

"*Too late,*" said Ikkita. No sign of Basan, though. Sabbath hoped he had gotten away.

The bots descended and passed through the door to a private side-chamber—evidently provided for confidential deals and quick

sexual assignations. The smart-matter furnishings had all with-
drawn, leaving nothing but smooth, soundproof walls and floor.

Six more Voskemats followed them in, accompanied by another
bot carrying what Sabbath's implant identified as a golf bag.

"First of all," said one of the Voskemats, "I wish to offer the
pair of you my genuine and sincere thanks. You have ensured
that this party will be talked of for the next Jovian year, if not
beyond. Thank you."

"I'm glad we—" Sabbath began.

"*However*," Voskemat continued, cutting him off, "for crashing
my party and interfering with my guests, I regret that I must
break as many of your bones as possible before I throw you out.
I'm sure you understand."

"We'll call for Juren security," said Ikkita. "You can't do this."

"You are both some kind of covert operatives, and I am entirely
confident you have absolutely no desire to attract the attention of
Juren security. Feel free to prove me wrong." Voskemat paused, but
when nobody said anything he continued, "In the absence of state
justice, I must resort to private vendetta." The six un-restrained
Voskemats took meter-long steel rods from the bag, and five of
them advanced menacingly toward Sabbath and Ikkita.

Before the beating began, the lead Voskemat hesitated and
frowned. "Wait—" he said, looking at the last clone, who stood
calmly by the door with his steel rod held in a defensive posture.

The stray clone smiled, and Sabbath's implant detected an
attack program trying to shut his brain down. But as soon as
the software recognized him it stopped—unlike the programs
afflicting the other Voskemat bodies and the two servitor bots,
all of which stood completely inert, with no more agency than
the golf bag on the floor.

"As you said, time to fade," said Basan. He slapped a smart-
matter patch onto his own face and Voskemat's features were
replaced by those of an independent gossip journalist who'd been
kicked out of the party twice already. He stuffed his toga into
the bag while his tights reshaped themselves into a pricey but
obviously mass-market set of mirrored scales. Sabbath and Ikkita
busied themselves doing likewise, and the three of them went
out of the room via the garden entrance, nodding and smiling
to the guests they passed.

They managed to get to within a hundred meters of the

edge of the disk before Sabbath heard a swarm of humming servitor bots approaching at top speed. His implant flooded him with adrenaline and endorphins, and the three of them sprinted across the garden at a good fifty kilometers per hour. Beyond the parapet at the edge was a sheer drop half a kilometer to the surface of the lake.

"Why didn't you get out on your own?" Sabbath said to Basan via implant as they hurdled over the parapet.

"I couldn't leave you two behind."

"You're mad, do you know that?" said Ikkita. *"Absolutely mad and I love you."*

As their bodies sliced into the waters of the lake, Sabbath had time to add, *"If Pavo and Ausarta aren't happy together I swear I'm going to kill them both."*

CHAPTER THIRTEEN

The group gathered in the atrium, sorting gear into three piles: essential, possible, and abandon-in-place. Anton kept moving things out of the first two piles onto the third. They wouldn't need food, or sleeping sacks, or entertainments. Just weapons, tools, and medical supplies. Solana kept her eye on Jaka, wondering what she would try.

Pera contacted Yanai on the group channel. "We're getting out now. There's a combat mech on the loose in the hab, probably with some serious cognitive bugs. Time to leave."

"*I agree. Never mind about the salvage. I'll send out some bots to bring you up with the hoist,*" said Yanai. "*It can probably manage two at—*" Her voice was cut off by a burst of static, followed by silence.

"Yanai? Yanai!"

A second later a distant rumble echoed through the hab ring.

"That doesn't sound encouraging," said Daslakh.

"Can anyone hear Yanai on comms? Yanai, are you there?" asked Pera.

"Could she have undocked? Maybe that was her drive firing," said Jaka.

"I cannot make myself believe that good Yanai would leave us here in peril of our lives," said Atmin.

"Any eyes up there?" asked Sabbath.

"I've got one. Tapped into one of her bots," said Daslakh, and shared the feed with the others.

It was jumpy slow video, but it was horrifying enough. Yanai's massive frame was completely severed, just behind the crew compartment. Her drive section floated free, tumbling and banging into the walls of the docking hub. Twinkling fragments looked like a heavy snowfall in the image. The tug powerful enough to move an entire hab was now just wreckage herself.

"Is this your combat mech at work? Could it have blasted poor Yanai? How can we fight against a foe like that, with weapons that can wreck a ship?"

"Kamaitachi didn't have any heavy weapons," said Sabbath.

"I know who did," said Pera, glaring at Jaka. "You're the one with the mine aimed at Yanai's processor section."

For just a moment Jaka's mask of perfect mastery slipped, and she looked on the verge of panic. "No! I didn't order—" She stopped and suddenly she wasn't just on the verge anymore. "It fired but I didn't do it! I swear! It said proximity alert and then it went off before I could do anything! It's not my fault—something got too close and it fired. It wasn't me!"

They all watched Jaka. Nobody said anything until she ran down. By the time she was done she was crouched on the floor, looking wildly from one face to another.

"Well, I guess we're stuck," said Daslakh. "I figure you guys have about six months before equipment failure and starvation get you. Forgive me if I don't watch. I'll find a place to hide in low-power mode for the next few decades. Nice knowing you."

Suicide, Solana thought. A quick death before we start to get sick and starve. Before we have to decide who to eat. She wondered idly if Jaka had actually triggered the mine on purpose, just to enjoy the experience of killing something as vast and strong as Yanai.

"Shuttle," said Adelmar. "The mine was aimed up, not down. Might be okay."

"If it wasn't crushed by the wreck I assume Kamaitachi is in the process of stealing it as we speak. It's the logical thing to do," said Daslakh. "Get out, get to someplace civilized."

"Ah, but you forget: it wants to kill us," said Sabbath. "One by one, just as it killed the population of Safdaghar. It will save the shuttle for afterward, when there's no one left to hunt."

"Not us," said Pera, gesturing at Jaka. "Her. She's the one who killed Utsuro. *She's* the one it wants. I say stake her out on the deck outside and leave her. Maybe the rest of us can get away."

"A plan I will endorse, so let us act without delay," said Atmin.

Jaka still crouched on the floor, but her expression of panic had vanished and now she looked positively feral. "I'm still in charge here, not any of you. Adelmar! Show this cocky lizard who's boss."

The chimp didn't move. "Got to save ammo. Might need it."

"Very sensible," said Sabbath.

"Solana! Tanaca! Protect me! Anton, get the weapons."

Tanaca moved hesitantly toward Jaka, apparently uncertain as to what she was supposed to do. Solana positioned herself between Jaka and the rest. Anton stood immobile, then twitched as his implant sent a jolt of agony directly to the pain center of his brain. The only limit to the pain it could inflict was his ability to feel it. But he had felt a lot of pain in his life.

When he still didn't move, Jaka increased the intensity. He dropped to his hands and knees but made no movement toward the closet where his laser backpack and Tanaca's plasma breacher were stashed.

"You'll regret this," said Jaka. A moment later Anton's implant took over control of his limbs. He stood and began to walk jerkily toward the closet.

Meanwhile Sabbath strolled calmly toward Jaka. "Let him go," he said.

Solana knew she had to stop him. Protecting Jaka was very important. She flung herself into his path, trying to block him like a Gendakhel goalie. Sabbath stopped and merely looked deeply into her eyes. In a calm, confident voice he said, "Solana, go sit down. This is no place for you. That's an order."

She smiled at him and walked away.

Jaka realized what was happening and scrambled away from Sabbath but with a swift lunge he caught her by the arm. Tanaca punched his shoulder but he ignored her.

"Stop it!" he shouted, finally showing a crack in his calm self-assurance. "You're not going to win and you're wasting everyone's time!"

Jaka writhed and struggled, twisting herself around to kick Sabbath in the face. But the suit he wore absorbed the blow as if she were kicking a stone statue. He frowned slightly and then smoothly shifted his grip, holding her in a modified half-nelson with her feet off the floor. She kicked helplessly and flailed with her free hand. Tanaca stood nearby.

Anton's body turned around, moving toward Sabbath with arms outstretched. Nobody else did anything.

"Stop it," Sabbath repeated, and kicked Jaka in the ass. Since the blow didn't shatter her pelvis he must have been using his own muscles, not the suit's strength. "There's no reason for anyone to keep you alive. Do you understand? *None.*" He kicked her again, and then a third time. "Now behave yourself. Stop it!"

Anton reached Sabbath and his hands grabbed the man's suited arm. Sabbath glanced at him, shook his head, and tossed Anton into the nearest couch. Then he sighed and touched one finger to the back of Jaka's neck. Her eyes unfocused and then she went limp, hanging like an empty suit in his grip.

For a moment nobody said anything, then Daslakh asked, "Why didn't you just tranq her right away?"

"I wanted to kick her first." Sabbath turned to face the group and raised his voice. "All right, time to get out of here. We need to get to the hub and there's a covert-ops mech trying to stop us. What's our ammunition status?"

"I've got four hundred and thirty-four seconds of laser power left," said Pera. "And a four-shot gas pistol loaded with shaped-charge rounds."

"Eight micromissiles, all explosive," said Adelmar. "Jaka's got two paralyzer missiles left."

"The laser backpack has only a hundred seconds of power," said Anton.

"Don't forget the plasma breacher. One shot, but it's a good one," said Pera. "Almost as much juice as that mine."

"What about you?" asked Daslakh.

"Me?" said Sabbath. "Oh, I've got a couple of stored megajoules I can use in various ways, and some darts. I won't bore you with details. Now: let us collect all the tools and supplies we have on hand, and decide what we absolutely can't leave behind. No time to waste!"

While he spoke Anton moved to stand near Solana. "Now," he whispered to her. "This may be our only chance."

"I still need my goggles," she said.

"Here." He unsealed his coverall at the ankle and pulled her goggles out, pressing them into her hand. "Don't put them on until we're out of sight. Upstairs bathroom. You go first."

As the others started moving around the medical center, Solana went briskly up the stairs. In the bathroom she put on her goggles and activated the visual filter.

Once again she lived in a safe world of shapes and objects. No faces. No desire to serve. She could be selfish again. It felt good—though there was always that vague regret. Could she be unselfish without her genetic programming?

Anton slipped inside and locked the door.

"How did you get them?" she asked, tapping her goggles.

"I didn't. Daslakh did. I wrote on its shell. This thing"—he tapped his forehead—"can hear what I say and see what I see, but it can't tell what my hands are doing behind my back."

"What does Daslakh want in return?"

He smiled. "When it gave them to me it said, 'Keep them on her face from now on.'" When she still looked suspicious his smile turned sad. "Not everything has a price attached."

"There's always a price. Sometimes you just can't see it until it's too late."

"If you don't help me I expect the price will be at least a couple of fingers when Jaka wakes up."

He lay down on the floor and they improvised a brace to raise and immobilize his head. Solana got her tool settings ready, and laid out her sparse medical equipment: wipes, tape, medical foam, a fistful of random drug patches. And then she knelt over him... and hesitated. "I have to turn off the visual filter again," she said.

"Are you afraid I'll go back on my word? Of course, you could do the same. Instead of deactivating the implant you could reset it, key it to yourself. I'm sure you've considered it."

"Yes," she said after a long pause.

"Well," he said, "I leave it to you. I'm going to concentrate on keeping my head very still and not thinking about the fact that you're poking around inside my skull."

She shut off the filter and then zoomed in on the top of his head between the ridge of his forehead and the crest of his skull. The pitted, hairy moonscape was nothing her brain recognized as a face.

Cutting a slit in the skin was messy but not hard. Like all scalp wounds it bled like mad. Solana had to swab and swab just to clear away blood as she cauterized the tissue with the hot tip of her tool.

"I don't mean to bother you," said Anton, "but my eyes are filling up with blood. Can I wipe them?"

Solana zoomed back out and nearly gagged. Anton looked as though he'd been murdered. The little one-centimeter slit in his skull had somehow generated enough blood to completely cover the upper part of his face. She rummaged in her pocket and found a sterile wipe. "Here, use this."

He got the worst of it out of his eyes. "I'll keep the scar as a souvenir, to remind me to keep my mouth shut."

She put a strip of tape across his eyes. "You may lose your eyebrows but this should keep the blood out. And now you really have to hold still," she said. "I've never worked on an implant before. I'll try not to damage you."

"If you do, I probably won't care," he said, and smiled. She zoomed in again and his face became nothing but a work site once more.

She made her tool into a drill and bored through his skull, going carefully, a micron at a time, and then pausing to check if she was through. Underneath the bone layer was the dura mater, a membrane thin enough to just poke her tool through, avoiding the blood vessels which showed up bright on infrared.

Inside the dura mater Solana switched to the eye in the tool tip itself, controlling it through her own implant instead of with her hands. At that scale the blood vessels in the pia mater layer hugging the brain looked like drain pipes. She was able to maneuver the tool tip around most of them but there wasn't much she could do about the blood getting into Anton's brain from his scalp. Either it would harm him or it wouldn't.

The tip of the tool extended deeper into his head, pushing gently between his brain hemispheres. And there it was: his compliance implant, nestled between them like a little gray millipede snug in a pink bed. Fibers led from it to his optic and auditory nerves, and down to the brain stem.

Her plan was to locate the implant's own tiny brain and disable it, leaving the comm interface intact. She switched the tool to ultrasound mode and fed the image to her goggles. Now she could see the implant's innards. The power tap extended down between Anton's frontal hemispheres to the top of his sinuses, generating a trickle of electricity from the temperature difference between the center of the brain and the nasal passages. Best to leave that alone. The comm used that same tiny gold fiber as an antenna.

She could make out three separate processors. One of them was obviously the basic implant device that nearly all humans had inside their heads after infancy. It had bundles of fibers extending to the visual, speech, and aural cortexes of Anton's brain, all leading to a conversion processor which turned electronic signals into nerve impulses Anton's brain could understand, and vice versa. That one could stay.

The other two were connected, and had fibers extending down into Anton's brain stem and thalamus. One of them was probably his bio monitor, providing information about the state of his body more useful than evolution's crude "I feel ouchy" signals. The other was the compliance device, the spy in his head. But they used the same basic electronics. She had no way to tell them apart.

The whole image trembled, and she realized Anton was speaking. "She's talking to me," he whispered.

All three tiny processors were active. Solana could see shifting patterns of heat and electrical impulses. "Try to stall her," she said.

Lots of activity, and then everything shook as Anton's whole body jerked. Solana lost her grip on the tool for a moment, and the only reason it didn't slip and tear into Anton's brain was the implant itself, anchoring the tip in place.

"Can't—make—me," Anton grunted. He tensed up again. This time Solana tried to pin him down, putting her entire weight on his chest. But as he jerked in pain she could see a little heat pulse from the active processor in the implant. The snitch.

She maneuvered the tool's micron tendril toward the traitorous processor, but she could see it sending impulses into Anton's brain stem. Something touched her back and she realized it was his hand. The hand bumped her, and then it hit her, hard. And again, and again. With Anton's eyes shut and no tactile sense, Jaka couldn't tell what the arm was hitting, but she could make it swing as hard as Anton's muscles could manage.

He wasn't a big man, but he had spent a lot of time doing physical drudge work and had grown up full of testosterone. He could hit hard. The blows were random, striking Solana's side and back, nearly knocking her off him. She got her knee onto his arm and put all her weight on it. The arm continued to jerk under her, and she simply wasn't big enough to hold it down.

Trying to ignore the commotion around her body, Solana concentrated on the image coming from inside Anton's head. His movements had shifted the tip of the tool nearly a centimeter from the implant, and getting it back to the device seemed to take forever.

"Stupid Jaka," he said through clenched teeth. "Ugly and—" His words became a groan and his whole body stiffened as the implant tormented him again. Solana realized he was doing it on purpose, goading Jaka into causing him pain to buy her time to work.

The quicker the better, then. The tiny tip of the variable tool found the implant again, and she directed it to the active processor. No time for subtlety; she cut the device's carapace open and plunged the hardened point into the layers of membrane-thin diamond wafers housing the processor.

Anton spasmed even harder underneath her, and Solana felt a stab of terror in her own mind. Had she killed him? All his muscles relaxed and he went limp.

He was still breathing, and she could feel his heartbeat. She quickly cut through all the snitch processor's connections, isolating it—inputs, outputs, power, everything. It would be inert matter inside his brain. When she couldn't find any other fibers to cut, Solana sealed up the implant's shell again with the broken processors inside it. Having bits of diamond floating loose in Anton's brain seemed like a bad idea.

She withdrew the tool and switched back to her goggles to look at Anton. Body temperature looked okay, but he was still unconscious. Had the implant done that? Or Jaka? Or had Solana damaged something and left him as good as dead?

She found the little canister of medical foam and filled the incision, just squirting it in as though she was caulking a leak. It was crude and sloppy but it would protect him against infection and stop him from leaking blood and cerebral fluid. Another strip of tape covered the wound, and then she peeled off the eye covering.

His eyes twitched back and forth under closed lids. Was that good? Solana didn't know. With mixed hope and dread she shook him. "Hey. Anton, wake up. Anton!"

The eyes opened, staring out unfocused, and her heart sank.

Then they moved, found her goggles, and she could see his attention lock on to her. The dried blood and gunk around his eyes cracked and flaked as he smiled.

"She's gone," he said hoarsely. "No comm, either."

"I must have cut something," said Solana. "I'm sorry. You can get it fixed."

"It's okay. Quiet in here. I like it." He cleared his throat. "Thank you."

She helped him to his feet. They both were covered in blood and foam. "You look terrible. How do you feel?"

He concentrated. "Bio monitor still works. It says I'm alive. I really need to wash my face," he said, and hit the sink icon on the bathroom wall. The sink extruded itself and he used about a liter of warm water to wash the blood off his face. Solana gave him a sterile wipe to dry off with, and when he was done he looked at her and grinned.

When they went back downstairs there was no need for any embarrassed explanations. "New hole in your head?" Daslakh asked Anton.

"I needed it."

"Fuel up now," said Sabbath. "We're moving out."

"Where's Jaka?" asked Anton.

For a moment nobody said anything. Solana looked around, her goggles sliding up and down the spectrum. "Not in here. Tanaca's gone, too."

"And the chimp," said Daslakh.

"The shuttle," said Sabbath. "No time to lose."

"They can go faster," said Pera. "No dead weight."

"Now, now," said Sabbath. "Don't be defeatist. Can Jaka even fly a shuttle? Maybe we can bargain."

"You're assuming she's thinking rationally. That's unwise," said Daslakh. "She's quite capable of persuading herself she's an ace pilot, and wrecking the shuttle before she can even get out of the docking hub. Still leaves us without any way home."

"Best get moving, then. If anybody's hungry you can eat while we walk."

Pera's size and horizontal posture created a tricky problem when it came time to help her walk. Her arms simply weren't strong enough to take the place of her missing leg, and they were in the wrong place, to boot. Even with stout aluminum poles in both hands she couldn't keep her pelvis from tilting sideways, and after just a few hobbling steps the strain meant she had to stop.

Sabbath tried to support her, with one of her arms draped over his shoulders, but she could only move forward in tiny hops, just a few centimeters at a time.

"This pace is like a glacier grinding over Pluto's plains," said Atmin.

"All right," said Sabbath with a sigh. "There's one other thing we can try."

He got Anton and Solana to brace Pera upright while he crept under her abdomen, legs and back bent. He got his back under her center of mass and then with a grunt lifted Pera off the ground. "How's this?"

"I feel like you're going to drop me," said Pera.

"Best I can do," Sabbath grunted.

With him—or, more accurately, his strength-amplifying smart-matter suit—carrying Pera the group could move at something like a normal walking pace. Atmin took the lead in his travel sphere, watching for traps ahead. Daslakh and Solana followed, using their augmented vision to look for hidden tripwires or triggers. To be doubly careful, Solana used one of Pera's discarded metal poles to prod the ground.

They went down the middle of the street, though Daslakh complained. "We're very exposed out here."

"Kamaitachi can hear us coming," Sabbath grunted.

"What's to stop it sniping at us from long range? We'd be safer with some cover."

"I don't think it has any projectile weapons still working," said Sabbath. "All its attacks have been with blades or traps."

"What about Ulan? It shot him with a tranq dart before killing him."

"Oh, that was me," said Sabbath. "The dart. I didn't mention it because I thought you'd figure it out once I revealed myself."

"We've been a bit distracted," said Daslakh. "So . . . did you cut him up, too?"

"I thought about it, but I didn't. Kamaitachi must have been somewhere nearby."

For a moment nobody said anything, then Solana spoke up. "Thank you."

"My pleasure."

They covered another couple of blocks in silence, and were more than halfway to the spoke when Daslakh made a discovery. It had gone off to one side to investigate something, and suddenly turned bright hazard red in the darkness. "Hey! There's blood on the ground here. Lots of it. Still warm. And I just found a finger."

Atmin's sphere gained altitude and he scanned the area with his searchlight. The rest of them hurried toward Daslakh.

"Whose finger is it?" asked Anton.

"The chimp's. Definitely."

They found the mech standing at the edge of a great red splatter ten meters across. It had a bloody finger in one hand, held away from its body so as not to get dripped on. Solana's goggles showed her a leg, the halves of Adelmar's split helmet, and a lump of organs, still hot. She fought a surge of panic.

"There's his head," said Anton, tonelessly. Someone or something had set it atop the leafless trunk of a potted shrub, looking at them with a look of dignified sadness.

"What about the other two?" asked Sabbath. "Anybody see anything?"

"Footprints," said Solana. She pointed. To her the tracks were obvious—still warm, traces of blood that looked black in ultraviolet—but the others peered uncertainly. Except Daslakh, of course, who scuttled over and took a closer look.

"Two sets of footprints. They went this way." The little mech pointed down a side street.

They all looked that way, but nobody followed.

"Keep moving," said Pera. "No time to search."

"Agreed," said Sabbath from underneath her torso.

"They may be dead, or hiding from the killer mech. Or perhaps could climb up to the hub and leave us here with no hope of escape," said Atmin. "We must away, no matter what."

"We could try comms," said Solana. "I mean, we can't just leave them here."

"I think we can," said Atmin.

"Look, I've got as much reason to hate Jaka as anyone, but she's had a pretty rough life. She doesn't deserve to die here."

"What rough life?" asked Daslakh.

"She said she lost her family, grew up in a half-wrecked hab full of gangs, had to do some pretty awful things to survive..."

"That's all a bunch of hot dust. I sent out some clever little queries after we left Scapino. Always a good idea to find out who you're flying with. Her real name's Ersi Duxtar, and she's from an utterly safe and comfortable Main Swarm hab called Ebut-huntu. Family sent her to Ceres for a high-status education but she ditched it after two years. Moved to a cycler on the Mars-Jupiter run, got herself kicked off at Juren for fraud. Grifted her way through the Jovian system to the Retro Ring and her own gang of pirates. She's no victim. Jaka put a lot of time and effort into becoming what she is."

Solana said nothing more and they quickened their pace.

As they approached the plaza around the spoke, Pera cautioned, "Go slow, check everything, eyes open. Prime spot for traps or ambush."

Daslakh examined the pavement and Solana kept her own eyes ahead, scanning in IR. She did keep tapping the ground with her pole. Ahead she could see the spoke, just like her last attempt to get away. But this time her goggles showed no human body heat around it. Jaka wasn't waiting to drag her back to the camp.

"Something moving left of us, between the café and the flower shop!" Atmin announced.

Sabbath pivoted so that Pera could point her laser at the contact. Anton did the same, and the emitter peeking over his shoulder locked in on some target in the darkness. Solana crouched by instinct as much as any tactical sense, but Atmin zoomed toward the little passage and illuminated it with his spotlight.

Two suited figures crouched in the mouth of the alley. Then Jaka stood, and without even hearing her Solana could see her bravado return, just from her posture.

"Hey," she said. Despite her air of confidence Solana thought she could detect a shakiness to Jaka's voice—and genuine relief.

"In truth we thought you both were dead. What happened? How is it that you remain alive while Adelmar, a bloody wreck, lies cooling in the dark?" asked Atmin.

"It caught us in the open and Adelmar decided to fight. We got away."

"You ran away and left him to die, in other words," said Anton.

"Shut up," she said.

"I don't have to listen to you anymore," said Anton.

"Hey, *I* didn't put that implant in your head. It was those totalitarian jerks in Fratecea. *I'm* the one who took you in and gave you an important job in my crew. You should thank me."

"Nice to chat but we've got to get moving," said Pera.

"You're not leaving us behind. That's my shuttle, remember."

"We're not leaving anyone behind," said Sabbath.

"Why not?" asked Daslakh. "More to the point: why aren't you just leaving by yourself? Kamaitachi will make sure none of us reveal any of the secrets you're trying to hide, and in thirty years your boss can send a message out to the buyers to let them know that oh by the way there's an insane assassin mech in that wrecked hab on its way out. Might want to be careful, and all that. What's in this for you?"

"I made my choice to screw up the mission when I stuck that bandage on Pera's leg. My boss will be furious but I haven't changed my mind." He gave a wry half smile. "I admit that I did have some second thoughts while Jaka had me stuck to a wall for three days with my own piss running down my legs. You might want to remember that," he said to her, the smile gone.

"I've got Adelmar's missile pods," she said. "He never wasted his time with tranq or tangle rounds. Maybe your suit could protect you, but I guarantee I can blow any of these others to bits with a thought. So I'm coming with you, or nobody is. End of discussion."

"Make yourself useful, then. I have to help Pera up the stairs. Daslakh's too small to carry much. That leaves you, Anton, Solana, and Tanaca to carry everything. We need weapons, tools, medical supplies, and water, in that order. Nothing else."

"We're going up the stairs?"

"We have to. Pera can't climb with only one leg."

"Seems like this would be a lot easier if we just left her behind."

"She knows more than any of us about spotting and disabling booby traps—and every minute we spend squabbling about this gives Kamaitachi more time to plant them." He turned and began laboriously lumbering along the street again. Except that instead of walking toward the center of the plaza where the spoke rose toward the hub, Sabbath followed the curving edge of the space, aiming for the opposite side.

"Where are you going?" asked Solana.

"This way," said Sabbath, pointing with his free arm down the main road to antispinward. "To the next spoke. Come on."

"That's another half a kilometer!" said Jaka, sounding almost on the verge of tears.

"Yes, and my guess is that Kamaitachi has concentrated its trap-setting efforts on this stairway. It's had weeks to prepare. The next one is likely to be safer."

"Makes sense," said Pera. "Fall in, everybody. We've got a longer walk than we expected."

CHAPTER FOURTEEN

The hike to the next spoke was nerve-racking but uneventful. They found no traps and Kamaitachi did not appear. Instead of a plaza this spoke rose from what had been a grassy park with fountains.

Daslakh—after a great deal of argument—led the way in, creeping along the wall or the ceiling. Atmin followed in his travel sphere. Pera and Sabbath followed, with the engineering laser powered up and ready. Solana, Jaka, and Tanaca were behind Pera, bearing most of the supplies and gear. Anton brought up the rear, wearing the laser backpack and carrying two large water containers which felt heavy enough to pull his arms off. He smiled in secret amusement at the marching order. Without any conscious thought the group had reverted to the pattern of a hunter-gatherer band on the plains of Africa fifty thousand years earlier: expendable men in front and back, women in the middle.

The staircase wound around the elevator shaft, inside the outer diamondoid wall of the spoke. Within the habitat ring, the stairway was more than just an emergency route. It doubled as a scenic overlook, and someone had taken the time to engrave pointers and labels on the inside of the transparent diamondoid, indicating local sites of interest. The labels were little fragments of Safdaghar's lost past. "Campanile: Full 10-bell peal rung nonstop over 1,004 hours, 9899-324 to 9900-001," one read. "Two-story green house: Birthplace of Mabikas Tao," said another. "Black dome: Concert hall, site of the Conclave of 9743-185." "Floral arch grown for the Sexual Games of 9881." "Obelisk: Monument to Lavibieno." "House with cupola: Flashpoint of the Aesthetic Riot, 9882-006." "Former location of the Bone House, built 9640 and demolished 9883."

After two circuits of the spoke the labels ended—but then a few meters beyond Anton saw words scratched by hand into the diamond, just at eye level. He read, "the poorest shelter me the weak stand guard fearful and unwilling yet refusing to betray no shield but right, no sword we will not win, we shall not yield" and then the writing stopped.

They climbed, and they climbed, and they climbed some more. Anton tried to breathe regularly. At first he inhaled when he put his left foot on the next step and exhaled when he put his right foot forward. Then he inhaled between steps and exhaled on the power stroke. Finally he was just panting. The muscles in his thighs and calves began to burn, then to scream.

He was determined not to complain, but still felt a rush of relief when Jaka spoke up. "Can we take a rest? Some of us don't have powered smart suits."

"Rest break, then," said Sabbath. "Be sure to drink something." He eased Pera down to the stairs. The dino went limp, lying as if she had passed out. Her big running-hunter chest was pumping hard and her leg spasmed.

"How high are we?" Jaka asked.

"Fifty-one meters," said Daslakh. "Halfway to the top of the ring section. At this rate it will only take us two hours to reach the hub. If you want to go even slower, maybe you meat people could take naps or make a nourishing pot of soup from scratch. I'm sure the tireless mech hunting us will wait until you're done."

"The gravity will get lighter as we climb," said Sabbath. "We won't need as many breaks."

Except for Atmin, the biologicals were mostly occupied in breathing heavily, but Daslakh seemed to be in the mood for conversation. It crawled over to Sabbath and displayed a question glyph on its back.

"Okay, let's be candid with each other. I know enough about what happened to Utsuro, and it's not hard to figure out how Kamaitachi got stuck here. But what about you? Why are you here, Sabbath? The real reason, not your cover story. If you came here to protect us against the mech you've done a pretty poor job of it. It's already bagged two of us and injured Pera, and we haven't even seen it."

Sabbath laughed. "Oh, I wasn't sent here to protect anyone. My job is to tidy up loose ends—in this case, Kamaitachi itself. You don't really matter to the people I work for. To be honest, my original plan was to just let the mech kill all of you and then dispose of it myself. Simple and tidy."

Anton moved closer. "Yet you chose to reveal yourself and save Pera."

"No need to rub it in." Sabbath was silent for a moment. "If you must know, I did a lot of eavesdropping on your various conversations, even the ones you thought were secret. At one point I overheard your friend Utsuro—my brother Basan—talking about the crime done here in Safdaghar. All the thousands of murders. He wanted to find out what happened, maybe bring the perpetrators to justice."

"You must have laughed at that," said Daslakh. "Given that he committed a bunch of them."

Sabbath looked at the mech sadly and shook his head. "No, it . . . it helped me realize something. All of us have programming, of one kind or another. Solana's got a compulsion to serve and obey. Anton had a spy in his head. You've got whatever heuristics guide your behavior. I have my own training and indoctrination. But Utsuro didn't. At least, he didn't remember it. The physical and psychological trauma stripped all that away."

He looked up at the ceiling and frowned. "What was left was a better man. Utsuro could tell good from evil, and he wanted to do good. He was better than Basan had been. I can vaguely remember when all my brothers and sisters were like that—before all our training in how to be amoral bastards. For a long time I told myself I didn't have any choice, but Utsuro showed me I still did. I guess I wanted to live up to his example."

"Who sent you, then?" asked Anton.

"I'll never tell," said Sabbath.

"Seriously?" said Daslakh. "You can't figure it out? Did Solana take out your frontal lobes by mistake? Who wanted Pasquin Tiu dead? Who has the resources for top-of-the-line gear like what this guy's got? He's got to be working for Deimos, and I can't believe he doesn't know it."

Sabbath made no reply.

"Deimos? Why would they kill a whole habitat just to get one person? It doesn't make sense," said Solana.

"You're thinking like a normal human," said Daslakh. "To one of the oldest and most powerful polities in the Billion Worlds it makes perfect sense. Everybody knows the Deimos Community are a bunch of ruthless bastards. That's not a bad reputation to have, actually. People don't cross you. I expect the original plan was to be ultra-subtle and sneaky. Pasquin Tiu just turns up dead with no explanation and everybody's suitably impressed. But something went wrong and the operation got blown. The team had to fight their way out, and didn't care how much carnage they left behind."

"And then Utsuro got injured," said Anton.

"Basan," said Sabbath. "He was still Basan then. Utsuro came later. He got hurt and left the station, signaling for a pickup that never came. That's the other side of being ruthless bastards: abandoning your tools if they fail."

"Kamaitachi stayed behind to finish the job," said Daslakh.

"But why? What purpose could it serve? Did the mech go crazy?" asked Solana.

"Again: you need to think like Deimos," said Daslakh. "It's okay if everyone in the Billion Worlds knows you're implacable and ruthless. It's even okay if they think you're a bunch of blood-thirsty monsters who deal out wildly disproportionate retribution for real or imagined slights. Those are all useful for the Deimos Community. They've been cultivating that reputation since before the Fourth Millennium."

"Old habits die hard," said Sabbath.

"What Deimos *can't* afford is for others to see them as incompetent or weak. That's just asking for trouble, even from allies. So once Utsuro—or Basan, or whatever you want to call him—was mission-killed, Kamaitachi had to eliminate the witnesses. *All* of them. It's fine if people suspect Safdaghar died because they pissed off Deimos. It's absolutely *intolerable* for people to know Safdaghar chased off a pair of Deimos operatives and hurt one of them badly."

"And I'm afraid Kamaitachi probably enjoyed doing it anyway," said Sabbath. "Having employees who love their work is normally a good thing, but when the job involves murdering people, well..."

"Bad PR. So they send you out to kill it—and us. By the way, I hope you've noticed a fundamental flaw to the whole murder-the-witnesses approach: it's hard to know when to stop. How do you know there won't be somebody waiting back home to break you down to basic elements to keep you from talking?" Daslakh accompanied this with a little stick-figure animation on its shell, showing little cartoon characters shooting, stabbing, and poisoning each other.

Solana interrupted. "You keep saying Deimos did this and Deimos did that, like it's a single person. There's a trillion people living in the Deimos Ring, and they have volunteer committees running everything. How could anyone even suggest doing that? How could it get approved?"

Sabbath just sighed. "You need to learn more history. My little section has been around as long as anyone can tell—since back when Deimos was just a rock with an elevator down to Mars. The bureau changes names whenever a new system takes over, and sometimes it gets disbanded, but it always comes back. There's probably more than one, operating unknown to each other. Deimos needs us. The ring around Mars is just a tiny part of Deimos. Most of its wealth is spread across the system, in millions of different financial networks and interlocking economies. You can't protect an empire like that with lasers and RKVs. You have to do it by eliminating problems, as cheaply as possible."

"Murdering people," said Anton.

Sabbath looked so surprised and hurt it might have been genuine. "Only as a very last resort. Killing's wasteful. Our primary weapon is bribery. Make it attractive to do what Deimos wants. One excellent bribe is simply to offer them the chance to join the Deimos Community. Turn enemies into assets. We tried that with Pasquin Tiu, repeatedly. Stubborn fellow. Wouldn't take our grants, wouldn't accept a cushy fellowship, wouldn't even be part of the Deimos counterculture."

"Almost like he noticed your edgy rebels are still part of your cultural empire," said Daslakh.

"When people can only oppose Deimos's economic and political power via memes crafted in Deimos, we've already won."

"How do you get any of this past the volunteer committees without someone revealing all your secrets?" asked Anton.

Sabbath laughed. "The committee system is a perfect environment, really. Who do you think volunteers to be on the Special Activities Committee? Spies, ex-spies, and wannabes. All the important stuff gets done via private networks, anyway. If there's any real opposition, well, the same techniques work inside Deimos as outside. Bribe, co-opt, blackmail, erase memories, fatal accident. We've got funding sources the other committees don't know about, so we're pretty much free to act as we see fit." He stood and stretched. "Come on, everybody. Time to keep moving. Stretch out and line up."

Anton tried to distract himself as they climbed. They were at about ninety-five percent gravity, but the brief rest had left everyone still sore and tired. Another fifty meters would take them to the top of the ring section. Beyond that was a four-hundred-meter stretch of spoke extending through space to the solar array access ring, halfway to the hub. Another four hundred beyond that, past the heat radiators, would bring them to the manufacturing and low-gravity living areas.

He wasn't sure which would be the most dangerous part of the climb. In the long spoke stretches they would be trapped in a tube, with no way to escape if the mech attacked. But in the warren of the hub they would have to worry about it coming from any direction.

The simple truth was that they were in danger everywhere inside Safdaghar. And in danger during the aerobraking pass through Jupiter's upper atmosphere. Even in the synchronous ring orbiting Jupiter Solana would be among a trillion humans, with only her goggles to protect her.

Was there anywhere at all she could be safe?

Anton smiled at himself then. Why was he worrying about keeping Solana safe? Surely that would be her responsibility. As soon as the shuttle reached the synchronous ring they would part forever, both free—and alone.

His thigh muscles and calves were screaming again long before they reached the top of the ring. Ahead he could see Sabbath plodding grimly along. He didn't seem to care. His suit—now in the form of a Deimos Special Forces formal dress uniform without insignia—could easily manage the load.

"Need...to stop," Pera gasped out as they approached the hundred-meter mark.

"Just a few more steps to the landing," said Sabbath. "You can make it."

"Trap!" shouted Daslakh, and everyone froze. Jaka dropped to one knee and dragged Tanaca down with her.

"Where?" Pera demanded, still a bit shaky.

"Right up ahead, ten steps up from the one under me."

Pera and Sabbath moved up to where Daslakh clung to the inner wall of the staircase. Atmin bobbed in the air next to the mech. "No peril to me does appear. What is it that you see?" he asked.

"That step's irregular. All the others are nineteen centimeters, tread to tread. But that one sticks up by about four millimeters."

"An error in construction, could it be?"

"Can't risk it," said Pera. "Daslakh, can you tell anything about its internal structure? Ultrasound or something?"

"It's solid," said Daslakh after a second. "Density's about point nine. There might be embedded circuitry."

"Do you think it is a bomb? Or some more deadly thing?" asked Atmin.

"Could be anything," said Pera. "Explosive, acid polymer, expanding foam...whatever it is, assume it's proximity-triggered. I think I can cut it out. Bunch up behind me, everyone. If it falls and explodes, the blast will be one turn behind us."

Everyone except Sabbath huddled together in the small clump of steps which were on the opposite side of the spoke from the suspicious one. For once Jaka looked serious, even worried. There was no way for her to bully a bomb, no words to manipulate it.

Pera sighted with her engineering laser and made a quick cut across the riser, about two centimeters below the top of the irregular step. She cut across the riser above it, so that the tread was supported only on the sides.

"Now the fun part. This might set it off." She hesitated, then made a quick cut down the left side. Anton could hear everyone around him holding their breath, and then all exhaled together after nothing happened.

She made a second cut on the right side, and the tread tipped, then fell through to the stairs below.

"Nothing happened," said Jaka. "Just a big waste of time."

"It's squawking," said Daslakh. "A short repeating code burst."

"Kamaitachi knows where we are," said Sabbath. "Time to move."

They all stepped cautiously over the gap left by the cutting. Ahead of Anton Solana couldn't help but look down. "It's getting—" she began, and then the fallen stair below them burst into flames. Fire jetted out from it in all directions, and hot smoke streamed through the gap in the stairs. More smoke billowed up the staircase behind them.

"No retreat," said Pera.

A dozen steps beyond the trap the spoke passed through a floor atop the habitat ring. The main purpose of the level was access to lights and environmental systems, but around the spoke the roof was transparent and the space was set up for recreation, with a couple of bars, a dining area, and a big open floor for dancing or sports. The tables and couches had all battered themselves to bits during Safdaghar's years of unstable spin, but Anton didn't notice. His gaze went upward to where Jupiter and all its satellites shone through the diamondoid roof, looping endlessly as the hab rotated.

They were close. At just under a hundred standard hours until Safdaghar's closest approach, Jupiter itself was a bright ball half as wide as Anton's outstretched hand, surrounded by the solid band of the synchronous ring, half again as big as the planet itself. He could see all four Galilean moons, and Callisto was near enough to show a visible disk of blue ocean and white cloud-swirls.

The backdrop for the planet and its remaining moons was a haze of orange pinpoints: the hundred million habs of the Jovian Great Ring, home to nearly two hundred trillion baseline beings. The Great Ring filled a fat torus around Jupiter, from about ten million to twenty million kilometers out. Seventy moons and hundreds of asteroids had been dismantled for the raw materials—supplemented by matter lifted from Jupiter itself—to build the structures of the Great Ring, ranging from village-sized microhabs to a few dozen planet-sized titans housing tens of billions each.

When Yanai had adjusted Safdaghar's orbit to pass through this cloud of worlds, she had made sure the doomed hab would not pass within a kilometer of any of the permanent structures circling Jupiter. But there was no way she could account for the billions of spacecraft—both intelligent ships and dumb ballistic payloads—constantly churning through the sky. Avoiding collision was up to them, and to the six mighty Ophanim who managed traffic control in Jovian space. The six of them had ultimate authority over spacecraft, and were famously remorseless about using their terawatt lasers to deflect or vaporize objects in danger of collision. Unpowered objects like Safdaghar had the right of way, but if it came to making choices about saving lives, a wreck with seven people aboard might easily be sacrificed to protect others.

"We've got to rest," said Anton, and nobody argued. They sat in the middle of the big dance floor, facing outward. So far all of Kamaitachi's attacks had been close up, cutting and smashing. No projectiles. That was a small mercy.

Sabbath checked the bar and came back with sealed cans of mors. "I'll be the taster." He peeled back the lid of one and sipped through the membrane, then made a face. "I forgot how much I don't like this stuff. It's fine, drink up."

Sitting with his back against Pera's torso, wedged between Tanaca and Solana, Anton felt himself getting drowsy. The adrenaline surge he'd been riding since Solana had cut into his skull was over, and his body was going on strike in protest. He didn't fight it. A quick nap was just the thing he needed before the next climb. His thoughts drifted and soon became dreams.

A sharp jab in his left calf brought him wide awake, to see Daslakh standing in front of him with words displayed on its shell: SOMETHING MOVING UNDER THE FLOOR. BE READY TO SCATTER.

It moved to show the message to Solana. The others were already moving slowly, irregularly, getting into position.

"Go!" said Daslakh via comm, and the eight of them scrambled and sprinted away from the center of the floor, just before half a dozen jagged meter-long blades punched through the polished surface.

Pera aimed her engineering laser at a spot in the center of the ring of blades, carving a hole in the floor and then firing into the opening. Anton didn't need Daslakh's hyper-acute senses or Solana's goggles to feel the enemy under the floor now. He could see the floor ripple as it surged toward Pera—only to stop when the dino drew a laser line in its path.

"Wait, stop!" Sabbath called out. "Kamaitachi! We want to talk to you."

"Is he insane?" said Jaka. "It's a killer!"

"I thought you didn't believe in killer mechs," said Anton.

The movement under the floor stopped for a moment, then with a great popping and splintering noise of cracking graphene, a pair of ropy arms pried up two of the floor panels, revealing a dark space below.

A second later Kamaitachi climbed up into the light, and Anton stared in fascination. The mech was smaller than he had expected, maybe half the mass of a human, no more than a meter tall.

Something had hurt it very badly, overwhelming its ability to repair itself. Its central body was blackened and fused, like sand turned to glass by intense heat. The damaged section was rigid, unable to change shape or even bend. Its surface was stuck in a chaotic swirl of mirror-shiny and utter black. The hard bits looked painful, like thick scabs on a human face. Limbs sprouted from one side of the damaged area, changing shape and length as the mech walked. Its movements looked drunken, almost random, but no less menacing for that. Like a wounded tiger. Anton didn't need Solana's goggles to see the air around the mech shimmering with heat. It was throwing off hundreds of kilowatts and probably had reserve capacity to draw on.

He was terrified, of course. Even damaged, Kamaitachi was still utterly deadly, and looked it. But he also felt a little surge of pride—pride for the people of Safdaghar. With their garden tools and improvised weapons they had almost managed to destroy this deadly mech. For eighty centuries every battle between living things and machines had gone to the machines. Even the Great War of the Fourth Millennium had been primarily machines against machines. But the people of Safdaghar had managed a draw. It felt like a victory.

"Kamaitachi!" said Sabbath. "Your mission is done. Time to stand down and leave this place."

After a second it replied. The voice was deep, mellow, almost musical, but the words were madness. "Never done nikty wan never leave keep segredo kill todos hurt todos punish todos punish punish kata kiru picar nero threads devour bloody ice secret forever."

"Listen to me. *Un assemblage de fous, de méchants, et de malheureux*," said Sabbath. "I speak for Deimos."

"A command phrase? You've got that poor bastard under external control?" said Daslakh, turning hazard orange.

"We've all got them. Goes with the job," said Sabbath. "Kamaitachi: go into hibernation mode now."

But instead of shutting itself down, the mech lashed out with an arm, which stretched three meters as it swung at Sabbath, its tip sprouting curved blades as big as Solana's forearm. "Can not, will not, are not, would not, is not, do not, am not, did not, could not, shall not, was not. Orokamono, jaakuna-sha, mijimena mono no korekushon!"

Daslakh had been standing still, stuck to the floor just out of Kamaitachi's reach. Now it jumped back, bouncing off the ceiling and sticking to the wall just next to the door. Its shell was bright orange again. "Comms off now!" it said. "That lunatic's full of attack code. The bad kind."

Sabbath's suit reacted to the striking mech faster than any human could, pivoting to take the blow on its right shoulder, the material turning hard and sprouting needles to catch the blades. Sabbath and the suit did a shoulder roll in the other direction as the blades hit, moving with the impact, while the needles bent and wrapped around the blades.

But Kamaitachi was braced, its other limbs stuck to the floor. A few seconds of desperate thrashing about followed as Sabbath's suit first tried to sever the killer mech's long ropy arm, then struggled to resist being pulled toward the flowering fractal blades of its other limbs. The suit finally got its feet onto the floor and stuck, letting the mech pull it upright. The two tugged and strained, and the air around them rippled with the heat they were throwing off. It was a contest that Sabbath's suit couldn't win without cooking him inside itself.

Sabbath slashed through the ropy arm gripping him and fell back as it parted. The bit stuck to him flowed out of his hands and leaped back to join the rest of Kamaitachi. "Tanaca! The breacher!" Sabbath shouted.

Tanaca moved with her usual sleepwalker's pace, raising the plasma breacher and staring as if she had never seen it before. Anton snatched it from her. Long ago he had done militia training, along with every other adult of Fratecea, preparing for the invasion of counterrevolutionaries which never came. He remembered the drill: flip up the panel on top of the breacher, look for the green light indicating full charge, click the mechanical safety from green to red, activate magnetic containment, place the muzzle between one and four meters from the surface to be breached, brace for recoil and—

He pressed the firing button and closed his eyes in the same instant. His training instructor would have hit him for it, but the flash lit up the blood vessels in his eyelids and Anton knew he would be blind for minutes if he hadn't shut his eyes.

When he opened them he saw a meter-wide hole in the wall, the edges still aflame. A couple of meters beyond that, a second wall showed a smaller hole, and three meters beyond *that* a black starburst on an unbreached wall. There was no sign of Kamaitachi.

"Did I get it?" he asked.

"Grazed it," said Daslakh, poking at a twisted bit of blackened smart matter on the floor.

"You idiot!" Jaka shouted at Anton. "That was our one chance and you wasted it!"

"No time for bickering," said Sabbath. "We need to get moving, as quick as we can."

They formed up into the same order as before without any discussion. The only difference was that Tanaca lagged behind Jaka and Solana, so that Anton had to keep urging her forward. He had never seen her look so blank. Compared to her normal vague expressionlessness, her face now looked like a corpse.

"It's all right," he said to her, not knowing what else to say. "We'll make it. You'll be fine."

"Why won't it stop?" she muttered, and then was silent again.

Beyond the roof of the lounge area, the spoke's walls were solid graphene, with layers of radiation and micrometeorite shielding on the outside. Anton's universe contracted to a dozen steps ahead and a dozen steps behind, with curving light-gray walls on either side. A light on the outer wall every six steps, an access panel on the inner wall every dozen.

When they stopped to rest, they just sat down on the stairs. Anton faced down the spiral, and barely rested, watching and listening intently, the manual control for the laser backpack in his hand. With his data implant dead, he had to actually press a button to activate it. Against Kamaitachi that delay might be lethal, so he couldn't afford to relax.

CHAPTER FIFTEEN

A hundred meters above the roof of the outer ring they came to a landing, where the spoke elevators could stop in case of emergency. Daslakh found a control which slid a pressure door into place across the stairway leading down. "It won't stop Kamaitachi forever, but it'll take a minute or two to hack through that."

"The gravity's lighter up here," said Solana. "I can feel it."

"Anybody have any painkiller patches?" asked Jaka. "I've run out." Nobody answered her.

Time passed weirdly. The climbs seemed to take forever, but when Anton actually timed the next leg of the ascent he found it only took five minutes to go up fifty meters. The rest breaks were as long as the climbing parts, but felt too brief.

The elevator landings were spaced a hundred meters apart, but as they approached the second one Atmin spotted something wrong. "The stair is blocked against us by a pressure door. I cannot say what lies beyond."

"Could be a trap," said Pera.

"Or damage to the hab," said Solana.

"Daslakh, can you tell if there's air beyond that door?" asked Sabbath.

"Of course," said the mech, and climbed cautiously up the wall to where the pressure barrier blocked the stair. "Pure vacuum beyond," it said after a moment.

"Seal up," said Sabbath. "We'll have to cut through."

"Still could be a trap," Pera pointed out. "Good place for one."

"What do you suggest, then?"

"Drop back a bit and cut through the floor, not the pressure door."

"Unless Kamaitachi thought of that," said Daslakh.

"Randomize," said Sabbath. "Daslakh, divide that ceiling into half a dozen sectors and pick a number from one to six."

"Right. Cut there," said Daslakh, pointing at a section of ceiling four meters away from the pressure door. Pera's laser made short work of the ceiling panel and then the sturdier floor deck above it. As soon as the beam cut through the floor layer a strong breeze began to blow toward the hole. Everyone sealed up their suits at once. The wind intensified as the cut grew bigger, so that Atmin had to land his travel sphere on the stairs and stick to the surface.

With the final cut the panel dropped down in front of them, and Daslakh scrambled up the wall to peer upstairs. *"I don't see anything. Just a lot of vacuum."*

"Laser's down to fifty seconds of juice," said Pera.

"Keep moving," said Sabbath. *"Solana, can you carry Atmin until we're closer to the hub? I'm guessing that sphere doesn't have much propellant for vacuum."*

"In zero gee, or close to it, my thrusters can support my sphere for half an hour or more. But here they would run dry much sooner leaving me imprisoned in a diamond cage."

The travel sphere plus Atmin massed about seven kilos—not too heavy, but the sphere was bulky and awkward to carry. Anton watched as Solana held it in her arms, then rested it on one shoulder, then transferred it to the opposite shoulder, and tried to prop it on her hip. Atmin was obviously not happy with the arrangement, and fidgeted in irritation every time Solana moved the sphere around. Finally the bird activated the sphere's manipulator arms and clung to Solana's back.

Climbing in the airless section of the spoke made Anton even more paranoid. The only sounds he could hear were his own breathing and the blood pulsing in his ears, and the whines and creaks of his antique suit as it labored to keep up with the demands of his lungs. He kept looking back, fearful that Kamaitachi could be creeping up behind him in the silent vacuum. When he looked ahead he found himself waiting for the thrust of a blade in his back; when he looked over his shoulder he feared turning back to see the others massacred in silence ahead of him.

The lighter gravity did offset the strain and exhaustion of climbing up three hundred meters of stairs a tiny bit. Tired and sore leg muscles didn't have to work as hard as their apparent weight dropped to only two thirds of what it had been at Safdaghar's outer rim.

About thirty meters above the closed pressure door they discovered the reason this spoke section was in vacuum. Daslakh, in the lead as usual, came scuttling back down the wall, its shell hazard red. *"We have a problem,"* it said over comms.

They followed it up the stairs until they could see the orange glow of the Great Ring and the circling bright dot of some large nearby hab through a huge gap in the wall. *"Looks like impact damage,"* said Pera. *"Not an explosion. Probably happened while Safdaghar was tumbling."*

Something had hit the Sun-facing side of the spoke a glancing blow, knocking away a ragged oval of the outer wall about six meters long and four meters high. Nine steps were completely missing, and another sixteen were attached only to the inside wall. Five of them were bent or partly broken, the others *looked* intact...

"We can climb up the inner wall to the end of the gap," said Sabbath. *"That seems safest."*

"Safest for you and me, and maybe the three female humans," said Daslakh. *"But someone's going to have to carry Atmin's fishbowl, Anton's suit doesn't have sticky surfaces, and you may have noticed that Pera's missing a leg."*

"I brought some cord, and Jaka's smart-metal strips," said Pera. *"With your suit helping, you can haul Anton and me up."*

"My travel sphere has low-thrust jets. I can expend some precious mass to launch myself up past the gap. You need not fear how I may pass this awful gulf." Without another word Atmin fired a burst of cold gas and shot himself upward at an angle, aimed at the intact stairs above.

Anton watched the sphere rise, and saw with horror that Atmin had misestimated the Coriolis effect. The diamond ball arced forward faster than it should, on a path which would take it under the bottommost step and off into space.

"*Pull up! More thrust!*" he shouted, and then remembered his implant was broken. He fumbled for the microphone control on his helmet.

Atmin himself noticed, just before it was too late. He fired the thrust jets at maximum power, pushing his sphere just high enough to hit the lowest step, bounce upward, tumble, and ricochet off another stair before starting to roll back down. On the second to last step Atmin activated the ball's sticky patch and it came to a stop, only thirty centimeters above the yawning gap into empty space.

After a couple of seconds the bird croaked over the open channel. "*I do not recommend the method I did use. All you who can should come some other way.*"

"*Jaka, you go next,*" said Sabbath.

"*Why?*"

"*You've got weapons. If Kamaitachi's managed to get above us, you won't be helpless.*"

"*I'm not going to be your human trap detector,*" she said. "*Tanaca, get up there.*"

Tanaca looked at Jaka as if she had never seen her before and couldn't make out what she was saying. "*I don't like this,*" she said to no one in particular. "*I want it to go back to before.*"

Daslakh scuttled up the wall. "*Traveling with you idiots is like having a cable welded to my leg. I could be up at the hub undocking the shuttle by now.*"

"*Go on, Tanaca,*" said Sabbath in an encouraging tone. "*It gets easier from here.*"

She shook her head, but started climbing up the wall. Jaka followed, but kept looking back at Sabbath as if afraid he was going to slip away when her back was turned.

"*Okay, I'll go next and pull you two up. Weapons hot in case Kamaitachi shows up.*"

"*Shut up and go,*" said Pera.

Sabbath simply walked up the wall as if it was a level floor. He paused just past the lowest step and attached one of Jaka's smart-metal strips to the wall, with a five-centimeter bulge in the middle through which he passed the end of the cord. He tossed the other end down to Anton. "*Hitch her up first,*" he said.

Anton started to loop the cord under Pera's arms but the dino stopped him. *"Won't work for me. I'll just slip through. There's an attachment point on my back; use that."*

He found the loop on the back of Pera's armored suit and tied the cord in an old-fashioned knot before sticking the end to the cord. Then he slid off the dino's back and stood with his back to the inner wall. He wished he could see in all directions at once, like a mech. He had to content himself with flipping back and forth between watching Sabbath haul Pera up and nervously eyeing the stairs leading down.

Sabbath's suit had sticky hands and feet, so he simply braced himself on the stairs and hauled on the cord hand over hand. Pera rose in short jerks, sixty centimeters at a time. When she got to the smart-metal loop, Pera stuck her one good foot to the wall and extended her tail to Sabbath. Hauling on her tail like a grabby toddler trying to catch a kitten, Sabbath dragged Pera up to the safety of the intact staircase.

Anton keyed his mike. *"Don't forget about me,"* he said, mostly joking.

As he spoke he caught a flicker of movement in the corner of his eye. But when he turned to look down the stairs, with his helmet lamps at maximum, he couldn't see anything. And then, all of a sudden, he could: that patch of discolored wall was Kamaitachi's fused and burned body, sliding slowly over the graphene.

Anton pointed the designator in his forefinger at the mech and activated his laser backpack. The little emitter ball sticking up over his shoulder locked on to the target and lit up Kamaitachi with a rapid series of pulses. The beam was invisible at first—just a scattering of intense white spots on Kamaitachi's body—but then the puffs of vaporized smart matter and soot coming off the mech's body became a series of dazzling grainy lines.

The pulses shifted suddenly as Kamaitachi threw a sliver of debris at Anton, too fast for him to see. The laser backpack spotted it, and went into defense mode automatically, vaporizing the projectile before it could hit Anton.

"Get me out of here!" he shouted into his helmet mike. Unable to look away from the killer he didn't dare move—not with broken stairs above him and an opening to space just a meter to his left.

Kamaitachi began to throw heavier pieces of debris at Anton. Not at hypersonic velocity, but a jagged chunk of graphene didn't need more than twenty or thirty meters per second to make a nasty hole in Anton's crude spacesuit and fragile body.

The laser couldn't blast the bigger projectiles into harmless dust, but its idiot-savant mind could knock them away by pulsing on one side or the other to deflect their path. And every time the backpack turned its attention to a thrown missile, Kamaitachi surged closer. It peeled itself off the wall and formed into a curiously flat shape, edge-on to Anton with the old damage in front as a shield, bounding toward him on three legs.

Just as Kamaitachi extended an arm tipped with a vicious-looking spike, something grabbed Anton from behind, and a moment later he was yanked upward. The spike jabbed at him but the laser saw it as a projectile and unleashed a flurry of pulses. He could see a second bright beam cutting through the haze around Kamaitachi as Pera's engineering laser opened fire.

Anton slammed into the upper stairs and through his suit and body heard whoever was holding him give out a grunt as they hit.

He felt a shock of panic when he realized his backpack had gone quiet, and then saw that Pera was no longer firing either. Kamaitachi was gone.

Sabbath hauled Anton to his feet. He turned and saw that Solana had been the one who had acted as a human grapple, with a line tied to the back of her suit so that Sabbath could pull them both to safety.

"*Are you all right?*" he asked her.

"*A few more bruises. I'll manage.*"

"*Got to keep moving,*" said Pera. "*It'll be back.*"

They moved out again, Anton bringing up the rear as usual. He did manage one look at the view through the gap in the spoke wall. It was lovely: the sky was golden with the glow of millions of habs orbiting Jupiter. Against that backdrop was the black disk of a major moon—he couldn't tell which—showing a bright crescent edge.

Ten meters of climbing brought them to the next landing. The pressure door there was sealed, of course, so Pera had to cut a way through again. As before, she picked a random spot to cut, in case of traps. But once they were through, she pulled a tube of sealant from one of the pockets of her armor and handed it to Solana. "*Put the panel back and seal it up. No sense wasting all this air.*"

This landing marked the halfway point between the habitat wheel and the hub. A small ring connected the spokes at that level, supporting and providing access to the solar panels and radiators in the space between the spokes. There was even a small lounge area with a diamond hemisphere window. Before the disaster someone had decorated the walls and ceiling with sculpted faces. Some looked like ceramic, others aerogel or foam, and a few were unnervingly realistic synthetic skin. Their expressions ranged from joy to anguish.

Despite their mounting fatigue, nobody wanted to spend a lot of time resting. The knowledge that Kamaitachi was somewhere close had everyone on adrenaline overload. The screaming faces everywhere didn't help, either. Sabbath had to insist that everyone pause long enough to drink some water.

"That way," said Daslakh, pointing with three limbs at the maintenance access passage leading spinward from the lounge area. "I generated a random number. It can't predict which way we're going."

Sabbath hesitated less than a second, then nodded. "Right. Let's move." He got Pera balanced on his back and set off at a brisk pace.

"Half a kilometer of extra walking just for a slight chance it can't track us? That means it'll be waiting at the hub," said Jaka.

"Best place to meet it," said Pera. "I won't need two legs in microgravity."

"My sphere will soar as well as I can do myself," added Atmin.

"What's your power level?" Anton asked Pera.

"Forty seconds. You?"

"Sixty. I hope that's enough. How many more doors do we need to cut through?"

"Four, probably more."

"That won't leave much if the mech comes back."

"No," said Pera, and that seemed to make any additional comment unnecessary.

The ring around Safdaghar at the half-kilometer height was a simple tube, with a flat floor covering conduits and the main structural members. The walls alternated opaque sections with stretches of transparent diamond, the north and south sides of the passage offset so that some parts were entirely sheltered, some had a window on one side or the other, and some looked like a footbridge through empty space. Hatches with pressure membranes every hundred meters allowed access to the solar panels and radiators above and below.

The group made good progress. A level floor and half-standard gravity meant they could move at a brisk pace, limited only by Daslakh's ability to watch for hidden traps as they progressed. The biggest difficulty was for Sabbath to avoid banging Pera's head into the ceiling, as there was less than three meters of headroom. He had to travel bent almost double, with the dino holding her head low and her laser powerpack slung on one side.

"It could be worse," said Sabbath. "We could be wading through sewage. I've done that a couple of times."

"Was it for work, or do you just like it?" asked Daslakh.

"Work. Had to get into a command post under a city on Earth—I can't say which one, of course, but it was one of the old ones. Still had a sewer system and centralized waste-processing. Thousands of years old. We crawled four kilometers through a one-meter sewer pipe to reach a spot where it passed over the bunker. Couldn't use a plasma breacher because of all the water, so we had to drill in and place charges. I had a mech with me made of smart matter, like our friend out there—" He waved vaguely to indicate Safdaghar around them. "It sealed off the pipe to shield the rest of the team, then set off the charge. We turned every drain for a kilometer around into a brown fountain."

As a tactical environment the passage was worrisome. Once Kamaitachi figured out which way they had gone, it could come at them from almost any direction—sprint ahead and wait in ambush, approach from behind by stealth, or break in through a wall. They could only plod ahead, confined in a tube, able to see only fifty meters ahead and behind before the floor curved up out of view.

Having air around them again meant it wasn't so unnervingly silent. All eight of them kept listening, speaking little. Anton wasn't the only one constantly looking back. The only exceptions were Sabbath, whose rear view was blocked by a dinosaur's hindquarters, and Tanaca. She plodded along silently, looking straight ahead and seemingly oblivious to everything. From time to time she slowed down until Jaka or Solana urged her forward.

They had covered about three-quarters of the distance to the next spoke when something came to a crisis inside Tanaca. She stopped walking, turned to Jaka, and said "I don't want to do this anymore. I want it to stop."

"No time for that now. You can rest in a little while. Come on, keep going." Jaka took her by one arm and gave an ungentle tug.

"No!" said Tanaca, showing more emotion than anyone had seen from her before. "I don't want this! I want to exit. Right now."

"Sweetie, this is life, not a sim. We are where we are, no exiting. Now come on and stop being silly."

Tanaca didn't move.

"I can't punish you now. We have to keep moving. I'll do it later, okay?"

Daslakh, clinging to the ceiling above Jaka and just out of her field of view, turned dark blue with a bright yellow timer on its shell, counting seconds down from ten. When it reached zero the mech went bright red.

"We need to go now. I don't know what bizarre meat-people games you two like to play but this isn't the time or place for that. YOU WILL MOVE NOW! MOVE NOW! MOVE NOW!" Daslakh's voice shifted from its normal neutral tone to a strident, harsh sound exactly matching one of the more common alert message voices.

Without really thinking, all of the biologicals including Tanaca began to hurry along the passage. Daslakh scuttled ahead to look for traps.

They were just a hundred meters from the spoke when Kamai-tachi smashed through the graphene wall between Daslakh in the lead and Sabbath carrying Pera. The air in the passage gusted out, carrying dust and bits of decades-old trash into space.

Entirely by reflex the dino snapped up her engineer's laser and put a spot of brilliant violet onto Kamaitachi's main body. Sabbath extended his left hand and unleashed a volley of hypersonic darts.

The mech dodged and twisted, turning the hard-fused section of its body to act as a shield. The laser left a glowing trail across the surface and a couple of darts struck there, each blossoming into a spot of intense heat that dug a fist-sized pit as it expanded and dimmed.

Kamaitachi *really* didn't like that. It jabbed a tentacle at Sabbath's face, and only his suit's quick reactions got his other hand up in time to knock the bladed tip aside. Pera shifted her laser to burn the tentacle.

The mech flipped itself back outside through the hole in the ceiling.

"*This way!*" said Daslakh. "*I can sense it moving behind us.*"

The others sprinted ahead, Jaka pushing past Sabbath and Pera to take the lead. Anton turned and walked backward, keeping his laser backpack ready to target Kamaitachi if it should appear.

He bumped into someone and found it was Tanaca, once again standing immobile. "*Come on,*" he said. "*We need to get out of here.*" A sound reached Anton's ears, carried through his suit and the decking underfoot: a creak, a rapid couple of snaps, and then a louder creak. A mech-sized hole and the strays from Sabbath's volley of mysteriously energetic little darts had compromised the structure, which was not a good thing in a narrow tube spanning a quarter-kilometer between supports.

Anton backed up past Tanaca and tugged at her shoulder, but she didn't move. The others were twenty meters up the passage and he had no idea where Kamaitachi was.

"*Please?*" he said, taking a reluctant step back away from her.

Just then the wall of the passage exploded inward, sending fragments flying as Kamaitachi burst through.

Tanaca was between Anton and the mech so he didn't dare use the backpack.

"*Make it stop!*" she said. She turned to face Kamaitachi. Anton couldn't tell if she was crying or laughing. "*Make it stop,*" she repeated, and began to walk calmly toward the mech.

"*Tanaca, get out of there!*" said Anton. "*We'll get you away from Jaka if that's what you want.*"

She made no reply, and spread her arms as if welcoming a long-lost friend.

Kamaitachi stopped. It had no visible eyes to watch her with—like Daslakh it saw with its entire surface. But its posture was intent, obviously focused on Tanaca. It even drew back half a step as she came nearer.

"*Please?*" said Tanaca, now just a couple of meters from the mech.

It shot out a limb, blindingly fast. What had been a foot at the end transformed into a hooked blade as the limb swung. For a moment it looked as though the blow had missed, and then Tanaca's head neatly parted from her body as she fell.

Underfoot Anton felt another crack, and this time he didn't

hesitate. He turned and sprinted along the passage away from Kamaitachi. The backpack hummed and popped as it targeted the pursuing mech with a steady barrage of laser pulses.

He made it ten steps before the passage broke in half just behind him. Anton felt a loud crack, then a second, then a dozen in quick succession and the floor dropped about a meter. He looked back to see that the floor had parted, and there was a gap about a meter wide stretching from one of the holes Kamaitachi had made to the other. Only the ceiling still held, and as Anton watched a bright violet spot appeared there and swept across it.

Ahead he saw Pera holding her laser. Sabbath held Pera in one hand and Solana in the other, while Solana clutched Atmin's travel sphere. Jaka was somewhere beyond them, out of Anton's view. The floor gave a final sickening lurch and then the whole passage began to pivot downward. Daslakh launched itself at Anton, trailing a rope back to Pera's combat armor. The little spider mech landed on his helmet, gripping it with all eight legs as the passage became a vertical shaft.

Behind Anton, Kamaitachi stood on the other side of the widening chasm, then leaped for the end of the passage as the section behind it—much longer and more massive—went into freefall. But just before it landed at the end, a spray of darts from Sabbath's weapon struck Kamaitachi in a perfect hexagon of bright spots, knocking it off course.

The mech stretched a tentacle, desperately trying to grab the passage end, but another violet laser spot from Pera vaporized it. Anton watched it fall, hoping desperately to see it tumble away into deep space, but its course curved back out of view so he lost sight of it before it reached the rim.

He found himself hanging by his helmet, looking down half a kilometer at the roof of the habitat ring. To his left, a sheet of photovoltaic cloth hung in shreds. To his right, the disk of Jupiter swung in and out of view every minute.

For a moment nobody said anything. Then Solana spoke over the comm channel. *"The poor thing."*

"We can burn incense later," said Sabbath. *"Now we have to get out of here before this section falls off the station as well."*

It proved to be a tricky problem in process management. Solana and Pera had suits with sticky feet and gloves, so they could stay secured to the walls and floor. Sabbath's suit could

do the same, and amplify his strength. Anton's kept air in, and
that was all. So first Sabbath hauled Anton—with Daslakh still
acting as an increasingly unhappy grapple on his helmet—up the
hundred meters to where the passage met the spoke. He more
or less tossed Anton through the open doorway into the spoke,
then went back for Solana and Atmin.

Finally the three of them hauled Pera up with the cable.
Throughout the whole process Jaka just hovered about—neither
helping nor willing to get too far away from the others.

"*Keep moving,*" said Sabbath once all were up in the spoke
lounge area. "*There's still half a kilometer to climb.*"

"*Can't we rest longer?*" said Solana. "*My legs really hurt.*"

"*No,*" said Daslakh. "*Kamaitachi could still be on board.*"

"*It fell away!*" said Anton.

"*It fell toward the habitat ring, which is half a kilometer wide.
I give it an eighty percent chance of still being on Safdaghar. Plus
or minus two percent.*"

All the humans sagged a little at that. After a couple of seconds Anton got to his feet. "*All right, then. Let's go. At least we've
bought a little time. It will be easier as we get closer to the hub.*"

Sabbath gave a dry chuckle and then hoisted Pera onto his
back once again. Solana picked up Atmin's sphere, and the six of
them trooped toward the emergency pressure curtain at the bottom
of the staircase, with Daslakh in the lead. Nobody even looked
at Jaka, who sat looking sulky and then hurried to follow. She
pushed past Anton on the stairs and gave him a poisonous glare.

"You let Tanaca die," she said, loud enough for the others to
hear now that they were back in atmosphere again.

"You drove her to suicide," he replied.

"That's impossible. Tanaca loved me. She was the only person
who ever really cared about me. You could have saved her but
you were too cowardly."

Now that she no longer had a traitor inside his brain, Anton
discovered that he didn't even hate Jaka anymore. He felt a considerable degree of annoyance, mixed with scientific curiosity
at how anyone could be so utterly solipsistic. Hating her was
like hating Kamaitachi—one might as well hate gravity, or the
vacuum of space.

CHAPTER SIXTEEN

More stairs. The terror of the collapsing ring passage had given all the biologicals another boost of adrenaline, so at first they climbed with new energy. But after the first landing, exhaustion came crashing back. By unspoken consent, they stopped to rest. Solana gulped water from her suit reservoir and massaged her legs.

"You think it's still trying to catch us?" asked Jaka.

"Not like it has anything better to do," said Daslakh.

"I think we have to assume it is," said Sabbath. "That's the wisest course."

"When it does come back, what have we got?"

"Twenty seconds of laser juice," said Pera.

"The backpack's got about a minute," said Anton over the voice channel.

"I've got plenty of dumb needles but those were my last anti-matter darts," said Sabbath.

"You carry antimatter?" asked Pera.

"I did. Just a couple of nanograms. It's expensive, but my employers are pretty rich. They can afford it."

"I think she means the hazard," said Daslakh. "No concerns about accidental detonation, or high-energy photons messing with your genetic legacy?"

Sabbath just laughed. "My genetic legacy's in a lab somewhere. And as to safety, anything that could cause an accidental release would probably pulp me and shred my suit in the process, so why worry? Anyway, they're gone now. What about you, Jaka? I seem to recall some unused micromissiles, and you haven't used them during these past few attacks. Saving them up for something?"

"I need to protect myself," she said.

Nobody had any reply to that, so they resumed the climb. The apparent gravity was down to Mars level, which was a relief to sore thighs and cramped calves. Ironically, it was Sabbath, whose suit was doing most of the work for him, who got the least benefit. He had to keep puffing along bent almost double under Pera's bulk.

At the next rest, a hundred meters up the spoke, Pera said, "I think I can make it on my own from here. My weight's down two-thirds and I've still got one leg."

"No argument from me," said Sabbath.

"How close do you think the killer mech is?" asked Jaka.

"It's been eighty minutes since it fell," said Daslakh. "That's enough time for something like Kamaitachi to make twenty round trips from the rim to the hub. It could be anywhere. No place is safe."

"It's up ahead," said Pera. "Basic tactics. Ambush in a prepared position. Probably in the hub structure—more places to hide."

Jaka pinged Solana privately. *"Do you want to get out of here alive?"*

"Yes," she replied cautiously.

"I can make it happen. When it attacks again, you and I can slip away. Let the others wear it down while we take advantage of the confusion. We'll move faster if it's just the two of us. I've got some stims left, and ammo if it comes after us."

"We can't just leave them."

"Yes we can! They were ready to ditch Tanaca and me after Adelmar died. They'll abandon you just as fast. You don't have any weapons, you're not powerful. The only thing they want you for is ablative defense—something to occupy the killer for a few seconds while they escape."

Solana tried to reject the idea, but found that she couldn't. Would Atmin or Pera abandon her? Maybe. Sabbath? The man was a self-described amoral killer. Anton? She hardly knew him. *"What do you want me for, then?"* she asked Jaka.

"You're very important to me, Solana. I'll do anything to get you safely off this hab."

Solana just looked at her. She certainly didn't trust Jaka, but the other woman always managed to sound so damned *plausible*. Maybe it would be prudent to break up into smaller groups?

She asked herself, what would Utsuro do? The answer was obvious: he would help protect the others even if it cost him his life. He had been trying to protect Sabbath when Jaka killed him.

"No, Jaka," Solana said aloud so that everyone could hear. "I don't want to sneak away and abandon the others. Don't speak to me again."

"You just made a very stupid mistake," said Jaka privately, but after that was silent.

They took a longer-than-usual rest at the final landing inside the spoke, a hundred meters below the hub. When they began moving again, they advanced military style. Pera and Anton led the way now, leapfrogging past one another with weapons hot. First Anton took a firing position, covering Pera's advance up the stairs. As soon as Pera readied her own weapon, Anton climbed up and past her, always staying within line of sight in case Kamaitachi made an appearance.

Daslakh stayed with whoever was in the lead, scrutinizing the steps and walls for traps or any other sign of Kamaitachi's presence.

Solana followed the second laser-armed shooter, carrying Atmin's sphere. Behind her, Sabbath and Jaka climbed the stairs backwards, keeping two sets of eyes on watch.

The grousing and banter was gone. Everyone was silent, tense, and alert. Sheer fear overcame exhaustion.

At Level 7 the spoke staircase entered the hub at a corridor intersection, so that they had five choices of route to follow: north and south along an axial passage running the length of the hub, east and west along a lateral one going around its circumference, or up to the center.

Daslakh generated another random number and pointed silently along the axial passage toward the north end, where the docking bay was. Solana adjusted her goggles and did a slow visual zoom down the passage in visual and infrared. No movement, no hot spots. She gestured thumbs-up and they moved out.

The entire level was devoted to storage: raw materials, unprocessed waste, spares beyond Safdaghar's ability to manufacture, emergency supplies, goods awaiting shipment, and all the miscellaneous stuff that might be useful on a hab. The axial passage was eight meters wide—big enough for a pair of cargo containers with some wiggle room. The ceiling was five meters up. The endless blank gray walls had big doors at irregular intervals, color-coded for what was stored beyond.

This section had air pressure, but they all kept their suits sealed anyway. Atmin's travel sphere hummed along above them once again. With only eight percent apparent gravity, Pera had no difficulty walking with just one leg and the aluminum rod for a cane. All of them had to make their soles sticky to avoid uncontrolled bounding. Their footsteps sounded very loud.

After the narrow stairway, that big corridor gave everyone including Daslakh a mild case of agoraphobia. The group clumped together, following the faintly glowing yellow stripe down the center of the passage.

With nice long straight sight lines ahead and behind, Pera and Anton could advance faster—but it also meant they had to pause at each door. Anton kept watch down the hall while Pera and Daslakh checked the flank, with Pera covering the door while Daslakh opened it just wide enough to stick in one limb for a look around.

This slowed their progress to a literal crawling pace. Nobody wanted to leave any of those dozens of doors unchecked. It was too easy to imagine Kamaitachi waiting with inhuman patience, listening for footsteps outside, and bursting out to strike after the advance guard had passed. A couple of them might survive, but not many.

When the axial corridor crossed a lateral one, they moved quickly, with Sabbath and Jaka covering the crossing while the others darted across. Solana saw nothing dangerous in either direction, but of course she could only see a bit more than a sixth of the way around the hub in either direction. Kamaitachi would know that.

The floor beneath their feet was relatively safe, as there was just a layer of drainage pipes and heat regulators before the outer hull. But the ceiling made them all nervous. So high above them, cluttered with pipes, structural beams, and dark panels that once had shed light. Anything could hide up there, even a human. A smart-matter mech like Kamaitachi would have no trouble. Solana kept her gaze up there, watching for warmth or the slightest sign of motion.

Moving just a couple of hundred meters from the top of the spoke stairway to the north end of the hub cylinder felt like walking around the Jovian Ring. By the time they reached the little access stairway leading up to the arrival concourse, all the biologicals were fighting a mix of panic and exhaustion.

Daslakh waved for their attention and displayed a message on its shell, for maximum silence and security. "Vacuum beyond this door. Most dangerous stretch. Freight elevator to docking. We just have to get to the shuttle. Just 30 meters. You can make it. Be alert, be cautious. Ready?" It waited for all of them to nod before it opened the door.

There was no way to avoid the gust of venting atmosphere, which blew a plume of dust and trash into the elevator shaft. Nothing with working senses could miss that. If Kamaitachi was above them, it knew they were coming.

The cargo elevator shaft was big, designed to handle full-sized cargo containers four meters wide. An access ladder ran up one side of the shaft, in a safety niche so that someone on the ladder wouldn't get hit by the elevator. It had been designed with humans and chimps in mind, not dinosaurs. Even with her body stretched out, Pera's bulky hips extended well past the edge.

With Daslakh leading the way, Pera pulled herself up using one arm and her remaining leg, the laser gripped in her other hand. This close to the hab's axis, each meter brought a noticeable reduction of the apparent gee force. Sabbath was right behind, with his powered suit ready to catch her if she slipped. Atmin followed, using the feeble manipulator arms of his travel sphere to climb the ladder. Solana was below him, also ready to act as a backstop if Atmin's grip slipped. Jaka followed her and Anton brought up the rear once again.

The decks in the hub area were all five meters tall, except for the big space right at the center. It wasn't a hard climb. By the time they passed Level 5 they could push upward and float free for a few seconds at a time.

At each level the big elevator doors looked more and more frightening to all of them. Was this where Kamaitachi would strike?

The answer came at Level 3, the upper level of the microgravity industrial section.

Daslakh, in front, alerted the others. *"Booby trap on the*

ladder! Tripwire and a—" It was cut off by the flash and bang of the improvised bomb going off. One felt the sound through hands and feet rather than with ears. With no air to carry a shock wave it was more distracting than dangerous.

Which was entirely the point. With all of them dazzled by the flash, or squeezing their eyelids shut to prevent it, nobody saw Kamaitachi pop out of an electrical junction box on the other side of the shaft and launch itself at Solana.

Solana only realized what was happening when she saw Sabbath turn and dive straight down at her, knocking Atmin's sphere aside. He slammed into her, shoving her out of the path of Kamaitachi, which hit him as Solana tumbled past Jaka and Anton before getting one sticky foot onto the wall to stop herself.

As she tumbled she got disconnected glimpses of what was happening. Headlamp beams swept around wildly, and laser flashes strobed, creating weird tableaux. Sabbath and Kamaitachi grappled with each other, the man trying to get free and the mech trying to crush him, while above and below the pair Pera and Anton snapped off laser pulses.

The comm channel was a jumble of shouts and cries. She heard Atmin cawing in terror.

She stopped herself in time to look up and see Kamaitachi wrap itself entirely around Sabbath. The mech constricted its body around his waist, and turned the inner edge into a molecule-thin blade. Pera actually jammed her laser against its body and switched to continuous beam, sending out a plume of steam and smoke.

Anton had switched his laser backpack to rapid-pulse mode, so that the underside of Kamaitachi's body churned in constant small explosions. Even Jaka fired off one of her micromissiles, blasting a fist-sized divot in the mech's smart-matter flesh.

Then the two halves of Sabbath's body separated, sliced apart at the waist, and fell spinning away from the staircase in a halo of blood.

"This way!" said Daslakh as it got the door to Level 3 open. Jaka dove through at once, followed by Atmin. There was no puff of air, as that section had been empty of air for years.

Above the door, Pera spun in place, pivoting on her single foot. She had been hanging head-down to fire her laser at Kamaitachi, but now she swung her massive tail, inside an armored suit, right into the mech. The blow caught Kamaitachi as it was changing form and off-balance, and knocked it off the ladder, curving down and back across the elevator shaft. As soon as it landed, Anton bombarded it with more laser pulses as Solana and Pera climbed through the door. Then he dove through just before Daslakh triggered the emergency pyrotechnics to slam it shut.

"*Keep moving! It's not going to quit now.*"

"*Which way?*" asked Anton.

"*I think to spinward lies a—*" Atmin began, but Daslakh cut him off.

"*Next lateral passage, left. Thirty meters. Go!*"

They went. As she turned the corner Solana could hear the creak of bending metal and the gunshot pops of cracking carbon polymers as Kamaitachi forced the door open.

They bounded up the stairs to Level 2, the microgravity residential area. As they climbed Anton struggled out of the laser backpack harness. "*I'm out of juice,*" he said.

"*I've got about ten seconds left,*" said Pera.

At the top she paused and waved the others past, keeping the engineering laser trained on the stairs. They rushed past, into the big open atrium in the center of the hub.

Solana had run ten meters before she realized Pera wasn't behind her. She turned and bounded back.

Pera sat with her broad pelvis wedged into the doorway, the laser in one hand and her wide-mouthed pistol in the other.

"*Come on, we're all out,*" said Solana.

"*Get going. I'm staying. That vicious asshole's taken a lot of damage. Can't have much energy left. It stops here.*"

"*But—*"

"*I'll catch up when it's dead. Now go. You're distracting me.*"

Solana tried to think of something to say but nothing sounded right. "*Good luck,*" she said at last, and then turned and ran.

Over the comm channel Pera began to sing: "*Iru infantoj de la Luna, la tago glorio e veni . . .*" Solana recognized the famous marching song of the Lunar Volunteers—the "tunnel rats" who had fought the Glorious Unique State's armies in the warrens deep below the Lunar surface, giving ground meter by meter until they all died. The tune was thousands of years old, with chords alien to modern music; the lyrics almost unrecognizably archaic.

Pera sang the first verse and the chorus loudly and defiantly, making the hairs on Solana's arms stand up inside her suit. Then the dino's breathing got heavy and ragged, with fragments of lines muttered out between grunts of exertion. When she got to the second chorus a gasp of pain choked off the first line. After that she didn't sing the words, just carried the tune between irregular breaths and more gasps. She managed to finish the third verse, then fell silent. No singing, no breathing. Pera was gone.

Solana knew there was no point to going back for her. If Pera couldn't stop Kamaitachi there was nothing Solana could do. She ran as fast as she could. The residential level was a bewildering series of passages, reflecting changes in use and fashion over the centuries of Safdaghar's history. She bounced off the ceiling and around corners, ignoring the bruises in her dread of feeling the mech's stabbing blades.

Her goggles let her see the faint infrared traces where the other two had passed, so she followed them, desperate to not be alone. But after half a dozen twists and turns she came to an intersection where the tracks split up. She chose to follow the trail leading toward where she remembered a stairwell.

In the airless maze the killer mech could be anywhere and she'd never know. Her goggles at least amplified the light, so that she wasn't blundering around in darkness the way she had down at the rim. She didn't dare try comms—any radio signal would be a beacon for Kamaitachi.

The infrared footprints were brighter ahead. Solana rounded a corner and then screamed as something grabbed her arm. It was Jaka. *"Where is it?"* she demanded. *"The mech!"*

Solana shook her head, panting too hard to speak.

"I split off from the others. Maybe it'll follow them. Hold still," said Jaka.

Solana felt a sharp jab in her shoulder, and then all her nerves tingled as if they had been asleep. She couldn't make her arms move, or even turn her head.

"Don't be afraid, it's just a paralyzer round. I kept a couple," said Jaka. *"Never know when you might need them. Now, before we do anything else, let me borrow these."*

She pushed her hand through the little pressure membrane section covering Solana's mouth and slid it up between the cowl and her nose. Jaka hooked her fingers into the top of Solana's goggles and yanked. The paralyzer kept Solana from screaming as some of the skin around her eyes went with them.

Jaka pulled the goggles out through the mouth membrane and tucked them into one of the pockets of her vest. "*Sorry. But these things are so inconvenient. I need you to do as you're told right now. We need to get to the shuttle.*" She pulled the paralyzer warhead out of Solana's shoulder and pointed her flashlight at her own face. "*Look at me. Come on. We've got to get out of here.*"

She led Solana toward the nearest stairwell, making long shallow bounds in the low gravity. But at the next corridor intersection the two of them were suddenly bathed in light as something came hurtling toward them. It smacked into Jaka's bubble helmet, knocking her away from Solana.

"*Leave Solana now and do not seek again to make her serve your twisted will!*" Atmin said over the comm, and Solana saw that the thing which had struck Jaka was his travel sphere. Inside it the bird looked furious, his wings extended and his beak open.

Jaka said nothing. Instead, two micromissiles left the pods on her arms and streaked toward Atmin. The first struck his diamond sphere at a shallow angle and caromed off down the corridor to explode against the floor. The second hit dead center and blasted the front of the sphere apart.

Atmin flapped his wings uselessly in vacuum, tumbling helplessly as he bounced off the ceiling and then fell. Jaka's flashlight showed the bloody foam at his beak and around his eyes.

"*No!*" Solana shrieked. While Jaka was distracted she began to run, and shut off the comm so that the other woman couldn't call her back. The stairwell was ahead, but Solana didn't bother climbing. She launched herself up to the hub level in one great jump.

The stairwell opened into the open circular concourse that ran around the entire hub just inside the docking bay. The light of Jupiter's vast disk shone in through the broken window, giving the whole place an orange glow like firelight. Solana could see that she was just spinward of the hab's launch tube, which meant the old emergency airlock was just beyond.

She got just past the launch room before Jaka slammed into her from behind. The other woman made her suit gloves sticky to pin Solana to the floor beneath her and jammed her bubble helmet against the back of Solana's head.

"Comms on!" Jaka shouted, and the contact of helmet to Solana's skull transmitted the sound well enough for her to hear.

"No!" Solana shouted, keeping her eyes clenched shut.

"I need you. I promise I won't sell you. I'll keep you with me forever. We can be best friends! Just listen to me."

Then Jaka shifted her grip and pulled Solana's head up. "Protect me!" she shouted, and then Solana felt her jump away. She risked a look. In the orange light she saw something moving ahead of her: Kamaitachi.

It looked bad. Pera had done real damage before dying. The mech had lost mass, and Solana could see more fused patches on its surface. It moved awkwardly, pulling itself along the floor no faster than a walk. But it could keep that up forever. Her mortal flesh would need food and sleep.

Jaka's last micromissile passed over Solana's head and struck the mech. The warhead blasted a chunk of rigid dead matter away, but Kamaitachi ignored it.

Solana grasped her multipurpose tool and it obediently shifted into a large knife. She backed up slowly, keeping the mech in view. Perhaps she could reach another airlock?

Her back touched something. One of the operating panels for the launch tube. Solana slid sideways and got behind it. Kamaitachi continued its inexorable approach. All Solana could hear were her own heart and breathing. "I'm not afraid of you," she said, though she knew it wasn't true. "Not afraid, not afraid."

She backed up another couple of meters and her foot touched something solid. The tube. Solana felt behind her with her free hand as she slid along it. There: the opening. A three-meter section of the tube's top half was open, the lid slid back for loading. She stepped over the edge into the tube. Could she seal it from inside? How long would it protect her?

No. She wasn't going to trap herself, not with a cargo pod full of dead children. Solana stepped out of the tube on the other side, keeping it between her and Kamaitachi. Stay mobile, she told herself. Protect Jaka.

The mech approached steadily. It hauled itself into the same gap in the tube.

Solana acted almost without thinking. One fast leap took her to the tube, and she grabbed the handle of the lid with both hands and slammed it shut with all her strength.

The mech battered at the diamond lid. Solana looked around frantically and saw the panel. She slapped the launch button.

It turned green, but her heart sank as nothing else seemed to happen. Too many years of jolting, too much vacuum exposure.

Then she realized she could see through the tube where the cargo pod had been. It was gone. So was Kamaitachi. Solana looked down the tube to the window at the end, where it passed into the docking bay. Far beyond the mouth of the bay she could just make out two tiny bright specks receding against the dim gold sky.

She stood still for a moment, trying to understand that the danger was gone. The killer mech wasn't hunting her anymore. She didn't need to run. With that thought, she began to shake all over, unsure of whether to laugh or cry.

A minute or an hour later—she couldn't tell—Solana felt Jaka's hand touch her shoulder. The bubble helmet pressed against her cowl. "Comms?"

She opened the channel but couldn't think of anything to say.

"Come with me. Let's get out of here."

Solana let the other woman lead her toward the airlock. But as they approached the door she saw a figure standing there. It was Anton.

"Solana got rid of the mech. Where were you hiding?" asked Jaka.

"I was looking for her, and you. I found Atmin," he said. His voice sounded like iron.

"Well, it looks like we're the only ones left. I guess you can come along if you behave yourself."

"Thank you," said Anton. He stepped aside to let them into the airlock. But as Jaka brushed past him he grabbed her bubble helmet with both arms, blocking her face with his hands.

"Stop him! Kill him!" she shrieked.

"Save yourself," said Anton, looking right at Solana.

She felt the handle of the tool in her hand. It obediently changed to the default form she'd picked. Keeping her eyes locked onto Anton's, she lunged, stabbing the ultrasharp blade through the skinsuit into Jaka's throat. The shriek turned to a gurgle as blood foamed out into vacuum.

Jaka struggled and kicked, but Anton didn't release his grip on the helmet until she went limp. He watched Solana the entire time, only closing his eyes when he put Jaka's body down.

"Do you know where your goggles are?" he asked after a minute.

She knelt and got them out of Jaka's vest, but didn't put them on. Instead she turned and walked into the airlock. Anton followed.

EPILOGUE

Sabbath pulled himself along the passage with his right hand, thirty centimeters at a time with long pauses in between. His left hand clutched his right ankle. His right leg, and the rest of his body below the navel trailed behind the ankle, bobbing along inside the bottom half of his suit in a soup of blood and urine.

The top half of his suit had sealed itself at his severed waist, clamping arteries to keep him from bleeding to death, closing off his digestive tract, and poking needles and tubes into him to keep him alive and conscious.

"Mind if I hitch a ride?" said Daslakh on a new private channel, dropping onto his back from the ceiling.

"Yes," Sabbath said in a kind of half moan.

Daslakh jumped off of Sabbath and took hold of his hand with two of its limbs. Its shell switched from stealth black to rescue orange with a green diamond symbol. *"I guess I'll have to give you a tow. Where's your capsule stashed?"*

"South end. Level 3. Section 235."

The mech dragged the two halves of the man along the corridor for about twenty meters, until they reached a radial shaft leading up toward the center. *"It's going to be tricky to drag you*

*up the ladder in two parts. Do you really need those legs? They'll
be pretty nasty before you can get yourself put back together.
Simpler to just print some new ones."*

"I like my legs. I'm attached to them," said Sabbath.

"That's a pretty lame joke."

Sabbath managed a faint chuckle, though it sounded a bit
like a gasp.

Daslakh said, *"Sigh,"* and then took hold of Sabbath's arm again
and began to haul him up the wall of the shaft, ten centimeters
at a time. Sabbath hung on to his severed limbs for perhaps half
a minute, and then with a genuine sigh he let the severed lower
half of his body drop. It fell a dozen meters, bounced off the
wall, and vanished into the darkness.

"Thank you," said Daslakh. *"That makes this a lot easier."* It
climbed faster now, and reached Level 3 after another minute.

"How did you know?" said Sabbath.

*"About your capsule? It's blindingly obvious. You got here, ergo
you came in something. I was kind of amazed none of those others
even thought to ask. If you mean how did I find you, well, I just
followed the trail of bloody goo you left behind."*

They scuttled along in silence to the next lateral passage, where
Daslakh turned left. *"Not far now,"* it said. *"How are you doing? Your
suit won't talk to me and I don't have time to crush its puny mind."*

"Still alive," said Sabbath. *"Need a medbot soon."*

"Hang on for another three minutes."

They turned right at an axial passage which led to the viewing
gallery at the south pole of the hub. The diamond-sheet windows
gave a glorious view of Jupiter, now spanning a quarter of the sky.
One window had been neatly punched out and a small disk-shaped
spacecraft, no more than four meters across, sat atop some broken
tables and chairs.

The top of the disk opened like a pair of beetle's wings as they
approached. Inside was a single pilot's couch, squeezed between
propellant tanks with a little power plant under the seat.

Daslakh dragged Sabbath into the seat and stood back as it
enveloped him from the neck down as the doors closed. A visual
display of Sabbath's vital signs appeared on the smooth white surface, accompanied by a long list of everything wrong with him. The
words "MASSIVE TRAUMA" were in bigger letters than the rest.

"Maybe I should drive?" said Daslakh, occupying the footrest since Sabbath's feet were half a kilometer away. "We're running out of time to get away."

"Fine," sighed Sabbath. A second later the spacecraft's tiny mind linked up to Daslakh's, granting full control.

Daslakh wasted no time, pivoting the disk with its gyros into takeoff position. A burst from the maneuvering thrusters pushed it out of the hab. Daslakh powered up the main engine, heating up a few grains of metastable helium metal suspended in water. The resulting blast of hot plasma kicked the disk well away from Safdaghar at a gratifying two gees of acceleration.

Once clear of the hab's debris halo, Daslakh plotted a path which would drop down into Jupiter's atmosphere and shed enough velocity to rendezvous with the Jovian Ring on the far side of the planet. It lined the little ship up with the proper vector, then used nearly all the propellant in a long burn to put them on the right course, keeping just a tiny reserve for docking.

With that accomplished, Daslakh looked at Sabbath, whose eyes unfocused as the suit stopped keeping him conscious. "Good thing you're going to be out of it. I expect we'll hit about fifteen gees during aerobraking," said Daslakh. "So if you don't wake up before we dock, here's something I pieced together on the hab. It's the last work of Pasquin Tiu. Be sure to tell your bosses."

Pride's eye inflamed by truthful dust
Hunts what it fears to see.

No hate as red and hot as love,
Hungry cubs born in blood,

But gnawing icy spite
And empty greed no feast can fill

Snap blind with broken fangs
Tearing with no care or will.

No mercy can I beg, no peace
From ceaseless silent chase.

The poorest shelter me,
The weak stand guard.

Fearful and unwilling,
Yet refusing to betray.

No shield but right, no sword.
We will not win, we shall not yield.

A BILLION WORLDS GLOSSARY

Aldakor: Shape-shifting smart-matter chassis.

Altok: Language based on English.

Baseline: An intelligence level roughly equivalent to an unmodified Homo sapiens; the legal minimum for personhood in most places.

Biara: All-Qarina hab in Neptune's leading Trojans.

Biologicals: Intelligent beings made of meat.

Borg: A cyborg, typically one whose body is mostly mechanical with only a small biological component.

Bot: A mechanical being with sub-baseline intelligence.

Centro: Boss (Rocasa slang).

Chac: Giant ring habitat a thousand kilometers across, orbiting Jupiter beyond the major moons.

Corvids: Intelligent species genetically engineered from ravens.

Deimos Ring: Large orbital structure extending all the way around Mars in synchronous orbit; one of the major powers of the solar system.

Ebuthuntu: Utterly safe and comfortable Main Swarm habitat.

Entertainment: Most common form of fiction, incorporating elements of novels, films, and interactive games.

Fangshuo: Team ball game in which contact is forbidden.

Fratecea: Medium-sized hab in the Main Swarm, currently ruled by a repressive regime.

Gendakhel: Zero-gravity ball game.

Gigajoules: Units of energy, or of purchasing power, very roughly equivalent to one-tenth of a US dollar in the early 2020s.

Glorious Unique State: Empire which ruled most of Earth in the post-Great War era; sometimes called the Tsan-Chan Empire.

Great War of the Ring: Massive conflict in the Fourth Millennium, between the Inner Ring and most of the rest of the solar system.

Hab: Short for "habitat," an artificial structure in space.

Inner Ring: A structure surrounding the Sun at a distance of 0.3 AU, made of the remains of the planet Mercury transformed into computronium. Home to the most advanced minds in the solar system.

Jiaohui: One of the larger Salibi habs, located in the Main Swarm between Earth and Venus.

Juren: Largest space hab ever constructed, located at Jupiter's L1 point.

Kendraraj: Large habitat in the Main Swarm, scene of genocidal violence in the 9890s.

Koenig: Design cooperative based in Plato, Luna, specializing in plasma drive and weapon systems.

Kreyda: Habitat orbiting Venus.

Kumu: Lawless hab in the Kuiper Belt where Qarina are made and trained.

Longwu: Martial arts for dinosaurs.

Magonia: Cycler hab circling between Mars and Jupiter.

Main Swarm: The collection of several hundred million space habitats orbiting between Mars and Venus.

Malapert: City near the Lunar south pole.

Martian redwood: Engineered redwood species growing on terraformed Mars.

Memetic Intelligence: A being capable of independent decision-making, embodied entirely in patterns of legal and organizational information rather than an algorithmic digital mind or a biological brain.

Mysteries of the Hidden Emperor: Cult founded in the Eighth Millennium, claiming an origin in the Fifth Millennium under the Glorious Unique State. Boasts about a hundred billion adherents, mostly in Jovian space.

Ningen: Language derived from Japanese.

Nuledor: Nulesgrima player.

Nulesgrima: Zero-gravity stick-fighting sport, uses graphene palos.

Old Belt: The original asteroid belt between Jupiter and Mars.

Osorizan: Hab dedicated to backup storage for digital intelligences.

Oterma: Comet converted to a habitat, in a cyclic orbit between Jupiter and Saturn.

Pasquin Tiu: Martian writer famous for his anti-Deimos lampoons.

Politica: Political prisoner in Fratecea habitat.

Qarina: Human created for sexual slavery.

Raba: Habitat at the Uranus trailing Trojans cluster.

Rebodar: Rocasa word for a drifter or transient ("ricocheter").

Retro Ring: The outermost ring of habitats circling Jupiter, orbiting retrograde.

RKV: Relativistic Kill Vehicle. The ultimate argument of worlds. A chunk of something dense traveling very fast.

Rocasa: Language derived from Spanish and Esperanto which originated in the Old Belt.

Sabela: Queen and hereditary owner of Oterma, of the matrilineal House of Buntala.

Safdaghar: Wrecked habitat formerly at the outer edge of the Old Belt.

Salibi: Followers of an ancient religion with only a few billion remaining adherents.

Saur: Hindi-based artificial language ("Solar").

Scapino: Habitat in the Jovian Retro Ring, notoriously home to criminals and shady mercenaries.

Scarab: Salvagers of derelict or obsolete habitats.

Sekkurobo: Ningen word for a sex robot.

Shikyu: Artificial uterus or baby printer (from Ningen).

Summanus: Large, old, and powerful space habitat orbiting in Jupiter's L2 position; also the high-level AI controlling the habitat.

Synchronous Ring: The lowest orbital ring around Jupiter, with elevator cables extending down into the planet's cloud tops. Home to about a trillion people.

Tiedao: Gambling card game, its origins lost in time.

Titan Psychoactives: A self-owning Autonomous Corporation. An example of a purely memetic intelligence.

Trojan Empire: Powerful government controlling thousands of habitats and asteroids in the Jupiter trailing Trojans cluster.

Ubas: Genetically modified fruit based on grapes. Commonly grown in space habs.

Woshing: Most common language on Mars, derived from Chinese.

Xiyu: Seldom-used language.

Washikyosho: Famed Lunar goldsmith of the mid-9900s.

Zukyu: Sport resembling rugby (from Woshing).

ACKNOWLEDGMENTS

All of the Billion Worlds stories rely heavily on Winchell Chung's magisterial "Atomic Rockets" website (at projectrho.com), the Orion's Arm project (orionsarm.com), and the very informative YouTube video series *Science and Futurism with Isaac Arthur*.

Dr. Diane Kelly provided helpful advice about brain anatomy, as well as ongoing vital support and encouragement.